For Joanna, Dominique, Stefan, Kristyna and Otis.

The Hotel Detective

and his Lover

Luxury stains everything it touches...   Cesar Ritz

Derek Picot

Copyright © 2020 Derek Picot

All rights reserved

The characters and events portrayed in this book are fictitious. Any similarity to real persons, living or dead, is coincidental and not intended by the author.

No part of this book may be reproduced, or stored in a retrieval system, or transmitted in any form or by any means, electronic, mechanical, photocopying, recording, or otherwise, without express written permission of the publisher.

ISBN-13: 9798669955670
ISBN-10: 1477123456

Cover design by: Art Painter
Library of Congress Control Number: 2018675309
Printed in the United States of America

Contents

Title Page	1
Copyright	2
Dedication	3
Chapter 1	7
Chapter 2	49
Chapter 3	85
Chapter 4	122
Chapter 5	161
Chapter 6	196
Chapter 7	235
Chapter 8	256
Chapter 9	284
Chapter 10	307
Chapter 11	332
Chapter 12	358
Chapter 13	391

Chapter 14	421
Chapter 15	450
Chapter 16	489
Acknowledgement	537
About The Author	539
Books By This Author	541

Chapter 1

As the privileged guests gathered by the pillared entrance to say their goodbyes from what had been another excellent select country house party, nobody took much notice of the stylish couple who moved from the portico and crunched over the gravel in the light drizzle, she putting on her blood red helmet and he striding purposely ahead to the potent black Triumph Bonneville. Kicking the bike into life, she waited as he moved it off the stand and gracefully slid one leg over the saddle as if she was sliding on top of him in bed. They roared off down the drive at speed, the noise causing only minor interruption to the murmur of the guests as they assembled themselves in the farewell line to leave.

The bike took the first few corners well and accelerated along the carriageway towards the copse that loomed through the biker's impaired rain-stained visor. His passenger, shifting her weight with the slope of the bike, gripped more tightly. It can be very dangerous driving a powerful motorbike fast along the Willows, especially on a wet moonless autumnal night when leaves are strewn across the path.

As they entered the left-hand bend just before the road straightened, the riders veered left with the bike and leaned hard over into the corner. Suddenly a series of bright sparks illuminated the carriageway as if a firework had been lit under the frame. The bike vaulted along the road, metal grinding tarmac, and as the front brake was applied the rear wheel jumped off the road. Sliding sideways in a heart-churning skid they both thundered into the verge as the bike, engine running, wormed over the embankment on its side. She flew the last few yards before crashing into the wall that ran close to the road. Her red crash hat split in two with a sharp crack as her head hit the oak. The stricken pieces of the helmet lay open like a split egg.

Indecision and consternation ensued, the biker picked himself up from the road and walked over to where the pillion lay. Looking down at her he could see that she was still breathing. He gently kneeled beside the body, lifted his visor to move a strand of blond hair from her face.

There was the thinnest trace line of bright red blood coming from her mouth. Standing up, he swayed with shock and looked around for any sign of car headlights that might indicate there were witnesses to this catastrophic mortal accident. It would be very awkward if someone appeared now. Night was falling on this deadly scene as he decided to exit the misadventure.

For this to happen at such a critical time with all the circumstances it involved for the family was a catastrophe.

Richard Marker was sitting in his office and reading the social column of his newspaper in the Security Office of The Adelphi Hotel.

As the Chief Security Officer he considered it important to keep up with the rich and famous, most of who favoured residing in the property. His workplace was as stained as his coffee cup and smelt like some of the best Soho nightclubs. Fag ends and last night's beer. On his desk was an ashtray fuller than an overflowing bath. On the walls were pinned various reports from his contacts at the Met and a number of mug shots of well-known hotel thieves. Most looked too well-dressed for robbery but Marker recognised that theft in five-star surroundings required some effort in tailoring.

Behind his swivel chair stood an array of dusty filing cabinets filled with reports of the misdemeanours of both the staff and guests. The drawers ran alphabetically from Arson to Zoo-sadism. There wasn't much that the clientele didn't get up to with anything ranging from setting a fire to accosting animals. Marker had seen it all. Some of them had money, some of them didn't but they all wanted to be there and to be noticed. From the sanctuary of this subterranean enclave he could file them in logical order, desirable guests, dubious guests, even dangerous guests. He had some excellent notes of those that he particularly wanted to follow, and it wasn't just the hotel guests either; he had an interesting set of folders on the hotel staff too.

There was the lovely Sandrine Parte for instance, the hotel's relatively new French Public Relations Officer for whom he harboured many carnal thoughts. He put down his newspaper, set his coffee cup on the ring stained desk and to remind himself just how attractive she was he unlocked his lower desk drawer. Flipping through the beige folders he kept on all the key managers he pulled up her dossier and glanced at the stapled publicity picture on the left inside cover. It was black and white and clearly a studio shot, Sandrine looked the image of a sixties model, modern, confident and sexy. Here was a woman of quality. Fine features, ample breasts, long legs and a cute bob haircut. Marker thought she had all the promise of a potential *femme fatale*...If only she would seduce him to show him a world he had only read about in books.

It was unfortunate that he spent so much time looking at her picture because he had missed something in the paper that he had now discarded. It would have caught his interest. James Egerton, the Managing Director of Broadman Development Corporation, was in the news again with his plans for the redevelopment of the Strand. And that meant the acquisition of The Adelphi Hotel.

Broadman were in the process of acquiring great swathes of the district to build a new retail shopping complex. The piece focused on the one impediment to their plans, the purchase of the hotel which was fiercely protected by its Chairman Sir John Bulling.

He replaced the file and standing away from the desk the hotel detective stood up in the cramped office. He picked up the Reception Office's daily arrival and departure sheet that had been printed out by the night reception. The stencil Roneo had smudged the house list but the date was still reasonably legible. Tuesday 14 June 1968. He looked over the page and glanced at the day's function list. Folding it in three he placed it in his inside pocket. Pulling his chest in and straightening himself to his full height he felt he looked good for his age. Early forties, a face with strong features set off by a firm chin and ruffled dark hair. He wanted a good solid look, as if he had filled his suit with muscular tone. A second look in the wall mirror made him realise that it looked more as if had stuffed a building inside the ensemble. The upper floors were in reasonable shape but the area around the mezzanine was hanging over the ground floor.

He put thoughts of this disappointing outline to the back of his mind. Time to focus on the present. The important issue of the day was breakfast.

Marker considered himself to be in a unique position, eating as he could pretty well anything he liked at the hotel and in one of the finest restaurants in London. Yesterday at lunch he had enjoyed the *Filets des Soles Veronique*, the fish as firm as youthful breasts and accompanied with what must have been white grapes stripped of their pips by hand, so beautifully prepared he had marched into the kitchen when he had finished to shake the hand of the Chef. He had done this without any word of gratitude, the silent and solemn gesture had signified alone the quality of what he had just eaten. Now he was considering an *Oeuf sur la Plat* for breakfast which might go well with a side of spinach. When looking approvingly at the breakfast menu he would choose Earl Grey tea to match the vegetable and now that he was avoiding bread he could eat with the comforting knowledge that the meal was all protein and no carbohydrate. His attitude to food was as focused as a Leica camera and his knowledge an encyclopaedia of *Auguste Escoffier*, the co-founder of the Ritz and great Chef of the last century who introduced the modern menu to the world.

The job suited this gastronomic character, one that he thought co-joined well with his pragmatic introversion. He enjoyed the discipline of working alone. Here he could work independently, seek out the malevolent, eat fine food and appreciate glamourous women.

He was, he considered, a man with virtue and integrity, his mother had certainly been responsible for his moral compass, but his introverted shyness had been created by her dominance, projecting as she had her fear of his growing independence. She did not want to face old age alone. His father had left when he was five years old and he and his mother had spent the war together in the London suburb of Pinner-. An area considered suitable for the middle classes, but his street had moved from white collar to blue. He was in his early teens when the first bombs hit in 1940 and he had excitedly hoped the war would last forever but the town had returned to pedestrian norm after the Blitz. When he was eventually called up, it was a relief to his mother that it was 1945 and the war virtually over. He left for Egypt and he started in the Military Police, hardly front-line, but the work taught him patience and tenacity. Military investigation and interrogation, he learnt, was all about going over the facts with the suspect time and time again until you got to the answers you wanted.

He was still a virgin when he finished his military service. He'd ignored risking the brothels of the Burqa in Cairo but now had the hungry appetite of a young virile man not yet fulfilled. That is when he met her. At a Saturday night dance in Leicester Square. Finally a girl who wanted to experiment as much as he did. They made nights into days when they made love. She was beautiful and smart too, he even got invited to meet her parents, but of course inevitably her family thought that he wasn't 'good enough' for her. Coming home he had taken a job with the Police. Her father had said she should aspire to someone above the class of a man who walked the streets. Marker simply didn't fit with a family tree that hadn't grown in the gardens of Surrey.

But he spent the next few years still walking the beat and when the realisation slowly grew that there was no promotion he eventually resigned the Force and moved to a private detective agency. There he found the work interesting and varied enough for him to let go of his first love and he found a new romance, a passion for food. Real passion. So as his career began to progress so inevitably did his waistline.

Then out of the blue, one day, after ten years of service, he was laid off.

'Not enough divorce cases to keep us going.' His manager had said. 'It's the Swinging Sixties, nobody cares who does what to whom.'

It was in June 1966 when he found himself once again pounding the pavements, unemployed and seeking work. Then, one day he had been getting off a bus in the Strand when he saw her again. She was just as slim, just as beautiful. She wore a light brown fox fur, and a tight blue dress that clung to her diminutive figure. She looked, to him, incredibly sultry and rich. She was just as gorgeous as she had appeared in 1947.

He pushed his way through the crowd standing on the quarter-deck to catch up with her. She was well down the street towards Waterloo Bridge when as she turned the corner, suddenly, she was shoved sideways by one of the filthy vagrants who habitually begged by the warm drain-covers. He made a grab for her handbag. It happened very fast, but she hung on and was screaming for help. The thief pushed her into the middle of the road. Marker was still down the street but not too far behind. He ran into the road, dodged two cabs coming in the opposite direction and flew the last yards finishing with a rugby tackle that would have impressed a Twickenham crowd. He downed them both. Together they rolled across the carriageway and landed in spectacular fashion right in front of a large red bus. It had screeched to a halt inches from their heads. Marker had the thief in his grip and she stood up dazed, unharmed but shaken, still with her handbag firmly on her arm. Marker heaved the thief back to the pavement and held him in a headlock. There was applause from the small coterie that had gathered on the street corner and some of the men helped him restrain the thief. It wasn't long before the Police arrived. Marker had him firmly in an armlock whilst they put on the handcuffs. He brushed himself down and then looking around realised that he couldn't see her. Had she gone? Then on the other side of the road he saw a small group of concerned women shielding the diminutive figure. He crossed over.

'An unusual way to say hello after all these years.' Marker smiled.

'God, how extraordinary! It's you Richard!'

She had taken a little time to recognise him. He had, after all, put on some weight.

'Thank you so much. I'm so grateful I have my bag. What have you been doing?'

'Catching wrong-uns' like him I suppose.' Marker glanced over to the Police van.

He told her that after they had broken up he had left the Met and had been a private detective, but now he had just been made redundant.

She told him that she had taken up selling real estate and met her husband who was someone important at The Adelphi, the grand hotel near to Charing Cross station. She had a young daughter. Then she told Richard that the hotel had a vacancy and was looking for someone of his ability and sense of civic duty. She promised to make an introduction for him. And so it was, with her overture to the staff manager that The

Adelphi welcomed him with open arms as their newly appointed Chief Security Officer. At his interview for the position, he had wondered if his modest social background would be an impediment, but his introduction appeared to be gold-plated and perfectly acceptable to the senior hotel management.

That was two years ago and looking to his desk, Marker pushed thoughts of his good fortune to the back of his mind and took that day's function sheets from his pocket for a last look before leaving his office. Making his way through the basement passages towards the kitchens, looming around the corner came the Chief Engineer, a man whose marked face wore the ravages of misspent youth. It seemed to Marker that his bulbous nose, which was located off centre, helped give an overall facial impression akin to a battleship with a couple of dents on the prow.

'Morning Klimp, got your grease-monkeys all in on time today? ...By the way, I'm having a problem with the air-conditioning in my office – any chance of getting it fixed?'

'Not today, we're servicing the air handling units all this week ...maybe back later tomorrow...in the meantime a little sauna in your office will give you a chance to get this down.'

Otto Klimp prodded Marker near his waistline. Klimp had seen wartime service too, as a young seventeen year old *Teufelhunden* marine on one of Grand Admiral Karl Doenitz's U-boats. Here was a man whose naval discipline was going to put order and inflexible discipline ahead of common sense with as yet unknown disastrous consequences for the hotel. His inability to grasp danger came from his wartime experience when being depth-charged at thirty metres was a daily experience. It was if he just couldn't see risk. He would tell anyone willing to listen:

'Only a third of us survived! It was fantastic, you never knew if you were going to see the sun again!'

And if given the chance would continue with his experiences with tales of blowing up Atlantic convoys or watching the Americans bomb the U-boat pens at St. Nazaire from 30,000 feet:

'*Ja*..Super impressive.'

Today Marker did not have time for the whole nine-yards of these stories and decided to walk briskly on.

'Bloody *Kraut*' thought the detective, pulled in his stomach and making a mental note to spend an additional fifteen-minutes of press-ups that evening, went looking for his favourite table in the restaurant.

∞∞∞∞

Sir John Bulling, the Chairman of The Adelphi, leant back in his chair, sighed and once again admired the river view from the other side of his oak panelled office. He stood up and walked across the thick pile dark green carpet to look out at the Thames. He thought the tide might be coming in judging from the debris floating up river. The recently redecorated room was appropriate in scale for a man of this position, neutral hues with some exceptional prints on the walls. He had wondered about hanging the Chagall but thought better of displaying a Jewish artist in what he knew was a Christian establishment; it might have sent a wrong signal to his influential City friends. He was keen not to disturb the processes in which he was involved, moving as he was through the Court of his Livery company. And, in regards to his bank facility certainly he needed the goodwill of his backers.

He had been unsettled by the latest conversation he had just had with the Managing Director of Broadman, James Egerton. He considered their persistent offers to buy the family controlling interest in The Adelphi as brazen and impertinent. The hotel was, after all, *his* inheritance, his by rights. He wondered how his father might have handled the disturbing and aggressive ambitions of what was, in his mind, just an East End builder with as much sophistication as a lead pencil. The hotel had been built by his father and when it opened it was innovation in all senses: the first with electric light throughout, moving rooms called 'lifts' and so many bathrooms that guests wondered if the hotel might be amphibious. It was outrageous to think that it would all be turned into a department store. He was an implacable foe of relinquishing his coveted shares, but he was on a path that was about to cross with a sharp and cruel chess game played out by an unknown nemesis determined to wrest control from the family.

Moving back to his desk, he passed the oval mirror and checked that his polka dotted tie and pocket handkerchief were suitably positioned. He was in character a distinctly unpleasant man. Someone so arrogant and full of pomposity that any Bridge player of quality would rather have just had him lay out his hand and leave the table as quickly as possible.

Balding, mid-sixties, not quite a museum piece, clean shaven and fastidiously traditional, here, were times different, he might have made a First World War General. He certainly possessed the psychopathic tendencies which seemed a pre-requisite for military leadership at that time and was applying the same ruthlessness to the way he ran the business. After all, it was he, with his father who had kept The Adelphi running in the war years. It was he who had suggested to the *Chef des Cuisines* that rabbit could be passed off as a quality meat if properly sauced. It was he who had virtually owned the black market to provide Churchill with fine lunches in order that the Premier could continue his fine war work on a full stomach. And he only rued the fact that all his fine war effort couldn't be mentioned in dispatches because his asthma had prevented him from being called up.

It wasn't just his secretary who found it strange that this particular complaint miraculously disappeared in June 1945.

Sir John's award of a knighthood in the Honour's List was believed to have been bestowed by the not insignificant influence of his father, Lord Bulling, sitting in the House of Lords. A considerable snob, utterly indifferent to the rich and privileged *milieu* of the Bulling dynasty to which he was born, Sir John personified the world he represented: vast corporate influence, unprecedented class power, high society and uncommon wealth unearned to a degree.

Since the devaluation of sterling and Prime Minister Wilson's heroic comment that 'the value of the pound in your pocket will be the same' London's hotel business was once again being badly affected by the absence of Americans. They accounted for more than half the hotel's revenue and Bulling wondered what other market could possibly supplant them. Before long the United Kingdom would be so far left of centre that there could be open revolution. There was little chance of sterling recovering and an enormous risk that business taxes would increase. Income tax was already an eye-watering 92% for high earners.

He had already decided to savage his staff numbers by 10%, the most expensive on the payroll requiring close scrutiny. Encouraging a higher proportion of female employees had allowed the opportunity to offer jobs previously taken by men at a lower rate. Mind you, his father would have thought it inconceivable to have waitresses in the restaurant. Now he was considering greater economies. He had already instructed the hotel management to reduce energy consumption by a fifth and the laundry costs by a similar amount. He could see that there were also further parsimony to be made in reducing food and beverage cost and he wondered if the urbane hotel General Manager, Timothy Patterson, had the ability to see all this through. And he, Patterson, was the most expensive on the payroll.

He looked out of his door for his young attractive secretary. He didn't know quite why he endured her. She appeared to be totally self-absorbed with her make-up. Striking as she was, this irritated him, but his intolerance was not yet stretched enough for him to fire someone who was the most appealing part of his office.

'Diana – get me the Accountant.'

She looked up from polishing her nails, nodded to Sir John and picked up the phone to David Farndon.

'Sir John would like to see you in his office… no, I don't know what about…but he looks anxious.'

Diana Spurling was an attractive girl; there was a little Essex in her that somehow successfully mingled with Mayfair. She was a reasonable personal assistant; did her job well, guarded Bulling's territory and probably knew more about the hotel and what really went on than he did. Beside all that, her best assets, from Sir John's point of view, were her looks and her loyalty What she lacked in brains she made up with simplicity and provocatively enticing short skirts.

She handled the telephone with care as the red nail polish on her right hand was still drying and although she had slipped the lacquer bottle deftly into her drawer, the smell of acetone hung in the air reminiscent of the glue-sniffers outside the Embankment tube station. Leaving her slender legs crossed well within view and with her engaging smile to the Chairman, there was, as yet, no negative comment about her worktime manicuring habits. She knew exactly how to handle the likes of Sir John Bulling.

Farndon arrived a little breathless. He was a middle aged man whose grey hair and pale complexion reflected his desire to fade into the beige of the recently replaced office wallpaper. His looks had all the right components but all slightly misaligned. It gave the casual observer a distant recollection of a face that might have been sketched by Munch. He was a cautious, judicious planner for whom a parapet was the last place he would consider placing his head above. Whilst he lived in fear of the Chairman, he still had his finger on the pulse and was aware that the hotel was close to the financial equivalent of cardiac arrest.

Bulling pointed him to a commodious leather seat by his partner desk:

'Don't make yourself too comfortable, Farndon. I'm thinking of firing some of the highest on the payroll – replace them with women perhaps...'

Farndon did indeed look uncomfortable but, on the positive side, more women would be cheaper on the wage cost.

'...and we can do more on the food and beverages costs,' continued Bulling, warming to his role of ruthless autocrat.

Together they went over the last month's trading and he again looked gloomily across to the South Bank. The Queen Elizabeth Hall, and the Hayward. Their bunker-like blocks, reminiscent of the war, surely made them the ugliest buildings in Britain.

'Broadman have called me again asking me to sell the controlling interest.'

Bulling pushed his chair back and standing up now took to vigorously pacing the office. This imitation of a caged beast was done more for effect than a desire to recirculate the blood in his veins. That usually ran much more slowly and with little heat.

'What would my father have done?'

He looked at the ceiling and scratched his bald head and then started fidgeting with his tie. The question was not directed at him but Farndon assumed it required an answer. He leaned back in his chair.

'Lord Bulling never traded in times like these, Sir John, but I think he might have considered a rights issue, but frankly with these set of numbers we would be hard pushed to provide excitement to our shareholders in terms of increased reward.'

Farndon then further considered the point.

'I think we need to talk to the bank, we can get a further loan at three points above LIBOR and perhaps secure it on a revaluation of our site – particularly if it's as valuable as Broadman believe it is.'

Bulling agreed that this was a good idea and feeling a little more relaxed he turned to the family pictures on his low level filing cabinets to the rear of his desk. There the history of his dynasty lay before him. His great grandfather, his father, and then a fine portrait of Lady Julia, his present wife, in that beautiful Amies dress. Blue suited her. Next to her, a picture of his twelve-year old daughter, he was lucky to have produced such a child considering he was not in the first flush of youth when he married his second wife. Of course there were no pictures of Cynthia. He didn't want to spoil the pleasant sweep of family portraits to be reminded of one of his gravest misjudgements.

The Adelphi ran like a very large Cunard ocean going liner of the very best luxury class, it sailed through periods of calm and times of turbulence with little cognizance to the elements of chance. A light lurch to port soon corrected by a slow swing to the starboard, its business heart beating like the quiet throb of large ponderous turbines. To its blissfully ignorant guests it created an aura of calm and tranquillity. A tremor to this establishment would require something of seismic proportions.

Timothy Patterson, The Adelphi's General Manager, was taking his breakfast in *'Leons',* The Adelphi's restaurant that overlooks the Embankment. He also looked immaculate in dark suit, white shirt, Brioni grey tie and blue cornflower neatly tucked through his buttonhole. Seated alone, he was irritated to see that Marker had once again slipped into the room from the kitchen and was indulging himself in the far corner. Up until then he had been enjoying his *Islay kipper* to a greater extent than the trading numbers he was reading in his daily report. Although sanguine about business prospects, the falling hotel occupancy gave sufficient concern for him to consider calling his number two, George Brooks, but only as soon as he had finished his Darjeeling and returned to the office.

Brooks was responsible for the day to day running of the enterprise and as adept at handling Timothy Patterson as he was at manipulating beautiful women. Impeccably dressed in long tailed morning suit, as demanded by The Adelphi standard, he knew enough to wear clothes that made him feel confident.

It was confidence, not the clothes, which made him so attractive. A man in his mid-thirties, he possessed film star looks with bay rum groomed hair and clear complexion. He was aware that he reflected the very best of what was expected of an Englishman and had invented himself using all his skill of an accomplished articulate actor. Sexually promiscuous, his louche personal lifestyle in the more dubious clubs of the swinging sixties will doubtless lead him into some tight spots but his sharp intuition and ability to make important influential friends meant he would survive. Here in truth was a man that blended Jeeves with Bond. For this was really who he thought he was.

And it was the arrogance that came with this

pastiche that had initially aroused the annoyance of Marker who now had quite a file on him and not just for reasons of professional interest. Mainly because he was conducting an affair with Marker's secret lust, that hussy of all-French promise, the Press Officer, Sandrine Parte.

Brooks arrived at Patterson's office, a room of auburn panelling and royal blue carpet just past the reception desk and next to the Cashier. He knocked and waited for the small red light on the corner of the architrave to turn green. As the traffic light changed he opened the brass door handle and entered the inner sanctum. He spotted the bottle of champagne that was always open with four glasses. This was used when important guests arrived for a welcome drink and were invited to meet the Man at the Top. As he pulled up a comfortable leather chair he looked over to the General Manager. Patterson was just completing *The Telegraph* crossword.

Brooks took in a breath and said:

'There's a gentleman at the cashier struggling to pay by cheque and who says he's your friend...'

Patterson glanced up from considering *4 across. Popular ointment.*

'Brooks, I do not have any friends, only colleagues and associates.' And with that filled in the answer to the clue. *'Topical.'*

Brooks noted the business report on the desk. He looked across at the senior executive who had now cast aside the paper and adopted a look of distant interest.

'It's the numbers,' said Patterson, unfolding his arms and leaning across his desk. 'What do you think we can do about them?'

Brooks looked mildly astonished; the sort of look an Oxford academic might give if asked what he was going to do about earning a living.

'The future of the business is secured because we know that even Johnson is going to have to end the Vietnam War. On top of that the pound is so low against the dollar that tourism will flourish in the summer.' He paused: 'You never know, we might get something from the Royals this year, a State funeral, another Royal marriage...' his voice tapered off.

'For God's sake, you're not asking me to rely on the Queen Mother dying to save the business I hope; although we could at least be sure that any ceremony would be held in the City rather than Windsor.'

Patterson moved in his chair and took a close look at Brooks. He always seemed somewhat affected, he thought, too good looking, too self-assured, generally a sort of candidate for a significant fall. He wondered about him.

'Next thing you'll be suggesting is that Wilson be shot alongside the Kennedys, mind you, not a bad thing some might say...'

'Well, it'll be either him or the old Pope...' Brooks' voice drifted off.

'Well that might suit hotels in Rome... but there will be no impact here. No one bothers with church anymore, and the Catholics that do are too busy trying to find heterosexual priests than to worry about a papal funeral.'

He paused and looked across to the picture of a naval frigate on his office wall. He had enjoyed serving in her. Pulling his thoughts back in line he then added:

'We have weighty issues Brooks and I think it will mean bringing our key department heads together to look at the situation. I see that Broadman Developments are still applying the pressure on Sir John and I am sure he is going to ask me what we can do to improve the cash flow; you know what a challenging man he can be. He's been on again about the payroll, he's looked at the utility costs and I half expect him to take an axe to the food and beverage costs. He's unpleasant and aggressive in this mood.'

At the end of the conversation, Brooks agreed to arrange a meeting with the key department heads that afternoon. He would look at the forward forecast of business and call together some of the team. As he left the office he spotted Sandrine Parte as she walked across the lobby floor, she was wearing a beautiful belted skirt and pastel cream shirt. He couldn't resist the temptation to invite her for some entertainment later that day.

'Sandrine....doing anything interesting this evening? I think my notes for the business plan need your expert eye over them. Despite being French you know your English is at a level that only an Apollo spaceship could reach. It's so much better than mine. Perhaps when you've decided on a few improvements your delightful fingers could come and work their magic on a rewrite with my typewriter.'

'The only thing you want my hands to work over is in your trousers...but I can manage a couple of hours perhaps...your place?'

'My place seven-o'clock.'

Sandrine was foxy, calculating and outrageously inclined to appear flirtatious.

Brooks gave her a broad smile and she gave him a delicious one in return, or at least it looked like that to Marker who was once again standing in his usual place across the lobby and slightly left of the two revolving doors. For it was there that he could watch all of the comings and goings without creating an impression of oppressive security. It was a good thing that he was that far away and couldn't hear the conversation for it would have raised his blood pressure and that would lead to the only other comfort he had... food. That was a bad thought, bad for his figure, and bad for his libido.

Brooks arranged his meeting in the Shaftesbury Room. A small private dining room just off the main restaurant where tables were being set for the evening's cabaret. In the centre of the room was a large mahogany table, so large enough that it would have required four men of some bulk to transport it. As Brooks surveyed its scale it occurred to him that it must have been assembled by a team of carpenters in the room for nothing of this gauge could have got through the door.

Calling his department heads together they assembled in a pre-ordained but officially unspecified order. The Head Housekeeper, Mrs Haul, being the only lady present, regally sat to the left at the top of the table.

Other department heads assembled and gave precedence to hotel royalty with the exception of the Chef who never gave way to a woman. They then spent an hour or so devising a suitable plan to address the declining profit. These meetings were generally a one sided affair with most of Brook's colleagues taking a non-communicative approach. This borne from the years of experience of the participants knowing that argument was futile and any positive suggestions were only likely to be attributed to them in the event of failure. Today was a little different however, Klimp, the Chief Engineer had several suggestions about energy costs and wanted to reduce the times the hotel was running air handling units for the air conditioning. This was treated with derision by Silvano Cornet, the *Maître Chef des Cuisines*, who said that the only things being roasted in the kitchens would be the cooks.

Cornet was a man of imposing presence and the kitchen operated almost as a separate state, a sort of Fourth Republic of the French Empire. A Gaullist, tall and nearing obese, he carried his weight with arrogance. As proud as Napoleon he had a stomach proportionate to his profession. His white uniform contrasting dramatically against the dark upholstery of the furniture; the only colour that radiated from him was puce from his overheated face. He glowered at the Chief Engineer. Brooks thought he had the appearance of a large iced bun with a red cherry on top.

As Ramadan was shortly finishing, the Rooms Division team, suggested that it would be good to raise all the suite prices. It would be just the right time to catch the Middle Eastern market. Brooks liked this idea as in his view visitors from the Gulf States were so immune from the reality of the cost of living that they were mercifully totally price insensitive.

Mrs Haul generally eyed the rest of her peer group with some disdain. A woman who was not unattractive but dressed as if captured in a time warp of the 1940s era. Her deportment came from a Swiss finishing school and as a consequence any entry to a room was always majestic. Outspoken but _never_ ignored, the inventory of rooms was her exclusive domain.

During the war she had trained women Special Operations operatives to jump out of Lysander aircraft at 500 feet and when considering the qualities of sheer nerve her agents possessed, thought in comparison that most of the hotel management lacked any semblance of courage. In her view they really hadn't a trace of an idea as to how to manage in a crisis and would, if anything calamitous occurred, doubtless be as terrified as non-swimmers running up the deck of the Titanic. 'LMF' she would mutter,

Lack of Moral Fibre, as she surveyed the collection of the all-male department heads around her. They were more effeminate than a Soho pub full of drag queens. She turned her attention back to her antagonist, Brooks.

'Are we to assume that as you are cutting my staffing and increasing the suite prices with the expectation of higher quality, my department will still be pushing our maids to clean more than fourteen rooms a day each?'

Brooks looked over to his left, eyed her up and after a pause laconically replied:

'Yes.'

Across the table Patrick Wildblood, the Adelphi's Irish restaurant *Maître d'* raised his hand. Sophisticated and urbane he was so suave he'd make water roll uphill.

'Is there any truth to the rumour that I am now going to replace my waiters with waitresses?'

He delivered this enquiry with a look of hostility that might have been more useful in Figger Magees, a real dive off Parnell Street in Dublin.

Brooks looked expressionless across the table and considered his answer carefully:

'Possibly...'

Wildblood looked uncomfortable but hesitated from enquiring further.

The meeting then moved on to discuss the upcoming important lunch in two days' time that was being arranged by the Foresight Insurance Company. This was a sponsored event called 'Heroes of Britain' and would be attended by the Prime Minister, most of the heads of the public services, and all the families of those that had helped create some of the epic life-saving moments of the previous year. This was to be a 'thank you' to the good and the great who had protected the Insurance Company from losing a good deal of cash by their rapid and effective response to a catalogue of emergencies.

Cornet told Brooks that he had it all under control and that the expected number would be in the region of 300 guests. Brooks noted this down into his leather compendium and calling the meeting to an end turned his thoughts lightly to the idea of stripping Miss Parte naked and bending her over his lounge sofa. He began to sense a familiar stirring.

George Brooks had a neat little pied-a-terre in John Adam Street. After he had finished for the day it was only a short walk along the Strand

and he wanted to get home before Miss Parte arrived.

He took the small elevator to the third floor and pushed open the door using the Yale. Looking around he cleared the glasses from the living room. He put them in the sink that fitted snugly into his kitchen. He hated the idea of being termed 'domestically disinterested', something his once a week cleaner had told the next door neighbour in describing his general approach to housework. He busied himself in the kitchen. The space was what estate agents would euphemistically call 'ergonomically designed' which meant that simply by turning around you could prepare, cook, clean and wash. It was a kitchen that no animal could swing in and certainly not a cat.

His sitting room was well proportioned and it led conveniently onto the 'Action Room', so named by a past lover after he had installed a large mirror on the ceiling in the bedroom. This had been dishonestly concealed behind a sliding blind that silently opened on a track. He found his own image naked on the bed erotic enough to be stimulating, but when viewed in combination with other bedfellows the vision drove him almost to orgasm.

Most who shared that experience seemed to find it more of a distraction, seeing Brooks' heaving naked body on top of their own could be sufficiently diverting to lose concentration.

He finished up and took one last look around the apartment to see it was all set for the evening, then he opened the door and left. He still had one or two things to address at The Aldelphi.

Sandrine was prompt and arrived as promised at seven, she had his spare key to let herself in. The apartment looked pleasingly fresh. She saw his business notes left next to the typewriter on the bureau. She picked them up and soon spotted several grammatical errors. Brooks, she mused, had trouble with his tenses. She picked up a clean sheet and rolled it onto the small portable. She quickly retyped the conclusions for him. She was well acquainted with Brook's flat; not only its layout but also its secrets. After all she had spent hours in there on her own and during those waits for him she had also worked her way through his library, his kitchen and his desk. In her previous life she had been an investigative journalist working for *The Daily Mail*, and a very good one at that. Some of her work had been dangerous, following the Kray twins for a story was one of her memorable press scoops. If she was sleeping with Brooks, she wanted to know everything, what exactly he was worth and who his friends were. Any woman would, she reasoned. Sandrine was rumoured to have a rapid turnover of lovers if her research disappointed her expectation of status or stamina.

After fifteen minutes had passed she looked out of the sitting room window and saw him crossing the street. As his key pushed into the latch she pulled the sheet from the roller, got up and moved to the small hallway.

They kissed and Brooks suggested a gin. As he poured the drinks and got the ice, Sandrine plumped the cushions. She wondered about the décor of this apartment, the greens and reds didn't quite work for her. She was more of a pastel person. All light lemon yellows and pale rose pinks. She didn't much like the prominence of the large television cabinet that filled the sitting room. It dominated the whole space and sat ominously and oppressively in the corner. She dismissed her thoughts of design and turned to a more pressing sensation that made her put her legs together. Although she really desired something a little fresher she would tolerate her current arrangements before embarking elsewhere. Brooks was attractive after all.

The drinks arrived rather pompously on a silver tray and when she took her glass she noted his erection pressing in his trousers.

'I see that you're ready for some excitement ...'

And her finger lightly touched the buckle of his belt. She stood up and taking the drinks she led him to the bedroom.

Sandrine placed the glass near the bedhead and unclipped her skirt and placing it casually on the bedside chair. Turning to George she slowly unbuttoned her tight shirt and revealed the very best of Maidenform lingerie.

'Are you unveiling the mirror this evening?'

She enquired looking upward at the beige curtain on the ceiling.

'I think we might, you know how turned on I get.' Brooks moved to pull the curtain across.

Sandrine slipped off the rest of her underwear and walked naked to where he had left his jacket. Pulling the white silk handkerchief from the top pocket she stood on the bed and stretched full height to wipe a smear off the glass.

In this pose she looked as magnificent as a figurehead on a ship's bow. Tall, exquisitely shaped, beautiful full breasts and completely confident. Indeed, Brooks, who was given to moments of historical fantasy, thought her beauty was reminiscent of Helen of Troy and the thousand ships that were launched to save her.

She then dropped the hankie and lay down seductively on the bed. Soon she was astride him and spotting his dressing gown on the floor lent over and picked up the cord. She then tied his hands to the iron bedhead. When she felt that she finally had him under control, she sat on top of him and began to move her hips so that he was comfortably inside. Brooks' mind was exclusively focused on mirrored carnal lust with this beautiful girl on top of him when the phone rang.

'I must answer that!' he cried.

'No need to.'

'But I must...it will be some disaster at the hotel.'

'I'll reply for you.'

And Sandrine took the phone from its cradle by the bedside.

'Mr Brooks' personal assistant – can I help you?' She wriggled her hips a little more... 'Hold on a minute... He's just coming... Georgie, it's someone called James Egerton.'

'I'm tied up,' he whispered.

'I'll hold the phone for you.'

Sandrine pressed the phone to his ear with one

hand and tried to make him hard again with the other.

'Hello Mr Egerton, how can I help you...?'

Sandrine didn't hear the rest of the conversation as she had already propped the phone against a pillow, pushed it close to his ear and moved further down the bed to deal with the matter in hand.

∞∞∞

Brooks had to consider the request from Broadman's Managing Director carefully. The relationship they had was certainly commercial but it occasionally moved into areas that were certainly unconventional, and the information requested mildly unusual. This time Egerton wanted him to 'take a cruise around Sir John Bulling's office and see if there is anything interesting'. Brooks was not a good sailor but felt he might be able to inveigle his way past the Chairman's secretary and navigate around Sir John Bulling's desk. Sometime back he had recognised the inevitability of a takeover of the hotel and had agreed to help Egerton and Broadman with some snippets of information from the inside. Brooks had considered that it was inconceivable that Sir John Bulling could hold the business together faced with the strength of Broadman's balance sheet; therefore his slice of cake was going to be better served from the victor in any upcoming bid for possession of the hotel. Not only that, but there was the nice piece of compensation that came into his offshore account every month that made exotic vacations so much more available.

The next day Brooks found a reasonable excuse to visit the Chairman's office and had planned his excursion into the Directors' corridor at lunchtime. The office personnel would be out food shopping or visiting the staff dining room and the last thing he wanted was to be greeted by Diana in the Chairman's office. Meeting her was always something that he held in some trepidation. She made him feel a little uncomfortable, there was that very welcoming smile given with a wry twist, it was as if she knew exactly who he was and what he might be up to. Anyway, if ever he was backed into a corner by her, he could just as easily confront her with what he knew about her love life. She was conducting a discreet affair with one of the 'gorgeous' boys in the kitchen. He had overheard that little piece of gossip from the staff restaurant when he had sat close to the lads from the pastry department. They were many good-looking young boys in that department he had reckoned.

He knocked on the Chairman's outer office door and was disappointed to find Diana still at her desk. He felt a slight pressure in his chest as his heart rate increased. He felt the instant need for a Rothmans.

'Sir John in?'

'No – he's at a meeting in the City with his bank.'

'Oh! I wanted to take a quick look into his office to see if the repair to the wallpaper had been done satisfactorily after that leak.'

'Go ahead – it's free, I'm off to lunch.'

She smiled back, but as she thought about leaving she wondered about George Brooks, and felt there was something about him, he was just too impossibly smooth, just too much of a slippery croissant. As she gathered up her handbag she wondered if she should stay whilst he went into Sir John's office, but looking at her watch she decided that if any of the decent salad was going to be left in the canteen she had better go now.

The empty office suited Brooks well as he moved around the room to look at what was in Sir John's desk. He tried the drawers but they were locked, but on the leather top there were a few files. Looking anxiously at the door to the outer office he flipped over the beige folder. He took out his pocket notebook and jotted down a few points that looked important from one or two of the more interesting sheets of paper. He forced back the rising sense of nervousness that he had felt earlier but there was a familiar weakening of the knees and his stomach contracted. It felt as if it was migrating towards his throat.

He looked across to the credenza on the rear wall. There were the family photographs – and he looked fondly at the one of Andrew Bulling, Sir John's son. He always took a good picture he thought. He briefly tried the cabinet drawers but they were locked too – and this was getting dangerous. At that moment he heard the outer office door open and he immediately turned his attention to the wall which had been recently repaired. Sir John Bulling strode purposefully into the room just as Brooks placed his hand on the wallpaper seam.

'They've done a good job here Sir John,' he said gliding his fingers along the paper. 'I thought I'd better come and check the work.'

'Thank you Brooks….occupancy better this morning?'

'We should fill tonight sir.'

Bulling looked pre-occupied and Brooks made his excuses and left with a heartbeat that had become dangerously high. It had been a close call.

Five minutes later Brooks rang Broadman and spoke to James Egerton from his office phone.

'Not much to report, there's an interesting document on restructuring, some notes on a rights issue and a revaluation – otherwise nothing of significance on his desk.'

Egerton was grateful. He considered the idea of a rights issue and instantly dismissed that but a revaluation of the hotel buildings was meaningful. It would certainly add pressure for them to push up their current offer and would not be welcome news. If a deal was to be done it had to be soon and certainly whilst trading was poor for the hotel. Brooks had told him that there was much anxiety amongst the management about business prospects. What was needed was a bit more leverage on Bulling, and when he got up from his office and looked out across the city, a thought occurred to him. He would need to find out more about the private life of the privileged Bulling family.

Chapter 2

The following day anyone entering The Adelphi would have sensed the change in atmosphere. Something important was obviously going to happen and the tension in the air was palpable. The doormen were ushering cars away from the River Entrance and there was a number of cleaners all immaculately dressed in black uniform busy with vacuuming the carpets and polishing the brass work. In the kitchen Chef Cornet was the only one of his brigade who took the luxury of sitting down. He was in his office on the telephone to the engineer.

'So why, Klimp, in the name of *mon Dieu* have you have chosen today to service the air handling units in the Banquet kitchen...You are a stubborn *kraut*! You knew we had the Heroes' Lunch today and the boys are already like *des porcs en sueur*. Can't you get the ventilation moving by service time at the latest?'

Cornet banged the phone down on the cradle before waiting for a reply and with a pock marked face that was turning dangerously close to the colour of a sliced *Pomodoro* tomato, strode determinedly out to the stoves of the main kitchen.

Timothy Patterson had finished breakfast and was reflecting on the grandeur of his position and the bruising meeting he'd had with the Chairman over the trading numbers. Was he really a man who time had almost forgotten? He felt that this was a most unfair taunt Bulling had thrown at him.

After all, admittedly he had started his career in the Navy wanting to be a navigator rather than an hotelier and although he had not come from any of the elite Clarendon schools the stripe of Eton or Harrow, he had benefitted from an education at Sherborne. There the Benedictine foundation had imprinted a sense of service to the community in his mind and at sea he had happily adopted the ethos in the ship's Wardroom.

This endeared him to his senior officers as

someone to whom the catholic mess menu could be entrusted, but not the direction of the vessel. At war's end, his parents, sensing that promotion was unlikely to arrive as promptly as a dinner gong, had arranged for him to meet Sir John Bulling's father to discuss an alternative career. Lord Bulling took an instant liking to the young Patterson, primarily because he too was a navy man, having spent time on a destroyer blasting U-boats from the Atlantic in the first war. So he could see that this Lieutenant understood ethics and had an aptitude for working in a team. Patterson, thought Lord Bulling, was a man he could trust, do what he was told, and might after a little training make an excellent General Manager, albeit that he might not know that a Manhattan was not only a place on the map and is served with bourbon and not whiskey.

And so it came to pass, a man with little experience of business but possessed with a sense of what made an Englishman achieved the pinnacle of his career; after a brief training in the various departments, Patterson was appointed General Manager.

And then within weeks of announcement on August 12th, Lord Bulling suffered a devastating heart attack whilst grouse shooting. Such was the severity of the pulmonary spasm the prospect of maintaining his position at the hotel became impossible to sustain and his son John Bulling was heralded in by the Board as his successor.

This was much to the disadvantage of Patterson as John Bulling's opinion of him was akin to those that played a poor game of golf. Bulling felt he was partnering someone with an ominously high handicap.

So Patterson continued his appointment under the new regime but with significantly more stress. Fearful of losing his position before it had barely left the City Appointments page of *The Times* he was aware that his numeracy and literacy might not be the required grade for the new man. So he searched around for some less obvious advantages that could be perceived as a virtue to the organisation. He thought, for example, that not having the encumbrance of a wife was surely an advantage to the enterprise; the Chairman could call upon his service at any time with the comfort of knowing he was not interrupting married bliss. Then he knew that he was able to bring a sense of elegance and artistic diversion to the hotel being as he was an aesthete. He was sure that it was important for the man at the top of this flagship property to know when the Summer Exhibition was on at the Royal Academy or the exact dates of Ascot a good year ahead.

What was unfortunate was that whilst the new Chairman enjoyed pursuits of various natures, the recreation of the arts and the single man was not one, and neither was horse racing.

Patterson's thoughts moved on from considering his reputation and the circumstances of his appointment towards the day's business and running the morning meeting in the General Manager's Office. He got up from the restaurant table and headed towards the Front Hall and his place of work.

Greeting his secretary, he opened the panelled door and tossed his copy of *The Telegraph* with that day's unfinished crossword on the side table. He now turned his attention to the line of expectant faces that were already seated across from his desk. Assembled before him were the hotel's department heads, the establishment.

They went through the arrivals list and picked out the most important guests. Lord and Lady Flatterley were coming, and Mr Van der Fleit was expected to arrive also. He was a director of Broadman and Brooks had already put a red circle around his name. He was an interesting guest of a certain age and prone to some unusual late night entertainment. The meeting noted that he was travelling without Mrs Van den Fleit so the Night Manager would have to be warned. Whitehead moved on:

'So today we have the Heroes' Lunch and the Prime Minister will be arriving at 12.45, I expect the usual security, Marker what has Special Branch told you?'

Marker pulled himself together from his reverie about Sandrine Parte and looking through his sheaf of papers found the function sheet.

'Dogs will be here at 11.30 to search the Crystal Room and the toilets then we get a three-car escort on arrival which I presume, sir, you will greet on the door.'

'Cloakrooms, Marker - not toilets. The Adelphi has cloakrooms and lavatories; the Strand Palace Hotel has toilets.'

Patterson gave a withering look at the detective who was seated, in his opinion, far too comfortably and who seemed to be growing plumper by the day on the generosity of the hotel restaurant.

'I will be on the door with you Brooks, and you Marker will escort the detectives – I assume that he is not with his wife Mary. She is as interested in politics as Liberace is in oil drilling. And considering Parliament is sitting he will probably want to go by 2.30pm after the principal awards have been given.'

After going over the menu and the other important arrangements Patterson dismissed the hotel team, closed his door and took up the crossword again.

Below the ground floor and in the huge labyrinth of the hotel's basements lie the kitchens with well on two hundred staff comprising *Chefs, Demi-Chefs, Chef des Parties, Commis* and Stewards. Built at the turn of the century they had only recently been refurbished to change the coal fired ovens to gas.

Every element of food served was prepared on the premises including a separate bakery in a further sub-basement. The closeness to the river and the poor cleanliness of the Strand also gave accommodation to a variety of wildlife in that subterranean wilderness that ranged from cockroaches to mice and rats. They had been there for generations and had even begun to adapt. Some which inhabited the insulation lining of the cold rooms were growing longer coats of hair.

In the kitchens the heat was beginning to build. The chefs were busying themselves with the *mise en place* and the air hung heavy with the smell of uncooked garlic. The banquet was a relatively simple affair with only three courses. The larder was already well ahead with the plated first course of a light *salade nicoise* cleverly created with exquisite french beans and finely chopped tuna.

Richard Marker had picked up the aromas as they wafted along the basement to his windowless office. With an almost automatic reaction he got up, locked his door on the way out and made his way to the banqueting department. Reaching the cold preparation area he paused by the raw ingredients that were to make up the salad and breathed in deeply. He looked over to see the Larder Chef, Maguire, finishing some of the plates. Marker had been watching Maguire for a little while as he suspected him of being responsible for the disappearance of various expensive items of meat from the cold rooms. He wondered therefore if it was sensible to ask him to put a salad aside for him later because Maguire was just the sort of person to remind him of that favour if he ever caught him red-handed.

'They look wonderful.'

He beamed at the cook, and at that moment threw caution to the wind.

'Would you put one aside for me for lunch?'

'Bugger off.' The chef replied and moved the finished plates further away from the detective.

Feeling the heat in more than one sense,

Marker moved on through to the main kitchen range. He began to sweat from the blast of heat given out by the stove tops and he felt a wet trickle slide down the back of his shirt and come to rest above his waist line. Forgoing the opportunity to see how the main course was coming along for fear of welcoming the police inspection team with a damp collar he made his way through the service exit to the ballroom.

The kitchen heat extractor was governed by the air handling units which were situated on the roof and the engineering team, as part of that week's maintenance programme were making significant efforts to change the filters as quickly as possible in order to get everything working in good order before midday. Unfortunately, they had come across an electrical fault that required a new fuse box and wiring. It was going to take longer than they first thought. Chef Cornet had already called Brooks' office and asked for him to push the Chief Engineer to get the units back in order as quickly as possible. Brooks was on the case and had gone to the roof to see the challenge for himself. As he stood on the roof gantry a room service waiter from the eight floor came up the stairs behind him.

'There's a call for you on my kitchen pantry

phone,' he told Brooks.

The Adelphi had a small pantry on each floor from which each floor waiter could prepare tables and deliver food to the premier suites and other rooms. Brooks went back down a level to take the call. Realising it was once again from Broadman's Managing Director, James Egerton, he turned to see if he could be overheard but the waiter had left the room rolling out a breakfast trolley for guests at the far end of the corridor.

'Morning Mr Egerton, what can I do for you?'

Brooks stood in the small kitchen looking at the four dumb waiter lifts that came up ten levels from the basement to deliver food and take back the left overs. Pressing the phone to his ear he was listening intently to his instructions. Egerton wanted to know about the Bulling family, Brooks felt it would be fairly easy to give Broadman a full run down on the Bulling set up – it was something about which he had intimate knowledge.

By midday the repair was still not fixed and the first guests had begun arriving, eager to take advantage of the champagne that promised to flow in liberal quantity. Chef Cornet called Brooks again and demanded that he appear in the kitchen to see just how impossibly hot the conditions were. Brooks told him he was staying on the roof to see the job done.

Cornet, whose face could change colour as frequently as a Piccadilly neon sign, changed from light burgundy to deep claret and now began to turn a deeper beetroot. Now emotionally stressed, he was moving from a pre-existing state of eruption towards a dangerously pyroclastic explosion.

By 12.30pm the sound of three hundred voices in the banqueting foyer had reached a certain crescendo. People were squeezed shoulder to shoulder as the white coated waiters moved amongst them with trays of Bollinger, their gold epaulettes catching the reflection from the lights of the crystal chandeliers. By 12.45pm, Patterson had appeared and looked immaculate in a pressed black-tailed morning suit, stiff white collar and grey tie. He stood away from the crowd at the banquet entrance and waited for Brooks to appear at his side.

Marker was already by his post and unconsciously moved a few steps away in respect for the General Manager and the magnificence of the senior team in tail-coats. Two members of the banquet team retrieved the red carpet and rolled it out across the pavement.

Just at that moment, to add to the tension, crossing the street entirely oblivious to the assembled pomp, an elderly couple ambled across the tarmac and onto the red carpet that was stretched out on to the road. Arm in arm they then walked straight across leaving a light trail of mud from their stroll in the park. Patterson flinched but didn't move an inch, he fired a look at the Banquet Manager that his gunnery officer would have been proud of as it hit the man's eyes centre bull. With less than a minute to spare the staff were sent back to fetch a vacuum. The clock was ticking dangerously towards the arrival of the Prime Ministerial motorcade. As they manhandled the machine out and plugged it in, Marker moved over to the General Manager and whispered in his ear.

'That security detail positioned across the road using walkie-talkies have told me they will be here in under one minute.'

Patterson blanched and seeing the cleaners still meandering over the carpet prodded Brooks who had just arrived from the roof:

'Get them moving.'

Brooks checked that now all was immaculate and ushered the cleaners away just as the Prime Minister's entourage rounded the corner from the Embankment.

In the kitchen the temperature was nearing 40 degrees. Despite the extreme heat the food preparation had gone surprisingly well. As the welcoming party took up their positions, the first course was being moved to the tables which left the kitchen 'pass' free for the chefs to finish the detail of cooking off the main course. The Chef had decided with the organisers that they would offer guinea fowl as the principal plate and this would require fast last minute roasting at high temperature to get a certain crispness to the bird's skin. The ovens would need to be turned up.

The Prime Minister's cavalcade arrived. Headed by a large Police Ford Zephyr and two motorbike outriders, the Prime Minister's dark maroon Austin Van den Plas followed. As the car pulled up next to the red carpet a detective jumped out from the front seat, walked to the nearside rear passenger door and looked up and down the street. The Adelphi doorman stood back with the hotel management team. When all looked clear the driver unlocked the door and the PM got out, Gannex mackintosh, pipe in hand. Patterson moved forward to greet him and Brooks, standing back, waited for the rest of the entourage to gather.

The welcoming party then moved through the foyer and into the ballroom. The Crystal Room is a large beautifully decorated space with a ceiling of *Trompe l'Oeil* painted as the sky. The Prime Minister was sat at the top table and after the welcome speech the meal service proceeded. In the kitchen the atmosphere was becoming unbearable, it was heated both in terms of temperature and temperament. If the air handling units were not going to go on the service would have to slow down whilst the team took it in turns to work near the stoves. The main *entrée* was just about to come out of the ovens and that would take the temperature even higher. Just as a moment of crisis was about to arrive, Klimp managed to get the power restored and started the units on the roof.

The fuse board was now allowing power and the Chief Engineer demanded full muscle via the controls in the electrical sub-station. At the precise time that the units returned to maximum extract, the banquet chefs were taking the roasting birds from the oven range. A young *Commis Chef*, nervously pulling out the roasting tray with his cloth then accidently spilled some of the sizzling fat from the pan and into the rear of the oven. It spilled straight onto the gas flame and there was an instant blaze.

Such was the scale of the flashover that it caught the bottom of the range hoods and engulfed the extract chimney. The kitchen instantly filled with smoke as the fire took hold against the grease laden walls of the stack.

What should have happened next never did. The panel controlling the fire suppression system had been switched off during the process of repair to the air handling system. The extinguishers on the kitchen hoods failed to activate and the sensors in the chimney which should switch off the enormous drawer of air created by the air handling units were still in hibernation.

Within thirty seconds the whole chimney was alight from basement to rooftop driven by the draw of the enormous wind pull created by the air handling units on full power.

In the Ballroom the clearance of the first course continued without interruption but a glance to the beautiful ceiling painted with blue sky revealed a certain change of atmosphere. There were large grey clouds of smoke rising from the service doors and gliding across its expanse in a strata of cumulus.

On the roof Brooks had returned to see how work was progressing and to have a quiet Rothmans. Whilst he was taking in the fine prospect of the South Bank he began sensing an acrid smell that wasn't entirely from his cigarette. Looking behind him he was astonished to see huge plumes of black smoke pouring from the main extract chimney. For the second time in so few days, a familiar sense of sickening tightness ran across his chest as a wave of panic washed over him. Grabbing the handrail he ran down the metal gantry now covered in black soot and ash back to the top floor hotel corridor. Shaking with fear he ran into the service area and called the switchboard to see if anyone had raised a fire alarm. They had not.

Patterson had by now returned to his suite on the seventh floor to take a little smoked salmon for lunch and at that precise moment was snoozing on the couch in his commodious sitting room. Brooks asked the switchboard to put him through to the General Manager's apartment. The phone rang and Patterson reached across from his light green sofa to the antique side table to answer.

'Yes...?'

'It's Brooks, I have just come from the roof and I think the kitchen extract chimney is on fire, but no alarm has been made – I'm going to call the fire team to assemble in the main kitchen but I thought it better not to raise the evacuation alarm until we've checked as we have the lunch in full swing downstairs.'

'God no! – Don't pull the general evacuation switch – we will have ten fire engines here and the Press in an instant. Check it out and I will meet you down there.'

Patterson looked out his window and could see great clouds of black smoke drifting across the Strand. Sighing, he put on his tailcoat and decided to take the lift to the ground floor.

In the banquet kitchen the situation had quickly become unviable and as the kitchen brigade tumbled into the Ballroom they let out clouds of smoke through the service door onto the diners. In full flight out of the kitchen one of the Chefs pushed the fire alarm and with no consideration for management's pressing desire to avoid any form of alert, the whole hotel filled with the ringing of bells and klaxons. The fire panel went into full evacuation mode. The uproar was instantaneous, some rushed for the exits; others fell to the floor under the tables. The Prime Minister's protection team ran to his table, grabbed him by his arms and bullied their way out through the scrambling horde.

Richard Marker was in ante-room finishing a plate that he had filled with the first course. Now he faced a dilemma; should he resist a final mouthful of the lightly poached tuna from the salad or run for the exit too? He looked at the plate thoughtfully and took another mouthful. Standing up and chewing appreciatively, he joined the *melee* that was pouring out on the street.

As the exodus bucketed into the Embankment Gardens, the hotel management was nowhere to be seen. Patterson found his lift was taken over by the automatic fire system and had descended to the basement. Brooks was still on his way to the ground floor and would be some minutes from getting to the Embankment entrance. By the time they had assembled the Prime Minister had been spirited away in a very fast moving motorcade of police cars, the Van den Plas having been modified for fast getaways, and most of the guests were standing bemused in the road. At that point, just audible above the crescendo of angry voices could be heard the sirens and bells of the arriving fire brigade.

Amongst the throng stood a man with an ashen face and balding head, it was Sir John Bulling. To his right was Diana, his assistant. A journalist with a hand held recorder pushed up alongside him.

'Hello Sir John, *The Daily Express*, what do you think that this will do to the share price?'

Bulling looked as if murder was crossing his

mind as he gave a stare so icy it probably froze the ink in the hack's pen.

Patterson and Brooks reconvened with Otto Klimp in the General Manager's office.

'So Klimp,' glowered Patterson, 'am I to tell the press that our kitchen chimney went on fire because it was filthy and that we switched off the alarm system because of maintenance?'

'Well sir.' Klimp started out bravely. 'You don't have to tell them that we switched the alarm system off as someone had the foresight to hit the fire button. That makes the siren go off regardless of what we had isolated on the fire panel.'

Klimp's expression somewhat morphed and he looked distinctly mournful as he nervously searched through his sheaf of papers for some shred of evidence to support his position:

'I think we should say that our extract systems are maintained by an external company and along with the Fire Authority we will be urgently investigating the cause.'

'Klimp you're an idiot for servicing those units

on such an important day. I'm not looking forward to the Fire Chief's report. Brooks – go and see the Press Office and sort out a statement. I have to go and see the Chairman.'

Patterson left the office and briskly made his way to the Directors' corridor. Diana was waiting for him. Putting down her nail file she said:

'Well he's not at his best as you can imagine,' she smiled and led him, Daniel like, straight into the lion's den.

'Patterson, it was unmitigated disaster, totally inept. Where on earth were you and your team?' Bulling continued:

'Beside the explanations that I have now to give to No. 10, I have to see the organisers of 'The Heroes' to offer my apologies and of course a full refund – and just hope that they will re-book. To cap that, I have had non- stop press calls and a plummeting share price.'

The phone rang and Bulling pulled the receiver from its base. Quiet for a second, he considered what Diana was telling him and decided to take the call. He signalled Patterson to leave and exasperated fell back into his chair. This call was important. It was James Egerton. Broadman was once again pushing for a sale against this latest piece of disastrous news.

∞∞∞

George Brooks was also sitting in his office, it had certain grandeur albeit was less imposing than that of the General Manager, but it reflected his status as the man that really ran the hotel. As he looked vacantly at the hunting prints on his wall he was reflecting on three things.

The first was the fire and how quickly they might be able to reinstate the banquet kitchen as well as clean the Ballroom ceiling of soot stains. Secondly he was considering the evening ahead with Miss Parte, one that would be doubtless satisfying in both a physical and emotional sense, and thirdly he was thinking of his upcoming vacation. Rome, he thought, would be an excellent idea.

As he glanced across the room he saw that the street lights were just coming on in the Strand. His phone rang and it was James Egerton again.

He took the call, listened and then replied:

'Yes Mr Egerton, unfortunate and especially with the Prime Minister there, I expect some awful report will appear in *The Evening Stand-*

ard, probably in Londoner's Diary,' he paused and listened as Egerton asked him again about the Bulling family.

'I don't need to do much research on the Bullings – I know a lot about their family, the Bulling dynasty goes back to when Sir John's grandfather made a lot of money in wool manufacturing and built the hotel. Its best years were when Sir John's father, Lord Bulling, was in control. The two of them ran it together for some time as Chairman and Managing Director respectfully, then old man Bulling died after a heart attack whilst out shooting. John Bulling then got his knighthood through has father's contacts in the House of Lords. Probably paid something to the Conservatives I expect. Usual drill.'

Egerton wanted more and asked about Bulling's private life. Brooks went on:

'As you know, Sir John married twice. His first wife, Cynthia, died in some sort of accident and he married again a few years after to Julia, Lady Bulling. He has one son, Andrew, from his first marriage and a daughter from his second. Andrew is estranged because he doesn't like his father, his father's choice of new wife, or his father's way of running the business. I was at hotel school with him. The daughter is at school somewhere I think...' Brooks waited for a reply and then added:

'Unusual?' He queried, 'well... unusual in what sense?....Oh, Andrew; well John Bulling is a bully and nowhere near the ability of his father, and he's aggressively uncompromising when under pressure. I think you'd put the relationship that he has with his son as the same that I imagine Prince Philip might have with Charles.'

When the call was finished Egerton reflected on what he'd heard. His first call to Bulling when he had learnt about the fire was useful in putting a little more pressure on him, his second call to Brooks had been more revealing. He considered his next moves and decided to call one of his more ambitious executives. He pushed the intercom and spoke to his secretary.

'Get me Adrian Archer.'

Archer was a director of Broadman and owner of his own property portfolio. He was a man of relentless drive and ambition who shrieked sharp business instinct. In the war years he had been fortunate to foster close relations during his Middle East posting as a junior intelligence officer. His charismatic approach as a savvy Captain in the 8th Army had won him the admiration of some close Saudi friends. Saudi Arabia, though neutral, was concerned with an Axis attack on the Suez Canal and young Archer's responsibility with his troop was to cut off any lightening assault. To achieve that he had built a strong relationship with the Al Mukta family who lived in Jeddah and as traders had specific interest in keeping the canal open.

After the war, at the suggestion of Abdulla Al Mukta, the father of his friend Hamsa, he took a directorship on the Board of Sol Brava, a company looking to make property investments in London.

After some success he formed his own property company. With his aggressive ambition he accumulated a large number of derelict and bomb damaged properties by London docks. He let these out to some of the poorest immigrants who had made it up the Thames from war-torn Europe. By the mid-sixties he was now one of Britain's biggest slum landlords.

His first commission with Sol Brava had been to acquire The Adelphi on behalf of the Al Mukta family. He had tried very hard to gain control, but the hotel had a complex 'A' and 'B' share structure. The 'A' shares held most of the voting rights whilst the value was retained in the traded 'B' shares. The Bulling family owned the majority of the 'A' shares and had these split across their extended household. He had met Lord Bulling and his son, James and found them intransigent, but he thought he had made some progress with his late wife Cynthia. He had found her charming and somewhat at odds with her husband. It had seemed to him that given the right offer she might have sold, left her husband and set up elsewhere with the proceeds. Then she was involved in an unresolved accident and the deal, along with her, died.

A dark undertone had been rumoured but not even the Coroner's report signed off by the Chief Constable made further enquiry of the possibility that she might have been in marital difficulties and considering to sell her shares. An action that would subsequently cause the Bullings to lose control of The Adelphi.

Now, as a director of Broadman, he was once again involved with an ambitious plan and this time it was for the Strand redevelopment and The Adelphi for the second time was in his sights. He was not going to let the Bullings get away this time.

Egerton called Archer to arrange a meeting. It was time to see if there was more that could be done to put pressure on Bulling to sell. The next day Archer was at Broadman's Head Office.

'Come in, take a seat...' Egerton gestured to the chair on the left of his desk.

Archer looked around the ultra-modern office,

walked over to the window and took in the rooftop vista of the City.

'Quite a view. It always impresses me.'

He moved over to the large desk and took the seat on the right.

'Yes, you know we are proud of what we build. Up in under three years with your help and it's a major landmark. I see that in that latest architectural magazine the press are calling it 'The Cup' as it looks like the Football Association Trophy; it's the small dome shaped viewing platform on the top that does it. You'll be pleased to know that all thirty seven floors are fully occupied and making good rents.'

Egerton moved back into his chair and placing his elbows on the desk leaned forward and looked directly at Archer:

'Developing the Strand is an attempt to improve the retail experience. We've got eyes on Coutts Bank opposite Charing Cross Station and perhaps could get that but it looks more likely that they will redevelop themselves. Then there is Charing Cross Hospital that is going to be relocated to Fulham soon. If we can get the Adelphi on the south side we can get all the views to the river stretching from Trafalgar Square to Waterloo Bridge.'

Archer moved closer to the desk and took out his notebook. He uncapped his Waterman pen and started to write. Egerton continued.

'If we want to persuade Bulling to sell The Adelphi, we need to understand his makeup. He's a stubborn and intractable man. What makes him tick, what are his weaknesses? He's a bit of a philanderer and on to a second marriage; I want you to find out what happened to his first wife and what his relationship is like with his second wife. He's got an estranged son, Andrew. Why? Where is he vulnerable? For a man like Bulling there is going to be a history. A cover story somewhere. Who has he angered? What kind of deals has he done in the past that he may not want to be aired with his Monday morning washing? Get the picture?'

Archer got the picture and it wasn't a masterpiece. When Egerton wanted to know about Sir John Bulling and his life, he probably meant shadowy life.

Archer considered all he'd been told and then asked:

'You have a man in the hotel on your payroll. Who's he?'

'The Assistant General Manager, George Brooks, we couldn't find anyone else so well connected.'

'And you say that Bulling has an estranged son?'

'Yes, I'm trying to find out more. Brooks knew Andrew Bulling as a friend, they had been in Switzerland together at the *Ecole hôtelière de Lausanne*.'

'I know Brooks, he looks after me at The Adelphi when I stay. Would you mind if I contact him directly? I have an idea.'

'Of course not, this is his direct line.'

And Egerton passed a handwritten note across to Archer. Egerton finished the meeting and making his way back to his office considered all they had discussed. It would be interesting what Archer might turn up he mused, but in reality he had no possible inkling of the devious plan that was now taking shape in his co-director's mind.

Later that evening Boardman's other director, Charles Van der Fliet had already checked into the Adelphi. He was an intelligent man but with an Achilles heel for unusual tastes and was already spending a happy night at the Rifta Bar in Mayfair's Hay Hill. A man who took partying to new heights, he had started the evening with a reasonable meal at Scott's in Mount Street, and had then wandered down across Berkeley square at about half past nine. It was now midnight and he had already paid for all the champagne that ten girls could drink, albeit that they poured most of it into the flower trough when he wasn't looking. Having settled a sizeable bill, he announced, a little unsteadily, that those who would like a light supper with him in his suite at The Adelphi could now join him. And with that asked the doorman to get two cabs.

The girls, who were dressed more for a discotheque than a luxury hotel all decided to go. After all, Charles Van der Fliet was known to be generous and there was safety in numbers. When they got to the hotel's Strand entrance the cabs were paid off and they all followed him across the marble floor to the riverside lifts. The night receptionist picked up the phone and called the Night Manager.

'Mr Van der Fliet has arrived with a collection of girls that look as if they have been on a hen night and they are all heading for his suite.'

The Night Manager decided to go to the fifth floor pantry and see what was going to happen next. After ten minutes or so the waiter's phone rang. The floor waiter answered:

'Fifth floor butler,' he announced and took the order.

'Well' asked the Night Manager: 'what was it?'

'Four bottles of Louis Roederer Cristal, scrambled egg and sausage, kedgeree, some minute steaks and a large plate of cut fruit with a lot of strawberries. He wants his dining room table extended for eleven places and set up for the meal.'

'Alright – you get on with that and keep me posted.' With that he left it in the good hands of the floor staff.

An hour or so later he had a call from Van der Fliet's room.

'Come on up!' He commanded, 'I've not been happy with the quality of the supper we've been served.'

The Night Manager made his way back to the fifth floor and knocked on the suite door.

'Come in.'

Van der Fleit appeared in a dressing gown that could have been on loan from Noel Coward. As he opened the door the Night Manager beheld a scene more appropriate to a Fellini film. Seated around the table with chairs at a variety of angles were some of the girls in various stages of undress but on top of the table, caught in an embrace as if some moving erotic Rodin sculpture were two naked girls making love to each other.

'What kind of eggs do you call these?' Van der Fleit asked pushing a filled yellow ochred plate into his stomach.

'Scrambled.' The Night Manager replied trying to keep his eyes on the plate rather than the scene behind.

'They are so solidly overcooked that you could plaster cracks in walls with these.'

'I'm so sorry sir. I'll get them changed and deliver them myself.'

With that he took the plate but perhaps a little shaken and certainly stirred, he went straight down to see the Night Chef. There he ordered a fresh timbale of eggs and as fast as he could, took the lift back to the fifth floor. He knocked on the door and one of the girls who was improbably wearing nothing but a silk dressing gown opened it.

'Come on in,' she smiled a welcome.'Charles, someone's here with the eggs.' She shouted in through the closed bedroom door.

'Tell him to take a seat and make him feel at home.'

With that she showed him a vacant seat. He put the fresh eggs on the sideboard and took the empty chair. She came over, slipped off her gown and sat naked on his lap. The two girls were still making love on the table, and he saw a considerable stack of brown ten pounds notes on the table. Not especially wanting to stop the entertainment, nor wanting the girl to get off, he innocently whispered in her ear:

'What are the notes for?'

'Oh' she replied. 'Charlie has a game where he puts out fifty pounds at a time until one of us decides that they are willing to go on the table naked. Then he starts another pile until one of the girls agrees that for that brick of notes she will make love to the other girl. It's a game of brinkmanship.'

'Have you had a go?' he asked.

'No, I really only like guys, and I can feel underneath that you like me too.' The Night Manager blushed and she slipped her hand into his trouser pocket to test his hardness.

'I don't think I'm allowed to indulge in this sort of way - on duty.'

The girl got up and knelt down in front of him and started to undo his trousers. The Night Manager, who was really only recently a young man, began to panic.

'Don't worry.' She said, 'Charlie's paid for this already.'

'What if he comes out?'

'Oh he won't, he's gone inside with Mercedes, and he'll be ages yet.'

But within a minute the lounge door had swung open and Van der Fleit was there with his dressing gown immaculately done up, just as before.

'I see you've made yourself comfortable.'

He smiled at the Night Manager who was leaning back whilst his companion enjoyed a very large mouthful of manhood.

'Have a drink.'

He lifted the champagne bottle, poured a glass and put it in his hand.

'I'm not supposed to drink on duty.'

He said, and Van der Fleit looked back over his shoulder and said:

'Well you seem to be able to do everything else.'

He sat down at the table and clapped his hands and made an announcement:

'Now girls all change. Let's see someone else.'

The girls got off the table and sitting down opposite still couldn't stop kissing each other.

Van der Fleit pulled out some more money.

'The wretched bank doesn't make twenties or fifties any more. You have to have a suitcase to carry this stuff around today. Ridiculous. Who would you like to see?'

The Night Manager was beginning to relax and with little concern for the consequences, took a swig of the champagne and selected a petite auburn haired girl.

'Alright Mandy, hotel management have selected you. £100 says you are on the table,' said Van der Fleit.

Mandy looked a little distant.

'Well as long as I can pick my partner, and she doesn't get more than me.'

'Olivia? Will you do it with Mandy? I know she likes you?'

'£120 for us both.'

Olivier was clearly commercially minded.

'Done.'

Van der Fleit counted out the money in two neat piles. Mandy stood up and unzipped her gown. She was wearing a light see through bra, nude stockings and a beige suspender belt but nothing else. She undid her bra and climbed on top of the table. The Night Manager worried that the table might give way, but it looked up to the task as Olivia got on at the other end. Standing three feet in the air she slowly undressed, peeling off her French knickers last of all.

Mandy cleared a space in the centre, and kissed her friend. Then she slowly moved her hand to caress Olivia's breast and squeezed her nipple. Olivia responded and felt an internal hardening between her legs. Slowly Mandy moved her other hand between Olivia's legs and began a slow circular movement. Olivia lay back on the table and Mandy put her head between her thighs. She wanted to make sure that that the two men could see her making love, so she arched her back and swept her auburn hair to one side so that they could appreciate the view.

Things were begin to get steamy when the Night Manager's pager went off. Irritated the Manager looked at the signal and frowned.

'All good things must come to an end Mr Van der Flcit, I have to go, don't forget the eggs, they will get cold.'

Mandy waved from her position on the table as he left the room, she couldn't say much as she was distracted elsewhere.

DEREK PICOT

Chapter 3

As day broke The Adelphi returned to its early morning routine and by eight o'clock the Night Manager had met up with George Brooks for a handover.

'Anything unusual to report?' Brooks asked.

'Nothing of any significance. Van der Fleit was entertaining and complained that the breakfast he was serving a group of his friends wasn't up to scratch. I changed the scrambled eggs and made an allowance on the bill. He got through a decent amount of Cristal.'

'He's a Broadman Director. Might be important if the takeover goes through. Best to look after him.'

Brooks added. The Night Manager said that he certainly would.

Later that morning another Broadman director got in touch. Adrian Archer rang George Brooks on the pretext of asking for his usual reservation. After he had given his booking details he asked Brooks:

'I think you're a good friend of our Managing Director, James Egerton'

'Yes I know him well.' Brooks was guarded.

'Come on George you know him better than that, you're helping us with our takeover plans and we are helping you with your bank account.'

Brooks felt a rush of blood and blushed even though no one was in the room. He had that unpleasant empty feeling in his stomach again.

'I'd like to ask you a question about the Bullings.'

'Go ahead.'

Brooks mouth followed his throat and went dry.

'So you know Andrew Bulling?'

Brooks relaxed a little.

'Oh yes, we studied together, we are good pals.' Brooks replied, careful not to slip into any vernacular that would betray his roots as coming from less than the best public school.

'Oh that's useful, tell me, how does he feel about his father?'

Brooks considered the question for a moment:

'Well that's an interesting comment Mr Archer, there seems to be a lot of interest in the Bulling family now that we have a hostile bid.'

'Come on Brooks, what's the real dope on Andrew?'

'Well he resents his father which is why he doesn't have anything to do with the family business. He's been disinherited because his father thinks he does drugs. His father lost his mother when she died in a motorcycle accident that was probably caused by his father's drunk driving. It's all pretty sad really. I see him from time to time, we meet at a pub in Earls Court.' Not all of this was news to Archer.

'I'd like to meet him. Can you ask him to give me a call, I think I have something of interest that might see him through to a brighter future.'

'I certainly will' replied Brooks.

'And keep this between you and me Brooks, I will make it worth your while.'

'I certainly will.'

Replied Brooks with more emphasis this second time round.

After he put down the phone he dialled the number he knew off by heart.

'Hi Andrew? It's George.'

'How's it going?'

'We're fine at the hotel. I've had a call from Adrian Archer, he's a director of Broadman who are making a bid for the hotel. He wants to talk to you, says he has something interesting.'

Brooks passed over the rest of the message and then said:

'I'm looking at Rome for that vacation. If Archer comes up with some cash you might be able to afford it after all.'

'Well let's see,' said Andrew and they finished the call.

Richard Marker was still nursing a grievance against Brooks caused by the slight of not being invited to his cost control meeting held the previous week.

'Can't see why you'd wanted to go.' Mrs Haul had said.

'They're just a bunch of ineffective homosexuals who've no real idea of how to run a luxury establishment of this calibre,' and after a pause added: 'especially that Brooks.'

Marker had bumped into the housekeeper as he was strolling down one of the hotel floor corridors towards the switchboard on the second floor and he'd complained to her that he hadn't been asked to join the departmental meeting. He thought it was just plain rude. But the Housekeeper's last remark had sunk in. Marker continued towards the telephone room pondering the idea that Brooks was homosexual. He was mystified, Brooks was dating Sandrine, what did that make Brooks?

He reached the panelled door to the left of the floor lift and entered the telephone room. Seated in front of an enormous panel with an array of plugs and cords were three operators. They spent all day taking incoming and outgoing calls for the guests as well as the hotel offices. There were over a thousand extensions and forty trunk lines coming in. He liked to sit there from time to time and talk to the girls who enjoyed a gossip. He had picked up a lot of information that way. Today it was the late shift who had just taken over at four o'clock and whilst he was talking to Mary, a large and comely woman who ate chocolate digestive biscuits as if they were the ambrosial of the Gods. Then he overheard one of the other girls put Andrew Bulling through to George Brooks.

Now that was interesting he thought. Why would Andrew Bulling want to talk to Brooks?

After fifteen minutes or so listening in to the non-stop action of international calls in from the States and local calls to a myriad of city businesses he decided to return to his basement room and complete the report he had made on the fire.

At about the same time that the team changed on the switchboard so eight fresh good looking male receptionists arrived to take over the Reception Desk in the lobby. The late shift were all dressed in evening dinner jackets and black bowties. The early brigade, who were fitted out with full tailed morning suits, were finishing up the arrivals book and completing the bill openings for the new guests. All bills had to be manually typed and passed to the bill office on the floor above. The Brigade leaders handed over to each other, and the remaining arrival list together with the guest profile cards were discussed.

The profile cards initially came from the Card Index, a large room that was filled with filing drawers alphabetically storing details on every guest who had ever stayed at the hotel. The room even contained a 'dead' file from which famous personalities who had stayed and since died were retained. The Index was looked after by Mrs Williams who took pride in showing visitors some of her 'treasures'.

Pride of place in the dead file was a card illustrating the stays of a certain Benito Andrea Mussolini. It noted his move to Prime Minister of the Kingdom of Italy, his various stays at the hotel, then his rise to life President and finally with a long red diagonal line across the whole card, the entry 'lynched Milan Square 1945'.

The cards provided a sort of idiots guide to who was who. Charlie Chaplin's card was noted as 'famous actor' in case some new receptionist might come across him signing in and not know who he was. Everything that happened was noted here and was the main port of call for Marker. If three coat hangers went missing, it was duly recorded on the card and a black tag attached. Steal from the Adelphi and you never returned.

That evening the Shift Leader noted that he still had a few rooms to sell and so when approached at the desk by a man in his thirties who was asking for a room for the night he felt he might take a chance to increase the evening's revenues. He called the Porters Lodge to see what luggage this new arrival might have and was told he only had an overnight bag.

Sensing that this client might be a 'skipper' (someone who might skip from paying the bill) he decided to take a large deposit of £200. He was surprised when the money was handed over in cash, but this suited both the client and the hotel accountant. He checked the registration. The form gave some brief details, the name was filled in as Peter Norman, his stated nationality British and therefore didn't require to show a passport. As such he could be afforded the 'British rate' a discount for those that spoke English properly and were clearly on the upper scale of social class. This guest looked the part and seemed to have the money. The address was given as somewhere in Southend. The box indicating method of payment was ticked 'cash'.

'That'll be a deposit of £200 please.'

The Shift Leader looked at the guest more quizzically than he might one who had taken the trouble to write a letter reserving their accommodation.

'That's steep.' Norman replied.

'Well we only accept cheques with a prior arrangement.'

'So I have two choices? Just take it or leave it?'

'I'm afraid so sir.'

The new arrival put his briefcase on the desk and opened it so that the flap shielded the receptionists eyes. He counted out the notes and passed them over.

Everyone who checks into The Adelphi is escorted to their accommodation by a receptionist and this guest was no exception even though he hadn't reserved in advance. The Shift Leader looked though the Witney racks which contained the name of every guest registered and where vacant rooms were kept to one side. He took a random vacant room and allocated it to the main house inventory. The room was not prime accommodation being located on the side of the hotel overlooking the Strand but it was comfortable enough to meet the standards of even the most demanding.

'It'll be apartment 743 and my colleague will show you up.'

And with that Peter Norman closed his briefcase and followed the dinner jacketed young man to his room.

Most of that day's guests had arrived by nine o'clock and the Shift Leader was finalising the large book that contained all the new bills that had been opened when his desk phone rang. The evening Housekeeper on duty was on the line asking for permission to let one of her maids stay overnight so that they could service some urgently required rooms early the next morning. There were still some vacant rooms left and with the approval of the duty manager the Reception Office was authorised to give her overnight accommodation. The room allocated was exactly opposite the room that had been given to the walk-in guest.

Norman had settled well into his room and after the Porter had arrived with his overnight bag he started to unpack. He placed a large bundle of £5 notes in the dressing table drawer, along with a large kitchen knife and his Colt Commander .38 pistol. He checked that the magazine was full. Then he pulled out the men's magazine that he had purchased earlier in the week that had all the numbers of the best escorts in town. He checked over the listings and was satisfied that the one that he had originally circled in black ink was the best choice. He reached for the phone and sitting on the side of the bed dialled the number.

'I'd like a girl for tonight please'

'Are you a client?'

'I'm staying at The Adelphi and my name is Peter Norman. My room number is 743.'

'We will call you back.'

Norman replaced the receiver and waited for

the call. It was their way of checking that they knew where he was and that he was *bonafide*. A gold plate address like the Adelphi was as good a reference as you could get. A minute passed then his phone rang. The hotel operator answered:

'I have a Mr Shah on the line from The London Agency, do you wish to take the call?'

'Put him through.'

There was a pause:

'Hello, Peter Norman here, yes that's right. A credit card? I'd rather pay in cash. Yes, I can leave it for collection in the next hour at the Enquiries desk in the lobby. You can pick it up anytime.'

'What type of girl would you like?' asked the caller.

'Well Mr Shah I want someone in their late twenties, experienced, blonde typically English, no foreigners please.'

'That's fine, let's say half past ten tonight. I understand, £50 for you in the envelope and I pay the girl £50 and anything extra is extra. How much is extra?'

There was another pause

'I see, it's up to me to negotiate.'

When he put the phone down he re-dialled the Enquiries desk and asked for someone to come up to take an envelope for collection. A few minutes later a liveried young boy wearing a pork pie hat knocked on the door and announced himself as a messenger. He took the envelope addressed to Mr Shah and bid Mr Norman a good evening.

Norman stripped naked and took a shower. He went over to his overnight bag and pulled out another magazine. This one was more of a specialist publication.

It was full of pictures of naked men in explicit positions. He turned the pages until he found the one of three men sodomising each other. He thought they looked very young, very muscular and very virile. He then lay on the bed and imagined himself as the missing fourth. If there were spare holes to fill, why not? He held the pages open and masturbated over the magazine. Just as he was almost at release there was a knock at the door, he slapped the pages shut and put the magazine under the bed.

He hoped it wasn't the girl he'd ordered, it was far too early but on the second knock he heard the word 'Housekeeping' and quickly put on the dressing gown the hotel thoughtfully provided for such moments. He called out 'Enter'. The room maid was quite attractive.

He admired all the curves as she turned down his bed and changed the bathroom towels for clean ones. Then she asked if he would like the curtains closed and he thought it would be a good idea, especially with what was going to happen. She reached up to pull the cord and he noticed the tops of her stockings where showing and there was bare flesh above. Shame she's working here he thought, because she's would have done nicely.

After she had gone he decided to watch television for a couple of hours. At ten o'clock he checked the bundle of notes, took them out of the drawer and left them on top of the dresser, he then slid the knife under the left hand pillow of his bed and decided to leave the gun in the drawer. He then went over to a side pocket of his overnight bag. He pulled out a cone of paper and poured the white powder onto the desk top. Taking his knife he chopped it more finely and looking at his watch decided to snort the cocaine immediately. It was almost time.

At ten thirty there was a knock on the door. He went over and opened it.

The blonde stood waiting to be asked to enter. She was the right age, well dressed in spangled blue boob tube and a tight fitting black mini skirt.

'Come on in'

Norman smiled and gestured towards the armchair which he had been sitting in to watch the television. The ten o'clock news had just finished.

'Would you like a drink?'

'That'd be nice. I'm Amanda by way.'

'Peter. Gin and tonic?'

'I'd prefer champagne.'

Norman looked at the contents of the minibar and found a quarter bottle. He slid down the gold foil and untwisted the wire cage. The bottle popped and whilst he was pouring the glass the girl was looking out of the window. She had, of course, already seen the stack of five pound notes on the dressing table.

'So what would you like to do?'

'How much is it going to cost me?' he asked

'Well just because I am here it's £50 and my taxis are another £8. If you want straight sex it's £50, if I stay the night, and that might be fun, it's £100. Any extras are £10 and I don't do anal.'

'Thank you,' said Norman as he handed her the glass. 'Cheers.'

She took a sip and put the glass down. He had

picked up a scotch that he had been drinking earlier and holding it in his right hand put his left on top of the banknotes. He wanted time to take her all in. She was attractive in a garish sort of way, her hair was obviously dyed but it had subtle highlights and her eyes were a piercing blue.

Her figure was all that a heterosexual could ask for, firm breasts, tight waist and rounded hips. But he wasn't a heterosexual, he was just curious.

'Would you like to freshen up in the bathroom?'

'Aren't we going out first?' She asked.

'Well I thought I might like a little horizontal relaxation beforehand,' he lied. 'I'd like to book you for a longer time, I want you to get to know me as someone that you wouldn't forget.'

Amanda made her way to the bathroom and locked the door. 'He's a right one,' she thought, 'but looks alright in a boyish sort of way.' She slipped off her panties, put them in her handbag and excused herself.

Whilst she was out of the room Norman could already feel the beginnings of his arousal, and he slid out the magazine he had under the bed for one more look. He put it in away in his overnight bag and by the time he heard the toilet flush he had a solid erection.

She came out, looked across to the money and said:

'It's payment in advance.'

'Count yourself out the cash.'

As she started to pick up the five pound notes he moved silently behind her with the hotel dressing gown cord in his hands.

'Here wait a moment,' she said looking alarmed. 'These are fake notes.'

Then she let out a scream as the cord went around her neck and she was jerked back onto his knife. He pulled tighter on her neck but she was still able to scream. Panicking, he pulled the knife out of her back and slid it across her throat until the screaming stopped and it was replaced by just a rush of air from her lungs through her sliced thorax. She slumped back in his arms and he laid her on the floor. He felt her warm blood run over his hands.

'Filthy bitch' he thought as he excitedly pulled her top down to her waist and plunged the knife into her breasts, stomach and thigh. He couldn't resist licking the blood from her thigh and savouring its metallic flavour. Looking up he saw that she was still alive as her mouth moved, she was trying to say something through the bubbles of plasma that were spilling copiously onto the carpet. So he took out his Colt and shot her once in the head. 'Pop' the gun went and the back of her head splintered ended up on the side of the furniture. Looking at his work he decided to pose the body and heaved it along the floor. He positioned what was left of her head so that she would be looking with those blue piercing eyes at whoever was the first to arrive on the scene. The outstretched arms were a nice touch.

Although the whole experience lasted less than five minutes he felt elated. It was better than he had ever imagined in his mind. He pulled down his trousers and lifted her skirt. He was surprised she had no underwear, but moving her limp leg sideways he sodomised her. After he was finished he unbuttoned his stained shirt and put on a clean one. Then he went to the basin in the marble bathroom and washed off his knife. He then packed his overnight bag and wrapped the pistol and the knife into his dirty shirt. He decided to leave the forged notes for the Police, it would give them something and nothing to go on. Looking around the room he was sure that he had left it exactly as he wanted them to find it, he then opened the door and left, slowly closing it behind him.

It was the series of piercing screams from the room that had startled the maid who was staying overnight and by chance sleeping in the room opposite. Realising the shouts were from the room next door she reached for the telephone to call for help, but when she heard a noise like a champagne cork and the crying stopped, she put the receiver down. A few minutes later she heard the door open in the next room. Getting out of bed she opened her door to see someone calmly walking down the corridor towards the lift carrying an overnight bag. Closing the door she thought through again what she'd just heard and seen and being a little concerned decided to call the Night Manager.

'There's been a commotion in the room opposite. Yes, 743 I think. A lot of screaming, then silence, then a champagne cork went pop. I was just going back to sleep when I heard the door close in the corridor and so took a peek. I saw a man walking slowly with a bag towards the lift. Maybe they had an argument and he's left without her.'

Despite his youth, the Night Manager was now reasonably experienced about Saturday night sex parties and this one didn't sound right.

'Sounds odd. I will give the guest a call.'

He put down the phone and looked up the

house register. Room 743 was let to Mr Peter Norman. Single occupancy. He picked up the phone and asked the operator for the room. If he had been 'entertaining' there would be a charge for double occupancy. There was no reply.

He then took the lift to the floor and walked to the room door. Knocking several times, there was no answer but as he looked down he saw a thin dark trail of liquid seeping out on the carpet from under the door. He reached down and touched it. It was red, sticky and smelt. This, he knew, was blood.

Using his Grand Master key he opened the door and was met by the naked body on the floor. The piercing blue eyes of a woman staring straight up at him from her lying position on the carpet, her arms outstretched towards the door her naked breasts lying at an angle. He wondered if she might even have been alive when her attacker had left the room and from the look on her face she wasn't pleased to see him go. Her body had by that time had lost a lot of blood and there was a dividing line of white and dark blue running laterally across her torso. The top half was ghostly, the bottom half a cold blue hue.

She could have been beautiful, but her body was now so full of stab wounds she just looked butchered. Through her head was a gunshot wound that had entered just left of her cheek and exited out of the back of her skull leaving half of her brain on the chest of drawers behind. Her eyes held the desperate look of someone wanting to grasp her assailant but had run out of luck. The carpet was drenched in her body fluids and the wall was splashed with red.

This had been a very violent attack indeed. He checked for a pulse, there was none but the warmth of her hand made him retch and he ran for the bathroom to throw up. He ran the tap, wiped the vomit from his mouth, pulled himself together and walked back across the room. He took one last look at the scene of devastation and, deciding not to touch anything else, he left the room.

Closing the door quietly behind him he turned to the maid who had been waiting outside her room in the corridor.

'She's dead.'

'I heard her scream, but then when she stopped I thought it was alright.'

He looked at her rather unsteadily and wiping his mouth with his pocket handkerchief muttered:

'It's not alright, it's ghastly.'

∞∞∞

Marker was appropriately woken by the stabbing rings of his bedside phone and gruntingly acknowledged the call. Swinging his legs onto the linoleum he climbed out of his pyjamas and put on his suit. It was now past one in the morning and he took a taxi arriving at The Adelphi's forecourt to see four or five police cars already parked up. Taking the Pierrot entrance he rode the lift to the floor and pushed his way through the gathering crowd.

He was surprised to find that the senior investigating police officer was a woman, DCI Amelia Bowen. He looked her over. Fortyish, a little frumpy but a woman who appeared to be competently in control. He went over to introduce himself.

'Marker - I'm the Chief Security Officer at The Adelphi. What do you need to know?'

'Names, addresses, we want to know who she is and who he was. Clearly the registration form will be a fat lot of use.'

Bowen spoke with a London accent and Marker could detect that as a North Londoner, she definitely came from south of the river.

'I will get the receptionist who checked this joker in to get out of bed and see if we can get a description. In the meantime I assume the Coroner's men will be here?'

'They are on the receiving platform already. We will have her bagged up and out the goods lift after we've finished the photos. Know anything about this?' DCI Bowen pointed to a pile of five pound bank notes on the dressing table.

Marker moved over to take a closer look.

'Well the one on the top is genuine, but the brick underneath all look false.'

The inspector moved over beside the hotel detective.

'Yes, that's right. My bet is she's a Tom and he was hoping for a free fuck when she got upset about the poor quality of the cash. She's been shot, possibly anally raped and then stabbed repeatedly. He's a jolly one whoever did this.'

After another fifteen minutes the photographer finished up and the black suited men from the Coroner's office arrived.

'You're a bit late tonight?'

DCI Bowen nodded towards them.

'Yes we've had a few tonight, just finished scarping one off the floor with a shovel. He was in a dingy flat near Hammersmith. Must have been there for a month or so.' Casting his eyes downward to the murdered girl he added: 'this one is a lot prettier.'

The DCI gave them a hard look.

'I want forensics to check for semen, what's under her fingernails and an analysis of the weapons used. Judging from the mess on the furniture we'll probably find the bullet in there rather than in her. So I want everything preserved carefully when you pick her up.'

With that they rolled out a long heavy duty black plastic bag, pulled the girl up by the shoulders and ankles and dumped her in the sack. Zipping her up they manhandled the body out of the room as if it was a joint of fresh meat from Smithfield.

With that Marker took one last look at the grisly scene and locked the room.

The next day found him bleary eyed sitting in front of the General Manager and Sandrine Parte. The main job was to minimise the publicity that would inevitably follow. Even though it was early in the morning, the sight of Sandrine's legs and the curtain pelmet she wore as a skirt brought a familiar feeling to Marker and he sensed the beginnings of warmth and another inappropriate erection.

Marker sat close to the window which was slightly ajar. He caught a whiff of the rubbish room that was further down Adelphi Hill. It made his stomach churn and he felt a familiar nausea creeping over him as he recalled the look in the girl's eyes that had followed him around the room. He promptly lost the promise from his cock.

'So Marker, what do we know?'

Patterson looked across his desk and folded his arms on top of it. He looked like a viper about to strike.

'We know that this was as a 'walk-in' all the usual precautions were taken, a £200 deposit and a freeze on the extras bill. The police thought the girl was an escort and we checked the number he called at eight o'clock and confirmed an escort agency was involved. The agency say that she worked part time to pay for the education of her eleven year old son who is at a public school. I don't know which one.'

'How was she killed?'

'She was probably stabbed first, had her throat cut for arguing and shot afterwards. There was a fake pile of banknotes. The police forensics are going to check if she was sexually assaulted.'

'Oh God.'

Sandrine choked and put her coffee cup down on the side table. She didn't feel up to hearing all the specifics of what was looking like a fatal rape. She looked over at Marker with an expression that seemed hardened enough to take a graphic description, but Marker hesitated on the detail and the moment passed.

Patterson turned back to Marker.

'What do we know of the killer?'

'Nothing much, but the receptionist that registered him is a bit of an artist and has given DCI Bowen a pretty good image. They are going to publicise that on the lunchtime news today.'

'Oh God,' said Sandrine again and looked down, this was not good news. 'I hope this story is not going to have legs.'

This was the term the press used when stories walked off in all sorts of different directions. Patterson considered this for a moment.

'Well you'd better put out a holding statement. Fill it with the usual stuff about thoughts with the family that are involved etcetera and our co-operation with the authorities.'

Patterson put his pen down and told them both to keep him informed as things progressed. In the meanwhile he would get the room stripped and redecorated as soon as possible and change the room number on the door. Room 743 wouldn't exist in the future.

Marker walked out of the office following Sandrine.

'That was rough on you last night' she said.

'I can cope.'

Marker looked into her eyes and she felt some sympathy for him. She could see sadness in this lonely man whose work kept him out of the mainstream of events and by its nature aloof and away from the staff. Looking at the way he was dressed he needed a bit of advice on how to smarten up, he needed to be taken in hand by someone but she couldn't imagine that literally.

'Pretty harrowing,' she added before they separated in the lobby.

Marker grasped the opportunity that was swinging in front of his face like the nipple tassels of a stripper.

'Fancy lunch?'

Sandrine eyed Marker as if it might be something she would regret but feeling another wave of sympathy flood over her she agreed. Marker felt a rush of emotion.

As he could eat anywhere he took her to the Pierrot, a thoughtful choice where he imagined Patrick Wildblood, the smooth Irish *Maître d'* would place him in a corner table, discreet enough to watch the clientele but not sufficiently well enough located to command the room. Wildblood worked the room as if on castors and had enough urbanity and charm to make him the perfect target of wealthy single ladies. He knew all his clients intimately. Possibly too intimately. The Pierrot was sumptuously decorated in harlequins and located with a separate entrance just off the main entrance. It enjoyed a clientele of stars from music, theatre and fashion all of them rich, for this was not a place for those without cash. Wildblood and his team of expert waiters could sell a timbale of caviar to the most frugal of diners.

As Wildblood greeted them, Marker glanced out to the forecourt through the large plate glass windows and saw a taxi draw up with a large colourful advert for 'Champion' pasted on its door. Pictured was a large breasted girl in short pants astride a huge spark plug. The slogan appropriately read 'Put the Spark back in your Life'. And that was exactly what he intended to do.

Their table was beautifully prepared with a fine Irish linen white tablecloth, overgenerous serviettes in the same fabric, and laid with Sheffield silverware. The glasses were lightly cut crystal. Sandrine sat on the alcove banquette and Marker took the generous dining chair. The room was becoming quite full for lunch and many of the city regulars had already taken some of the reserved tables. Nothing was allowed to be an assault on the sense of well-being that was generated by the calm atmosphere. The smooth movement of the service was as exceptional as the food which passed from silver salver to porcelain plate.

Marker called the *Sommelier* over.

'A Chardonnay?' he asked Sandrine.

'Why not?'

'Then it's a premier Chablis please....the '65 should be good.'

The *Sommelier* nodded and moved from view, and Marker continued to look over the compendium of wine he had been handed.

'Not everyone knows that all the white Burgundies are exclusively chardonnay grape you know.'

Sandrine smiled and corrected him.

'That's not strictly true, Sauvignon Blanc is found in the *Saint-Bris Appellation*. You forget that I am French.'

Marker blushed at his ignorance and sought to change the subject.

'Tell me more about yourself, it seems to me that rather than promoting the hotel to the Press, you do exactly the opposite. You keep the Press at bay.'

Sandrine dropped her menu and giving a gorgeous smile lent forward onto the table. Her elbows resting gently near her napkin and her hands folded neatly under her face. Marker noticed the colour of her lips, the lipstick of which he had seen when she applied some just before they entered the room. *Chanel Rouge Alure.* Her breasts appeared to rest on the table. Very tempting he thought.

'My job is to protect the reputation of The Adelphi and that of its guests. I spend most of my time denying that we have any celebrities here at all. At the moment we have Bob Hope and Bing Crosby staying and no one except the floor staff and the doormen knows they are here. Richard Harrison is in residence as you know and he gets pretty drunk and doesn't pay his bill. That won't be in the gossip columns either. After that there is a host of B-listers who want exactly the opposite in terms of press attention.'

Marker was aware of who was who but hadn't been able to think of a better opening line. He looked across at Sandrine and considered how it was ever going to be possible to seduce her. She was bright, vivacious looking and well-connected. His mother had warned him about this type of girl. Wasn't she just a bit too 'racy'? The sort that sowed her wild oats on Saturday night and then prayed for crop failure the next day?

The waiter approached the table and took their order. A simple *Sole Meuniere* for Sandrine with *haricots verts* and *Truite Bonne Femme* for the detective. He enjoyed nothing better than the lightly browned mushroom sauce on poached trout. The Chef had to get the right amount of egg into the liaison of cream to get it to lightly toast under the Salamander.

'How will you handle the murder?' He asked.

'We need to see what the police will say to the Press. I have asked them to refer to us as just a West End hotel. I think I have enough influence with the editor of the *Evening Standard* to keep our name out of the paper. Sir John rang me anxious about the impact this might have on the share price and I've told him I think we can come out with minimal damage. That's what I'm paid for.'

Marker was thoughtful.

'We have some good news that the receptionist who took the guy to the room is a bit of an artist. He's done an excellent drawing of our suspect which the police will issue as a sketch on television. I imagine on the regional news. Will that be a problem?'

'Not if they avoid the name of the hotel.'

Marker changed the subject.

'What are you involved with in the Broadman romance at the moment?'

'What? Are you insider trading?'

'I don't hold any shares...'

'The Chairman and I are trying to talk up our business to the FT and other financial Business pages. George Brooks doesn't think we are trading too badly at the moment.'

At the mention of Brook's name Marker was challenged to swallow and the poached spinach he had ordered as a side plate seemed to glue to his teeth.

'Ah, Mr Brooks, I know he called a meeting the other day to discuss cost controls but didn't invite me. Probably because he knows my department is so pared down it has as much meat left on the bones as that fish you're just demolishing.'

'Well yes, that's affecting us all. We'd better avoid a dessert in that case.'

Marker rather rued that last remark as he had been wondering about a *flambé crepe suzette* but decided to forgo the temptation of two delightful dishes on his table at the same time. At that moment Wildblood came across to the table. He elegantly enquired if everything had been satisfactory and then announced that there was a call for the detective.

Whilst he had gone, Sandrine reflected awhile on the latest turn of events. She rather liked this detective, she didn't think he was as sharp as she was, not the brightest spotlight on the stage, but he had something most women might find attractive. Not that she had a maternal instinct, being that her real preference was for young, lean-bodied men. But here was somebody that she could improve, and that might be the beginning of an interesting relationship, especially if he offered her a little more excitement. Maybe she could persuade him to let her get more involved with his investigation. The idea of getting back to something with intrigue would be entertaining, and maybe along the way there was bound to be a few evenings out judging from the potential his stomach had for nourishment.

She saw that the call was going to take longer than a few minutes, so she got up and left the bill for him to sign.

She crossed the chequer board marble floor of the lobby and headed to her office located on the Mezzanine floor next to the card index. The entrance wall was one large noticeboard which was filled with pinned photos of all the good and the great who had ever stayed. Several had personal messages and signatures on them. Richard Burton and Elizabeth Taylor's shots from the set of Cleopatra had 'wish you were here' inscribed on them. Miss Lollobrigida had written 'All my love to you Sandrine' and the latest pictures from the Bond movie - Goldfinger were signed 'Sandrine– thanks a million Sean'. She sat at her desk with this backdrop of glossy black and white which gave her the appearance of a Hollywood talent agent, but her taste wasn't for things of sophistication or the rich and famous, she preferred something a little rougher.

Turning to the events of the previous night she asked her assistant to switch on the office television and watch the next local news bulletin. In the meanwhile she picked up the phone to speak to the William Hickey column on *The Daily Express*.

'Nigel Dempster please, thank you. Nigel, its Sandrine. If you print the name of the hotel in your story about the murder here last night you will be off my Christmas card list and you know that means no more exclusives for you. *Capice*? Excellent – thank you Nigel.'

That was the first off her list, next was the Londoner's Diary on *The Standard*.

Then the television news came on and it showed the sketch that had been made of the suspect. Thankfully the broadcast didn't mention the name of the hotel and everyone in the office sighed in relief, but wondered if this case would be quickly solved.

DCI Bowen had returned to West End Central and was also looking at the television broadcast, and wondering if the sketch was good enough to get any response. It didn't take long. A barman rang in from Earl's Court. He was working at 'The Boltons' that lunchtime and as he served a man at the bar the image came on the screen opposite. He said it was almost an identical likeness to this 'bloke'. He remembered that the man turned around to listen to the news item and promptly left, leaving his untouched drink on the counter.

The Met knew that The Boltons was a well-known pub for homosexuals and an occasional hangout for the underworld, not that there was any direct connection between the two, apart from the Krays. Bowen shouted across the office.

'We're going to Earl's Court.'

The squad left in two unmarked car and sped along the Fulham Road, parking up outside the corner pub.

'He'd bandaged one wrist.'

The barman was leaning on the counter and thoughts of an attempt at suicide crossed Bowen's mind.

'But I've seen him here before, he's a queer and hangs around with some of the more dangerous of our customers.'

'Who are they?'

'You know them, The Firm.'

Bowen knew this to be the Krays, and they were close to an arrest there. She was sure that one of those two were homosexual and decided to talk to CI Read who was leading their investigation.

Back at the station DCI Bowen called home and told her teenage son that she will be home late. It came as no surprise to him so he took some frozen sausages out of the freezer and started to cook dinner for his younger sister.

Bowen looked and felt tired but she was effective at work, a strong no nonsense leader who has gained respect in the force for her integrity and her intuition. It certainly wasn't for her looks.

'So we know that this guy is a fag and that he may have tried to top himself.'

Bowen was talking to 'Nipper Read' on the internal phone. Read was working on an arrest and the Krays were top of his list as members of 'The Firm'. She nodded as he told her about the connection the Earl's Court pub had and said she would await the file. In the meanwhile she was also waiting for the autopsy people and any forensic information that they had. So far all they knew was the length of the knife that was used and a single low calibre bullet they had retrieved from furniture in the room. It had passed straight through her skull. Blown a hole the size of a cricket ball out of the back of her head before embedding itself into The Adelphi's finest oak.

'Let's try the local hospitals, anyone with a wrist injury...'

She barked like a Doberman at her assistant. Good job they hadn't nicknamed her 'Pincher', there was already one of those at the Yard.

Chapter 4

It was Thursday 23 June and at West End Central DCI Bowen has had a breakthrough in her investigation. She had eventually got home the previous evening to Shoreditch just in time to check on her two children and see them in bed. Shame she had no man to help, but relationships that last require compromise and she really wasn't good at that. With this new case she needed some help and the next morning it arrived. The phone in the lounge rang just as she was getting the kids ready, and she answered it with all the charm of a British Rail ticket collector who had heard it all.

'What is it?'

It was her office. She listened as intently as if war was being declared.

'I'll be straight over. Meet me in Fulham.'

The Chelsea and Westminster hospital had reported a man who had attended A&E in the early hours of the morning with a wrist infection caused by a razor blade. The hospital had kept him in for observation. He'd appeared drugged and confused on admission. It didn't take long for him to be picked up and brought in for questioning.

'Where is he now?'

She asked her assistant whilst throwing her bag on her desk as if it was a bowling ball on its way for a strike.

'In the reception suite.' Replied Sloane, a man of few words and even less charisma.

'Let's roll him in and get a team over to search his address. We have prints from the registration form that will help.'

The tape recorder was set up and the suspect observed through the two way mirror. There was a lot of denial, but that wouldn't last when the fingerprints came back positive.

'So they have their man.'

Patterson was sitting across his desk with

Marker standing up and giving a brief explanation of the update he'd had from DCI Bowen. Across the office Sandrine was sitting with a biro and metal spiralled notebook.

'It looks as if he did it for a novelty, kicks, and a kind of new thrill. Apparently it was something he'd always wanted to try while high on cocaine. It seems he was homosexual or perhaps bi-sexual. He wanted to fool an escort girl into sex without having to pay. When she cut up rough with his false pile of banknotes, he did the same but with a knife. Of course he shot her just to make sure she was actually dead.'

'Pretty disgusting,' Sandrine commented, 'and those poor maids who had to clean up the mess. I feel most sorry for her little boy. Do we know anything more about her family?'

'We assume that her parents who are quite middle class will look after him.'

Marker shot her a glance and wondered what class she thought he was. Patterson then asked:

'What are the implications for the hotel?'

Marker considered his next words carefully, because he wanted them to have the maximum effect on Sandrine and her relationship with Brooks.

'Well the killer was asked why he chose The Adelphi. He told the police it was a random thing. Any luxury hotel would have done but several weeks before he'd met the hotel manager of The Adelphi at the Boltons and had, what I think is euphemistically called 'a one night stand.'

'You are not, I hope, inferring that I spend my time in Earl's Court?'

Patterson looked deeply taken aback. The sort of look a priest might have after being accused of having his hand on the knee of a choirboy.

'No sir, but George Brooks certainly has.'

Sandrine visibly paled, and although her mind was spinning like a playground carousel Marker couldn't readily gauge her reaction. Patterson continued:

'Well that is a revelation. What are the police going to do about it? It's only just become legal hasn't it? What was it that MP said in the House last week? Homosexuals are the most disgusting people in the world... Prison is much too good a place for them; in fact, that is a place where many of them like to go - for obvious reasons. Good grief Marker this will be bad if it gets out.'

'Oh I think we can leave Miss Parte to sort that out sir, she has all sorts of relationships that she keeps from the Press.'

Sandrine glanced in his direction with a quizzical look that clearly requested a meeting outside of the current venue.

After a few more enlightening pieces on the same subject, Patterson decided to call the Chairman and keep him abreast of the situation. It wasn't going to be easy and he picked up the phone as the two left the office. They walked together down to the tea foyer.

'What do you know Richard?'

Sandrine stared him straight in the face.

'I know that you and Brooks have an interest in each other.'

'That may not be for too much longer.'

She turned on her Manolo heels and walked purposefully back to her press room.

It wasn't until later that day that she rang Brooks to suggest a light supper. Brooks returned to his apartment to get ready. As he applied the last of his cologne he gave the rooms a glance to see if they were all set for a little entertainment later that evening, and then left for the restaurant. He arrived a little ahead of time and was surprised to see Sandrine already at the long zinc bar of the Embassy Club with a large glass of her favourite Cabernet Sauvignon.

'You're early!'

He gave his most welcoming smile.

'Yes,' Sandrine replied: 'We've had an interesting day. The police have our suspect for the murder.'

'Really! That's terrific!'

'Yes George, it is, but it's more complicated than that. You're involved.'

'Involved? How could I possibly be involved?'

'Because the killer has told the police he chose The Adelphi as he had slept with the hotel manager. Now that wasn't Timothy Patterson although I am never sure of his sexuality and neither by any stretch of the imagination was it Sir John Bulling. It was you George.'

Brooks reddened and looked compromised. His mind collapsed like a dynamited cooling tower and before he could re-assemble his thoughts and a reply of any consequence Sandrine emptied the glass of wine over his head. As she walked out she said:

'You're a shit George. I'm going to get myself tested for the clap.'

That evening Adrian Archer was thinking about the call he wanted to make to Andrew Bulling. He picked up his desk phone and dialled the number that George Brooks had supplied. The phone in Andrew Bulling's apartment rang for a long time. Stirring from his doze Andrew woke with a head that was blurred and he took a little time to orientate himself. He sat up rubbed his eyes and finally worked out where the noise was coming from. He reached out across the sofa and picked up.

'Uh...hello?'

'Hello Andrew? Adrian Archer, I'm a friend of George Brooks. I'm sorry have I woken you up?'

Andrew Bulling had indeed been woken up from a drug infused dream that was so disorientating that he thought he was actually in Liverpool's Strawberry Fields.

'No that's fine,' he lied. 'Who did you say you were?'

'I'm Adrian Archer and I am a friend of George Brooks.'

Andrew now remembered the conversation George had with him. Archer continued:

'I have a business proposition for you that I think you might find financially very beneficial.'

For Andrew this was a whole new term he was not used to. The only propositions he'd recently dealt with were drug deals.

'What is it you want to do?'

His mind was clearing. Shaking his head he felt as if he was coming round from a knock down blow in a boxing ring. God how he hated the aftermath of heroin.

'I want you to come up to see me in Leeds tomorrow. I'll pay your expenses.'

Archer replied.

'Well I'm in London – you must have known that from my number.'

Andrew's head was clearing and he now remembered that he was in his apartment in Fulham. Coming around from his high was depressing to remember where he actually lived.

'Yes, I imaged from the number you were somewhere west. Take the tube to King's Cross and see if you can get here as early as you can.'

The next day Andrew Bulling woke at ten which was an unusual time for him and he was unaccustomed to the bright morning sunshine that streamed through his windows when he opened the bedroom curtain. He dressed in what he thought might be suitable for a business meeting and searched out a tie to go with the clean shirt he had washed and pressed. He sat down on his sofa and picking up his diary tore out the pages that he'd made some notes on for the Leeds address and put the book back down on the cushion. He then walked out on the street and hailed a cab. Expenses were, in any case, being paid for. The cab dropped him in Euston Street and he made his way across the road to the station and looked at the departure board. With ten minutes to spare the board flashed up the platform number for Leeds and he walked over to find the train.

Discovering a suitable seat in First Class he made himself comfortable and slept most of the way to Leeds City station. He joined the queue for taxis and gave the driver the piece of paper he had torn from his diary on which he had written Archer's office address. The taxi drew up at an anonymous office building and he walked over to the Porter's desk in the lobby.

'I've an appointment with Adrian Archer from Archer Developments.'

He returned the stare of the uniformed concierge.

'Name?'

'Andrew Bulling.'

'Fifth floor, the lift is to the right.'

Andrew took the elevator and was met by an attractive girl who introduced herself as the receptionist. She took him through to an area where he threw his coat onto a seat and picked up a copy of a local property magazine to read whilst he waited. He wondered what this could possibly be all about. George Brooks had probably told him that he was looking for an opportunity in the hotel business and wondered if Archer had some sort of hotel project for him to consider. It had been a while since he had been gainfully employed but with his family pedigree he felt he might be qualified for some sort of management role. After a wait of fifteen minutes the same girl asked him to follow her and led him to Archer's office.

Adrian Archer stood up when he entered and shaking his hand asked him to take a seat in one of the armchairs that was positioned to the left of his desk in a separate sitting area.

'Coffee Andrew?' Asked Archer who indicated to the receptionist that a service of two would be required.

'Thank you for making the journey. It's not too bad if you take the fast train.'

Archer made his first impressions of Andrew Bulling from the chair opposite. He was young, quite good looking in a feminine sort of way and he could see that from his dress style that he certainly didn't look heterosexual. Andrew had chosen a bright pink tie with a matching pocket square. And he was, in Archer's opinion, pretty much made for unemployment.

'I wanted to meet you because I think that you can help me with a business venture I am engaged with as a director of Broadman, the development corporation that is currently acquiring property on the Strand.'

Andrew's pre-conceived bubble of aspiration for a job in hotel management popped.

'I'm not sure I can help,' he said. 'My father is the Chairman of The Adelphi and I hear that Broadman is making a hostile bid for control.'

Archer didn't take to the rough vodka driven tone of Andrew's voice but ignored the reaction that it registered.

'Yes I am aware of your father and it's about him that I want to talk to you about.' Archer paused, 'I understand from George Brooks that you are estranged from your father and that you probably haven't seen him in some time.'

'My father is not my favourite person.'

'And why is that?'

'He hasn't seen me since I dropped out of hotel school and although he helped me when I was a student he's cut me out off from his second family.'

Archer considered this for a moment and then asked:

'How do you manage financially?'

'I do a little part time work and I'm trying to find an opportunity in hotel management. I was wondering if that was the reason you might have wanted to see me.'

Andrew looked uncomfortable and crossed his legs.

'Well I do have a proposition for you, but tell me more. It must have been interesting being brought up in a dynastic family like the Bullings and I'm surprised that you aren't being groomed to take your father's position at The Adelphi in due time. He is, after all in his sixties.'

'I don't have a relationship with him since he was rumoured to have deliberately killed my mother.'

Archer looked a little stunned. He knew his mother had died but he hadn't suspected that Bulling had deliberately killed her.

'How did he do that?'

'An accident whilst riding his motorbike back from a party.'

Andrew looked expressionless as he imparted the details as he knew them. He crossed his legs again.

'So you resent him because he killed your mother and he's cut you out of the family business? Surely your mother's death was a proven accident.'

'I'm convinced it wasn't.'

'Why?'

'Because I think it was all too convenient. At the time there was another takeover bid led by a Spanish company just after the war. You know that General Franco was well in control of the country. A company called *Sol Bravo* had strong government connections and owned the Ritz in Madrid. It was making overtures to the family. My mother was intending to sell her stake to them and presumably it would end up with the Spanish dictator's family business, but her death prevented the transaction. Although I was young she told me I was to benefit from that and that we were going to live away from my father. She told me that she was tired of him bullying us and intimidating her.'

Archer showed no reaction as he knew more than most the disappointment he'd had twenty years ago when at that time he couldn't wrest control from the Bulling family. He nodded in a way that he hoped showed only a distant interest. He remembered that Cynthia Bulling was carrying an agenda but he never knew the plan. Andrew continued:

'On top of that I am pretty sure that my mother was or had been having an affair and that my father found out. It was a good way to get rid of a problem that had become both emotional and financially dangerous.'

That was news to Archer.

'Why do you think your mother was having an affair?'

'I remember once that we went to Aylesbury on some sort of shopping pretext but we never went to the shops. We met a man and she gave him a letter and kissed him.'

'Hardly grounds for a divorce or evidence she was having a relationship.' Archer interrupted

'Well it was the impression I was left with, I felt that there was something more to it.'

Archer considered this for a moment and then continued:

'What do you make of your father's second wife?'

'The Lady Julia? Well she's pretty ineffectual. He bullies her like he bullies everybody. I think she's good wallpaper for him. He lets her out occasionally when he wants to impress his friends. She is fifteen years younger than he is.'

Archer changed the subject:

'I've an idea that could get you your inheritance back.'

Archer waited to see Andrew's expression lift.

'And what is that?'

'As you know Broadman is making a bid to gain control of the hotel. They could get the majority of the voting 'A' shares if they had your father's share. Currently they hold a majority stake in the non-voting 'B' shares.'

Archer considered his next words carefully.

'If we could find a way to coerce your father into selling his controlling interest we could proceed with our redevelopment plans. We have made an attractive offer to him but at this time he has no compelling reason to sell. If you were to disappear, say be held to ransom, he would have to sell his stake to pay for your release.'

'Well he's not going to sell to save my skin.' Andrew said decisively.

'I think perhaps you may be wrong. I think from what you've told me we might be able to play to his conscience, but these are details you have to leave to me. Tell me, if I were to arrange for you to disappear for a couple of weeks and we paid you all of the money that you might have gained from an inheritance that is now unobtainable, would you be interested in working with me?'

'Why not? I've got nothing much on...'

Archer considered his next moves and gave Andrew a set of clear instructions.

By the time the young Bulling had left the office there was still an hour for him to get the four o'clock train home. He thought about the details he'd been given and decided he could prepare over the Saturday and Sunday. Maybe he was going to be rich after all.

Andrew returned to his apartment in Fulham and put a few things together. He re-read the notes he'd made from his conversation with Archer. Picking up a pencil he wrote a number down on the notepad in his sitting room and tore the top sheet off and stuffed it in his jacket pocket. Although he was a junkie and led a chaotic life he still had pride. So before he left with his bag he made sure that everything in the flat was left tidy. It was the only discipline he had. Tidiness. Tidy home, tidy mind. But unfortunately Andrew's mind wasn't as tidy as his housekeeping.

He made his way over to Covent Garden and finding the address he used the small key he'd been given by Archer to open the mailbox. In there he found the Yale and Chubb fobs to open the third floor apartment. He climbed the stairs and looked for the door. He walked along the corridor and found the flat. He pushed the key into the lock and discovered the small but comfortable accommodation. The apartment was well equipped and he had all day to sort out anything he thought he might need. He would have to get the food and drink supplies too that he needed for the next couple of weeks.

After Andrew had left Archer considered his next move carefully. With the disappearance of Bulling junior agreed, things were beginning to take shape. On top of that he now knew much more about what had happened to Cynthia Bulling. He could see a clear way that this might be very helpful in persuading Andrew's father to part with his coveted 'A' voting shares.

Yes, he thought, if there was any doubt that he might throw his son to the wolves, he may not if he has a dirty little secret. Archer opened his humidor and lit a fat cigar. He was going to be very relaxed about all of this. He was just in the mood to dial his mistress and talk dirty to her for half an hour.

The weekend had passed quickly and on Monday morning Marker had risen early and made his way to the hotel before eight. He was now sitting in his basement office after once again enjoying a light breakfast of scrambled egg and smoked salmon which had been delivered by room service. He hadn't appreciated the dark looks the General Manager had given him the previous week when he slipped into the breakfast room. He preferred the eggs to the kedgeree which was a little too filling, it left one's palette feeling too smoky from all the fish. After he finished the dish he decided to take the dirty plate and cutlery back to the stewarding area behind the main kitchen. He dropped them into the dishwasher basket and made his way through to the ranges. There he asked the Chef about the smoked salmon. Cornet extended himself to his full height pushed out his stomach. Marker delighted in the fact that he was clearly fatter than he was.

'Come with me.'

And with that the hotel detective had been invited to the 'Holy of Holies'. The Chef's Office. The walls were decorated with a few well-chosen colour prints. One of the Chef meeting the Pope and another shaking hands with Princess Margaret. Marker couldn't make out the characters in the third frame but the picture involved an enormous cake with a girl hanging out of it. The remaining wall space was taken up with clipboards for each day of the week from which hung all the function sheets which detailed every event, its menu and the numbers involved together with the all-important timings.

Cornet, flushed from walking too close to the ovens, picked up the large market list sheet that was waiting for his approving signature in order that the provisions of that day could be delivered and seated himself next to Marker.

'You see here,' he said pointing to the smoked fish section of the list. 'I can buy smoked salmon, Scottish smoked salmon, and smoked Scottish salmon. What do you think is the difference besides the price?'

'Well presumably two are Scottish and one isn't.'

'Correct, but you're not much of a detective

if you can't spot the difference between the Scottish ones.'

'Enlighten me.'

'As always, dear Richard, you need education. Scottish smoked salmon is smoked in Scotland and smoked Scottish salmon is smoked elsewhere, probably London. The flavour you've just enjoyed can only be achieved in the smoking kilns of Inverness.'

'Most revealing.'

'Now tell me Richard, what is the latest on the murder. Are *les flics* on the case any good?'

'Good enough. They have a suspect.'

'Excellent – you must keep me up with events.'

And with that the Chef pushed open the door with his stomach and the detective was shown out.

Marker returned to his office, threw his jacket over the chair and passing over his in-tray, looked at his watch. It was surely time to pay a visit to Miss Parte to check what the morning papers had to say. Before he left his desk he picked up the house list and cast his eyes over the past weekend arrivals. There were the usual selection of weekenders who had come. He was glad of the two days he'd taken off as those type of guests could be much more troublesome than the regulars. They had expectations that were way higher than the price they paid. They wanted to ride the Rolls Royce of hotels on a bus fare. The Adelphi was expensive but some of these people expected it to be the dining hall of the Gods. Just as he was closing his door the phone rang. He retraced his steps and took the call. It was Diana Spurling from the Chairman's office with a request that he pass by immediately. 'Well', he thought, perhaps a little late praise from Sir John for a job well done in catching our murderer. He hurried along to the Directors' corridor.

Diana was looking as immaculate as ever and greeted the detective as he arrived a little puffed from the three flights of stairs that separated their workplaces. She put down her pocket mirror and smiled. Marker smiled back.

'Is in a good mood?'

'Mr Marker it's barely ten o'clock and he's never in a good mood before lunch.'

She told him he could knock and go straight in. When Marker entered Sir John Bulling indeed looked far from happy, in fact he looked decidedly pale.

'Ah! Marker. Now here's a tricky problem that requires your expertise. What do you make of this?'

Bulling handed over an envelope and a sheet of foolscap on which was a typed message.

Marker read it over several times.

Bulling:

Your son has been kidnapped. Call the police and he dies.

Co-operate: He lives

Ransom: £250,000

There will be no negotiating. Payment in Gold Bars. Remember the Willows?

All we want is the money. He will be released as soon as we exchange. Wait for our next instructions

'Can I see the envelope?'

Bulling passed it over. It was typed in the same bold courier script and had one of the brand new first class stamps that had just been introduced. The stamp sat neatly in the top right corner and had a grumpy picture of Churchill.

Bulling paused whilst Marker looked over the items again and then emphatically added:

'We can't involve the police.'

'Why not?' asked Marker.

'Because this is a most delicate time in dealing with the attentions of Broadman Developments' Board. If they find out that I am facing personal difficulties it will weaken my position.'

'But why would the police tell them?'

'Because they are corrupt. I know that there is going to be a major investigation into how most of the Met detectives work and you mark my words those that will go to gaol will be in their hundreds. Under no circumstances are you going to tell them. What you are going to do is find out who has set this up.'

Bulling emphasised the words 'you'. The detective thought it would have been better if there was a 'we' instead of a 'you'.

'Does he owe money to anyone?'

'My son is a waster Marker, he probably does and is up to his ears in drink and drugs. He lives at this address in Fulham and I haven't seen him in years.'

Bulling passed Marker a scrap of paper.

'Why not?'

'Because he's a layabout and bats for the other team. This is where he was living.'

Bulling wagged a pudgy finger at the slip that Marker was now holding.

'What more do you want me to tell you?'

Bulling passed over a sheet of paper that identified an apartment in Iffley Road. It eventually occurred to him what 'batting for the other team' meant was and wondered at the Chairman's range of venacular.

Marker folded the paper and put it in his inside pocket. 'What is this mention about the Willows?'

'I have no idea.'

Bulling huffed and turned to his desk. Marker stood his ground.

'I will need this demand and the envelope, it may have fingerprints on it'

'Well leave it with me for the time being, you have the gist of it now get on with your enquiries and report back to me as soon as you have something concrete. I will let you know if I hear anything.'

With that Bulling showed him the door and after closing it collapsed into his chair and took another familiar long look across the Thames. He stood up, sighed and walked over to the credenza. He picked up the photo of Andrew and muttered 'Bloody fool' and put it into his desk drawer.

He then pushed the intercom switch to his secretary.

'Get me Farndon.'

A few minutes later the accountant arrived in the outer office. Diana looked at the red light on the Chairman's door, closed her lipstick and pushed the intercom key.

'Mr Farndon is here for you.'

The red light turned to green and she told him to go in.

'Ah Farndon, come in, come in. Now tell me, you're a man with your finger on the pulse, what is the value of my family holding?

'About £1 million.'

Farndon knew his numbers but knew those of the Chairman's even better.

'Remind me, how much is the value of my controlling interest?'

'The critical number that you have to possess is ten thousand shares to keep control. At today's price of £22 a share. That would give you £220,000.'

'If I lost control, what would I have in the way of pension?'

'Well you have the benefit of a considerable accrual that would give you and income of over £50,000 a year.'

Bulling considered the numbers and there was

an unpleasant silence in the air. It reminded Farndon of the atmosphere that might appear at the Old Bailey when a murder trial jury is about to return a verdict of 'guilty'.

Eventually the Chairman thanked the accountant and showed him the door.

By that time Marker had retraced his steps to the basement and thought through what he knew. Kidnapping was illegal, but paying a ransom was not. He turned his thoughts to the reference on the note about the Willows. That was odd. What were the willows beyond trees? He had no idea. Deciding that he needed a little light relief he went to visit Sandrine in her office. As he got to the Press Office corridor he saw her coming down the other way.

'Can we chat?' he asked.

'Sure.'

She showed him into the office. He still looked scruffy she thought. Marker closed the door behind him and looked again at the photo wall full of celebrity.

'I keep seeing more people I know on that photo wall but can't put a name to.'

'Who don't you know?'

'That one with the bowler hat.'

'Oh he's John Gielgud.'

Marker still didn't know who that was and decided to change the subject.

'Tell me about Brooks - you seem to know him quite well'.

He didn't want to let her know of his deepest suspicions, but it would be useful to have Brooks out of her affections if his own plan of seduction was to have any success.

'Well I would never have thought he was bisexual.'

'Apart from the fact he bats for both teams, is there anything else that's not kosher with him?'

'Where did you get that term from? Cricket?'

'No, the Chairman this morning.'

Sandrine couldn't make out the connection and decided not to pursue it. The English could sometimes be obtuse. She thought hard about Brooks and then said:

'He's got a relationship with the CEO of Broadman, James Egerton. He calls him from time to time.'

Marker reflected on that for a second or two and

wondered if Brooks could be passing on confidential information, but then what information did he possibly have that could be of any use?

Sandrine continued:

'He's a bit of a shit really Richard. I mean he is fun, quite flash with money but he's misled me on one or two things recently.'

'Oh! What things?'

'Personal ones.'

'Fancy dinner?'

Marker had decided to finish with the cross-examination and considered that the best way into getting his hands anywhere near the Press Officer's lingerie was to follow the trail of food.

'Possibly.' She replied.

The hotel detective felt his body move into another unwanted arousal. Well, unwanted at that time.

Marker left the office and walked through the Front Hall. It was quite busy and he had to wait his turn at the Hall Porter's desk. He ordered a taxi and stood out front until it arrived. He then made his way to Iffley Road.

The street was full of 1930's built terrace houses and the house that Andrew Bulling lived in had a ground floor and a top floor flat. They both looked empty but he tried the doorbells for both anyway. There was no reply. He looked through the letterbox and saw a neat pile of what was most likely junk mail on the side wall radiator. Slipping a plastic card along the door frame he found the latch and pushing hard was able to open the door. The mail was all for Andrew Bulling. Straight ahead of him was a staircase, he ignored the ground floor flat entrance door and he took the stairs two at a time. He used the card again on the first floor latch. The flat smelt musty but it was surprisingly well ordered. There was a small living room that looked over the road and a bedroom with a double bed at the back. The bathroom was pristine, and unusually for a man, the toilet seat was closed. There was no signs of a struggle.

He went back to the bedroom and checked the bedside table drawer. Nothing of any value was there except a couple of used tubes of lubricant. Back in the bathroom he noticed that there was no toothbrush or toothpaste. Bulling had packed for a journey. He walked back to the living room and noticed a pad by the telephone. It appeared blank, but he tore off the top sheet and put it in his pocket. He gave the apartment one last look over and left the way he had come in.

∞∞∞

The next day was Tuesday.

'Are you going to the funeral?'

Sandrine was looking across the table in the staff restaurant at Marker who was sitting opposite. The detective was finishing his meal of *toad in the hole* and a dessert of apple pie. They were up to his expectations which given the location weren't very high. He wiped his mouth with a paper serviette which he pulled from the chrome container on the table. He hated staff lunches.

'They aren't my thing. Too much black crepe and too many dark ties.'

'It's this afternoon, come on, I know that you never met the girl, but Whitehead wants me to represent the hotel and I need you to see me through this. Funerals aren't top of my list of 'things to do' either. It's a trade off against the benefit of taking me out for dinner.'

Marker thought it through and wondered if he was being unreasonably used but decided that in the interests of his pursuit he would go. It would be churlish to refuse.

'I need a black tie.'

'The linen room will give you one, they use them for the barmen. Surprised that you hadn't noticed that considering the amount of time you spend in the food and beverage department.'

Having got himself equipped by Mrs Haul, Marker passed the Press Office to pick Sandrine up and they left The Adelphi to make their way by taxi to Ealing. They stopped at the church where they saw the hearse and two black limousines parked up. The family had already arrived.

'Thankfully it looks as if there is no Press.'

Sandrine said as Marker paid off the cabby.

'There's bound to be a number of people going, her being only in her twenties.'

'Yes, if you want a good attendance at your funeral, die young.' Marker added dryly.

'Let's make our introductions.'

And they walked through the granite archway that led to the main church door. To their left was a small group of mourners who were standing near a cluster of gravestones. Marker wondered why gravestones never seem to be in the perpendicular. This collection were pointing in most directions but none were true vertical. They went over and he introduced himself and Sandrine to the gathering.

'She was a wonderful mother' her father said, 'it's too tragic for words.'

Marker felt that he would like to be anywhere but here and having stayed long enough to be polite he took Sandrine by the arm and led her into the church. They took a pew at the rear and watched the rest of the congregation arrive. They were typical of a middle-class set. A lot of suits and smartly dressed women who were out to make a day of it. He decided that he although he wanted to be like them he surely wasn't yet in their division. And what league were the managers at the hotel? Premier he thought. He became depressed at the idea of trying to climb two levels to become socially acceptable. He wondered what Sandrine thought of his position on this social scale and hoped that as she was French the English class system might have passed her by. Across the aisle Marker saw a group of younger people. Her friends, he mused and wondered if any of the girls amongst them were also 'on the game'. They looked more the type from where he came from, blue collar turned a paler shade. Periwinkle perhaps.

It was a miserable way to spend an afternoon and when the service ended everyone trooped out after the coffin. Marker went with Sandrine to offer their condolences to her parents once more and say they were going. They were with a little boy of about eleven years old. Marker assumed this was the lad who had lost his mother. He looked totally fazed and still in shock so he said 'Hello' and ruffled his hair and instantly sensed an affinity when he remembered how he had felt when his father had disappeared from his life. They declined the sandwiches and drinks on offer at the family house and made for the road and a cab to take them back to the Strand. When they got there they saw Brooks in the Front Hall talking to Timothy Patterson.

'Where have you been?' Patterson asked Marker.

'The murdered girl's funeral. Pretty emotional actually and Miss Parte needed some support.'

'Rum business.' Replied Patterson and headed for his office. Brooks looked at the pair.

'Must have been difficult,' he muttered. Sandrine gave him a challenging look. 'I'll see you later,' and he followed Patterson to the back of the lobby.

Sandrine turned to Marker.

'So it's a dinner for our next rendezvous?'

'It certainly is.'

∞∞∞

The next day, Archer checked into The Adelphi with his wife Carol and was greeted by Patterson who suggested a welcome glass of champagne in his office.

'Good to see you again Mr Archer and I hope that business is good for you?'

'It's satisfactory, you know that we are making an improved offer to your Board and I wonder if one day we will be working together.'

'Well I am merely a servant of my masters.'

Patterson who despite feeling a rising anxiety in the pit of his stomach continued as if he was at a cocktail party.

'The hotel is running very well, although I must admit the past few weeks have not been without their surprises.'

'The fire and the murder you mean?'

'Yes, it's all been most unfortunate, but The Adelphi sails on through, there's isn't much that can disturb our equilibrium.'

'How about the new American competition – the Hilton on Park Lane and I see the Sheraton is making some building progress in Knightsbridge?'

'Yes, but they are all very *nouveau*, not our clientele.'

They finished their glasses and Patterson called for the receptionist to show them to their accommodation. They were then escorted to their river suite on the fifth floor accompanied by the Brigade Leader. Whilst he was showing them all the facilities, one of the other members of the reception team was opening the door of a suite of similar quality on the floor below to allow a certain Miss Dorothy Robinson to enter. She had arrived separately by taxi and been ushered with some discretion to her rooms whilst the Archers were in the General Manager's office. Within the next hour Archer, his wife and mistress were all comfortably installed with Carol Archer blissfully unaware that as she would sleep tonight, fifteen feet directly below her on the other floor, would be her nemesis.

Archer continued with his business whilst a large number of suitcases arrived the contents of which were installed in the bedroom closets by the floor staff. He took several calls and emptied a number of files from the briefcase that he had personally carried. Carol took the opportunity to look again at the magnificent view across the river. The rooms were decorated like an upside down wedding cake, all twists and curls of plaster that added an elegance similar to that of Versailles. In the centre of the sitting-room was a large crystal chandelier by Baccarat. All the doors were curved like those in a French chateau and the whole room was painted in light restful hues of grey. The furniture was equally sumptuous with deep English rose-garden patterned cushions on the sofas which almost enveloped those that plumped themselves down on them. A colour television had been especially wheeled into the room and installed at the far corner by the picture window.

The suite phones rang in unison and Archer picked up from the desk in the sitting room.

'So it's come along nicely. I'm glad you're comfortable, you have a full service apartment and if this goes well it might take less than two weeks to sort out. Yes, yes. _Of course_ I understand, but you must stay indoors and sit this out. In the meantime, I know it's a pain, but _don't go near the windows_ and certainly _don't_ go out!'

Carol appeared at the door. She knew her husband well enough to know that he was probably going to lie but still ventured a question.

'Who was that?'

'A business acquaintance. He's in Lebanon and we're worried about him after the El Al hijacking by the Palestinians'.

She doubted that.

The following day Archer left his suite dressed for the City. His wife was bid farewell and he told her that he wouldn't be back until late afternoon. He took the west lift to the floor below and walked the short distance back along the corridor below the fifth to his mistress's apartment. He knocked twice and Dorothy opened the door still in her nightgown.

'Had breakfast?' he asked.

'I'm just about to.'

She let her negligee fall open to reveal her naked hour glass figure, breasts that stood firm and a small triangle of blond pubic hair. Closing the door she led him by the hand and he felt the longing that had consumed him so many times before with her. They fell into bed and it was the most he could do to restrain himself before he heard her familiar deep throated groan. Now was the time for his release.

After an hour lying together, he kissed her on the forehead and said it was time for him to go. He had to see someone north of Covent Garden in Long Acre. They arranged to meet for lunch and perhaps, he added, some light horizontal refreshment afterwards. He got up and slipped back into his city attire. A white shirt, gold cuff-linked, to which he added a dark striped tie and matching pocket handkerchief. All set off by a dark blue double breasted pin stripe suit. Slipping on a pair of the finest Lobbs and making a last quick check in the mirror, he made his exit quietly back onto the fourth floor corridor. He took the stairs to avoid running into Carol in the lift which would be most unfortunate, whilst if he was to meet her in the lobby he could prevail upon her with some reason for his early return, a lost paper perhaps.

When he was next to the Enquiry Desk he asked the Chief Enquiry Clerk if he could use his phone to make a city call. The Clerk had appeared at the desk as soon as he had spotted Archer on the staircase. He was a good tipper.

'Of course sir,' he passed the receiver over.

'May I dial the number?'

Archer gave him the Broadman number and when it answered Archer asked to speak to the Chief Executive, James Egerton.

'Ah! James, it's Adrian, my advice to you is that today may be good time to increase your offer to our target. Say half a million for the lot. I think he'll take it this time.'

He finished the call and passed the phone back.

'Many thanks!'

He smiled, and gave a cheery wave to the clerk who returned the greeting with an imperceptible bow.

He made his way out across the Strand and took the street that led behind the Strand Palace opposite. From there he made his way through Covent Garden market full of fruit and vegetable wholesalers with their customers. He was almost knocked over by an overloaded barrow in the traffic congestion. This will all have to change he thought as he battled through the delivery vans queuing up for their load of green grocery. Finally he arrived at the address he knew well. It was, after all, a property that his company owned. He rang on the third floor bell. The door buzzed open. Climbing the stairs he knocked on the door marked '3b' and waited.

'Hello Andrew – how are you?'

Chapter 5

Sir John Bulling looked at the envelope marked 'Personal and Confidential' which carried the same stamp and postmark as the previous one. Taking his letter opener and handling the envelope by the corner he tore it open and took out the folded sheet of paper.

Talk to the police and your son will die. Remember the Willows. Expect a call.

The truth of the matter was, of course, that it wasn't his son he was worried about it was the threat that the letter contained. That was a secret that just could not come out. A few minutes later the desk phone rang and his secretary put James Egerton from Broadman through.

'Morning Sir John, I have some good news for you.'

Bulling thought that he could do with some at

that precise moment.

'I've been meeting with some members of the Board and we think that the hotel is worth more than the amount we discussed the last time we met. We are prepared to buy your family interest at an increased offer. Say £500,000 for the whole lot? That's a 20% improvement on our last offer. On top of that we can offer you a place on the new Board for two years at a highly respectable remuneration.'

Bulling thought that through and realised that if he wanted to settle the problem this was a good offer.

'Alright Egerton. Let me think about this. Are you offering to keep the hotel as is for at least the next two years?'

There was a long pause. Egerton sensed he might be near an agreement.

'Yes, it's possible.'

'Let me come back to you early next week.'

He put the receiver back down and pushing his office intercom asked Diana to get hold of the accountant. Farndon arrived just as Diana was closing her lipstick and almost as breathless as the previous time.

'Can you check the valuation on the shares this morning?'

'I've already had a look, the 'B's slid after the fire and the murder but are steady at £1/12s/6d' the 'A's are still at £22.

Farndon, a man who was never quite certain which direction the Chairman's thoughts might move in, looked anxiously across the desk.

'Can you arrange a meeting with the main Board members? I'd like to discuss Broadman's revised offer.'

'Yes.' Farndon replied, relieved that this was a simple request. 'That'll be fine and I will fix it.'

Farndon left the office door open as he was dismissed and Bulling asked Diana to get hold of Marker. Ten minutes later the hotel detective arrived in the outer office.

'What's his mood like today?' he asked.

Diana crossed her legs and swung them out for Marker to get a full appreciation.

'You always seemed concerned with his health! It's as well as can be expected before lunch.'

She swung herself back to her desk and pressed the intercom.

'Mr Marker is here sir... yes I will.'

She cast her arm to the right as an indication that the Chairman was ready to receive guests.

'It's another letter.'

Bulling passed it over to Marker just as he had closed the office door. The detective studied it for a little while.

'Good English, but not much more. We will have to wait for a call. What are you going to do?'

Bulling didn't like the impetuousness and went on the attack:

'What have you found out?'

'Well it appears your son hasn't been doing much. I've checked his apartment and he's not there. There was nothing in it of note. It looks to me that he knew he was going somewhere. Not many kidnappers allow you to take your toothbrush with you.'

'What do you mean?'

'I mean that he was probably grabbed whilst on a trip somewhere, the flat was immaculately clean and there was no sign of any struggle. Any ideas who's behind this?'

Bulling looked across the desk and added:

'I think this is all drug related. My bet is that Andrew got himself into trouble with debt. He was asking me for money again just a month or so ago. I don't think this has anything to do with business. I think this is a problem that he's got into.'

'What is this threat about the Willows?' Marker asked.

'I've no idea what that means.'

Bulling replied curtly but didn't like the detective's tone. He turned his back and looked at the array of family photos on his credenza. Marker noted that they were all there with the exception of Andrew.

'I haven't got a picture of Andrew – do you have one?' Marker asked.

Bulling looked flustered and looking in his desk drawer pulled out the framed picture that had stood with the others of his family.

'Take this and let me have the frame back.'

He passed the image over to Marker.

After the interview Marker decided that he needed some help and a little more education about the Bulling family. The clock was ticking. He turned left out of the Directors' corridor and went straight onto the mezzanine floor and the Press Office. Seeing Sandrine with her door open he went in and closed it behind him. She was on the phone and glanced up over her glasses and gestured a seat.

'Here to fix that dinner date?' She asked.

'Yes and no. I've got a more pressing problem and I need your help to illuminate something for me. Business first. I want to know as much as you can tell me about the Chairman's family.'

'Officially or unofficially?'

'Both.'

'Well here is the standard press release we have on him.'

She pulled a one pager from her desk drawer. A bit of history on the hotel and its Board. A nice piece on Lord Bulling and a small bio on Sir John.

'I am pretty guarded about his private life, what specifics are you wanting to know?'

'Tell me about Andrew Bulling.'

'Well, he's the son from a first marriage, I know he went to Hotel School with George Brooks, I saw a photo of the two of them in George's apartment. I don't know if they are in contact. The word on the Strand omnibus is that Andrew is a little limp wristed and does a few psychedelic drugs like LSD. A bit of a loser.'

Marker had difficulty controlling his instinct when he heard of this connection but changed the subject.

'Does the word 'willows' mean anything to

you?'

Marker looked directly at her.

'No not at all, beyond trees.'

'How about tomorrow night at seven o'clock? I will take you for a couple of pre-dinner *Mai Tais* and a little Polynesian at Trader Vics in the Hilton.'

'Done.'

Sandrine returned to reading *The Evening Standard* that had been delivered by the page boy earlier.

Opposite her office and just further up the corridor was George Brooks' work place. He knocked on the door.

'Enter.'

Marker stepped in and stood whilst Brooks remained seated.

'What can I do for you?'

Marker became aggressive.

'Well, I have several questions, the first is that whilst homosexual acts are now only just legal, well in principal, you have put the hotel into a very difficult position. What on earth were you doing at the Boltons?'

Brooks looked ashamed and whilst he gathered his composure the detective looked around the walls. He saw a certificate from Lausanne Hotel School on the wall.

'It's not something I'm proud of,' he said.

'I met this bloke at the bar and I fancied him. We went back to my place and we did it there.'

'He's a druggie you know. You into drugs?'

'No I'm not.'

Marker took a long cold look at him.

'Do you know Andrew Bulling?'

Brooks looked a little surprised.

'Yes, I was at hotel school with him.'

'Personal friends?'

'No not really, haven't seen him recently at all.'

The phone rang and whilst Brooks expected the detective to leave the room, Marker held his ground.

'Hello Mr Egerton, what can I do for you today?'

Brooks made some notes on his blotter and after the call Marker asked:

'Know Mr Egerton well do you?'

'He's a client.'

Turning his back on Brooks, he left the office with a mental note to come back later to see what he could find from what was written on the desk compendium.

Saturday evening and it had been raining. At 6.30pm Marker walked to Trafalgar square and got the No 6 Willesden Routemaster bus to the Dorchester Hotel and then walked down Park Lane. Turning sharp left when he reached the bright lights of the Hilton he took the side entrance and down the stairs to another world. Trader Vic's was decked out as a South Pacific island. Above the bar was a huge canoe that looked as if it would fit ten rowers. All the furniture was made of comfortable rattan and across the room he could see two large clay baking ovens where the Polynesian specialities were made.

Taking a seat at the bar he ordered the *Mai Tai* and waited for his date. She arrived on time, and judging from the fact that her coat wasn't rain soaked he assumed she had taken a taxi. Such was their difference in salary.

'Ever eaten here before?'

'Only when it opened, but I love this sort of food.'

'Well there's maybe too much pineapple in it for me.'

Marker passed her the menu, pulled out his cigarettes and offered her one.

'Rothmans! My favourite.'

He offered her his light and she took a long drag before exhaling across the bar.

'I wanted to ask you if you would like to help me on a particular challenge I am having.'

'Is it about the murder?'

'No, it's delicate and confidential and about the Chairman.'

He then went on to describe the two notes and the ransom demand made for Andrew. He told her that the Chairman hadn't wanted the Police involved and that to make some progress he really needed more background on the family.

'Then there is another thing,' he continued, 'would you help me with some information about George Brooks, I know you knew him a little better than you've illuminated him to me so far.'

Sandrine blushed and thought things through. It had come as quite a shock to know about the kidnap but she could understand why the Chairman didn't want the Police involved. Any publicity like this would be bad publicity.

Then here was the hotel detective telling her that he knew all about her affair with George. But the idea of being almost back as she was when an investigative journo sounded very appealing and before she realised where she was going, she agreed.

'But total confidentiality! I will tell you, but this is just between you and me.'

Marker was pleased with the outcome so far. He had this beautiful creature almost where he wanted her. He believed the next thing to do was to give her a good meal and see what followed next.

Dinner started with the detective ordering for both of them. A first course of rare beef skewers with a soy-sake glaze which was finished at the table over a flaming *hibachi*. For her he ordered salt and pepper calamari whilst he had the jalapeno cheese balls. Then the next dish of spiced chicken came with yoghurt coriander and cumin. On the side was a small plate of spicy spring rolls. They finished the meal off with a *Verviene* tea for her and an *espresso* for him.

During the meal Marker expanded on what he knew and it was decided that Sandrine could find out more on the family. If she came across anything that connected them with 'The Willows' that would be of prime interest.

When they left, Marker was disappointed. She wanted him to hail a cab and she wanted to leave alone. So he turned around and walked down to the Hyde Park Corner and the tube. He decided to go back to the hotel, it was the weekend after all and it would be very quiet.

Deciding to use his master key to open the side entrance in Adelphi Hill rather than the staff entrance where the Timekeeper would see him. He walked past the Chairman's office and made his way up to the first floor via the west staircase. From there he took the east staircase on the opposite side of the building and arrived outside Brooks' office. Using his master key again he opened the door and walked over to the desk. Leaving the light off he picked up the blotter and shone a torch across the writing. He could just make the word Archer and the numbers 1230.

On Monday morning he had got to work early and made his way to his pigeon hole where the weekend mail and messages are stored. There was the usual late night delivery from the clerks in the Reception Office, the House List headed with its *advenis et exitus*, arrivals and departures. The Adelphi used Latin as frequently as the Pope. Marker assumed it was to differentiate between non-clerical employees like him who had been to a secondary school and those who worked at a higher echelon who had gone to public school. Then there was the '*factum negotium*' or business done sheets, and underneath all the office paper, an envelope addressed in handwriting. He put the Xerox aside, tore it open and took out the plain card.

> '*Thank you Richard for a lovely evening Saturday. Sandrine X.*'

That was thoughtful of her, he reflected and put the card in his drawer. He then looked at his diary and wondered what the day would turn up. It wasn't long before his phone rang. It was the Met and they wanted to talk.

DCI Bowen arrived within the hour. She told him that she was making some progress, but the murderer was not revealing what he had done with the gun.

'Obviously scared, and I wouldn't be surprised if it was connected to the Krays. Those evil bastards have contacts in and out of prison, so if he squeals he's going to get more up his arse than he'd bargained for, bloody cock jockey.'

Bowen took a long drag on the Rothmans that

had been offered.

'What else goes on here?' she asked.

'Well we are in the midst of a takeover bid from Broadman and we have the Chairman under heavy pressure to sell out. On top of that he seems to have got himself into a little bit of personal bother which I'm looking into.'

Bowen's ears picked up.

'What sort of bother?'

'Well he has a wayward son which I need to know more about, Andrew Bulling.'

Bowen took out her notebook from her voluminous handbag and jotted down the name.

'I will see what I can find out.'

Marker walked her back to the lobby and as she left via a parked up Police car, Sandrine appeared at his side.

'I've something for you.'

And together they went back to the basement and his disorganised office.

'My God Richard you live in a dump.'

He nodded in agreement and mumbled something about Mrs Haul refusing to clean up for him. Moving several weeks' worth of house lists off the only spare chair, she tossed them in the wastepaper basket.

'What's this? Doodling? You have too much time on your hands.'

Sandrine picked up the notepaper that the detective had taken from Andrew's apartment. He'd used a pencil to scribble all over it.

'Don't throw that away!' He suddenly became animated. 'I can just work out a trace of a number on it – what do you think they are?'

'It's a telephone number COV and four numbers, looks like 4366 or maybe the last two are 55. Covent Garden.'

'Thanks, might be useful.'

She then told him what she knew.

'Sir John Bulling had a previous wife, Cynthia, this was before he was knighted. Her only son was Andrew. His daughter is by his second marriage to the Lady Julia. Cynthia died in a motorcycle accident about twenty years ago just after the war. I then looked in our archives which we keep in the Card Index for anything that was happening here at that time.

Unbelievably the hotel was the subject of another takeover bid, this time from a company called *Sol Brava* and Lord Bulling was fighting that out tooth and nail. The Board minutes at the time indicate that the Bulling family was split on what to do.

Cynthia Bulling was keen to sell her shares that she had received after she married, but her death happened before she could sell. That effectively saved a tricky situation. What is interesting is that the board members of *Sol Brava* include several of our clients. There is Adrian Archer for example and an Arab sheikh called Hamsa Al Mukta. Adrian Archer is also a board member of Broadman as is an Al Mukta. A son I believe.'

'What do you know about Cynthia Bulling?'

'Well she was a well-known face on the London modelling scene at the time and came from quite an ordinary working class background. She has dazzling looks. Here have a look at these.'

Sandrine passed Marker a couple of glossy black and white portrait shots that she had retrieved from her archive. Marker flipped through them and could see the attraction. She had a beautiful face and he felt an instant affinity. Perhaps it was the class where they both came from.

Sandrine continued:

'I think Sir John must have met her here. The Adelphi was the absolute epicentre of the social scene during and after the war.'

'And what about our friend George Brooks?'

'Well George has more money in his bank than he should have judging from the statements I saw in his flat. He's also a bit of a deviant – likes kinky things, he has a mirror hung on his bedroom ceiling.'

Marker wondered what making love to Sandrine would be like using that arrangement and had to sadly push the image from his mind.

'Thanks for all that Sandrine, I'll keep you posted with stuff as I get to know it.'

She picked up her clutch bag and moved to the door.

Marker reflected on what he had heard and decided that he'd have to make a call. This time it was to DCI Bowen. Before Sandrine left he asked:

'What about dinner again – it was fun.'

'I have a waistline to consider – but a cocktail would be good. How about tomorrow night?'

'Be great.'

When the door was closed he picked up his phone and dialled West End Central.

'DCI Bowen please, yes I'll hold.'

'You're fast,' she said: 'I've only just got back to my desk.'

'I've found out that Andrew Bulling's mother

was reckoned to have been killed in a motorcycle accident about twenty years ago. Can you let me have some more details on that accident? She was involved in some potential share dealings at the time with a client we have in house who is now tied up with the current bid. I wondered if you could tell me <u>who</u> was riding the bike. It couldn't be her surely?'

DCI Bowen took her shoulder bag off and put it on the office floor. Marker waited a minutes as she processed this latest piece of news.

'You wanted to know about Andrew Bulling and now you want to know about his mother. You're a bit Bulling focused aren't you? I will see what I can get for you.'

The next day, Marker climbed out of bed early and, opening his blinds, was depressed to see that the sky was its usual grey hue. He felt as if he had missed summer entirely as the day before he had been taking a shower on the only morning he could remember the sun shining. Every day in London seemed to bring a dawn of gloomy skies. Throwing off his pyjamas he gave himself a casual glance in the hall mirror. Sandrine was right, he need to smarten up and lose a few pounds.

He made himself an instant coffee. He opened a new jar as it always tasted so much better. That was why he only bought small jars. He didn't like the flavour of instant that had been left for weeks on end in half-filled screw tops. He was lazy because his preference was really for fresh brewed given his high expectations. But he basically just couldn't be bothered to go through the palaver of making fresh coffee from beans. As he stirred in the brown crystals he reached for the open pint bottle of milk in his small fridge and poured it in. Sitting down on the kitchen chair he thought again about how he was living his life and what he really wanted to be. He had two overriding desires. The first, most urgent one, was to sleep with Sandrine Parte. The second was that he wanted to be rich. He came to the conclusion that neither were in his easy grasp.

His thoughts moved on to the kidnap. It was a strange affair. The Chairman had things to hide and it wasn't going to be possible to keep the Police out of the whole affair and he was not being realistic in thinking that Andrew Bulling had been ambushed in some predatory raid. The neighbours would have heard or seen something if there had been a commotion in his flat. There was no evidence that he was planning a holiday, but it was true that the items one would expect in a bathroom were missing. The question was who would want to do this and why? The drug story suggested by his father was the most plausible but the full magnitude of the threat was not yet out. How much money did the kidnappers want and where and how was he, Marker going to solve this? There was very little to go on but he did have two advantages. He had what he thought was part of a telephone number and a good deal of information from Sandrine. He put his coffee cup in the sink and finished dressing. Fifteen minutes later he was in the tube on his way to the Embankment station. He took the steps up from the District line and headed towards the Adelphi across the Embankment gardens. On the way he picked up a copy of *The Daily Express* and folded it under his arm.

When he arrived at the Adelphi Lane entrance for the staff he took a brief look at the thousand odd clocking in cards that were mounted of frames next to the Timekeepers office. He was pushed aside by a group of three Italians who were late for their breakfast wait-shift. He noticed that they clocked in four cards and wondered if he should take some action. Clocking in someone who wasn't there meant that the hotel would be paying for labour that hadn't yet arrived. Thinking about the day ahead, he had enough challenges without making more trouble for himself. Who cared if someone got a paid for a few more hours than they were actually present for?

Going back through the subterranean passage towards his office fumbling for his key he opened the office door. He was greeted by the same overflowing wastepaper basket and the smell of stale dog ends.

He left his overcoat on the hat stand and sitting down at his desk flicked through the rest of the mail he'd received. Finally he started to read the pages of *The Express* that he'd picked up and it wasn't until he'd reached page three that he sat up and paid attention. Someone had leaked details of the kidnapping to the paper. Now who would do that and why?

Almost as he had finished reading the piece about Sir John's son and the unfortunate angle that had been put on about the relationship he might have with his father, the phone rang on his desk.

'Richard, its Sandrine. Have you read this morning's *Express*?'

'Just doing that now. Did you leak this story?' Marker asked her aggressively.

'It wasn't me that leaked that.' She sounded equally hostile, 'I need you to know that when I make a promise I keep it.'

Marker calmed down and had to admit it was an intuitive reaction. Maybe he didn't trust her as much as he thought he did.

'I believe you, but who would want this out? It's as explicit as that rock show Hair!'

He was looking at the third page of the paper and an article that was headed *'Son of Adelphi Tycoon Kidnapped'*. The piece went on to describe Sir John Bulling's current challenges with Broadman and made a reference to the fact that Andrew was a product of his first marriage.

'You'd better call his office and suggest putting together some sort of holding statement. I am no doubt going to get a call from the Police and will have to think how I field that.'

He put the phone back down and leaning back on his chair reflected upon how he was now going to handle both the Chairman and The Met. The phone rang within a minutes of him having finished the last call.

'The Chairman wants to see you,' Diana Spurling then added, 'before you ask, no he's not in a good mood.'

Marker fairly well sprinted up the three-flights to the Directors' corridor and wheezed into the Chairman's outer office. Diana put away her powder puff and looked at him quizzically:

'It's those lunches in Pierrot,' she then added, 'a little more time for exercise perhaps? He's ready for you now.'

And with that she pulled out her nail file. Marker knocked on the door and the light went from red to green.

'How the hell did this happen Marker?'

The chairman was waving a copy of the paper in his face. He had already turned aggressive.

'I can assure sir that as far as I was aware this was something only you, me and the kidnappers know about. So I am pretty sure it's been leaked by the kidnappers to put pressure on you.'

'Who would do that?'

'Well my instinct has always been that it is tied up with the hostile bid. I can't prove that, but there are a several things all swimming around in my investigation that seem to point to that direction.'

'To hell it is. My son is a homosexual drug addict, I can't believe you are seriously suggesting that the kidnap and the bid are inter-related? It's his druggie friends. He's been unable to pay his debts and they are squeezing me for the bill.'

Marker was cool in the face of Bulling's rage. He

waited for the tirade to finish and then continued:

'I'm pretty sure that I will get a call from the police, how would you like me to handle that?'

'Keep them out of it – I've told you _that_ before.'

'That maybe not so easy, kidnapping is an offence, but paying a ransom isn't, they are bound to want to interview you. I suggest when they do I attend as well. It won't do any harm to show them the evidence you have, in fact it might be helpful to see what their take is on it.'

Bulling became defensive.

'We are going to have to do this ourselves. Involving the police will make it dangerous for Andrew.'

Marker stood his ground.

'I don't think we have a choice. I think the kidnappers leaked this story and it will make it more dangerous for you to get this to a satisfactory conclusion. By the way, Sandrine Parte is going to produce a holding statement for you, we are going to need that to field the rest of the press pack.'

'Well then at least someone is being helpful.'

Bulling glowered at Marker.

'The bloody phone has been going off the hook. We have a press pack at the back door and they need to be kicked out. Get it sorted and keep me up to speed on what happens next.'

With that the detective assumed it was time to leave.

When he had gone Bulling tapped the intercom switch through to Diana. He shouted so loud he didn't need to lift the phone.

'When are we having that bloody Board meeting!?'

'Friday ten o'clock,' she coolly replied.

By the time Marker had got back to his office his phone had rung several times. He picked up.

'Ah! DCI Bowen' he answered, 'I wondered how long it might be.'

'Yes Richard, I've been reading *The Daily Express* over my boiled egg this morning. How long has this been going on and it obviously has something to do with why you asked me to find out about Andrew Bulling and his beloved deceased mother?'

'Ah yes, well it was client privilege, I couldn't tell you by reason of my instructions. It hasn't been going on long, and yes, I knew a little about this when I spoke to you last. I assume that you will want to get the story first hand from the boss?'

'Be helpful. Tell him I'm coming over this morning at eleven. Murders, kidnaps, motorbike accidents what else are you planning to fill my Christmas stocking with? I hope that you will be a little more forthcoming if we are going to work together.'

At the mention of stockings Marker thought fleetingly of what might be Miss Parte's lingerie and who would be pulling her cracker come the festive season.

'Well he may be busy.'

'Tell him it's unwise to keep a woman waiting, especially a Detective Chief Inspector.'

After the call, Marker fixed the arrangements with Diana and when DCI Bowen arrived he joined them in the main Boardroom. Sir John was sitting at the top of the large highly polished dark wood table and to his left was the police inspector. Diana was sitting a few chairs further down with a large spiral notepad and pen. When he opened the door, Bulling indicated he should take a seat to his right. Bowen was already seated and had already berated the Chairman for not having immediately involved the Police.

The conversation had subsequently become a little stilted and the hotel detective attempted to improve the atmosphere.

'Sir John, I think we should hand over the messages and the envelopes to the DCI so that they can have forensics to look them over.'

Sir John handed over the two letters and envelopes he had received. He had already resolved that he was not going to tell the police what he planned to do but he indicated he was going to co-operate with whatever was required.

'We take a dim view if any ransom is paid.' Bowen warned the Chairman. Looking over the messages again she commented: 'Well written, the English is all in good order, which is a little unusual for my friends of the criminal fraternity. What is this reference to the willows?'

'I've no idea' Bulling lied again.

'Well we will make immediate enquiries with the company that your son keeps. That may lead somewhere, you may be right that this is all drug related. Please keep me informed of any developments, what do you plan to do next?'

Bulling looked uneasy and searched across to the prints on the wall for answers. It was after all a fine series of hunting scenes. The Adelphi must have bought a job lot. Hunting scenes appeared all over the hotel corridors. He considered his reply and then looking as submissive as he thought appropriate.

'Keep you informed, as you requested.'

That was another lie. DCI Bowen looked at the letters and the envelopes.

'Let me take these from you and I will get them checked for prints and anything else we can find.'

Bulling asked Diana to take a Xerox copy for his own file and let the policewoman take the originals.

The Chairman asked Marker to see the Chief Inspector out and Marker led the way to the Adelphi Hill entrance of the hotel. When they left the building they found an aggressive group of press waiting for photographs and there was an explosion of flashes as DCI Bowen and the detective appeared.

'Do you know who the kidnappers are?' One shouted.'How much is the ransom being asked?'

The chorus was getting out of hand. Marker noticed that Sandrine Parte was talking to two or three determined looking journalists to his left and the camera flashes popped again when the DCI's car turned into Adelphi Hill to pick her up.

'Can we have a statement?'

Shouted one of a group that were being shepherded by a uniformed officer.

'Is Sir John paying the ransom?' Another shouted.

Bowen pulled Marker aside as her car rolled up.

'It was your Chairman who was riding the bike. She was the pillion and I find it a very convenient solution for a difficult woman.' She said looking the detective straight in the eye. Marker couldn't think of any reply but his mind was spinning like a fairground ride. Bowen gave him another long gaze as he watched her get into the back seat of her car. Just before she closed the door she said:

'...and you know that I can be difficult too Richard. As for Andrew Bulling he's another of your twink friends and hangs out at the Boltons. Didn't seem to have a job. I'm going to find out a lot more about him before this is over.'

With that she slammed the door of the black Wolseley saloon and drove off at speed.

He then made his way over to Sandrine who

was handing out a press release. Although he had all the intentions in the world to fend off unwelcome reporters his mind was elsewhere. He was as agitated as a butter-churn as he considered what he'd just heard. Bulling had been responsible for his first wife's death and that at a critical time for the survival of the hotel and the family dynasty.

He went back to the entrance door and attempted to fend off the Press as Sandrine took the opportunity of some protection and get back inside. He had taken the initiative to ask the Hall Porter to provide a uniformed doorman who was briefed to keep everybody out. Not that it would do much good. He thought The Adelphi doormen were very able to let in undesirables if pound notes were pressed into their hands.

When the door had been firmly shut behind them she then passed him a copy of the release to read.

'It's a good holding statement.' He told Sandrine.

'Just the right touch of concern and sentimentality. Who do you think leaked the story in the first place?'

'No idea, but it was obviously done to put pressure on the Chairman. I hear he's having an emergency Board meeting soon to discuss the hostile bid, I wonder what will come from that?'

Marker considered that and his thoughts turned to Brooks and Broadman.

'I asked you a couple of days ago about Brooks and you gave me some answers but what more can you tell me – he seems to get regular calls from Egerton at Broadman?'

'Well he certainly knows him. Maybe he's lining himself up for promotion if they take over.'

'He might be lining himself with something else'. Marker looked thoughtful:

'He's flush with cash - right?'

'He has a lot of it' she replied.

Changing the subject the detective asked one more favour:

'Can you do some more work on the family? Let's find out a bit more on the late Cynthia Bulling, there's further to come on her.'

They both walked back to her office and squeezing her hand he thanked her for her note and left her at the door.

'Tonight Richard,' said Sandrine. 'That cocktail, I'm afraid I'm going to have to cancel. I'd forgotten that I have an invite from *Vogue* that

I'd accepted. It's a party for their new editor at Manchester Square.'

'What about meeting up after?'

'The only thing I'm meeting up with after Richard, is my bed. Sorry!'

After he had left her outside her office he felt a rush of disappointment and wondered if his pursuit was a bit too intense. He decided to lay off for a day or two. Turning his thoughts to the hotel he wanted to make an appointment to see the General Manager to bring him up to date on his various activities. Making his way into the General Manager's office he passed through the hotel typing pool where six girls were busy on the latest Olivetti machines, typing all the reservation correspondence the hotel received. In the corner was a fast telex machine that was pushing out international bookings with the staccato rhythm of a machine gun.

Every client was expected to write in with their accommodation request and each confirmation letter was personally signed by the General Manager after it had been checked by the reception office. On the far side of the office sat the General Manager's secretary and she controlled the traffic light system that allowed access down the short flight of stairs to the inner sanctum. Above the noise of all the typing he asked if he could see Mr Patterson as a matter of urgency. She pushed the internal intercom switch and picked up the receiver. Whilst she was still speaking she waved Marker directly through.

Entering the office, Marker was not invited to sit and found himself like an errant schoolboy standing in front of the Headmaster's desk.

'I've come about two issues sir. The first is about the kidnap of Andrew Bulling that's in the Press.'

The General Manager put down his fountain pen with which he had been signing a very large compendium of reservation letters.

'Go on.'

'The Chairman is quite convinced that this is all drug-related. I am not so sure, and despite police advice I think he is going to make arrangements to meet the ransom demand. This doesn't affect the hotel directly, but it is clearly putting him under pressure in regards to the hostile bid'

'Quite so, Marker, quite so.'

'The second issue is I would like to know what you intend to do with Brooks now that we know he had a homosexual relationship with a murderer.'

'I don't see it's any of your business.'

Patterson eyed Marker. It was a rather rheumy eye thought the detective looking across to the champagne bucket and the two half-filled glasses.

'Well it is, because I also think that he's running with the hare and racing with the hounds.'

'Explain yourself.' Patterson sounded bored.

'He's having conversations with the hostile bid. Boardman Developers and their Managing Director, John Egerton.'

'Egerton is a valuable client. I've had conversations with Egerton, it doesn't mean that I am disloyal to the hotel.'

Marker wondered where his own loyalties should lie. Was there a difference between loyalty to the hotel and loyalty to the Chairman and his family? He was beginning to feel a little lost. The General Manager continued:

'Your job is to look after the safety and security of the guests of The Adelphi Hotel, you are not the Staff Manager and neither should you be involved in the machinations of Boardroom politics.'

Marker could see that this was going nowhere fast and thanking his superior for his time, bid him a good-afternoon and left back up the stairs from which he had so keenly descended not five minutes prior.

So he was out on his own then.

Chapter 6

The next morning Archer put on his suit, said good-bye to his wife before once again ostensibly making for the City. Closing the suite door he made his way along the sumptuous corridor to the lift. When the elevator cruised to his floor, he got into the cabin and pushed the fourth floor touch button. It illuminated a dull orange. Getting out he made his usual detour to Dorothy's suite.

She was not in such an accommodating mood today and rather brusquely met him at her door.

'Anything the matter?' He tentatively enquired.

She sat down in the most comfortable armchair and he took the seat on the sofa closest to her.

'I'm worried about my future with you. You tell me you are leaving Carol, but this never seems to happen. I love you Adrian, but you are not giving me any security.'

'But I do love you Dot, you know I do.'

'Maybe, but not enough.' She knew this man was not to be trusted on delivering all that he promised.

'Come here.'

Archer stood up and going over to her chair, leant down and kissed her. It was the beginning of what was to come, and he then stooped down and scooped her up in his strong arms before leading her to the bedroom.

At about the same time as Archer was working through his set of seductive moves, Marker was in his office also thinking about how he was going to lead Sandrine astray. He looked vacantly at himself in the mirror. He saw a tyre of fat around his waist. Klimp was right he thought, and he didn't want end up looking like Bibendum, Michelin Man. The telephone rang and he picked it up.

'Marker.'

'DCI Bowen. We have someone in Aylesbury who knows more than just where the local pubs are. The desk sergeant tells me that the Willows is a road that runs to the north west of the town. It was where John Bulling lost control of his motorbike and killed his wife. Now why would someone put that in a ransom note? To apply a little pressure I think. It's called the 'frighteners' in our business. You see Richard, the trouble with being a Policewoman is that I am actually suspicious of everything, my children, my boss, even my own shadow, and that's only because it follows me around.'

Marker also had an issue with trust and distrustful women like DCI Bowen made him uncomfortable. She was the sort of person that made you believe that even when you were telling the truth it was probably a lie. He remembered how the Military Police had often been able to turn fiction into truth by applying a little torture and a large amount of repetitive questioning.

'And another thing,' she continued 'I will be going up to Aylesbury to check that accident out. I don't think the investigation was particularly thorough at the time.'

He thanked her for the update and sat back in his chair to contemplate this latest piece of information and to think about his stomach, the ponderous weight of which he had once again caught sight of in his cloudy mirror and which this time, because he had leant forward, looked less like a tyre and more like a sack of potatoes.

Little time had passed before the phone rang. It was almost lunchtime and it was the Reception Office. This was irritating as Marker was just considering that he might enjoy a *flambe steak Diane* with some green beans for lunch and he had already felt his stomach flinching in anticipation. They were ringing to let him know of a small challenge that had befallen the guest on the fifth floor. Apparently he had been visiting his assistant on the fourth and his trousers had been thrown out of the window after an altercation. They wanted permission to ask Engineering to get a ladder and retrieve them from the top of a tree in the Embankment Gardens. Marker reached for his printed house list and saw that the suite was allocated to a certain Mr and Mrs Adrian Archer, whilst on the fourth floor directly below, the suite was occupied by Miss Dorothy Robinson. This is the same man that Sandrine had mentioned was a Board member of Broadman. There was something about the name that Marker couldn't quite place. It was buried in memories from years before. Looking down the house-list again he noted that Mr Archer was paying for both rooms. He picked up the phone and asked to be put through to the fourth-floor suite. He wasn't surprised when he heard a male voice answering his call.

'Can I speak to Miss Robinson please?'

'This is her friend, whose calling?'

Marker introduced himself and Archer explained that he'd had a little bit of fun with his business assistant. He said he'd been trying on some new clothes that he had wanted to surprise his wife with and in a little 'horse play' his suit trousers had been thrown out of the window whilst he was changing.

He was a good liar thought Marker.

Archer continued.

'This is a matter of some delicacy and I need your discretion. My wife will find it very odd if I reappear in our suite without my trousers wearing new clothes with which I want to surprise her. She is so critical of what I wear she thinks I'm a hopeless shopper. So I have been out to acquire a new wardrobe and wanted to show my colleague to make sure they fit well. Miss Robinson hadn't realised the window was open when she tossed them aside whilst I was changing. I would be very grateful if they could be retrieved and returned to me.'

Marker smiled to himself and agreed that he would try to resolve the problem. Half an hour later he found himself in the park outside the River Entrance of the hotel together with a team of Klimp's men who arrived carrying a long ladder. The ensuing performance to retrieve the trousers took on the appearance of a high wire act performed by the fittest of the Engineering troupe. Swaying from the top of the ladder which was held by three of the team, the staffer hung precariously between a long fall to the ground and the top of the tree just below the hotel suite. Eventually having embraced the nearest branch so closely as if it was a new lover, he grabbed one leg of the trousers, pulled them clear and dropped them to the ground. This elicited excited applause from the small crowd of onlookers that had gathered below. The team re-assembled and accepted the audience's appreciation as if they were a street cabaret act.

Marker, who had been watching at a discrete distance took the trousers back to the fourth floor, got the valet to press them and put them on a trouser clip. Knocking on the fourth floor door he was not surprised when a very attractive girl opened it.

'Come on in.' She gave Marker a small smile and left him in the sitting room.

'Adrian, a man is here with your trousers.'

He sensed the atmosphere and it felt like the calm of the eye in the middle of a fierce storm. A moment later Archer appeared from the bedroom dressed in one of the hotel's monogrammed snow white dressing gowns.

'Thank you very much Mr Marker, job well done I'd say.'

Archer handed him a ten pound note. It was the size of the tip that disorientated Marker. He had wanted to deliver the trousers personally to get a measure of Archer, but had not expected to be so genorously rewarded. His thoughts were thrown between accepting it from politeness and refusing it on the grounds of incorruptibility. Avarice took the better of him and he shook Archer's hand and pocketing the note.

'Everything alright up here?' He enquired, not moving from his position near the coffee table. He had noted the magazines thrown on the floor and an upset cup of coffee that was at this very moment staining the Tai Ping carpet.

'Yes fine thank you. Miss Robinson is just a little upset at the turn of events'.

Archer showed Marker out.

The detective made his way back downstairs and to the bill office. There was something a little disturbing about Archer, but he couldn't quite understand why he felt chilled. He asked one of the accountants to go to the in house bill tray and find Archer's account. When it was retrieved he saw that he was indeed a big spender.

He was running up quite a list. There was valeting, hairdressing, laundry, meals in the restaurant and an endless list of telephone calls. And just then a number caught his eye, COV 4365. He asked for a copy of the bill and decided to take the late lunch he had been promising himself since mid-morning.

That afternoon Mrs Haul was having a challenging day discussing the quality of the Irish linen with Patrick Wildblood. The issue was the standard of pressing that was coming back from the flat ironer at the hotel's laundry in Kennington. There were over 3000 individual pieces that left the hotel every day of which the restaurants were only part, and the property had to allow six 'turns' of linen to support the operation. That was 18,000 pieces in total. One was in use, the second was dirty on its way to the laundry, the third was being washed, the fourth being ironed. The fifth-turn was on its way back to the hotel and the sixth was in cupboard storage across the building. The scale of the operation was so large it needed separate premises to operate the large boilers, washing machines and presses.

Wildblood explained that whilst he had an electric iron to smooth over the tables when the clothes had been laid for dinner, the stock was coming from the linen room creased diagonally instead of squared.

Just as the discussion was getting a little heated, Sandrine Parte arrived at the Pierrot entrance and lent her arm on the *Maître d's* podium. Waiting for their conversation to finish, she spotted a picture of a very handsome boy attached to a resume that was resting on the stand. Before she would read much of the detail, Mrs Haul imperiously sailed past her like the Royal Yacht.

'Afternoon Mrs Haul – you well?'

'God save me from anything Irish.'

She gave a withering look in Wildblood's direction and navigated her way past the potted palms into the corridor.

Sandrine smiled at the Maitre d' and Wildblood turned on his charm:

'Hello Sandrine, you're looking gorgeous, what can I do for you? How about a date?'

She gave him a playful smile and said:

'You're too old but I like the look of him.'

She pointed to the resume.

'Ah! That's my son, Eion, I'm trying to get him a job here but Brooks tells me that the hotel will not allow relatives to work in the same department. In this case, he said, it was a double negative a definite 'no no' as it smelt of nepotism. So I'm looking out for an opening for him elsewhere.'

'I've been going through my files and I have an old archive picture of you with Cynthia Bulling. Must be twenty years or more when it was taken. I didn't know you knew the Chairman's first wife. How did you know her?'

Wildblood smiled a little and folding the resume up stuffed it in his inside jacket pocket.

'She was Cynthia Hampton then, a very well-known London model on the scene just after the war, did the odd *Vogue* shoot here in the Pierrot and I couldn't resist a picture with her for my album. I was young in those days and had no idea of all the celebrities I was going to meet in the coming years, so a picture of a girl like that was one of the first I had.'

'Where did she meet Sir John?'

Sandrine's question was phrased as one more of curiosity rather than anything akin to a cross examination.

Wildblood relaxed and pointed to the circular banquette in a corner of the room.

'Well over there actually, I introduced them when he was passing by and he invited her for lunch. You know that she died in an accident?'

'No I didn't know until yesterday. Very sad.'

'Yes, she was a beautiful woman with a lot of talent going for her. Terrible what happened.'

Sandrine asked whether he'd like the copy of the picture she had and he said he would, for old times' sake.

'Let me know when your son gets a job, he looks rather dishy.'

She smiled, turned on her high heels and walked back to her office. When she had settled herself down behind her desk she picked up the phone and asked for the Security Office.

'Richard, Sandrine. Wildblood knew Cynthia Bulling and thinks he was the catalyst in introducing her to Sir John.'

Marker considered this and then replied:

'That's interesting, presumably he knows about the motorbike accident and who was riding then.'

'Probably.'

'Something else Sandrine, I met your friend Archer today. Lost his trousers when his mistress threw them out of the window after a lover's tiff. I got tipped for getting them back.'

'Good you can buy me that cocktail later from the windfall, it will make up for last night.'

'I was rather hoping dinner.'

'No wonder you're fat,' she giggled. 'Alright let's do it, eight-o'clock?' This time Marker refused to survey his profile in the office mirror. It was becoming too much of a habit. 'By the way did you see on today's arrivals that Sheikh Al Mukta is due to check in?'

'No I didn't. He's the other Board member of Broadman Developments isn't he?'

'His company Al Mukta Holdings has a substantial holding'

'I must try and see what he looks like, thanks for the heads-up. Tonight at eight then. The Ivy?'

'Fine.'

He put the phone back down and felt a little insulted. Sandrine was the third person in so many days who had made a reference to his weight. He was hurt and beginning to have his doubts about her. Maybe he didn't know enough about the people he worked with. What was it that DCI Bowen had said? She didn't trust anyone. It was about time that he upped his game to that of Bowen's level. He made a note to pass by the Staff office and take a look at Sandrine's file and whilst he was at it, he'd look at Wildblood's file too. A man of surprises he thought and a woman of mystery. He picked up the phone and asked for the Staff Manager.

Taking his time he wandered down his usual corridor and turned left heading for the staff exit and the Timekeeper's office.

Marker walked past the clocks and cards and into the recruiting department. The larger outer office had three women seated at desks interviewing what looked like a motley collection of more Italians asking for casual waiting jobs in the banqueting department. The queue stretched out into the corridor. A younger woman was addressing those standing:

'Solo a quelli che parlano inglese verrà rilasciato un colloquio' she shouted. Only those that spoke English will be given an interview. Upon which two or three sallow faced individuals turned to leave. Behind the recruitment section was the Staff Office. Posted on its opaque glass door was the opening and closing times that they would see the hotel personnel.

Marker walked straight in and acknowledging the secretary who was seated behind an ancient but obviously reliable Remington typing up a large pile of notes.

The Staff Manager came out of his small office. He was used to odd request from the Security Office and offered up two large buff folders that he had retrieved from a locked cabinet in his office.

'These are the files you wanted to see.'

Stamped in large red letters 'Private and Confidential' they were reasonably substantial.

'Can I use this desk to read through them?' Marker asked and the chair was pulled out for him.

'Go ahead, looking for anything in particular?'

'I'm not sure.'

Marker took the seat and started to read. The look and feel of Wildblood's file was like that of an old encyclopaedia and it represented a good twenty years of various issues. There were the annual salary reviews, a tax inspection on the amount of tips he was declaring, early on in his time a few cautionary letters regarding his timekeeping and lack of supervision at breakfast time. But overall, the Irishman seemed to have kept out of trouble. Then there was one thing that he noticed, he was asking for regular payments from his salary to go to his mother in Ireland. That was something with integrity, more than Marker did for his mother. But despite flipping over the pages several times, there was nothing on Cynthia Bulling.

He turned to Sandrine's file. She had only been at the hotel for two years and had clearly made a good impression judging from the notes that were on her annual evaluation. Her work visa showed that she was born in Nantes and came to the hotel from *The Daily Mail* who had originated her paperwork for emigration. She had worked there as a correspondent reporting on European affairs and helped the paper rid itself of its fascist history promoted before the war by Lord Rothermere. Her application letter for Head of Public Relations also noted that she had also done some good occasional investigative work around the Kray Twins. Marker thought that that might be useful.

The detective then looked for her next of kin. None were recorded. He thought that a little unusual. Sandrine had no friends or relatives, odd for a girl with such good looks and charisma. Then he glanced over the next few pages and was irritated to see that her first interview was with Brooks who highly recommended her. He was not surprised as he imaged what she might have worn for that appointment. But her final approval for hire came from the Chairman's Office. The necessary two letters of recommendation were from the French Ambassador whose reference was full of Gallic charm and the other was from the editor of *The Daily Mail*. He praised her as someone who was diligent, intelligent and discreet. Then before he closed the file he also saw that she got a considerably higher bonus than he did last year. Sandrine Parte was richer than he was. Now that was even more irritating.

He noted down her last address in Nantes and her passport details. He wanted to know more about her background and looked again at her reference letters. He had missed one that was slipped in behind the page from the newspaper editor, but he picked it up now. It was from the *Lycee* that she had attended in Paris. It seemed less positive than he imagined and she might have wished for. He fished in his pocket again and pulled out his Kodak Instamatic camera. Moving the documents to the window he took a picture of each and put them back in the file.

He stood up, put a large red elastic band around the paperwork and handled the bundle back to the secretary before making his way back to his office.

In the late afternoon an important arrival came in through the revolving doors. Sheikh

Al Mukta had turned up in an extremely large Rolls Royce, followed by two other Daimler limousines. He was dressed just as if he had come straight from the desert. Patterson and Brooks had both already received a signal in their offices from the doorman's discreet buzzer which signified important arrivals. They were now waiting outside on the forecourt in their tailcoats, stiff collars and grey morning suit ties, ready to throw open the doors of the Adelphi to the large entourage and Al Mukta dressed in a diaphonous khamis.

'Don't be fooled by the wealth Brooks,' said Patterson, 'they still have sand between their toes.'

Brooks was unlikely to be fooled by much. As the Sheikh walked towards them in his robes and sandals he had a young girl on his arm.

'Brooks! Brooks!' he called.

'This is Miss Julia Blackston, and I am going to be taking her to the Moon and back!'

He shouted the words as if there was going to be lift off imminently in the Front Hall.

Brooks glanced at Patterson who had visibly blanched. Miss Blackston was wearing very little. She had a skirt on that was so short that it could have doubled for a sweet wrapper.

'Welcome to London and the Adelphi your Excellency and Miss Blackston, you know the General Manager, Mr Patterson of course.'

As he welcomed the Arab so he executed the most miniscule of bows and leading with his left-hand directed everyone inside.

When the General Manager had made his welcome known and disappeared back to his office to the crossword, Brooks continued:

'Tell me Your Excellency, how exactly are we going to achieve blast off for you and Miss Blackston?'

The Sheikh squeezed the young girl by the waist and continued:

'I want a bath of hot milk and Cristal Champagne to start with and then rose petals on the bed.'

'My pleasure,' said Brooks who when the formalities were concluded made a straight line for his office where he picked up the phone.

'Reservations please... yes, I will hold.'

He tapped his Parker fountain pen on the desk blotter.

'Yes, thank you. Tell me who is paying the Sheikh's bill? I see, do you have a number? Yes, I'd appreciate that.'

He scribbled down the number and before making the outside call rang the sixth-floor pantry kitchen.

'Sheikh Al Mukta has arrived in the company of someone who looks familiar as the daughter of a guest of ours. He wants a bath of hot milk and Cristal champagne. Yes I know, I imagine it's a bit sticky but what can you do? How much will twelve bottles of champagne be together with fifteen-gallons of hot milk? Yes, I will hold on.'

A minute passed and he was eventually told the cost. Brooks noted down the amount. He then called the external number he'd been given for Lt. Colonel Jones. Jones was working for Hawker Siddeley and was the contact for the entire account.

'Colonel Jones? It's George Brooks from the Adelphi in London. I am terribly sorry to interrupt your evening but we have Sheikh Al Mukta who has arrived and he is accompanied by a certain Miss Julia Blackstone. By chance I know her to be the daughter of a good client of ours. His Excellency wants, in his words, not mine, 'to take her to the Moon and back'. I don't have an issue with the Sheikh's own idea of space exploration but it will require a considerable amount of champagne and hot milk... Yes sir, hot milk... the process apparently involves using a bath. Cost? Oh I think the bill will be in the region of £300. I want to know if you are happy to pay it.'

There was a pause and before Brooks put the phone down Jones asked a question. After a short time to consider an appropriate answer Brooks replied:

'I don't think it will be possible for us to keep the bath plug in for you to come over and as you say: 'Have a go', but I am at least grateful you'll pick up the cost.'

He finished the call and then went down to see the General Manager.

'I don't know if you recognised who the girl was sir.'

Patterson gave Brooks one of his rheumy stares and said:

'No, I didn't recognise her, should I have?'

'She's the daughter of our most beloved client Roland Blackstone. I only hope that she's told her father. He's a minister in the government!'

'Yes well Brooks, you of all people should know that we aren't running a church here. It's a hotel and what happens within our walls is not for us to make commentary upon. I'm not playing the Archbishop of Canterbury.'

With that Brooks was dismissed and Patterson

retrieved a copy of *The Evening Standard* from his in-tray.

Richard Marker had booked the Ivy and thought that Sandrine would enjoy seeing some of the late theatre crowd that came on after performances finished in the West End. Many of the stars frequented the green banquettes and the food was more supper than a four course dinner. He walked up shabby West Street in Covent Garden and arrived at the restaurant ahead of his eight o'clock booking. Taking a place at the zinc bar and ordering a Manhattan, he took the time before Sandrine's arrival to look over the menu. Arriving fashionably late, Sandrine made the venue by 8.15. The detective could sense the eyes of the room on her as she strolled up to him and gave him a kiss on the cheek.

'What have you ordered?' She asked looking at his glass.

'It's a Manhattan, Bourbon and red Martini with a maraschino cherry.'

'I'll have one too then.'

Marker put his arm on the bar and raised a finger. The barman came over and repeated the order. When the two of them had tipped glasses and Sandrine had taken in the surroundings Richard asked her what she might like to eat.

'The joint does lighter food, mainly for the late set.'

He put his glass back down.

'Have you a *clop*?' she asked.

'A *clop*?'

'Yes it's French slang for a cigarette.'

He fished in his pocket and offered her a Rothmans.

She took the cigarette between her red lips and drew in deeply as he lit it from his Colibri.

'Well I think I'd like something light, maybe the *Eggs Benedict*, I know it's usually for breakfast but it might be fun. Perhaps a *Welsh Rarebit* for afters?'

'You're not going to put on much weight with that, but I think I will have the same.'

Marker smiled into his drink and then looking up called a handsome young waiter over to give the order. Sandrine almost dropped her glass. This fresh faced server looked remarkably familiar and very much her type. It was when he asked her in a soft Irish brogue that she made the connection.

'You aren't, by any chance, Patrick Wildblood's son are you?' she enquired.

'Why? Do you know him?' he replied with a mild lilt.

'Well I only work with him. I saw your picture on a resume the other day.'

'Yes it's me, Eoin. How well do you know my father?'

'Very well indeed. Congratulations on getting the job, he told me you were looking.'

'Well it's grand here, and I'm enjoying my first few days.'

Sandrine delved into her handbag and pulled out a business card.

'Here, this is who I am, I will tell Patrick that we met up!'

Eoin showed them to their table and the detective noticed that Sandrine had become a little flushed.

'Attractive boy?'

He looked at her.

'Yes, isn't he.'

She dismissed the comment.

Then they settled into their table.

The food arrived promptly. The eggs looked

as if they had been carefully hand-poached and then gently nestled onto a bed of bright green spinach. On the top a light hollandaise sauce drizzle of butter and egg yolk had been blended over the egg and the taste was delightfully smooth with a slight bite of vinegar from the sauce. The Rarebit was another triumph. A clever *béchamel* white sauce had been mixed with warmed cheddar and then lightly toasted under a salamander to give a light brown glaze. It was all finished off with a dash of Lea and Perrins Worcester sauce on the top.

At the end of the meal Marker looked in seventh heaven and pouring the last of the St Emilion Bordeaux into her glass wondered if they might continue the evening at a small club he knew in Soho.

'Why not?' said Sandrine.

After the bill was settled Eoin brought over the coats. When the detective had gone outside to hail a cab she squeezed Eoin's hand and said:

'Give me a call.'

And Eoin said he would.

In the cab Marker took her hand and explained that he had wanted to take her to the Flamingo Club but that had just closed, so he had decided to go to Ronnie Scott's. The jazz wasn't quite as good, but it would have to do. They got a good table and ordered some more Manhattans. "Tubby" Hayes was there playing tenor saxophone with Ronnie Scott and trumpeter Jimmy Deuchar. Marker told Sandrine that Hayes had only recently got over a drugs rap but seemed to be playing well. He put his arm around her and she didn't pull away. A few drinks on and she had her head on his shoulder. By one o'clock it was time to go and the hotel detective wondered how he might progress this advance.

'Shall we?' he asked.

'Shall we what?' she smiled back.

'Shall we go back to my place for coffee?'

'As long as it's not in the same filthy condition as your office.'

'I have a cleaner.'

And they left the club arm in arm.

When they got to his address, he put the latch key in the lock and swung open the door to reveal his private world. Sandrine looked around and was not unimpressed. His apartment overlooked the river and had a fine view of Hammersmith Bridge in the distance. The sitting room was tastefully done with a large comfortable sofa and two armchairs. In the corner was a cabinet with his books and some army memorabilia. On a desk stood a picture of his mother.

'You've done the dusting then, looks quite neat, quite homely.'

'Glad you like it. I make my own espresso, do you fancy that or tea?'

'Earl Grey please.'

It was fortunate that he took care of what he ordered for his provisions and he had a caddy with most varieties of tea.

'The bathroom's that way.'

And he indicated the room to the left before he went into the kitchen. Whilst she heard the rattling of cups and the water boiling she took a close look at the bookcase. Her experience had taught her that you tell much from what people read and the books they collect. The detective had organised his volumes into a logical order. There was a shelf dedicated to Conan Doyle which she assumed to be 'professional' because alongside them were several large reference books. Burkes Peerage, Who's Who and surprisingly, a book on etiquette by Debretts. On the shelf below were a series of cookery books with Escoffier's *Repertoire de la Cuisine* taking centre stage. But more revealing was the shelf below that contained a number of Len Deighton books. Sandrine pulled out the 'The Ipcress File' and opening the fly leaf saw that it was a signed copy.

When Marker reappeared with the late night drinks she asked him:

'Deighton a friend of yours?'

'I read him for advice and you will see that he has written a book called 'The Swinging Sixties' very useful!'

Sandrine put the book back took a sip of her tea and then moved to the bathroom. She reappeared with her blouse undone by two buttons. Walking over to him she put her hands around his waist. Then he turned and gave her a deep kiss. They left the cups in the lounge and made their way to his bedroom. He slowly undressed her until she stood in just her lingerie. She looked stunning and Marker picked her up and laid her on the double bed. He quickly undressed and felt an undeniably urgent passion rising as he lay alongside her. They slowly kissed and he slid his hands around her to remove the last of her underwear. She moaned a little and he moved on top of her. He tried to pace her, but as he moved inside her she gripped him firmly with her thighs and took up the rhythm. He held himself back until she gave a small cry of orgasm and then he finished too. He lay back in elation. Sandrine squeezed him and then turning over he put his arm across her and they fell asleep.

The next morning Marker woke late and was surprised to find the bed empty and putting on his gown he walked into the kitchen where there was a note left propped up against last night's teapot. The pot had been used again and was still warm.

It said: '*Thanks for the experience XX*'

Marker just couldn't believe he had been so lucky. He dressed quickly and just could not stop a smile.

He made it to the Stand but stopped at the Chemist in Charing Cross station and paid for the folder of photos he had arranged to be developed. He arrived at the hotel late and more than a little light-headed. He went straight to his basement office and sitting in his chair closed his eyes, leant back and tried to remember every detail of last night. When he thought of how wild Sandrine had been in his bed he became misty eyed and decided that maybe there was perhaps a benevolent Guardian Angel that had been helping him last night. He had been truly blessed. Had he actually fucked her? But there was something else nagging in his mind. A man as fat as he was couldn't really be that lucky to come across a rampant French woman with a serious sexual interest. And there was much about Sandrine Parte that he didn't know, it pulled on his subconscious. She was still a woman of mystery. He resolved to look a little deeper and took out the folder of photos in his desk drawer. Selecting just one, he then decided to ring someone whom he felt he could ask and now almost regarded as a friend. He reached for the phone and dialled.

'DCI Bowen please. I'll hold.'

He waited to be put through.

'Hello? It's Richard. I need your help again. I wondered if you could run a check on a French national called Sandrine Parte? I'm completing a review for a new position for her and the Staff Manager needs a security clearance...relevance? She's helping me with the kidnap.'

He then passed over the french passport details and her place of birth that he had from the photo he took of her file.

After the call the detective congratulated himself on how well the mendacious side of his personality was coming along. He then gave some thought to what he knew so far. The telephone number from Archer's bill matched the numbers that were visible from the telephone pad in Andrew's apartment. Should he call it? There may be nothing lost and decided to use one of the phone boxes on the Strand later that day.

And then there was Brooks who was getting calls from Egerton of Broadman and clearly they had discussed Archer being in house. That wasn't unusual in itself, it was probable that Egerton would ring to make sure that he was well looked after. But the numbers 1230 weren't a room number, Marker wondered if it could be another meeting time or perhaps a telephone number. He would try that too with a Covent Garden code. He completed his last patrol around the building he took the staff exit out of the building and walked the few paces to Shell-Mex House where he found a vacant telephone box. He put in a coin in the slot maked 'A' and dialled COV 4365. It rang and when it answered he pressed the button. He heard his florin hit the cashbox.

'Hello I'd like to speak to Mr Archer.'

Marker ventured this name as the most likely to make some connection with the anonymous person who had answered.

'You have the wrong number.'

The call hung up. He pushed Button 'B' but his coins had already been consumed. He refilled the phone and tried COV 1230. The call rang out. He pushed button 'B' again and this time his money was returned. Returning to the hotel he went straight to the first floor switchboard to speak to Mary whose knowledge of telecommunications was almost as broad as her backside. He found her sitting precariously on a stool in the middle position on the board with her large bottom flowing over the edges of the frame.

'Mary, is there any way you can tell me if a line is connected on the telephone exchange, or indeed who owns a particular number?'

'If the line rings out it may have been in use at some time but has no current subscriber. I might be able to find something out by asking the central operator. I have a friend at the exchange I can ask.'

'It's COV 1230. Another thing, can you find out who the subscriber is at COV 4365?'

'That's more difficult, but I can try. What's it worth?'

'I'll take you to the Simpsons for dinner.'

'It's a deal'

Marker left the switch-room and its heat. Closing the door behind him he rather dreaded the thought of asking Mary for dinner rather than Sandrine, but that was what duty involved.

Deciding to start a patrol of the rest of the hotel he again reflected on what he knew but this was rather what he suspected. By the time he had completed all eight floors of the main building he had come to the conclusion that the kidnap had to be related in some way to the take-over bid and being used to coerce the Chairman to sell his shares and lose his controlling votes. Then there was Archer, whom he hadn't been impressed with even though he was £10 the richer. Unlike himself, Marker, who occasionally tossed coins into the hats of the homeless, didn't perceive Archer as a man of natural charity. He wondered what he might have to do with the Broadman takeover strategy. The Met had explained the mystery of the Willows, but why would the Chairman be threatened with that news, certainly he would not have wanted it to be made public that he was responsible for his wife's death but the accident was that - just an accident. Whilst lost in his thoughts he somehow found himself on the first-floor corridor and once again passing the Press Office.

'Miss Parte in?'

He asked the young girl who was typing quickly with the new IBM golf-ball machine, addressing a large number of envelopes to send out for a Press party invitation.

'Go straight in.'

She waved vaguely at Sandrine's door and set about her keyboard with renewed fury.

'Morning Sandrine.'

He greeted her as she looked up from a pile of press cuttings she had laid out on her desk.

'Thanks so much for last night, it was just great.'

Sandrine looked up and smiled.

'Oh, I'm glad you popped in, close the door.'

Marker turned and closed the door and the noise of the machine next door faded away.

'I've got some news. Did you hear about Sheikh Al Mukta and our client's daughter upstairs? That'll be something that we have to keep out of the Press.'

'No, I hadn't.'

'He's ordered a bath full of milk and Champagne, it's the talk of the stewards' dining room!'

Marker smiled and looked thoughtful. Sandrine continued:

'Anyway, something else for you. He and Archer have known each other a very long time. The Al Mukta family partially owned *Sol Brava* though one of their Middle East companies, and Al Mukta's father and Archer were behind that takeover bid just after the war. The father has since died and his son, the present

Sheikh, has a large shareholding in Broadman. You know they are also both directors.'

Marker looked thoughtful.

'Well not a coincidence that they should both appear here together then, just as things are hotting up. I remember what it was about Archer now. He was in the Middle East during the war. Army intelligence I think. Ran an outfit that was semi-anonymous keeping the *Krauts* off the Suez Canal. Worked with some private army out of Jeddah. I heard all about it when I was serving in Cairo just after the Germans capitulated.'

Sandrine then said:

'Maybe he'd worked with Al Mukta during the war then. The Sheikh's from Jeddah judging from the address he's given on his registration card.'

Sandrine tossed the index card over to Marker and he looked at it in more detail.

'Seems to spend a lot.'

Marker passed the card back. He then moved over to the window and looked out.

'I've been thinking about this kidnap. The ransom is being demanded in gold bars. How will the Chairman get hold of that and where will it be paid over?'

'Well obviously with exchange controls he's never going to get cash with the Police breathing down his neck, so gold is the best thing. He can buy that at any Bullion dealer. I don't suppose it's that difficult.'

Sandrine leant back in her chair and Marker got yet another appreciation of her figure.

'Fancy another Polynesian?'

'No, let's try one of those restaurants in Covent Garden.'

'Fine, tomorrow night? Eight o'clock?'

'Perfect.'

After he left Sandrine considered where she was at in this new relationship. Richard Marker was an interesting man. A little too focused on his appetite perhaps but she enjoyed his company. It was going to be fine as long as he didn't put his enquiring mind into her past. She certainly didn't want that to interfere with the new opportunities his investigation might open up. She was looking forward to getting back to her investigative journalism days and there could be some extra compensation to be enjoyed. And he was, in his own way, a reasonable fuck too.

Coming to London after France had been like starting a new life. She had a history and she had made a mistake in Paris. No one in London knew she had a little girl who was looked after by her sister. She was now just about to go to school and was beginning to be seriously expensive. The last thing she really wanted dredged up was the issue of the student fund she had plundered at the *Lycee* in a stupid attempt to pay the bills. She would never have been found out if she hadn't fallen for the game they played to catch her. It had been her pride in wanting to win.

Everyone knew that the money was kept in the student union safe and she had learnt the numbers of the combination by watching the union secretary over a number of days going in and out of the strongbox. She had taken the opportunity when the office was just closing for the weekend and there was no one around. She had only skimmed a few thousand francs or so and left the rest of the notes. Not enough to be noticed she thought. But on the Monday the shortfall was picked up and an enquiry began.

Then they ran a quiz night later that next week. She enjoyed those evenings, but one of the puzzles was to ask the gathered students if they could guess the combination the thief used. Everyone had to guess the right order from a collection of ten numbers put on a board. She couldn't resist putting the numbers down correctly. She won the quiz but realised that by being the only one to guess with deadly accuracy the finger of suspicion was upon her. Of course they never proved anything but her head of department was not a stupid man. He knew that she had an illegitimate child and needed the money. He had known about her arrears of rent which she had surprisingly repaid the weekend after the robbery. Stupid.

And now her sister had called that morning to say she needed more money. Sandrine had already some ideas about how she might cover the shortfall. She hadn't told the hotel detective that she knew a little more about George Brooks and his relationship with Andrew Bulling. When she had gone through Brooks' diary on one of those visits to his apartment she had seen that he was planning a vacation with Andrew in Rome.

Brooks never mentioned this to her and now she wondered if their friendship was more physical than emotional given his exposure as bisexual. She needed some revenge and alongside his diary in his desk at his apartment had been Brooks' bank account details, and she had carefully noted them down. Because the two things that Sandrine needed most was sex and money, and of those two, money certainly came first. She wondered if the adventure she was on with the hotel detective might also be worthwhile.

She would keep Richard warm and cosy, If things turned out well and they uncovered the kidnappers old man Bulling might be generous with a reward.

Mary rang Marker in his office and asked him to pass by the switchboard. He made his way up via the west staircase and as usual found the telephone room a hive of busy activity.

'Morning Mary, what have you got for me?'

Mary swivelled her commodious body around on her stool, giving the appearance of a bulbous spinning top about to lurch off its pivot.

'Well COV 1230 is a dead line. It hasn't had any recent subscribers. COV 4365 is registered to a company called Makeley Properties and it's a flat, I have the address here.'

She passed a page from her notepad over to Marker. He noted the address, Flat 3b, Betterton House, Betterton Street, Covent Garden.

'Well thank you very much Mary.' Marker got up and started towards the door.

'What about that dinner?' Mary looked hurt.

'Oh yes! Delighted!' Marker lied and inwardly groaned. 'When does it suit?'

'How about next Wednesday?'

'I'll make the booking.'

Marker replied and opening the door, blew a kiss in her direction. He thought he saw Mary blush.

Chapter 7

It was Friday morning and James Egerton picked up his papers and made his way to the Broadman's meeting room, a large room with an oval table that could accommodate fifteen impressive chairs. Already seated were several of the salaried directors and the non-executives. Archer was near the top of the table in deep conversation with Sheikh Al Mukta who was looking remarkably fresh after his encounter with Miss Blackston. Across the way was Charles Van der Fleit looking none the worse for wear either, but presumable a few pounds lighter. Not in weight but in wallet.

'Good afternoon everyone.'

Egerton took the seat at the top of the table and began his address:

'I wanted to bring you up to speed with where we are on the Strand development.'

He picked up a crystal decanter which was near his blotter and poured himself some water.

'I took some advice from Adrian and increased the offer to Bulling at The Adelphi. He's gone away to re-consider his position. As you know from the papers he's got a nasty situation that has arisen with the kidnap of his son, but I think that might have the benefit of putting more pressure on him to sell.'

These opening remarks were met with approving nods around the gathered ensemble. One of the directors asked if it was appropriate to negotiate with these new circumstances. Addressing the whole table Egerton replied:

'It is indeed unfortunate but in business we can't be distracted from our end goal. Without The Adelphi the whole scheme is in jeopardy and we need to start work on that side of the Strand sooner rather than later. I am concerned that we will have enough challenges with planning, especially as we have to be aware of the provisions of the Town and Country Planning Act. We don't want a preservation order slapped on us at a later date and there are moves afoot in Parliament to put a tighter rein on buildings with architectural or heritage merit.'

Sheikh Al Mukta asked:

'What's the deal James?'

'Well I've upped the offer by 20% and offered him an Adelphi Board position at the hotel for a further two years.'

'Very generous.'

The meeting continued for the rest of the hour and at the end as they were saying their goodbyes, Archer approached Egerton.

'I think we've got him under quite a lot of pressure and if we keep the foot on the pedal I am confident we will get a result.'

Egerton looked up from his notes.

'I think you're right too Adrian, he seemed in more assuasive mood when I made my last call.'

Archer picked up his briefcase and walked to the lift. He left the building from the main entrance and gave his pass back to the doorman. He hailed a cab and made his way back to the Adelphi. It was still early and he would have time to pass a couple of cocktails with Dorothy when he got back. He wondered how Andrew Bulling was getting along in his little nest in Covent Garden. Probably quite well he thought. Then his thoughts turned lightly as to what Andrew would do with all the money that he was getting from the ransom. Probably spend it he decided.

That same day the Adelphi Board gathered in the Baccarat room. A smaller private dining room next to the restaurant that could seat all the Directors and from which the room was sufficiently remote to be soundproof. The Board sat in some trepidation awaiting the Chairman. Many of them hoped that he wasn't going to be in his usual aggressive mood post alcoholic lunch. Sir John strode in late with a face of thunder and took the large chair at the top of the table. Seated across from him were two executive directors whose main responsibilities were wine buying and operations management, and they sat shoulder to shoulder with the two hotel bankers. Taking the dangerous seats next to Bulling were the lawyer and the outside accountant. Bulling opened the meeting without a welcome and cast his eyes onto the notes that had been provided earlier by his secretary.

'It's a good offer, twenty percent up on their last one but I don't need to sell.'

'You may not, but what about the other 'A' shareholders. Will they be so loyal?'

Asked the lawyer.

'Well they are City friends, but we are not trading well, so I suppose it's a risk. The question is are we going to reject this bid or accept it?'

There was a general discussion about Broadman's plans and what it meant for the ongoing business. One director asked if the hotel would close entirely.

'That's isn't necessarily true.' Bulling rudely interrupted. 'The plans still call for a hotel, but it would mean that the Strand side of the building, some one hundred and fifty rooms, would go. But those are the smallest of our accommodation and it would leave the original hotel that was built at the end of the last century intact.'

'How many rooms will be left?' Asked the accountant who was already scribbling some numbers on the notepad that had been provided.

'Well it takes us back to two hundred and sixty.' Bulling replied. 'You must remember that we are in difficult trading times. If we reduce the rooms count we can effectively manage the rest of the inventory with an increase in price.'

'With Broadman in control, how many directors will they want on the Board?'

The question came from one of the executives in full time employment.

'Well they want two to start, and I imagine it will become a full subsidiary. However they are not hoteliers and the smaller hotel may be allowed to float off as a separate identity in two years' time when I resign my position. There will be casualties unfortunately, but they have promised to look at who will be laid off and what they can offer in their organisation.'

That reply did not seem to offer much hope for the future careers of those around the table.

'Well Sir John, I suggest that you get some clarity on the situation from Broadman before you agree to accept or reject the offer.' The lawyer suggested, and then added: 'You will need to see what the terms are and get more focus on the process.'

The meeting finished and the attendees left considerably more down-hearted than before they had arrived.

Bulling returned to his office and asked Diana to call James Egerton at Broadman. He waited for him to come on the line.

'Egerton, it's Bulling, I've just had a meeting with my Board. They are interested to hear more of your plans. I suggest that we arrange a meeting between us to see exactly what the agreements look like and you can outline how you specifically want to take over the hotel. I have already given them an idea in line with what you've told me.'

Bulling listened a little more and then finished the call. When he was free his secretary called through on the intercom:

'There is a Stefan Hofer here to see you, he's your 3pm appointment.'

Bulling told her to bring him in.

A thin tall man casually dressed strode purposefully into the office and shook the Chairman's hand. After he had been offered tea and Diana closed the door, he took a seat on the other side of the large partner desk that stood in the centre of the room. Bulling opened the conversation:

'So Mr Hofer, you will know about the predicament I am in with the kidnap of my son.'

Hofer said that he knew something of it, but not any of the detail. Bulling continued:

'I'm told by my City friends that you are a specialist in dealing with kidnapping and kidnappers. I don't want the police involved, but as it's already been in the Press, I am somewhat exposed.'

Hofer nodded and taking out a packet of cigarettes offered the Chairman one.

'I prefer cigars.'

Bulling pushed over a large glass ashtray that had a half-smoked cheroot resting on one of the sides.

'What do you want to achieve from the negotiations?'

Hofer pushed his flowing blond hair back behind his ears and leaned back in his chair waiting for Bulling's reply:

'Well I have the money to pay the ransom and I want this whole thing to go away. In particular I am being threatened about a tragic motorcycle accident I had years ago. I think the inference is that I was responsible. I can't afford to have all that dredged up at this time as we have a hostile takeover bid going on.'

'Yes, I've read about that in the financial papers. If I am to be in charge of these negotiations I have to be left entirely alone and allowed to make arrangements without interference from you or anyone else. It's a risky business and people can die. I don't want that to be me, Andrew, or you.'

Bulling considered this for a moment and then asked:

'You mean that I have no say?'

'You have no say.'

'What are your fees?'

Hofer passed over an envelope and Bulling opened it.

'That's pricey.'

'Yes' replied Hofer. 'It's the rate I get paid by insurance companies who use my services. I assume that you don't have kidnap insurance?'

'No I don't. I never imagined anything like this happening otherwise I would have!' Replied the Chairman.

'There are a surprising number of international companies that do provide cover for their talent.' Hofer replied.

Bulling looked thoughtful and picked up the cheroot and chewed Churchillian like on the butt. He was certain he was talented.

'Alright, the fees and expenses are agreed. How do we proceed from here?'

'Who else, apart from everyone who reads a newspaper, knows any of this detail?'

'Well the police and my hotel detective know the detail of the ransom notes.'

Hofer considered this and produced a small notebook from the inside of his linen jacket pocket.

'Names?'

Bulling provided the detail. Hofer then asked to see the copied ransom notes and took a small camera from his pocket.

'Do you mind?'

Bulling looked at the camera and said it wasn't necessary. He had an extra Xerox for him.

Hofer put his camera back.

'The next message you receive must not be shown to them. I have to be able to communicate in complete secrecy. Please contact me as soon as they reach out to you and do nothing until I arrive.'

Bulling looked humble, something that wasn't a natural occurrence and hadn't happened for some time. He said he understood and standing up he went to shake Hofer's hand.

'It's a deal.' He said.

The meeting finished abruptly and Hofer gave his card with his contact numbers. Bulling put it in his pocket.

On his way out Hofer was wondering how he was going to make contact with this malevolent group, but assumed the Chairman would keep his word and call him, he was ,after all, being well paid. He took a cab back to his office. It was a discreet bureau. No name plate on the door and to all intents and purposes looked like any ordinary mews house, but once inside he had a number of staff who were intently busy on telephones and telex machines. This was the hub of London's Risk Management Associates business and Hofer was in charge of its European operations.

DCI Bowen had returned to West End Central and decided to take a look at Andrew Bulling's apartment to try to get some handle on his abduction. She wasn't surprised that Sir John Bulling seemed more pre-occupied with the implied threat in the letter than he was about getting his son back and she was sure he was going to pay the ransom for some silence. But Andrew Bulling had gone AWOL and she had already put out a missing persons notice to all stations. She decided to take her number two, DI Sloane, with her to Fulham.

When they got to the address they parked up opposite his block. They rang on one of the two doorbells until one answered. A frail voice came over the door intercom.

'Who is it?'

'Police.'

'I'll come to the door.'

A few minutes later, through the frosted glass they could make out the fuzzy shape of an elderly woman making her way up the corridor. When she opened the door she was surprised to see a woman and a man rather than two men. She asked for their warrant cards which they both flashed.

'Good afternoon, come on in and I can tell you all about Andrew Bulling,' she said, 'he's been kidnapped you know.'

They were shown into a cosy sitting room on the ground floor. Bowen and Sloane took their seats whilst she asked if they would like some tea.

'No thank you,' the DCI replied. 'When did you last see Andrew?'

'Well he kept himself to himself you know, I know it's just legal now, but you see he is homosexual, so he didn't have many girlfriends. Well, come to think of it, he didn't have any, well there was the cleaning lady of course and there then was that nice woman from the clinic that sometimes came around.

He is always very courteous, wouldn't harm a fly, quite sweet natured boy really. What was it you asked me?'

Bowen and Sloane looked at each other. Then Bowen said:

'DI Sloane is going to ask you some more questions and I am going to have a look in his apartment.'

'It's locked you know.'

'I have a key.'

Bowen didn't, but it would be an easy enough job for her to get in the door as she was more skilled at breaking and entering than most of the thieves she caught.

When she had forced the lock with a plastic card she kept specifically for the purpose, she found the flat exactly as it had been left. Everything in its place, if a little dusty. She took a camera from her briefcase and snapped away until she was satisfied she had a view of every physical angle. After she had finished she sat down on his sofa, and looking around spotted the corner of a book that had appeared between the cushion she was sitting on. It was just by the edge of the settee arm. She pulled it out. It was a diary of sorts. Relaxing a little more she began to turn the pages and most interesting reading it made. She put the book into her briefcase and went back downstairs to pick up Sloane. They said their good-byes to Andrew's neighbour and made their way across the road back to their car.

On the way back to the station Bowen turned to Sloane and told him she had what appeared to be Andrew's diary or at least a notebook of some kind.

'Well let's look it over. Chuck it here.'

Sloane held out his hand.

'I already have' she replied. 'And there are pages torn out around the date he disappeared. He seems to have had a lot of friends, and one of them is George Brooks from the Adelphi.'

'Oh that's interesting. Brooks who fucked the guy who murdered the tom?'

'That sounds convoluted but the very same.'

They both returned to their office and the DCI picked up the phone to Marker. When the hotel detective answered she told him that she had been to Andrew Bulling's flat and had found that he was friends with Brooks. Marker told her that he was aware there was a relationship. Bowen continued:

'You wanted to know about Sandrine Parte?'

Marker waited in anticipation at the end of the line.

'No criminal record here in the UK, but something came up on her visa application. Do you want me to make some enquiries with my counterpart in *La Surete*?'

'Yes please, I want to be sure that I know everything I can.'

Marker was intrigued.

After the conversation he rang through to Sandrine's office. He was curious to know more about how the papers had got wind of the kidnap story.

'I want to know how *The Daily Express* got hold of the Bulling kidnap story. Can you find out? Maybe the paper's diary will know. Or maybe that bloke you know on the crime section. Might be more up his street.'

It didn't take more than half an hour before Sandrine rang back.

'It was an anonymous tip off by phone to the crime reporter. A bit of an East London accent apparently.' Marker took that in and then added:

'Let's discuss it tonight, I've booked Rules.'

The restaurant had one of those old-fashioned rooms, a lot of dark red velvet banquettes with walls full of old prints. The menu was of traditional British fare. The detective had arrived early and wanted to be sure that he had a discreet table. The restaurant was, after all, close to the Hotel and on a Friday night one was never certain quite who else might be dining that they knew. After being seated in one of the alcoves he studied what was on offer. There were the usual selection of grills, and he was particularly drawn to the lamb cutlets. If they were cooked pink he would choose those with red currant jelly and a little mint sauce.

The vegetable selection looked good too. The *petits pois a la flamand* were attractive, peas with small poached white onions accompanied by a light green sauce. Then there was a choice of potato, the *pommes marquise* looked especially inviting. Rounds of piped mash potato with a centre of pureed tomato.

Turning to the wine list he selected a 1966 *St Emilion*, the ideal red Bordeaux that he was sure she would like. A little lighter than the other clarets, it would go perfectly with the white burgundy.

At ten past eight the restaurant door swung open and there she was. She looked almost as good with her clothes on as she did with them off. The Maître d' took her coat and she came over to the table and kissed him on the cheek.

'Hello Richard, you're always prompt and I'm always late.'

'Fashionably so.'

He smiled as he stood up and pulled out her chair.

'I imagine you'd like the view of the room and I'm fine with that.'

Sandrine made herself comfortable and asked:

'I suppose you got here half an hour ago to study the menu?'

'Correct.'

'So what am I having?'

'A cocktail.' He suggested.

They ordered two Negronis and Sandrine looked around the room.

'Mostly weekenders.' She ventured.

'Yes, you probably right, I think this is one of the oldest restaurants in town and it's been here since 1798, they serve oysters which I thought you might like, good for your libido and all the traditional British fare. It also has game from its own estate, Lartington in Teesdale.'

'I'm glad you're keen to see I keep my libido up.'

'I am and I'm thinking about a Macon Villages and a St Emilion to keep you going.'

'Sounds great.'

Marker wanted to make an impression and thought of something cultured.

'It's got a good clientele too, apart from you I see Laurence Olivier over there.'

Marker twisted in his chair and nodded towards a table close to the door.

'Olivier's dining with his wife Joan Plowright.'

'Yes I see them. He's at the National isn't he?'

'I'm not as sophisticated as you Sandrine, but you're probably right.'

A waiter came over dressed in a short black jacket and long white apron. Marker gave his selection and Sandrine as if by command, ordered oysters and a grilled Dover sole.

The *Huitres Belon* arrived very fresh. Sandrine said she could smell the sea air from them and she ate a half dozen flavoured with raspberry vinegar. Marker had a grilled slice of *foie gras* that came with toast and a light chutney.

After the plates were cleared the fish was presented and prepared at the table. Four firm filets were put on a white plate and offered with tartar sauce. The detective's three cutlets came out beautifully grilled with black lines from the brazier impressed on the sides, they were cooked to a perfect medium rare.

The detective asked about the anonymous call to the paper.

'The accent?' asked Sandrine. 'Probably put on, but it does mean that the kidnappers are local, we aren't dealing with Sicilian body snatchers.'

'Yes, and it points more to gangsters rather than anything to do with the bid.'

Marker continued:

'Well we have to put it on the back burner – for the moment.'

Marker then told Sandrine most of what he had now found out.

'More importantly I want you to help me look into this apartment. I've got the address and it's somehow tied up with Andrew. I traced a number that he had left in his flat. You need to dig around the company that owns it and then we are going to visit. I say we, but actually it's you.'

Sandrine blanched a little at the plan.

'What if something happens to me?'

'Well you're a big girl Sandrine, and you've done investigative work before. I suggest that as it has a few flats at the same address you can make out you're looking for a neighbour and knocked on the wrong door. Be interesting to see who answers it.'

'Who do you think will answer it?'

Marker retrieved some black and white photos from his pocket. They were thumbnail shots of several Broadman directors and one of Andrew Bulling.

'Let me know if any of these mug shots fit.'

Sandrine put the photos into her bag.

'Are you coming back for a little late night entertainment?'

Marker thought that he might strike lucky a second time.

'Not tonight Richard, too much of good thing might be bad for you.'

Marker wondered if this rejection was because of his weight, his seductive skills or his social status. He hoped it was none of these, but concluded it probably was.

'Shame.'

He picked up the bill and taking her by the arm he collected the coats and left the restaurant to call two cabs.

Chapter 8

The Arrivals List at the hotel the next day looked impressive. The top guest was Frank Sinatra and his entourage. He had just divorced Mia Farrow and it was assumed he was coming unaccompanied. A private trip with no London concert planned, as this year he had been making a number of films. Brooks was agitated and wanted to make sure that the visit went well so he made several important points during the morning meeting. It was established that he would be flying and arriving with a fleet of cars and in the rear would be a baggage van that had all of the group's luggage.

'So which floor are they all going on?' Brooks asked.

'It's unfortunate that we have Adrian Archer in house as he has the best suite on the fifth.' The Reception Manager replied.

Mrs Haul looked up from the list of rooms that had been allocated.

'I suggest we go for the third floor of river suites and put his 'hangers-on' into the rooms on the opposite side of the corridor.'

'It will mean a few guests in house will have to move.'

Brooks studied the floor-plan of the hotel lying on the desk.

'Well let's get that done by lunchtime and offer those that have to shift an upgrade to suites or something.' Mrs Haul added.

Brooks looked across to the hotel detective.

'Marker – what security arrangements are in place?'

He looked up from his house list and said that Sinatra's team usually contracted with a local security firm that provided the 'heavies' for his concerts.

'He'll be using those when he goes walkabout outside, but I don't think he will need them in-house. He has a personal valet who looks after his stuff and an assistant who handles the business side of his visits.'

'What's he here for?' asked Brooks.

The meeting participants looked around at

each other rather vacantly.

'Amusement?' Offered Fellowes, the Hall Porter who was sitting across the room.

He was the only one dressed in a hotel uniform. A long livery frock coat with matching waistcoat. The rest of the team wore morning dress or similar attire. The comment went by with no response from the gathering.

'Alright' Brooks began:

'Let's make the arrival seamless. Registration in the room. Full VIP amenities, champagne and fruit replenished every day, turndown to be at a requested time. Security to be around Marker, on arrival and departure, including any planned trips out during the day.'

The hotel detective nodded.

'Sandrine.' Brooks looked at her plain faced.

'What are the Press arrangements?'

'It's a private visit – no press and the rooms to be listed in the exchange as incognito. We are using the name 'Mr Marks' if anyone wants to be put through.'

The meeting eventually broke up and Marker walked out of the office with Sandrine to his side.

'What have you got on that address I gave you?'

'Well I asked a friend who has access to the Land Registry and it's owned by one of Archer's companies.'

'That's interesting, I think we need an early visit to Betterton House.'

Sandrine looked at Marker.

'By that I know you think 'me', you said as much last night.'

Marker wondered if that had been the cause of his rejection. He just couldn't fathom women out. Who wouldn't want sex after a perfectly good meal? Dropping the thought he asked:

'When can you do the visit?'

'I thought I might go now, before the fertiliser hits the ventilator with the Sinatra arrival.'

'Great, let see what happens. Remember you can gain entry by just pressing any of the intercom buttons and make your way up to 3b and knock on the door.'

Sandrine returned to her office to brief her staff about the outcome from the morning briefing. When she was satisfied that everything was in order, she left, with some trepidation, for the walk to Betterton Street. She crossed the Strand and made her way through the mass of vans picking up deliveries from the market. Most were going to drop off their goods at local restaurants and hotels, but a few were making longer journeys to the suburbs and the outer markets elsewhere.

Finding the street she looked at the bland front of the red brick building of flats and walked up to the main entrance. Just as she was thinking of pressing the intercom button the door opened and a woman with a shopping basket on wheels pushed out. Sandrine took the opportunity to walk in unannounced and made her way up the carpeted stairs to the third floor. There she saw a number of flats all with a letter of the alphabet following the number 3. Turning down a side corridor she came across flat marked 3b and walked straight past it. At the end of the corridor she hesitated and then ignoring the growing sense of tension in her chest she walked purposely back to the door. She put her head scarf on and knocked.

There was a noise, and then the sound of a chain being put across the door. As it opened just a few inches a man's voice asked:

'Hello, can I help you?'

Sandrine's mind was in overdrive but focused. She had thought this part of the exploit through. She used her best french accent.

'I'm looking for Madame de La Plance, is she in?'

'No one of that name here, try the Concierge on the ground floor' and with that the door began to close.

'Oh! I wondered if you could tell me which direction the emergency stairs are. The lift is being used for furniture removal from a flat upstairs.'

A head then moved closer to the door frame and Sandrine just caught a glimpse of its owner. She instantly knew who he was.

'To the left and at the end of the corridor.'

And with that the door closed.

She made her way back to The Adelphi and walking into the Front Hall saw Richard Marker in his usual discreet position. She went over to him and said:

'I'm pretty sure it's Andrew Bulling.'

Marker was going to reply, but a receptionist came over from behind his desk to say there was a call from Brooks who needed to see him urgently. He was so excited with Sandrine's news that he was tempted to kiss her but resisted the urge and said he had to dash.

The Chairman was reflecting on his situation. The last thing he wanted was the police and the Press raking over Cynthia's death. All that had been neatly dealt with years ago. He was innocent of any blame. But it was better to be take the insurance of hush money. Someone out there knew there was more to the story. So now with the bid for the business and the threat of exposure to some unpleasant news,was this a good time to make a move into retirement? Like a football manager the role of Chairman in any organisation had a shelf life. The tricky part is knowing when your time was up. He was going to have to handle the ransom and the hostile bid. The offer was a good one, and it had the advantage of two more years at the helm and a good follow-on pension.

There were several considerations to be made: how was he to convert the cash from the sale into gold bullion? He decided that it would be best to create a company that the funds could ostensibly invest in, and what better idea than for it to create an offshore investment trust. In that way it could trade in all sorts of securities and could be used to purchase gold bars.

Then he began to consider the implications of selling his shares. For the price on offer he could happily retire and take full advantage of a lavish lifestyle into his dotage. He pushed the intercom switch.

'Diana, tell Farndon to come on up when he has a moment.'

His secretary picked up the internal phone and asked for the Controller's office.

'Mr Farndon? He wants you.'

The accountant arrived a few minutes later and as there was no red light showing on the Chairman's office door, went straight in.

'You remember we talked about selling my shares?'

The Chairman asked:

'Well I want some of the proceeds to invest in an offshore investment company that can trade stocks, shares and that sort of thing. Can you fix it?'

Farndon felt surprised, but he had held his job long enough to show no emotion.

'We have shell companies with Articles that are widely written. I think we can use one to operate securities.'

'Excellent Farndon. I will let you know how to proceed'

Sinatra and his group arrived after lunchtime in a fleet of Daimler limousines. There were a number of large heavies dressed in light bright coloured suits with shoes more appropriate for a round of golf. The doormen who took note of these sort of things at the Front Entrance could tell more about someone's worth from what they wore on their feet than what a bank credit check could discover. The star VIP came straight into the lobby flanked by his men. Behind came his personal assistant carrying a large briefcase. They walked over to the East lift that was being held on the ground floor by a liftboy. Brooks had missed the arrival but run on behind and barely made it to the lift before the doors closed.

They went directly to their suite of rooms. Brooks was able to get ahead of the entourage when the lift doors opened and with a grand gesture opened the river suite door. Sinatra knew the room well and waved him away heading straight for the whiskey bottle that had been thoughtfully provided by the management. He barely noticed the large arrangement of cut flowers that the hotel also provided and had taken much of Mrs Haul's time to properly position.

Closing the door behind him, Brooks ran into Sinatra's personal assistant.

'I've all the passports and filled in the registration forms I took with me last time and got them all signed on the plane.'

Brooks thanked him and took the sheaf of papers.

'I want a number of suits unpacked and pressed and we will use this room as a baggage room as well as a wardrobe.'

He pointed to room 334.

'That'll be fine,' said Brooks, 'what about lunch?'

'We had it on the plane, I think he's going to take a nap. Let's not disturb him please!'

'I've put the telephone under the name of 'Marks', so you will need to tell him that if he wants any personal calls. I will send along the housekeeper to work with his valet.'

Sinatra's valet together with Mrs Haul unpacked all ten suitcases. The suits were sent for pressing in the lower basement and the laundry was rushed to the Kennington premises.

Later that day all the items were returned and hung on temporary clothes racks that had been wheeled into 334. It was later that the assistant rang Brooks and said:

'We've lost $100 that was in the green suit pocket. I left it there by mistake but assumed you would have found it before the jacket was pressed.'

This sent a shiver down what would have normally been his cool spine, and so he went up to the floor to meet Sinatra's valet and his assistant. The money had been inadvertently left in an inside pocket of a favourite blazer. It wasn't going to be easy to find as there had been a number of hotel staff who had handled the item before it had been returned. This was a job for the hotel detective and Brooks lost no time in getting in touch with Marker.

'It went out to the laundry and came back within three hours.'

Brooks was back in his office and had called Marker in from the lobby. Marker took out his pocket notebook.

'Well I will need to know the names of all the staff who were in involved both here and at the laundry, can you get hold of the staff rotas from the floor, the linen room and the pressing room at Kennington?'

Brooks thought that could be reasonably accomplished.

This incident was an inconvenience. Marker had other things on his mind such as why Andrew Bulling was in a flat owned by Archer and he wasn't in the mood to start conducting a full scale investigation as to where $100 had been lost.

'How are you going to handle Sinatra?' He asked.

Brooks considered this for a minute and then said:

'I think we will reimburse him on his account. It's not worth doubting their word it was there, but in reality it could have been one of his people who took it just as much as it could be our staff. His business is worth too much to us to start an argument.'

'I wonder how you would feel if I set up a honey trap?'

Marker looked Brooks straight in the eye. Brooks looked a little uncomfortable.

'What are you suggesting?'

'Let's send some more stuff out with some notes in it and see if the same thing happens. I can mark the notes with an invisible marker and when watch to see if and when the notes disappear within set steps of the process. Then we can do a search and see if the notes turn up in someone's pocket. If we keep this just between you and me and Sinatra's assistant, it might bear fruit as long as the thief doesn't realise we know about the missing money.'

'Ok let's do it.'

Brooks nodded his agreement.

When Sandrine returned to her office she was also considering what finding Andrew Bulling meant, but she was immediately distracted when she sat at her desk for there was a telephone message that had been taken by one of her staff. It was from Eion Wilding. Now there was someone really worth pursuing. She dialled the number.

'Hello Eion, it's Sandrine Parte, how are you?'

The young Irish voice came back over the line.

'Great, you asked me to call you, so here I am.'

'Well I was wondering if you have any time free from your busy job at the Ivy to have a drink?'

'I'd love that.'

It was all set up. Putting down the phone Sandrine felt her heart rate move a little faster and she felt a familiar rush of excitement as she considered what she would like to do to Eion and how she might surprise him. She decided to meet him at a bar near her place, if it all worked out well she would take him back there.

She thought about her all the opportunities that were now ahead of her. Would this new relationship just be physical? That in itself would be very welcome, but she found the boy very charming for the brief moment that she had met him. Maybe there might be more to this. She could think of nothing better than relaxing on a beach in Juan les Pins with someone as attractive as him lying beside her beach towel. It might be difficult to keep this from his father, but she would have to make that perfectly clear right from the outset. She was good at that, laying down the boundaries.

She let her mind drift on.

Then there was the excitement of the kidnapping and discovering Andrew Bulling hiding out. Maybe a chance of that little pay-off she had been thinking about before for all the information she had found out so far. She could certainly keep one step ahead of the hotel detective, he was kind and paternalistic and she was happy to fuck him, but here was a limit to how far that was going to go, and if he kept insisting on inviting her to restaurants she was going to need a larger dress size.

The next day another note had arrived in the Chairman's Office. Bulling rang Hofer and told him to come straight over. Hofer arrived within the hour and when he got to the hotel he was met by Diana who showed him into the boardroom. Bulling was sitting at the top of the mahogany table with the latest message and a telephone.

'Have a look at this.'

Bulling passed over the note:

12.30 Today on your direct line

Hofer read the message and then running his fingers across the page passed it back.

'Quality paper.' He looked at the Chairman, 'can't tell much from that, I suppose if it was perfumed you'd think it was a woman behind this.' Hofer smiled and continued, 'so it's 12.15 and I assume that your secretary can pass over the direct line to this extension?'

Hofer pointed at the phone. Bulling nodded and asked:

'What are you going to say?'

'I'm going to do a lot of listening and then tell them that we need more time. Maybe reassure them that the police are out of it. They won't be long on the line as they will suspect that you will try to have a trace on it.'

Bulling looked momentarily uncomfortable and pulled himself up in his chair. He thought he should tell Hofer how he was going to settle the ransom.

'I think I can get the money into an offshore company in the Caymans. In that way they can make the transfer of bullion to anywhere in the world.'

Hofer considered this and then said:

'I'm going to give them a way to contact me so that I can negotiate out of the limelight. I might be able to get the ransom down more easily that way.'

Diana brought in a tray of coffee and Hofer helped himself. As the Boardroom door closed the phone rang. Hofer picked it up and heard the tone of money being deposited in a phone box.

'Bulling?'

'No, it's Stefan Hofer, I am your contact in this negotiation.'

There was a brief but painful silence and Hofer detected a strong East End accent.

'Tell Bulling that we want the gold transferred in Menton on the Monaco French border seven days from now.'

'I'm afraid that timescale won't be possible, but I can get you what you want with more time. Before you put the phone down I am going to give you a number that will always be answered by me for one hour from six o'clock any evening. It's Whitehall 2435.'

The pips went and no more money was put in the box.

'He's using phone boxes and he's got a strange Cockney accent I think he's putting on. Phone boxes make it difficult to trace. I think this is a small operation. Let's see what happens when he calls me back.'

Bulling considered this and then said:

'Making Menton for the handover is clever. It is going to be much easier to get bullion into Monaco than anywhere else in Europe.'

'Yes, I think he's more sophisticated than he would like us to know.'

Hofer picked up his briefcase and saying goodbye to the Chairman told him he would keep him up to date as events emerged.

Bulling returned to his office and picking up his phone got through to his lawyer.

'Are we set up with that Cayman company yet?' He asked.

'I'm getting my co-respondent to lodge the

papers in the Caymans and we should be able to transfer funds within a few days. I've draw the Mems and Arts so that they are as broadly based as possible. The new company should be able to do pretty much anything from selling bicycles to buying super yachts.'

'Well all I need at the moment is to buy and sell bullion.'

'Understood, provided that it's not moved to a country where there are exchange controls.'

'Monaco?'

'That'll do.'

Bulling finished the call and then considered when to make the share deal. Tomorrow would be good.

Marker wasn't concentrating when he was planning his trap to catch the member of staff who had light-fingered Sinatra's pocket money. He was pre-occupied with what to do now that he knew where Andrew Bulling was hiding out. What he didn't know was if he was alone or not, and in truth whether he was being held under duress. He thought that unlikely as he had opened the door himself, but you never know.

Finally turning to the problem of the lost cash he placed a $50 bill into the inside pocket of another jacket and sent it off for pressing in the same manner as the first had been dispatched. After the housekeeping porter took it from the third floor room Marker walked the four-flights of stairs to the basement linen room. There he spotted the jacket tagged and hanging. There were several linen room staff in the vicinity, but when no one was looking he checked that the note was still in the coat pocket. It was. Just at that moment the large laundry truck drew up onto the goods receiving platform and the long rear doors were swung open. The driver then loaded the van with a number of metal trolleys that carried all the dirty bed linen. The linen porter told him that the jacket was for a VIP and to be expressed pressed. He took it into his cab, closed the rear doors and drove off to south of the river.

Meanwhile Marker went to the linen room office and picked up the phone.

'Hello Mary, can you put me through to the Laundry in Kennington please? Dinner-? Oh yes, that's booked at Simpsons, tomorrow night.'

He felt a little gloomy about the upcoming rendezvous but held the line.

'The laundry manager please. I will hold'

He tapped the desk with his pen and took out his notebook. He looked up the pressing tag number. After a minute the line was answered.

'Hello, it's Marker at the hotel. I want you to check that a jacket with the number 5283 has a $50 note in the inside pocket. It will be arriving with you in the cab of our truck registration number 345 HLY. Let me know if it's missing, and if it is I will be over straight away. Tell the truck driver to wait for me.'

The call came through half an hour later. There was no money. Marker waited for the next truck to arrive at the back entrance and took the ride over to the laundry. When he got there he went straight to the manager's office where he found the driver and the supervisor.

'Has he been anywhere after you checked the jacket?'

He looked at the rather neatly turned out laundry supervisor. Clearly he was getting his laundry done for free. The manager shook his head. He turned to the driver:

'Empty out your pockets please.'

He looked the driver up and down. He was slight and gaunt and spoke with a south London accent.

'What's this about?'

'It's all about $50 that you took out of this jacket!'

Marker pointed to the jacket now on the supervisor's desk. The driver blanched and felt sick. It was the sort of feeling that was familiar to those who run for a train that might have already departed. Marker found the note tucked in behind the man's belt when he frisked him.

'Make a habit of nicking guest's money?' he asked

'Nope' the driver replied.

'Well I think you do,' said the detective, 'because yesterday the same guest lost $100 from a similar jacket.'

He moved over to adopt a more threatening stance and could smell the tobacco on the driver's breath. He grabbed him by the lapels and lifted him off the floor. They were face to face and Marker felt a bit nauseos being that close to foul breath and yellow teeth.

'Now tell me what are you doing with the money you're pilfering?'

The driver looked scared as the supervisor closed the door and Marker let him drop back to the floor.

'I've had to pay a bet that I lost.'

The driver looked down at the floor.

'I found the $100 on the floor of the cab yesterday and I realised it must have fallen out of a jacket I had put on the seat, so I was just looking to see if I might be lucky today.'

'I bet you thought it was lucky.'

Marker looked at this shrunken heap of a man and would have liked to have hit him.

'What was the bet?'

'I bet that the hotel wouldn't change ownership and I lost.'

Marker's thoughts moved from middle gear into overdrive.

'But the hotel hasn't been sold to Broadman.'

'It will be, I bet with one of the office cleaners and they clean out the Chairman's office. She's got a letter that proves it.'

Marker guessed she was reading the stuff from the wastepaper bin.

'How much was the bet?'

'Well it wasn't as much as the money, so I thought I would cover my loss and a bit more.'

'I'd say it sounds like quite a bit more.'

The driver's face looked more sheepish than a lambing station.

'Who is the cleaner?'

Marker thought that the cleaners were doing a better job than he was in finding out exactly what was happening to the future of the hotel.

'If I tell you can I keep my job?'

Marker thought this through and made a decision.

'If you give me all the money back and you make a statement to say you found it on the cab floor I can see what I can do.'

'It was Anne, you know the fat black one who does the Directors' corridor.'

Marker didn't much like the description but it certainly fitted the overweight girl he had seen waddling around with a large plastic bag of rubbish and a vacuum cleaner.

When he got back to the hotel he took back the dollar notes and went straight to Brook's office. He found the manager going through several papers that looked like the hotel's month-end reports.

'Well here's the loot.'

He threw the money on his desk. Brooks picked it up and looked at Marker with some bewilderment.

'How did you do that?'

'Well, let's say that the finder was a little delayed in passing the cash back, but I am sure that he had every intention to do so.'

'Anyone I know?'

'A driver. I'm going to put a note on his file but let's be benevolent. There's not much work around these days and I don't think being a day late in passing back lost property is so much of a crime.'

When the detective left he made his way directly to Mrs Haul's office and finding her there he asked if he could interview Anne. The cleaner had just arrived for work and they waited for her to be found. She arrived at the Housekeeper's office looking considerably worried and squeezing in between them she arranged herself on the only spare chair. Marker thought that after he had finished with her she would doubtless be seeking the solace of more chocolate. The interview took less than five minutes and ended in tears. Anne would not be taking the Chairman's correspondence from the waste bins in future, she would be transferred to cleaning the staff changing rooms at the end of the week.

It was four o'clock in the afternoon and the boat train arrived at Waterloo disgorging a large number of Adelphi guests from the States on to Platform 8. The Cunard's Queen Elizabeth II had been delayed docking the previous day and all her passengers stayed overnight on board. It had become marooned on a sandbank in the Solent and probably saved the employment of the Reservations Manager who had inadvertently overbooked the hotel by twenty rooms the evening of the ship's planned dis-embarkation.

This was something unheard of in the history of the hotel. The mistake had happened when, executing 'the count', the addition of all the room nights booked that was carried forward by mental arithmetic every day for a view of the seven-day forward rolling forecast.

Although the hotel always left three rooms deliberately empty for the unexpected arrival of a well-known guest, or to accommodate any additional space required by guests in-house, it was not enough to provide for all the expected arrivals that day. Four days before the Cunard was due to dock two pages of the reservations book had become stuck together and as consequence thirty reservations remained uncounted.

The mistake was discovered only whilst the liner was two days out from New York. The situation was compounded as the reservations department had kept taking bookings whilst the mistake lay undiscovered. However, when Brooks was made aware of the problem he had come up with an inventive solution.

Looking through the following two-day arrival list he picked out those clients who were of little importance, some of whom had never stayed before, and only those who had booked for no more than three nights. The room where the murder had been was already stripped and he instructed Klimp, the Chief Engineer, to flood the bathroom floor above so that water came through the ceiling into the room below.

In this way, over the coming next two days, unsuspecting first time clients who were considered of little worth would be met by an extremely apologetic receptionist and told 'their' room was drenched in water with no carpet. There then followed an explanation that their accommodation would unfortunately be 'out of order' for a week. A great misfortune which had happened when a forgetful guest had left the taps on the bath above whilst taking a long distance call. They were then told arrangements had been made for them at a nearby hotel at no cost and that on their next visit to London they would be upgraded to a river suite.

When Mrs Haul had found out about this scheme she had demanded to see Timothy Patterson and raise the strongest possible objection on the grounds of the enormous flagrant dishonesty and deceit that was involved. She was not surprised to learn that he was going to do very little about it. In this way guests who might have occupied accommodation that was sorely needed for the trans-Atlantic arrivals were moved to other hotels and room space opened up sufficiently to meet the forty strong contingent that was due to arrive later in the day.

The fleet of taxis from the station took the doormen by surprise. There was considerable confusion on the forecourt, luggage, American guests and the usual regular tea time patrons all came together at the same time. There was a terrible clash of fashion as loud checks sported by oversize New Yorkers ran up against the best of Hardy Amies being worn by the English afternoon tea set.

Patterson had always thought that these ladies had greater breeding than the stockyards of Texas, albeit that they didn't have anything like the cash. Brooks was on hand to alleviate the congestion and whilst some guests might have had to wait fifteen minutes to get a receptionist to show them to their reserved lodging, the hotel lobby returned to its normal tranquillity before the restaurants had finished serving the last of the admired cucumber sandwiches.

That night the hotel slumbered peacefully, a deep sleep in the knowledge that it have never been known to overbook and that all of its important guests were assured of comfortable and reliable accommodation in the finest style. It didn't seem to matter about those of no consequence who had been forced unknowingly to stay elsewhere.

Chapter 9

The hotel detective woke late and opening his curtains was not surprised to find it raining again. It had been a busy day yesterday and he now had a few things to follow up. For a start there was Andrew Bulling sitting it out in Betterton Street, then there was the Chairman probably selling his shares and tonight he had to take fat Mary out for dinner. Finally he still had the erotic vision of sexually liberated Sandrine in his mind that must have been a cast-off from a dream he'd just had. It was disappointing that she hadn't come back with him the other night. She was a sexy minx despite her inclination for dangerously handsome young males of whom there were probably many.

He padded off to the bathroom, showered and changed quickly into his suit. Before leaving the apartment he looked through his notebook and realised that he hadn't heard anything from DCI Bowen about Sandrine in a couple of days. He resolved to ring her when he got in.

Bowen had also left her apartment in Elephant and Castle early after making breakfast for her two children who had complained about her early start. She and Sloane were on their way to Aylesbury and were taking the 08.15 from Marylebone. They arrived at Aylesbury Town Station just as the tail end of the daily commuters were leaving for the opposite direction. The platforms were relatively empty and they made their way out through the Victorian ticket hall to get a taxi from the forecourt to the police station. Bowen announced herself to the desk sergeant and they were shown into a bland interview room. Bowen put her briefcase on the table and took out her notebook. A young faced detective opened the door and introduced himself.

'Hello, I'm DS Mills, I understand you are here over the Bulling accident, I have the files here.'

He put a slim buff file on the table. Bowen nodded and offered an introduction

'DCI Bowen and DI Sloane from West Central. We want to understand the exact circumstances of this motorbike fatality and if there is any remaining evidence.'

Mills took a seat and opened the file.

'Well it seems reasonably straight forward. Mrs Bulling died as her crash helmet split open as she hit a tree. It was a wet road and there were no skid marks but the tarmac was dug up as the motorbike frame gouged it before it went over the bank.'

Bowen looked through the file and read the notes. Then she made a close inspection of the pictures.

'I don't suppose you have the helmet still?'

'Well we don't, but I'll check the central evidence library but it's twenty years ago.'

Bowen considered this for a moment and then looked again at the pictures.

'Well the photos are reasonably clear enough, quite odd to see a straight line split virtually from the centre right to the centre back. I wonder if it had been deliberately weakened.'

'Are you thinking that this was a murder?'

Mills looked a little shocked.

'The Coroner and the Chief Constable signed it off as an accident'

He passed them the relevant copy of the form. Bowen realised that it was probably because of her age that she wasn't surprised any more by cover-ups, but Mills was still young enough to be ignorant of convienient arrangments within the establishment.

'Bulling has the kidnap of his son to deal with at the moment and he's being threatened by this accident in the ransom demand. It was certainly convenient for Bulling to be rid of his wife. The family had another hostile bid they were fighting off and she had a good quantity of controlling family shares, I read him as being frightened by this accident re-appearing in his life twenty years later. Maybe he was having an affair, he married pretty soon after the crash. Maybe <u>she</u> was having an affair. I don't think it was a marriage of unmitigated bliss.'

Bowen fleetingly thought of her own situation and the misery her marriage had been. She turned to the photos again and passed the file to Sloane.

'I see she was declared dead at the scene.'

'Yes.' Mills replied. 'It took some time for an ambulance to arrive. Bulling was the first to raise the alarm but he had to walk to a nearby house. It was at least half-an-hour before anyone got to her.'

'From the photo I can see a large rock that has blood on it.' Mills looked at the picture.

'Probably hit it on her way off the bike.'

Bowen was sceptical but then she was always suspicious.

They asked for copies of the notes and Bowen took out her camera to photograph the pictures. She asked the sergeant again to check the evidence room and get her the helmet if it was still available.

On their way back to London they found a quiet carriage and Sloane took out the copies of the file.

'Interesting reading. But there isn't anything in here that looks new.'

Bowen looked across at Sloane.

'Well Bulling is scared. I'm tempted to push him along a bit but we've not got much to go on. Maybe he was drunk, maybe he hated her enough to just let her die at the roadside. Maybe he thought it was better for him and the family that she just bled to death. His father was a man of influence and twenty years ago it might have been easier to put some pressure on those responsible for the investigation.'

Bowen looked out of the carriage window as the grey office buildings of Wembley began to flash past. They would soon be back in London. Sloane followed her gaze and asked:

'What have you thought about the kidnap?'

She brought her thoughts back into focus.

'Well the missing book pages are interesting, but only if we knew what was written on them. My gut tells me that this kidnap doesn't have a feeling of violence running through it. More a sense of obediant cooperation. A set up maybe?'

Sloane closed the file and looked out of the window as the train pulled back into Marylebone and he could see the green of Regent's Park.

'Nice place to live up here.'

'Beats the grime of Shoreditch.' Bowen added.

When they got back to the station there was a message waiting from Richard Marker. Bowen picked up the phone.

'Richard, what can I do for you?'

'I wondered if you had anything back from the French.'

'I sent the request off. I got some information back yesterday. Apparently she has a file. She was the suspect in a theft from a student union safe at her *Lycee* in Paris. Nothing proved.'

The hotel detective considered that for a moment.

'Not enough for me to be careful?'

'Not enough for you to find her guilty of theft. But there is usually no dance without some kind of music. What news on the kidnap? You've gone rather quiet the past few days.'

Marker had already thought this question through before he had called earlier. He wasn't going to sell the Crown jewels.

'Well I think the Chairman is going to sell his share of the business, so he must be building a fund. He's kept me out of it so I'm not in the story.'

'Tell him that he's not to deal with kidnappers unless he involves me.'

'Of course.' Marker lied.

The telephone only rang two times.

'Hofer.'

He heard the telling pips as money was deposited in the coin box.

'We want the gold bars delivered in two weeks' time. Menton at the *Statue St Michel, Quai Imperatrice*, by the public phone boxes. Noon. You will pass over the gold. We will test it. All clear then Bulling will be released at Victoria

Station London.'

Hofer took out his pen and made rapid notes whilst replying:

' My private Post Office box is P.O.Whitehall 3000 I want you to write to me with the detail of the release, timings and your requirements together with the security that you have Bulling.'

'We've noted that.'

The pips went and no more money was deposited. Hofer thought through what he had heard. The only way he could make this happen is if he was completely in control of the gold until he had confirmation from London that Andrew was free. A plan began to formulate in his mind. But he would need to fly to France to understand the geography.

He picked up the phone again and dialled Sir John Bulling's direct line.

'Sir John? Hofer. I've had a call. Same accent, same man. I need to fly to Nice and get down to Menton and understand where they want to do the handover of the gold. They are suggesting that Andrew would be released at Victoria station. I guess they will choose rush hour so that they can make an easier get away.'

'Have you a time frame?'

'Two weeks.'

'Not much time to get organised.'

'We might extend but my recommendation is not to string this out.'

Bulling considered his options.

'Well I think I've got things in place. The bullion will be delivered to Edmund de Rothschild Bank in Monte Carlo, you will have my letter of authority to pick it up.'

'I'll visit them on my trip to make sure that there is no hitch in the pickup. I will be doing the handover personally on the day.'

Bulling took a few minutes to think it all over. He couldn't really care less about Andrew, but it was a deep worry that now it was very likely what he did to Cynthia was going to resurface. Then he doubted that anything could be proved given the length of time that had passed. And what would Lady Julia make of it if he was declared a murderer? He dismissed the idea from his mind with an arrogance that matched the hubris of Oedipus. How *could* the Chairman of The Adelphi have murdered anyone, he reasoned?

He picked up a piece of scrap paper and wrote the salient details down that he needed to handle in order to facilitate the transactions. Looking at his notes, he re-read them then screwed up the paper and threw it in his bin.

It was half-past-ten and Adrian Archer was meeting Sheikh Al Mukta in the tea lounge at the Adelphi. After they had placed their order, Archer sat back in the armchair and opened the conversation.

'I need a little of your help.'

'Yes dear Archer, what can I help you with? You doubtless need a little *wasta* from my friends.'

'I do indeed.'

Archer looked out across to the gazebo full of flowers that were the centre piece of the room.

'Confidentially, I'm acting alone and I'm in the middle of a plan that is persuading Bulling to sell his shares. You remember when we did something similar during the war with those difficult Palestinians?'

'Ah yes, *sadiqi,* I remember it very well, we kidnapped their father and held him until they paid.'

'Well I have Bulling's son on our side and he is

willing to act as a hostage, Bulling would have to sell his shares to pay the ransom. I need some help with the arrangements. I'm planning the ransom to be handed over in Menton.'

The Sheikh moved forward in his chair.

'Menton? France?'

'Yes. I need two men to pick up gold bullion, test it, and then move it across the border to Monaco. From there I am going to liquidate it and then pass some of the cash proceeds back to his son as a payment for his co-operation. I've made arrangements in the Channel Islands.'

'Dangerous?' the Sheikh asked.

'Not especially, but Bulling has hired a kidnap specialist whom I am wary about.'

'My dear *zamil* we have to be careful. Does Egerton know of this?'

'Only you and me Excellency.'

The sheikh looked thoughtful and poured himself a cup of Jasmin tea that had just been delivered to the table by a white jacketed waitress.

'If The Adelphi is now going to employ girls to serve tea then they should at least be sexy don't you think?'

Archer glanced at the well turned out woman who had just passed their table.

'Well she's ugly but at least she's well groomed.'

Al Mukta gave her a long look as she moved across to another table.

'So Archer, I can help, I have good contacts with some Italians who make a living out of this kind of thing who are in Nice. They have an Algerian team they work with. Let me have the details and I will let you know the cost. Services like these are cash on delivery. It can't be paid in gold bars and must be transferred at the same time.'

Archer considered this and agreed.

There was considerable activity on the Directors' corridor as Marker passed by on his rounds. He saw Farndon, the accountant, sitting nervously in the Chairman's outer office, and Diana was busy making Xerox copies of a large amount of paperwork.

'Any news?'

He asked her as he stopped to catch a glimpse of

what was being reproduced.

Diana slid a beige folder over the visible typed script.

'Nothing to concern you <u>yet</u>'.

Marker made a mental note that he should meet Anne the cleaner one more time. As he walked on, Diana was called by the Chairman on the intercom. She knocked on his door and went in. Taking out her notepad and pencil she waited for his next instruction.

'Come in Farndon.'

He beckoned the accountant over to his table through the open door.

'Let's get this signing done. Diana can do the witnessing.'

And within a few minutes the Chairman had effectively and dramatically relinquished control. Within the hour Broadman's stockbroker had picked up the shares and paid the premium. The announcement hit the Stock Exchange by midday, but it would take a few hours yet before anyone in The Adelphi knew what seismic event had happened.

Marker made his way to the Housekeeper's office and asked the duty supervisor to send Anne to his office. It was only a few minutes after he himself had arrived before there was a soft knock on the door.

'Enter!' he shouted

'Ah! Anne – come in and take a seat'.

The corpulant cleaner looked very anxious and slowly took the only seat available.

'I've done nothing wrong.' She whispered.

'No you haven't Anne, I'm going to forget all about our little incident if you can help me with a top secret investigation I am carrying out.'

Intrigued and flattered to be asked about anything 'top secret' turned her mind into a whirling windmill.

'You know that the Chairman's son has been kidnapped. I am tasked with finding out who the kidnappers are. As you know it can be a very frightening thing... kidnapping...'

Marker paused and Anne nodded vigorously. Marker continued:

'I think the Chairman is too frightened to tell me something I need to know and I want you to empty his rubbish bin like you normally do, but bring all the paper back down to my office tonight. Can you do that?'

Anne looked uncomfortable.

'Are you sure that this will be alright?'

'Well you are not beyond reading the contents on previous occasions are you Anne? So I don't think you have a moral problem, and in this way you will be helping the Chairman and I catch the criminals!'

Anne looked reassured.

By late afternoon the hotel shifts had all changed and Marker walked one more time through the restaurant to see Patrick Wildblood supervising the room set up. He was standing by a *commis* giving a final wipe to the table glasses. He was dipping them in champagne bucket filled with hot water and using a fine linen cloth to get rid of the last smears.

'Busy night?' Marker asked.

'We will fill.' Wildblood replied.

'Are you joining us?'

'Regretfully not, I'm taking the switchboard supervisor to Simpsons for dinner. Doubtless she will order the beef trolley and a small pile of Yorkshire puddings.'

'Fancy large ladies do you?'

Wildblood looked at Marker's stomach.

'Make sure you don't order the same.'

Marker blanched and then smiling made his way out of the Pierrot entrance and up to the Strand. Turning right he entered Simpsons and was immediately impressed with the sense of age. Here was an establishment that hadn't changed since it was a seventeenth century coffee house.

He saw the *Maître d'* who ran the upstairs room and settled on a table near the window. He called for the menu and waited for Mary to arrive.

Had he been in the forecourt five minutes later he would have spotted Sandrine leaving for her dinner date and it would have aroused his curiosity. She had made a special effort and was dressed especially youthfully, a short skirt and tight fitting top amply displayed the promise of her figure. She was dressed to kill and looked ready for the hunt.

Walking down the Strand she made her way quickly to the tube at Charing Cross. She didn't want to be late. She had arranged to meet Eoin at a bar she knew in Chiswick and it was important to get a certain seat. One she could eye the room from and keep her guest in focus. She made her way by District Line to Turnham

Green and then turning left headed for Scarlett's. They made the best cocktails.

She was early enough to get her choice and within a few minutes the bar was beginning to hum. By seven o'clock it was so full she only just saw Eoin come in. He looked gorgeous. Dressed on trend, his clean dark hair cut to the right length, he manoeuvred his way skilfully amongst the crowd and sidled up to her stool.

'Take a seat!'

Sandrine moved her clutch bag off the empty stool next to her.

'Well Hallo!'

He replied in a soft Irish brogue.

This was going to go extremely well thought Sandrine and she pressed her legs hard together and felt a distinct surge in affirmation.

'So tell me all about yourself.'

'There's not much to tell, I'm here on an adventure really, my father has got me the job, I don't have many friends in town and I'm looking for some fun.'

Sandrine thought she could help him there.

'Are you enjoying the Ivy?'

'It's good, you see lots of theatre celebrities and a few television people. We had Alan

Whicker in the other day.'

Sandrine was impressed.

'Ask him for his autograph?

'We aren't allowed.'

'Any plans?' She asked.

'Well yes, actually I do now that I am in London. I am curious about my mother.'

Sandrine was interested and asked for more.

'My father has never told me exactly who my mother was. He's always been evasive and although he never married her I know that she died just after I was born. I have the impression that she didn't want to keep me and wanted an abortion. My father, being a Catholic, was dead against that and so she went through with the birth on the condition my father took full responsibility for me. I think it was a 'one night stand'. So I was brought up by my grandma in Ireland and it has always been a taboo subject in our household. I can't discuss it with Dad. I thought I would start with my birth certificate and take it from there.'

Sandrine was now intrigued.

'Well I can easily get that for you' she said. 'I used to do some investigative stuff when I was a journalist. I will call Somerset House in the morning. I assume that you were born in England and not Ireland?'

'Yes, England, because I tried in Dublin but there is no record there.'

As the evening wore on she thought that Eion was exactly what she needed. He was just the right personality that she found irresistible. He was amusing and vibrant and had all the good looks to match. By the time ten o'clock arrived they had enjoyed a number of the drinks on the list and also finished two plates of sliders and a couple of burgers. Eion looked as if he was going to suggest going home.

'Would you like to come back for some coffee?'

Sandrine pouted her lips a little.

'Can I?' he asked.

'Why not?'

Sandrine took him by the hand to the door. On the High Road she told him that she just lived across the way and she led him to a delightful terraced house a hundred yards further down.

'I live in the upstairs apartment.'

And putting the key in the lock she made sure that she was a few steps ahead of him on the stairs so that he might just get a glimpse of her underwear. Eion moved on up behind her and was in a state of confusion. He wasn't sure if this was really his lucky day or if she was intending to simply show him her latest press cuttings. At the top of the stairs there was a delightful well-spaced sitting room and on the walls were large framed black and white prints of American stars. Several informal photos of the 'Rat Pack', Sinatra, Sammy Davies Jnr and Dean Martin. To the left was another shot of Dick Van Dyke. Eion noticed they were all signed.

'A lovely room'. He commented. Sandrine nodded and asked how he liked his coffee. Whilst she was in the kitchen he took in the rest of the room. It had touches of France, there was a small bookcase with some Moliere and Hugo, across the room were a neat pile of *Paris Match*. He noticed a picture of a small girl on the bookshelf. Sandrine came back with two mugs and made him sit next to her on the sofa. She put her hand in his and offered him a *Gauloise* from a packet on the coffee table. He took out one of his own and she lit them both. Putting hers down on the ashtray, she blew out a thin line of blue smoke, leaned over and kissed him.

Eion was now clear as to his role and moved his arm across her shoulder.

'You really are very attractive,' he murmured.

'You're not too bad yourself.' And stubbing the cigarettes out she led him towards to the bedroom. Sandrine wanted to be lead astray...

Richard Marker had passed an evening where the enjoyment had been focused on the food rather than the company. Mary had arrived in her best flower print frock that stretched to breaking point when she sat down. Her large cleavage was amply displayed and wobbled as dangerously as a milk pudding released from a mould when she settled into her chair. They had looked over the menu, the front of which used an H. E. Bateman cartoon as an illustration. It was a picture of a Simpsons carver with his trolley looking horrified with his arms in the air waving a carving knife and fork at a thin diner and his large wife. The caption read: 'The American who asked whether the beef at Simpsons was English'. So that was what they had ordered. It came with a well-made cauliflower cheese lightly *gratinee* on the top, some English peas and a red wine gravy. For desserts Marker had ordered the steamed plum pudding. Although she was exceedingly unattractive, it had been a pleasure to sit with someone who shared the same love of indulgence.

At the end of the meal they both felt considerably fatter than when they had originally walked in. Not that the evening had been entirely gluttonous. The hotel detective had learnt more about telephone switchboards than he thought it possible to absorb in three hours. Most interesting was the secrets of how operators listened in on calls. The skill lay in making sure that the connection and disconnection cannot happen whilst the parties are on the line. Leaving a line mid-call gives a definitive 'click' and the eavesdropper exposed. Marker thought it had been worthwhile ordering a second bottle of red to elicit that snippet and it might come in useful.

It had been late by the time he made his way home and passing Charing Cross station he saw the first edition of the papers had arrived. He bought a copy of *The Daily Express* and took the last tube. When he got home he decided to make a cup of tea and reflect on his meal. He again wondered if he really was getting too fat and spontaneously got on to the floor to start some push ups. That seemed to be fine, albeit a struggle and after ten he resolved to do the rest in the morning. Sitting back down a little breathlessly on his sofa he casually picked up the paper and turned the pages. There wasn't anything of much interest until he reached the business section and his attention was drawn to the small headline:

'Adelphi Chairman sells controlling interest to Broadman Developments'

Chapter 10

The Adelphi dynasty had been taken over by a different cohort. The next morning the news ran out across the hotel faster than prisoners from a jailbreak. The collapse of the family control was not what had been anticipated and most were in fear of losing their jobs. It called for a steady hand on the great rudder of the ship. Timothy Patterson finished his breakfast and strode to the Crystal room where like the Master of the Titanic he addressed the complement of staff that had come in for the early shift.

'Fear not! This is a new chapter in our glorious history and we will survive this exciting challenge and embrace it with all our professionalism of quality and service. Remember the company motto!' Patterson paused: 'For Excellence we strive!'

He continued to warm to his theme until the

Chairman, Sir John Bulling arrived and took the stage. With grace Patterson gave up the microphone and stood back, a little deflated.

Bulling spoke with a measured voice and stood as like Nero addressing the hordes of Rome.

'I will not be leaving this great establishment, and it will be in very good hands with the formidable strength of a company like Broadman Developments in control. The Adelphi Hotel will survive, albeit in a slightly diminished form but an establishment of this nature will not lose its stature as the best hotel in the world.'

Marker, who had been leaning on a convenient pillar, lost concentration and wondered how this new development would influence the outcome of the kidnap. He could see how the money was going to be created, but wondered how it would be converted to gold and where the handover would be. He was dragged back to the event unfolding before him when the drone from the stage became more animated. Bulling was giving reassurance to those assembled that there would be no forced job losses. Marker thought that this sound bite had the same insincerity as Harold Wilson's when he had made a promise about the pound in the pocket.

After the meeting he went back to his office.

Sitting on his desk was a large bag of paper rubbish and a note from Anne. '*As requested*' it said.

He sat down and painstakingly took each piece of paper and sorted them in two piles. Interesting and uninteresting. When he was finished he had a lot more in the Interesting pile. Of greatest importance was a scrap of paper that the Chairman had written. On it were the details of a Monaco bank and what looked like the name of a bullion dealer. He put the slip in his pocket. The rest of the papers referred to the share sale. He kept the pieces he wanted of those and filed them in the back of his cabinet. He then looked at his own overflowing basket and decided to take all his own rubbish and the unwanted papers from the Chairman to the skip on the receiving platform. After he'd done that he went to see Sandrine in her office.

Sandrine looked very fresh this morning he thought and he felt an unwanted arousal.

'Good night last night?' He asked.

'Very relaxing.' She replied.

'Well that meeting was not a complete surprise. I think the ransom will be paid shortly. I've got some interesting detail on a Monaco bank and a name of a bullion dealer. Can you see what you make of it?'

Sandrine looked at the paper.

'The Chairman's handwriting?'

'Yes, I believe so.' Marker replied.

'Been on a fishing expedition in his wastepaper basket?'

'Not me exactly.'

Marker hesitated to take a seat. Sandrine looked up at him and said she would make some enquiries but that her hands were full with calls from the Press regarding the takeover. Marker decided that it wasn't time for a coffee and said he would catch up with her later.

That afternoon a further meeting was called when James Egerton from Broadman would speak to the staff. They all duly reassembled in the Ballroom and waited with anticipation as to what else was going to befall them. At three o'clock, Egerton and some members of the Board including Archer and Sheikh Al Mukta trooped onto the stage.

Sir John made a polite introduction and Egerton took the microphone.

'Our plans for the hotel will include a re-development. In two years' time we intend to convert the Strand side of the building into new apartments and sell those to raise funds for the redevelopment of our retail plans along the street to Waterloo Bridge. We expect there will be some shrinkage of the establishment, but jobs are not at stake. It may well be that as people leave of their own volition so their jobs may not be replaced. In the meantime it's business as usual as we assess the structure and viability of the hotel operations.'

After a few more platitudes and some reassurance the meeting broke up. Marker decided to see what progress Sandrine had made. He found her on a call to Somerset House.

'Yes, that's correct,' she said, 'I want to have the birth certificate of Eion Wildblood please, date of birth 11 March 1947. Born London. I will send over a courier with our cheque and he can wait for you to make a copy.'

She put down the phone.

Marker was a little mystified.

'Eion Wildblood?'

'Yes, he's Patrick's son and I ran into him the other day, remember him from the Ivy?'

'I do.'

'Well he wants to know who his mother is and I said it was easy for me to help him. He says his father said he was the product of a one night stand.'

'Oh' said Marker. 'Typical Wildblood. Any

news on my bank?'

'You're pushy,' said Sandrine: 'But yes, it's the Rothschild bank there and they correspond with bullion dealers.'

'Bingo!'

Marker and gave Sandrine a kiss. She looked a little startled and, regaining her composure, added:

'I'm going to find out more as I have a friend from Paris who works with Rothschilds Monaco.'

'Good girl!' said Marker.

'In the meanwhile I am getting on with this takeover if you don't mind.'

George Brooks was idly sitting in his apartment wondering when Timothy Patterson would be fired and he would take his place. He'd enjoy a larger office and a decent hike to his salary. The phone rang.

'Brooks.'

'George, it's Andrew.'

'Andrew! I've been worried sick for you. I assumed you'd disappeared over some money problems, then there came the news of this kidnapping. Where are you? Are you safe?'

Andrew Bulling then proceeded to tell his friend that he was perfectly safe and expected to be released in a few days provided his father paid the ransom. He told Brooks that he couldn't give him any more details but that he was hoping that he was still planning a holiday in Rome with him. The call finished abruptly as the pips went and no more money was added.

Andrew had taken quite a risk, but he was bored sitting it out in Archer's apartment so he had slid out in the late afternoon when the early commuters were making tracks homeward to mingle with the crowd. It was then he had the idea of calling George Brooks as he had a little coinage in his pocket. He thought he had made it back to the apartment with no one seeing him, but when he got back Archer was waiting for him.

'That was foolish.' Archer looked him over.

'Anyone from the Adelphi could have seen you. You face has been in the papers you know.'

'I'm sorry.'

'Not as sorry as you will be if you screw this up.' Archer continued:

'I came over to give you some instructions.

Next week we will be making the transaction. I am going to pick you up in a taxi. We will drive to Victoria station and at eleven precisely you will walk onto the main station concourse and proceed over to the phone boxes by the large hanging clock. Someone will be waiting for you and I will give you a description as to whom you're to meet and what you will say. At that point the ransom will have been paid at midday in France. There is an hour difference between the two countries.

When you re-appear like that there will be considerable Press interest and the police will be wanting to know all about where you have been and what you have been doing. Here is a file which is your effective cover story. Read it. Re-read it. And then read it again. I will be over next week to test you on your answers.

I am arranging a Jersey Bank account to be opened in your name that your funds will be transferred to, hopefully within three days of your release. Spend the money wisely. You father had resigned as Chairman of The Adelphi by the way.'

'That's a lot to take in. So the bastard will pay up? He's such a shit you need to be sure that he does.'

'Yes – I think he will pay but we will only get

away with all of this if you stick to your story.'

Archer tossed the file at him and made to leave. Turning at the door he said:

'Don't go out again.'

The last message was menacing.

After he had left Andrew opened the file. The first section contained details of how he had been abducted, then there was a section on how he had been looked after, and finally on how he had been delivered blindfolded to Victoria Station. In the rear of the file was a comprehensive selection of pictures showing a set of squalid rooms in the East End. It was his task to memorise every detail. He was grateful the file made it clear that he had been blindfolded most of the daylight hours and his room had no window. It would be useful to also know he had been handcuffed to a large old fashioned radiator. Archer had thoughtfully left a set of handcuffs with the file for him to wear twenty four hours before his release. It would be something to show the Police.

He settled down to read it all again, this time more thoroughly.

Sandrine Parte was looking a little startled. But there it was in plain black and white. Eion's birth certificate and under the heading 'Mother' was listed the name as Miss Cynthia Hampton. What a shock that was. She had remembered what Patrick Wildblood had told her. That picture was of Cynthia Hampton before she was married and became Cynthia Bulling. The Chairman's future wife obviously had an illegitimate child with Patrick Wildblood. No wonder they all wanted to keep that quiet.

Several conflicting thoughts rushed into her mind. Did the Chairman know she had a child from the Restaurant Manager? Could it have been after she was married? Was her death actually an accident? Was Eion related to Bulling? Was he a stepson? She wasn't sure how the English regulated these things. She reached for her copy of Debretts Peerage. After reading it through she concluded that although Eion was illegitimate he was certainly Andrew Bulling's half-brother by nature of having the same mother. He could only become legitimate if Sir John Bulling had accepted him into his family and that was certainly not going to be the case.

Putting the book aside she wondered what her next steps should be. She was the only one who had this information so there wasn't any need to tell anyone, and it might be useful. Power was knowledge and that could be turned into cash. And she needed some of that, her sister had been on the phone again asking for more support. It wasn't going to change anything if she kept her mouth shut whilst she worked things over in her mind. But she would have to tell Eion soon because he could just have easily found this out for himself. She wondered how best to handle the situation. She wanted to see more of him. A lot more of him. He was, after all, very energetic, and she didn't mind going through that experience again.

Just then George Brooks came into the office and she shuffled the certificate into a pile of papers in her in-tray.

'I wanted to know what feedback we can give the boss this evening about press interest in the takeover.'

He was wary of Miss Parte since that unfortunate altercation in the bar had abruptly terminated his relationship.

'Pretty considerable and I think we will get more as Broadman get going with their publicity machine. It's a story with legs.'

Sandrine eyed him suspiciously.

'Bet it suits you rather well, what with your connections.' She said.

Brooks worried about what she meant by that and felt a nervous reflex in his stomach. He felt it best left unanswered. He doubted she knew anything of his arrangements. As he left the room, Sandrine got up and closed the door after him.

'Must have been born in a pigsty with no gates.' She thought.

Brooks made his way slowly back to the office. Her remark had troubled him and he decided that she just might know something and that something might be connected to the piece of paper she shuffled out of his view when he had entered her office. He decided to take a closer look after she had gone home. After all, he had all the master keys of the hotel in his pocket.

DCI Bowen felt that there should be some news from The Adelphi and reading the paper about the share sale prompted her to ring the Chairman's office and tell them she was on her way over to see if there were any further developments on the kidnap. The police had not been idle but they had not been able to tap the forty odd trunk lines that ran into the hotel's switchboard. Tracing the kidnapper's calls to the

Chairman's office was therefore impossible. On top of that the DCI was convinced that Bulling was going to make it difficult for them. She suspected that he knew they would trawl over the motorbike accident. Still they had made some progress with the tip off to The Daily Express about the kidnap. They were looking for an East Ender and it all sounded very local.

Then there had been the diary that Andrew had kept. She now knew that he had some sort of relationship with Brooks and a tap on his private apartment phone had revealed that he took calls from Broadman and one other that was a real surprise. It was from Andrew Bulling himself, placed from a phone box. Now that was certainly strange. The team had concluded that if he was being held under duress this box must have been in a private residence somewhere and they had made a list of doss houses in the East End where such phones had been installed by landlords.

But she was suspicious. All a bit too cosy she thought, Andrew was a flake and from the recording of the call he didn't sound too stressed. She wanted to know about the relationship of father and son.

Shouting at Sloane to join her they took the station car to Adelphi Hill, parked it on the double yellow lines and jumped out. They pushed past the top hatted doorman and walked straight up to the Directors' corridor and the Chairman's office.

DCI Bowen spoke to his secretary.

'Did you get our message?'

Diane put down her compact and looked up at the two CID officers.

'Yes we did, and I've freed up fifteen minutes for you. I will let him know you are here.'

The light above the Chairman's door turned from red to green.

'You may go in.' Diana said.

The Detective Inspector and her number two walked in and Bowen took a seat without waiting to be invited. Sir John looked flustered.

'Good morning, and what can I do for you?'

'This is DI Sloane who's helping me with my enquiries.'

Bowen waved a hand in Sloane's direction.

'I think you can give us a briefing on what has happened so far in the kidnap, you don't seem to be keeping me as closely informed as I would like.'

The Chairman looked uncomfortable.

'I've had one more message. If you people can't

solve this I am desperately worried about my son and I can see that I am going to have to settle to make sure he's safe.'

Bowen eyed him.

'I wouldn't do that Sir John. Promotes criminality.'

'Well what progress have you made that would give me some assurance not to?' Bulling turned in his seat.

'Well we think this is local, we think your son is presently unharmed and being held in the East End. We don't know if this is related to a debt or if it has something to do with putting pressure on you during the hostile bid. Your son isn't too keen on you is he Sir John?'

Bulling looked more uncomfortable and moved back in his chair.

'I'm very fond of him and I want to see he's safe.' He lied.

Bowen changed tack.

'Tell me about that motorbike accident, it was in the Willows wasn't it. Why would the ransom note refer to it?'

Bulling had prepared for this type of question and was well versed.

'Well I think it's just to put pressure on me. It

was a very tragic event. I loved my wife very much and it was a terrible accident to happen.'

Bowen thought she might apply a bit more pressure.

'Yes, her helmet split. Unfortunate to be wearing a defective helmet when motoring at speed.'

Bulling looked up.

'Are you inferring that this wasn't an accident? I think you will find the Coroner's report is unequivocal.'

Bulling still had some confidence that the family influence was sufficient to see off the impertinence of a working-class flatfoot acting like the Gestapo.

Bowen looked him in the eye. Bulling blinked.

'I think the kidnappers are. You say you are very fond of your son, but I'm not sure why he is estranged from you.'

Bulling thought carefully about his reply.

'I think it's his choice, we don't exactly share a similar lifestyle.'

Bowen felt that the conversation was going nowhere and decided to leave.

'Before I go, I want to remind you that you should not pay a ransom and that we want to catch these people. If you make moves without us we lose the chance. If you don't keep us informed step by step inch by inch we can't help you...and I think you need a lot of help.'

The police officers left the office and Bulling considering his options.

It was after seven in the evening and the Press Office had been locked up. George Brooks took out his master key and opened the outer door. He quickly slipped into Sandrine's office and started to look through her in-tray. He was surprised to see the birth certificate. He remembered the name, it was Patrick Wildblood's son who had wanted a job in the hotel. What was the interest in that? He looked it over again and then looked at the names of the parents. He especially noticed the mother's name. Cynthia Hampton. There was something familiar about that name but he couldn't quite pinpoint it. He quickly shuffled through the rest of the papers on her desk. After a few minutes he felt a sense of relief as he realised there was nothing incriminating there.

∞∞∞

The South of France, in the words of Somerset Maugham, was a sunny place for shady people. Today was no exception as Hofer took a taxi to Heathrow and caught the BEA flight to Nice. Pushing his way through Customs he hailed a taxi to Menton. The car took him along the straight road of the *Boulevard des Anglais* and then through the old port. After that the road became a torturous sequence of tight corners as it wound along the littoral through Beaulieu and Monaco. After an hour the taxi pulled up outside the *Hotel Splendide* in the town centre and he paid the it off. He checked into a sea view room and unpacked. When he had tidied everything away he pulled aside the net curtain and looked for the *Quai Imperatrice*. Picking up the binoculars which he always carried as an essential, he focused on the view of the marina and easily recognised the *Statue St Michel*.

He decided to take a walk over and after changing from his suit he put on a casual 'T' shirt and shorts. As he crossed the road to the harbour he looked like any other tourist. Walking onto the harbour wall he lifted his camera and took several shots of the statue and the phone boxes nearby.

There was car parking all along the stone quay with an entrance protected by barriers and there was a list of restrictions that only allowed boat owners parking after eleven o'clock. It occurred to Hofer that the kidnappers could well be using a boat. A car get away might be problematic.

After he had made a full survey he decided to go back to the hotel and change. Then he would get a taxi to Monaco and visit the Rothschild bank.

It was a beautiful sunny and warm day with clear blue skies and as he came over the hill and dropped down to Monte Carlo he saw the sunlight catching the rooftops of the Grimaldi Palace. The large harbour was already full with large yachts chartering for the summer. The cab drove him through Casino Square and finally drew up outside the *Entrée de Banque.*

He introduced himself to a receptionist and said he had an appointment with the Chief Cashier. He was shown into a small but elegantly designed office with a dark mahogany desk and three regency chairs. He put his briefcase down and took out a file. After a few minutes the Chief Cashier, Monsieur Blot arrived and enquired if he would like coffee.

'A cup of tea would be fine.' Hofer replied.

Monsieur Blot pushed a button and took a seat.

'Tell me Mr Hofer, what can the bank do for you?'

'I explained some of that on my call to you earlier last week. I'm here on behalf of Triangle Gold Holdings, a Cayman company that wants to place an order for export gold bullion. Is this something that you, as a merchant bank, can arrange?'

'It's not an everyday request, but provided we complete the appropriate paperwork and there is sufficient time it can be arranged. I want you to meet my assistant Monsieur De Freynes. He is our gold specialist and can make the arrangements for you.'

Blot picked up the phone and asked his assistant to come in. A young man in a light linen suit came in just as the tea arrived and Hofer stood to shake hands. Monsieur Blot continued:

'Yes, Monsieur De Freynes is new with us but he's been in our Paris office for a year or two. He's very well qualified from the *Institut Européen d'Administration des Affaires*.' Blot went on to explain what was required and the necessary documents were prepared and presented for signature. De Freynes looked over the order details.

'That's a very large amount of gold bars at today's price of $44 a troy ounce. I calculate you will need something of the order of thirty four bars.'

Hofer nodded.

'Yes, it's the problems of exchange control and gold is such an international currency. I know they weigh a few kilos each.'

They continued to discuss the delivery details and eventually Hofer stood to leave.

'So it will be Thursday week. I will arrange the order for you and the appropriate off shore payment.'

They shook hands and Hofer turned left out of the bank and walked on down to the Louis Vuitton store. There he looked over a few trunks and finally selected two suitcases large and robust enough to take the weight. He asked for them to be delivered to the Hotel Metropole under his name in seven days' time.

He then walked to the taxi rank and getting in the front car asked the driver to pass by the Metropole and then drive on to Menton. As they cleared the hotel Hofer started his stop watch and kept it running until they had reached the *Quai Imperatrice*. The journey had taken three quarters of an hour.

'Too long' thought Hofer. He paid off the driver and walked across to the *Capitainerie* and asked where he might hire a fast boat.

Marker picked up his mail and was surprised to see an envelope marked 'Private' and with no stamp. It had only his name and position on it. Obviously a note from someone in authority at the hotel. He returned to his office and tore it open.

It took a little while for the contents to sink in. So he read it over again. The hotel staff manager had written to him to advise him that with the change of hotel ownership his job was to be made redundant. Broadman Developments had their own security department that was going to take control at the month's end.

Now he hadn't seen that coming and it hit him like a karate chop from behind. His immediate response was one of rising anger, but he was able to restrain himself from any instant reaction. He sat back and quietly simmered.

'How dare they do this to me? I've been loyal and given good service. I bet that bastard Brooks isn't going to get fired, and who else are they going to let go? How right was I to not believe a word from them? No job losses indeed.'

The hotel detective quietly mulled over his options. If he was going to lose his job he'd have to get some kind of security and like the rising sun it slowly dawned on him that if he could deliver those who were behind the kidnap he might get a decent reward. But now he felt he could trust no one. It was true, he was by the nature of his job an outsider and not one person in the whole hotel had taken the time to give him any helpful advice as to how he should do the job. He'd had to teach himself everything. He'd been excluded from meetings, treated with disdain by the management, cast aside by the Chairman. His thoughts turned murderous and he began to think of those closest to him. Even Miss Parte was untrustworthy given her record, he decided instantly to throw some cold water on his fiery passion.

He got up and poured himself a glass of water but instead decided to drink it.

Pacing the floor his thoughts turned to the kidnap. He felt sure that he knew where Andrew was being kept and he also knew that the Chairman was probably going to pay the ransom thorough a Monaco bank. If there was anything dishonest going on it had to point to Archer and Andrew Bulling working in tandem to the disadvantage of the Chairman. And as it stood he wasn't especially in favour of helping someone who might have deliberately killed his wife and by his actions put Richard's job on the line. From now on he was going to work independently and an idea came to mind.

He went back to his filing cabinet and took out the remaining papers that he had filed from the Chairman's wastepaper basket. He flicked through them and pulled out the one that he had remembered. It was the handwritten Chairman's diary note that Diana prepared for him each day as an *aide memoire.* There, at 11.15 was the name 'Hofer. Risk Management Associates. He put the paper down and reached for the telephone directory. He gave them a call and asked to speak to Hofer's secretary.

'Oh hello, it's Sir John Bulling here, I have the information that Mr Hofer was asking for, can I speak to him?'

'I'm afraid Sir John that he's in Menton as agreed. He's making arrangements for the bullion.'

'Oh, I'm sorry I forget that was this week, I will call back tomorrow.'

Marker put back the receiver. So Hofer was the go-between and Menton was the location-. That made sense if the bullion was coming from Monte Carlo. He looked up Risk Management Associates in the yellow pages and noted their advertisement as an 'International crisis agency'. They must have a kidnap specialist he concluded.

He would need to know the date of the exchange and he decided that if it couldn't be in Menton, he could follow Andrew's release from Betterton Street. But that would require some planning.

Closing his file he left the office and went to see the Staff Manager. They were going to have some discussion about his impending departure.

Chapter 11

Sandrine Parte put down the telephone and considered what she had just heard from her friend at the bank. Rothschilds was small and there weren't too many personnel. Claude De Freynes had been a past lover she knew at the college and a fairly good one at that she had considered. It had been serendipity that it was he that was handling the bullion transfers by a certain Mr Hofer. So now she knew the date of the transfers and assumed that the final day of collection was the date for the kidnap transfer. She wondered how she might get her hands on some of this money that was clearly going to be very mobile. She called the Security Office.

'Richard, it's Sandrine.'

Marker had answered immediately and had been expecting the staff office. A call from the gorgeous Sandrine was more welcome.

'My man at the bank tells me the bullion is due to be collected by next Thursday week from Monte Carlo. A guy called Hofer is handling it.'

'I wonder who that is?' Lied Marker, relieved that the problem of getting a date appeared to be resolved.

'What do we do next?' Sandrine asked.

The hotel detective was cool in his response.

'Let me think this over. I'll come up and see you.'

On his way to her office he passed the Smoking Room. This was a small stuffy lounge serviced by a long term employee called Enzo. He spent his day charming elderly ladies into drinking gin at any time. To line his own pocket he would smuggle in his own gin bottle and serve it whenever anyone looked as if they might pay cash rather than put it on the hotel bill. The scam operated quite easily. He opened one bill for a gin and tonic and never closed it. In this way the same bill could be presented time after time and the cash earned pocketed. It would be eventually closed at the end of the shift with the last cash customer. The hotel would make the money for one gin and tonic and Enzo might have sold as many as twenty.

'Morning Enzo.' Marker greeted him with a mischievous look.

'Good morning Mr Marker, have you caught any miscreants this morning yet?'

'I'm looking at one Enzo, but I like you too much to ask why all these bills are left open on your counter.'

'It's a good job you aren't asking then.'

As Enzo shuffled them all together and put them back in his drawer. When Marker reached the Press Office he was quite pleased with his new found benevolence. What did he care? He was fired anyway. He continued down the mezzanine corridor to the Press Office.

'Morning Sandrine.'

He greeted her and despite his conviction to be distant felt a familiar urge beginning to develop which he couldn't easily control

'Well Richard, what do you make of it?'

Marker had thought this through.

'I think that Bulling is paying the ransom and I think Andrew is in this with Archer. I think that Andrew is going to get a payoff for his trouble.'

Sandrine looked a little puzzled.

'What are you going to do with that information? Tell the police?'

'My friend DCI Bowen? I don't think so – at

least not yet.'

After they had talked it through a little longer, Marker got up to leave and when he had got back to his office he found an envelope pushed under his door from the telephone exchange. Inside was a message to call DCI Bowen. He picked up the receiver and dialled the number.

'Hello it's Richard.'

Bowen had answered the call within two rings.

'Yes Richard, I've been giving some thought to the kidnap after my visit to your Chairman, or should I say ex-Chairman. I have information that Andrew Bulling and George Brooks are friendlier than one might believe. What can you tell me about that?'

Marker took a moment before replying because the opportunity to put his nemesis in trouble was indeed tempting:

'Well Brooks is a faggot and probably corrupt. He has a relationship with the Managing Director of Broadman that I don't like. He went to hotel school with Andrew Bulling and given his promiscuity I wouldn't be at all surprised if he sucked his cock if that's what you're implying.'

'It is indeed,' she replied. 'See what you can find out.'

'Anything else for me?'

'I'm watching your ex-Chairman's every move. I don't much take to him.'

Bowen hung up the call.

The hotel detective recalled what he knew about Brooks and Andrew Bulling. He remembered the certificate from Lausanne that he had seen on Brooks' wall and wondered how close they might have been on the sunny lakes of Switzerland. Then there was that gay pub in Earls Court. Perhaps they met there. Sandrine knew more about Brooks. He would ask her for some more detail.

He went back up to the office but Sandrine's door was closed. He was just about to knock when he overheard part of the conversation. She was talking about a birth certificate and Cynthia Hampton. That name, he knew, was the Chairman's first late wife. When the call was over, he knocked on the opaque glass and went in.

'I've had call from the police, they think there is more to the relationship of Brooks and Andrew Bulling. What do you think?'

Sandrine thought for a second.

'Well I think they may be right.'

'What can you find out?' Asked Marker, 'I think

it might also be a good time to put Brooks under the spotlight with his connection to Egerton at Broadman.'

'You asked me that once before, and I said that I didn't know he was queer. I've quite a bit of stuff on him that might be useful. His bank account details for one but not much more that seems relevant.'

The detective considered this and asked:

'What bank?'

'Barclays' she replied.

'Be useful to see the detail – I will need the account number.'

Sandrine agreed to let him have this when she had a moment. He left the office having decided that he wouldn't let Sandrine know about his impending departure she might lose interest in someone who was shortly going to be unemployed.

Back in his office he picked up the cup of tea he had brought from the canteen. He put it back on the table as he suddenly remembered who Cynthia Hampton was and like a set of railway trucks all coming together in a series of loud clunks, he made the connection to Patrick Wildblood. The pieces suddenly fitted together. He had come to the conclusion that he imagined Sandrine must have arrived at. And she hadn't mentioned any of this to him. The Chairman's first wife had an illegitimate son and the father was bloody Wildblood. Bloody Hell. Who knew that? Not the Chairman he guessed, because unlike him, Wildblood was still gainfully employed.

After the detective had left her office Sandrine considered that she knew quite a bit about Brooks as he had been careless with what he had left around his flat. He hadn't calculated on someone like her being drawn like a magnet to odd bits of documentation left lying around. Then there was the information she had on Andrew. Andrew Bulling had money, but not much of it according to the bank statement and odd paperwork he'd casually left at Brooks' apartment. Brooks had offered to help him set up a hire-purchase with the company the hotel dealt with for all its electrical hardware. She wondered if Andrew was capable of paying it off.

She decided to wrap up as much of the takeover work as she could before thinking more about this troublesome duo. Putting the last of the press releases to one side she eventually unlocked her lower office desk drawer and took out a small diary. It was where she had made a note of all of George Brooks' personal details.

He had two accounts. There was one with Barclays in London and another in Jersey. It was the latter that she had seen statements for which showed deposits from a Broadman's offshore account. She had stolen several cheques from the back of both cheque books and had a sheet of paper on which she had pasted several examples of his signature from some hotel documents. She had practised the script multiple times and was now pretty good at it. Good enough, she thought, to get it passed by a sleepy bank cashier.

She toyed with whether to let Marker have the account numbers and decided that if she gave him the Jersey one it would do no harm. His friends in the police had no jurisdiction over there, and it would take a court order to open up the details for the United Kingdom authorities.

She picked up the phone and dialled his line.

'Richard? I have the detail on his Jersey account that gets the cash from Broadman? It's Barclays International, St Helier, Account 40515568. It's in his name.'

'Great thanks Sandrine. I will get straight on it.'

Sandrine then thought carefully about her next call. It was to her new friend, Eoin. She picked up the phone again.

'Eion? Hello, it's Sandrine again. How would you like to see me tomorrow night? I want to show you that certificate I called you about.'

Eoin was delighted and with agreed more with lust in mind than any news that Miss Parte might bring about his mother. Whilst he was curious to know who she was, he wasn't passionate about someone whom he had never known. In fact the only thing he was passionate about at the moment was Sandrine. They agreed to meet the next evening at a bar just off Covent Garden.

Marker looked at the details he had written down and considered his next move. If he could prove Brooks was getting illicit payments he could get him fired, but if he wanted to use Brooks to get closer to Andrew Bulling that wasn't such a wise move, well, not wise just yet. He decided that getting the evidence wouldn't be that easy given that Barclays Bank Jersey was a separate entity from Barclays in London. But perhaps someone could impersonate Brooks and might be able to get hold of a statement if they turned up at the branch. He presumed George Brooks had never been to the Channel Islands. He would give that some consideration. It was possible to do a day trip there and there was no reason why he shouldn't take some of his holiday given that he was leaving shortly in any event. Nice morning for a stroll around the town and the afternoon on the beach. All he would need is Brooks' passport, and maybe he could learn to copy his signature.

He decided to pay Brooks a visit and called him up for an appointment. The detective told him that with the changes in ownership he need to see him about some necessary security paperwork for a new bank account. Brooks told him to come straight up. That rushed him a little, but he had enough time to take some headed notepaper and type up a certification request with a space for Brooks' signature. When he got to his office he found him signing a few letters. It was good he already has his pen out. Marker came straight to the point:

'I've been asked by Farndon to make a new bank mandates for the hotel signatories now that we are being taken over and it's necessary to make you a signatory.'

Brooks looked up and began to feel rather important. The detective continued:

'They need to have your passport for forty eight hours in order to copy the details and make a Notary copy that has to be filed. Can you let me have it by Thursday? Should have it back at the weekend. Just in case you were thinking of flying off anywhere? Could you also sign this letter and put it back in my pigeon hole? I will need it with your documents.'

Brooks seemed quite happy to comply and Marker left the office with a wry smile. His next stop was the travel agent across the road where he paid for a day return ticket to Jersey leaving Heathrow next Friday.

When he got back he thought he would see if Sandrine would like another evening out. He rang her up but she said that she had another date for tomorrow. That was a shame he thought and wondered what he might do to rekindle her interest. There was something about her he just couldn't get over, was it the way she moved, or something about the way she wooed him. She was like no other. He pushed the thought out of his mind. Where did that come from? Probably a James Taylor song he thought.

∞∞∞

Hofer was studying the anonymous letter that was waiting for him on his return to London. With it was a grainy Polaroid of Andrew Bulling holding up a copy of the Times with a headline that was the banner two days ago. It proved he was still alive.

Time: midday French time

Place: Statue St Michel

32 Gold bars of 40 troy oz.

The quay is secured. <u>No police. We have guns.</u>

Bulling will be released on Victoria station concourse after we verify receipt of the gold. 11.00 London time

We will call for your confirmation on usual number. Date to follow.

He'd need to get over to Victoria Station, but he was beginning to understand how this was going to work. He wasn't happy with that location, too many people and too much that could go wrong. He needed more detail. Where was Andrew to be released precisely and how could that be done securely?

Then there was the Menton end He had concluded that the ransom would most likely disappear with the kidnappers by boat. The traffic in Menton was unpredictable and it would be too risky to take it by car up the tortuous route to the main throughway to the Italian border or to Monaco. Besides which they would probably put a couple of strongarm guards on the quay entrance to stop any movement during the handover and they wanted this at the far end of the quay, not near the road. Then there was the problem of testing the gold. That would be done by them, but it would take time. It then occurred to him that he may well be taken hostage whilst that process was happening, he'd have to plan for that eventuality.

He picked up the phone to Sir John.

'Hello Sir John, Hofer. I've been to Monaco and Menton and made the arrangements as we had discussed. The handover is agreed, but I haven't got a date, it must be in the next ten days or so. Your son will be released in London whilst we release the gold in France. Not ideal, but do-able. It's essential that the police know nothing. These guys will be tooled up and I don't want to wind up dead. Do I have your assurance?'

Bulling sighed on the other end of the line and confirmed that no one else was aware of their arrangements.

'Good. Well I will keep you informed as I know more.'

Hofer hung up and called in his secretary.

'Get my usual two associates to come and see me tomorrow please. We have a little job for them.'

The next day the usual department heads gathered for The Adelphi morning meeting. They habitually met in the General Manager's outer office where the typists were already busy with letters of confirmation for upcoming reservations. The talk of the day centred on a report of food poisoning from a private dinner and the loss of a certain amount of silverware from the fourth-floor pantry that had been spotted in the overnight bi-annual stocktake. Marker was one of the first to arrive and had been looking through the list of those in residence on the fourth-floor and had already formed an idea.

Chef Cornet arrived looking as if he'd just left a sauna and was already vehemently denying any involvement of his food and the idiosyncrasies of just one diner's stomach. A whole host with food poisoning would be quite a different matter.

At nine o'clock precisely the light above Patterson's office changed from red to green and they all trooped in to take their allotted seats. Marker noted that the champagne bucket had been refreshed by Enzo, but that it hadn't yet been opened. 'Give it an hour,' he mused.

Patterson opened the meeting.

'83% occupancy, good rate at £75, important departures today are the Smyths, Barton-Claircourts, Lord and Lady Pevensey and Sir Hugh McDonald. I assume the accounts are to be sent on. Arrivals look a bit thin, but I see the Jesseys are coming, we need a decent suite for them, and special pillows please Mrs Haul. Anything else of note?'

He looked at Brooks.

'A report of food poisoning from the oysters last night in the private dining rooms.'

Patterson looked at the Chef.

'Well?'

Cornet put a look on his face that was one of sheer astonishment.

'*C'est impossible, les huitres Cancale*? These oysters are as fresh as a sixteen year old virgin.'

'My apologies Mrs Haul.' Patterson looking at the Housekeeper whose expression of studied experience seemed to imply that virginity wasn't just confined to younger women. He looked back at the Chef and continued. 'Less of that kind of talk please Monsieur Cornet, it's before midday. Do we have any other reports from anyone else? It was just the one diner in a large party?'

Brooks answered:

'Just the one, they all ate the oysters. It could be just a bad one, but more likely the guest was allergic to shell food. I will write to him and advise that we have tested other oysters from the same suppplier with no negative result, and that others who had them last night were not similarly affected. Our apologies and I will send the usual food poisoning letter.'

'Fine,' replied Patterson.

Brooks continued:

'There appears to be an ongoing theft of silverware from the fourth-floor waiter's pantry.'

Patterson looked across to the hotel detective:

'Any ideas Marker?'

'Yes sir, we have Margaret Droitwich on that floor, she's been here for her concert. I had some trouble with her the last time she stayed. She has a tendency to take the silverware off her breakfast trolley and pack it in her suitcase. I'll go up and check it out when she has left for the theatre.'

Sandrine looked at him from across the office.

'Richard, does she do this all the time? I hate the Press to get hold of a story like that.'

Marker looked at her and annoyingly felt that familiar sensation. Ridiculous, it wasn't even ten in the morning yet.

'Well last time I took out two silver salvers, about four egg cups and their associated spoons, three sets of cutlery and a silver pepper mill. She had them all wrapped up in one of our towels.'

Patterson asked Brooks for her card. The guests in house had all their information cards from the card index in an in-house card box that was carried to these daily meetings. Brooks passed the yellow card with a red VIP tag on its corner.

'Yes' said Patterson. 'I see that she's been a guest here since before the war. Must be getting on a bit. She stole a few towels the time before I see. Any relatives here that we can make a quiet suggestion to?'

Brooks volunteered that he knew her agent.

'Well that settled,' said Patterson, 'Brooks talk to her agent. Marker get the stuff back out of her bag and put it back in the pantry.'

'Shall I leave the towel?' Marker enquired.

'Clear it all out' replied Patterson. 'Bath robes, towels bed sheets – whatever you find. In the meanwhile put an additional £50 on her account as a miscellaneous charge for 'lost inventory' after all she has no idea about the bill and we don't know what else she might have taken.'

When the meeting had finished the detective couldn't resist asking Sandrine out Saturday evening. He'd be back by then. He told her he had some more news for her. Sandrine considered it for a minutes and decided that as she was seeing Eion on Friday, he probably worked a Saturday night, so she accepted.

A little after ten the Fellowes the Hall Porter rang Marker in his office to tell him the Diva had just left the front entrance by cab. Marker put the phone back down and ran for the lift to the fourth floor. He opened the door using his Grand Master, and proceeded straight to a stack of leather suitcases that were in the corner of her sitting room. By the time he had reached the third he had collected quite a haul of silver, some towelling and a bathrobe.

He carried the collection back to the waiter in the floor pantry.

'Here you go. It's all yours. I suggest that whoever serves her meals is the same person who collects the trolley to check that whatever goes into the room comes out again.'

'Well yes.' Replied the fourth-floor waiter. 'But you see Mr Marker, she's a very good tipper.'

So there you have it, thought Marker. They are feeding her the stuff.

The afternoon dragged a little for Sandrine who spent most of her time wondering how she was going to play her meeting with Eion that evening. It was going to be news that his mother was The Adelphi Chairman's first wife. What would the young Irish boy do with that information? He would soon find out who his step brother was. The kidnapped Andrew Bulling. She didn't think that this was going to be particularly helpful. If she wanted to continue her relationship with him she would have to get some control over what he did with this dynamite news.

'Never start without the end in mind.' Wasn't that what her newspaper days had taught her? She was pretty clear that she wanted to continue this hazardous liaison but on her terms. Sandrine took several minutes to think it all through and eventually settled on a plan.

They met in a bar behind the Strand Palace Hotel. It was close to The Adelphi but Sandrine didn't fancy a trip out to Chiswick in the Friday rush hour. When he had walked in she instantly remembered how attractive he was in a raffish way. He came up to her and kissed her on the cheek.

'You look great.' He said.

'So do you…'

They ordered. He a beer, she a Manhattan.

'Eion.' Sandrine opened the conversation. 'We've had a really good time and I want to know if you want to continue to see me?'

'I'd like that very much.'

'Well, I've some news for you that if I tell you and it doesn't remain between us I won't be able to see you again.'

'Why is that?'

'Because it would compromise my job at the hotel if your father knew I had told you more about your mother. I don't think he would forgive me, and as much as I find you super-attractive I can't afford to make my working relationships difficult. I told you your mother's name but I didn't tell you exactly who she was. If I tell you a little more you are going to have to promise not to confront your father. Would you tell your father?'

'Not if it meant I couldn't see you. I mean I'm interested, but I never knew her and I'm not on a mission of zealous discovery.'

Sandrine was relieved that what she said next wasn't going to be too emotional for Eion to handle.

'Well Eion, Your birth certificate has the name of Cynthia Hampton. She was a very attractive model just after the war. She met your father at The Adelphi and they must have had a brief affair. I think she was already married.'

Eoin smiled:

'The dirty dog!'

Sandrine continued.

'I think she then died just after you were born in a motorcycle accident.'

'Wow!' Eion looked stunned. 'Well that all fits in with what he told me. What did she look like? Do you have a picture?'

Sandrine showed him the picture she had of

Cynthia taken with his father in the restaurant. She had been careful not to give him any more details of this *menage a trois* and who the third man was because if the Irishman knew the rest it could certainly be dangerous.

'Now' said Sandrine. 'If we are to have a relationship it's essential that you keep your promise not to tell your father. It would put me in an impossible situation. I like you very much Eion, but I don't want to lose my job. So what is it to be? Do we kiss goodbye now and you go off to cross examine your father on how he slept with your mother and under what circumstances, or do you want to fuck me now and again?'

'Is that you condition?'

'Yes it is.'

Eion hardly considered this for a moment before agreeing to Sandrine's terms. He wouldn't confront his father, and anyway he now had some information and a picture. He could make his own enquiries without either of them if he wanted to.

He smiled:

'I want to fuck you now and again.'

They ordered another round of drinks. They were seated near the window, it had been the only table close to the bar when Sandrine had arrived. It was still early and whilst they were talking with heads close together, Timothy Patterson passed by on the pavement with Brooks walking alongside.

'Isn't that Miss Parte?'

He asked Brooks. Brooks glanced through the window.

'Yes sir, in the company of a young man.'

'Good on her!' Replied Patterson.

And they continued on their way to the Garrick Club where Patterson in a moment of unusual largesse had invited Brooks for a Friday evening glass of sherry.

Sandrine had been looking away when they had passed by and would have recognised the danger if she had seen them, but her mind was set on heading off to Chiswick and sharing the warmth of her well sprung mattress.

It was Friday morning and the hotel detective looked out from his bedroom window. The weather looked reasonable. He didn't want fog on the island to disturb his schedule. He'd picked up Brooks' signed letter and passport the evening before from his pigeon hole and spent the evening copying the signature until he felt it reasonably accomplished with good handwriting speed.

The picture on the travel document might be a challenge, but although he was older, the black and white image of Brooks did have some uncanny features close to his and he considered that if it was given just a cursory glance he would be fine.

He took the bus and tube to the West London Air Terminal on Cromwell Road and checked in. He took a seat on the top of the double-decker that took him to the Queens building for his flight. Heathrow was a building site, with Terminal 1 promising to open later that year. He boarded the Viscount turboprop and the one hour flight was uneventful. He cleared Customs and took a taxi to St Helier. Stopping at the Weighbridge he decided to walk to Library Place where Barclays had its branch. He weighed up the situation before he approached the door and judging it to be reasonably busy, busy enough for there to be a queue at each of the cashier desks. He joined the nearest line. After five minutes he arrived at the glass divide.

'My name is George Brooks and I'd like to have a copy of my statement please.'

He passed over the slip of paper with the account number and name.

'Do you have any identification?'

'Would my passport do?' he enquired.

'That'll be fine,' the cashier replied.

'Do you want to know just the balance?'

'No, I'd like the last three months, I have to show I have funds for a loan I'm taking out.'

The cashier closed her cash drawer and went over to a printer that was located in the back office. She took the passport with her. After a few minutes she returned with some papers.

'Normally we send these out quarterly and I've noted these as duplicates.'

With that she passed them through the sliding drawer under the glass together with the passport.

The detective thanked her very much and left, resisting the temptation to put a finger across his collar that had become quite warm. Taking a seat on a bench across the road he carefully reviewed what he had been given. There in black and white were the entries he expected from Broadman Developments. The total on the account showed a balance of just over £2000. Tucking the papers into his briefcase he decided to have lunch at the Grand Hotel at

West Park as a celebration before taking a taxi back out to the airport.

Taking his seat near the panoramic windows that look out over Elizabeth Castle, the weather could not have been better with a clear blue sky reflecting on the high tide that was very near the sea wall.

He ordered a plate of Jersey ormers, cooked in a light sauce and served in a casserole, followed by the Canker dressed crab. To make the light lunch palatable he decided on just a half bottle of Chablis making sure that his budget was not exceeded. Still the wine was cheap and duty free on the island so there was little danger of him breaking the bank, although he was quite capable of deceiving it. Having finished with an Earl Grey tea, he paid the bill and found a taxi to the airport. By eight o'clock that evening he was already home in Hammersmith.

Chapter 12

Sheikh Al Mukta had been as good as his promise to Archer and had indeed been busy. He'd been in touch with his Italian friends whom he knew were members of the *Unione Corse* a loose union of various criminal families who made a living along the Riviera in the same fashion as the Italian Mafia. The most notorious of the families were the Francisci and it was this part of the organisation that Al Mukta gave the job.

For a payment of ten percent of the bullion it was agreed that they would provide men to secure the quay, a boat to take the gold around to Genoa and from there convert the gold bars into American dollars at the daily rate for onward transmission to a Jersey bank account.

Al Mukta picked up the phone from his office in Jeddah and asked for a long distance call to Leeds.

'Hello Archer. I'm calling to let you know that it's all done. You will need to tell your associates that the gold be taken to Italy and from there it's going to be divided up and deposited for exchange with some tame brokers. Gold is an international currency my friend. The US dollars will be credited over four days to the account you nominated in Jersey. It was Barclays right?'

'Yes, Your Excellency. It's the Jersey account in Andrew Bulling's own name. It all sounds very good. Do your people know that we have to co-ordinate the handover?'

'Yes Archer, they understand that the gold hand over will be coordinated with confirmation that Andrew Bulling has been released.'

Archer contemplated this for a few seconds and then added:

'We can't have any shooting, it can't be messy.'

'Dear Archer, we can't always wish for ideal outcomes and my dear friends the Francisci brothers don't offer guarantees, but they are very professional. The Algerian mujahedeen are good operators. They are recognised by a tattoo on the inside of their arms. It's a black head with a white bandana.'

Archer made a note of this to tell Hofer. He didn't want the gold disappearing into someone else's welcoming arms. They finished the call with a few *'salams'* and Archer made his way out to pick another public phone box he'd spotted near his office. He had been careful not to use the same box twice, and anyway, his first calls had been from London.

He dialled and waited for the call to be answered. He pushed button 'A' and put on what he thought was his passable cockney accent.

Hofer answered.

'You have got our message from your mailbox?'

Hofer confirmed.

'Good. There will be operatives with a black head tattoo on their arms, do not deal with anyone else. We will have secured the area. We need five minutes to test the gold. The handover starts after the test is positive. When we are satisfied you will see Bulling at the station and we will simultaneously start to load the gold. If you pull a surprise when we are transferring the bullion we will shoot you. You will have Bulling before we have completed the operation as an act of good faith, but if Bulling is grabbed at Victoria before we have started loading the gold you will be the first to die. Bulling will be second. We want to do this in seven days time.'

Hofer interrupted:

'How are we going to be in communication?'

'Not us Hofer. You. You will be responsible for your own arrangements. We have no interest in how you work. All you need to know is that we will be informed in London when the gold has been tested positively and starting to be transferred.'

'Bulling is concerned about your threat. What comfort can we take about your silence if we pay up?'

'We aren't bothered if you pay. If you don't you'll read more about it in the press. We have some good contacts at the *Daily Express*.'

'That's no guarantee you'll keep your word.'

'No it isn't. But we will. We want this finished in seven days.'

'That's impossible.'

'Make it Hofer, or Bulling will be on your conscience, I will not be calling again.'

The receiver was replaced before the pips signalled the call was ending.

Hofer rang through to his secretary and asked if his colleagues had arrived and to show them into his office. Two younger well-dressed men came in and they all shook hands. Hofer asked them to sit at his office table and put an Aldis projector at the far end and switched it on. He was toying with the piece of typed paper of instructions that had been posted to his post box by the kidnappers.

'Gentlemen we are assisting in the Bulling kidnap.'

He read them the contents and began to explain his plan.

'You, John, will be at Victoria Station where Bulling is to appear when the gold is being transferred. We need to go over there later today and survey the area I have in mind.'

John was shorter than his colleague and had the sort of face that could be lost in a crowd. His features simply didn't stand out, they were as bland as an October sky.

'Michael, you and I are on a trip to Menton in the south of France.'

John muttered something inaudible that indicated he rarely got the better locations. Michael was a good French speaker but in any other sense could also be described as undistinguished. Hofer then put on the slides he had taken on his trip and described how he thought the operation was to work. The three then discussed the details at some length before Hofer wound up the meeting:

'So it will be next Friday for the handover. Michael and I go over on Wednesday to organise the transport and the gold. In the meantime, John, let's take a taxi to Victoria. I want to see what the best solution is for communicating. It looks as if it's all going to be public phone boxes, and that's risky.'

The ride over took a little time as they were held up in Whitehall by a troop of the Household Cavalry passing through Horse Guards Parade. They eventually cleared Westminster Square and drove on up Victoria Street. They pulled up at the bus station and walked through to the station concourse. They checked out the phone boxes nearest to the central clock and took down the numbers of each. Hofer would ring them Monday with John in place to check they all received calls. John would arrange for one box to be locked with an out of order sign at ten o'clock to make sure it was vacant and usable at eleven. They had agreed that the best solution for communication was through the office switchboard. Their operator would patch the calls through from France and Victoria. They had used this method before.

Hofer knew that Andrew Bulling must be accompanied for part of the handover. There were several entrances from which they might appear, but the position of the boxes made it easy to see in most directions as they were up against the East station wall.

Satisfied that they understood the geography they went their separate ways.

The next day was Saturday, but Marker had decided to go in to the hotel in the morning, just to check out anything that had happened the previous day. He may be fired, but he was still diligent. He picked up his mail from the General Manager's outer office and found the typists still working hard churning out confirmation letters for upcoming visits. He decided to pass by the Lounge Bar where Tony worked. He was famous for his cocktails and he found him at ten o'clock, setting up the bar.

'A good barman,' said Tony looking a little tired, 'really requires everything a diplomat should have and something more.'

'Good night last night?'

The detective asked, making a judgment more from the smell of stale beer and cigars than the report of the night's takings he had seen earlier.

'Yes, a fine one indeed. Here's an odd thing

though – have a look at this.'

And Tony passed over a silver measure that they used for pouring the spirits they put in cocktails. Marker looked at it closely.

'Ah yes,' he said, 'the shilling stuck to the bottom. Give me a knife.'

Tony passed over a thin bladed fruit knife and Marker levered it out. It had stuck in place with a small piece of chewing gum.

'Very nice. It's been done by someone who wants to get more than sixteen measures out of the bottle. They can pocket the money for the seventeenth. The shilling reduces the amount of spirit that you can get in the measure. Audit only check to see that you've taken the money for sixteen measures and so the takings marry with the stock you've used. Where did it come from?'

'Well we had several staff behind the bar and it would have come from a casual barman I had on last night, but there's no proof.'

'Well you need to watch him. If the Weights and Measures people come in to check what you're serving you might get into a bit of trouble.'

Tony thanked him for the advice and said he'd keep his eye out for anything similar happening. Marker made his way down to his office.

When he was sitting down he opened up his mail which was the usual mundane operational fodder. He then fished out Brooks' bank statements. They made much more interesting reading. Broadman Developments appeared to pay him regularly and it was the only credit that appeared. There were very few withdrawals, but he noted one to a Rome hotel that obviously was made as an advance payment to avoid exchange controls. A holiday perhaps? He thought.

He then recalled what he now knew.

Andrew was holed up nearby in Archer's flat. Hofer, some sort of kidnap specialist, had been appointed by Bulling to go to Menton where presumably there was to be a handover involving the Rothschild bank. Brooks and Archer were both directors with Broadman who had now successfully persuaded Bulling to sell his shares. Andrew and Brooks might be more than close friends. On top of that the Chairman appears to have a stepson who was fathered by Patrick Wildblood. That, he considered, might make some people's thoughts turn lightly to murder if it was inadvertently revealed by the offending party.

The detective began to think about the size of

the ransom. It was a huge amount of money and he decided he needed to focus on how it was going to be moved around. After all, if he was able to recover even some of the cash there might be an award, and he will probably be needing some extra funds after he left the hotel. He knew where to begin. A closer look at Archer was a good starting point. He wondered if he might use Sandrine for that, and he was seeing her tonight.

He had chosen Annabel's, the high society discotheque on Berkeley Square. They had a reasonable supper menu and the club was full of the good and the great. Well the great anyway. It was members only but he'd spoken to Michaele, the restaurant *Maître d'* about getting a table. He'd worked at The Adelphi before and would let an old friend like him in, even if it meant the detective had to bung him a fiver-. He'd arranged to be there for eight, and he walked up from Green Park tube to the square. He crossed the road over to the green portico which covered the steps down to the club. When he was there, the porter signed him in and he left Sandrine's name with the desk. He then went through to the Bar and ordered his usual Manhattan and lit a Rothmans. The walls were covered floor to ceiling with good art. Oils mainly, and there was a degree of comfortable seating, but he chose to sit at the bar and reserved a stool for Sandrine next to him.

After ten minutes Sandrine arrived looking terrific. She was wearing another Quant miniskirt and light silk blouse. Her hair was immaculate and she smelt gorgeous. She turned heads.

'Hello Richard, you a member here?'

'I have my contacts,' he replied and helped her onto the stool. 'Manhattan?'

'Please.'

'Rothmans?'

The detective offered his pack.

'Please, I passed Mark Birley on the way in. He's the owner, named it after his first wife I think.'

'He's doing very well, great sense of design.'

They continued with small talk until a waiter came over dressed in an immaculate white jacket to offer the menu and take the order. They moved to a table opposite the dance floor. They both sat next to each other on a banquette.

'This is cosy Richard.'

And Sandrine moved a little closer to him. She had ordered the Risotto and he decided on the grilled lamb chops again. Lamb was becoming a habit. Richard looked at the small booklet of wine and decided the prices had no relation to the real world. He ordered the house claret.

'Now dear Sandrine, business before pleasure. We know that Brooks is on the Broadman payroll and is close to Egerton and Archer. We know that Archer has the flat where the beloved Andrew is resting up. It looks as if this is, despite the Chairman's denial, a stitch up to get him to sell his shares. Which, of course, has happened. I'd like to know how the money from the kidnap is moving around. My guess is that if Andrew in working in tandem with Archer then he'll be getting some of it.'

Marker was careful not to mention that he knew something of the handover and that he'd made a trip to Jersey where his relationship with Barclays seemed on a steady footing. He continued:

'I wonder Sandrine whether there's any way you might be able to help in getting Archer's banking details. You've got some good contacts.'

'Well,' Sandrine considered her next words carefully.

'The ransom is being paid in gold and we know that the transaction is in Monaco for the conversion of cash to yellow metal. It will not be possible to trace that after it's liquidated unless we know what Archer has arranged for it after it disappears. That is if Archer is arranging anything. I agree that if the beneficiary in total or in part maybe Andrew Bulling we have a better chance to start at that end of things rather than with Archer. I think that is where to start.'

Sandrine was surprised that her strategic target was exactly where Marker's was aiming and if she was to get her hands on some of the money then she was going to have to be abstemious with passing out what she might learn.

The food arrived and was impeccably cooked. The *risotto printemps* came with a light shade of green that looked almost white under the subdued lighting. The lamb chops were cooked *a pointe* and were suitably succulent. They shared the green beans and for dessert they ordered a *Grand Marnier soufflé* which came as light as a cloud and was rich with the orange liquor. Afterwards the detective who had spoken little during the meal suggested a dance and Sandrine was surprised at the quality of his moves. There was a little more to this man than she had thought, but he couldn't beat the energy of Eion, her young male most wanting.

When it was after midnight, Marker suggested a taxi to his place. The claret and the liquor had done the trick and they fell into a cab. He put his arm around her and kissed her. She kissed him back biting his lower lip. When they got back to his apartment he didn't switch on the lights, he simply pulled down the zip of her skirt and let it fall to the floor. She stepped out of it and undid her blouse. Standing only in her negligible underwear she led him to the bedroom. And yet, although Marker thought it was 'love' and not food that was the true key to his 'French Squeeze'...it was actually money.

Andrew Bulling had been spending all of his time alone. It was a lot of time he thought, and he was bored. Still there was a considerable amount of money coming his way and he had calculated that for two weeks work it was indeed a very profitable enterprise. He had read his folder several times and was now confident that he had the story straight. In this fiction he had been abducted by a group of East End gangsters and spent his time handcuffed to a radiator. He had been fed, but the food had been poor. His time indoors obviously hadn't helped his pallor and the beard he'd grown added to the general impression that his time incarcerated had been one of hardship. Well that was what he thought when he's looked at himself in the mirror.

He'd been thinking things over. What a miserable bastard his father was. Sitting as some kind of plump Mandarin at The Adelphi, making stacks of money with no consideration for his first born. Over the days his hatred had grown. His father had murdered his mother just for money. When he got out there was going to be retribution. Andrew's problem was that he wasn't sure how this was going to happen. He was too much of a coward to do it himself, but he was determined that his father was going to die one way or another.

Archer had been to visit him again and had gone through what was going to happen next. Archer would arrange to meet him on the day of the transfer at the flat and together they would take a taxi to Victoria. Andrew would wear a hooded duffle coat and they would wait for a phone call in an office space that Archer had rented for the day. When they received a confirming call that the transfer was in progress, Andrew would leave the flat and head across the street. He was to use the separate Victoria Station underground entrance to gain access via the subway up to the main underground exit of the mainline station concourse. Then he was to make his way towards the large clock that hung in from the station ceiling. All this was to create the illusion that he had come off the tube. There he would put his hood down and wait until someone come across to meet him.

Archer told him the real challenge was going to be to get his fictional story straight. The police will want all the details at the Press conference that was bound to follow. And then there was his father to deal with. How was he going to be treated by him? The return of the prodigal son perhaps? Archer knew that Andrew might be too vunerable under pressure.

When they had gone overall the details again Archer left and Andrew began to think about a vacation. George Brooks had suggested Rome. It would be good to be with George and he wondered how he was coping. He had sounded alarmed when they had spoken. He hoped that he hadn't done anything stupid like talk to his father or worse, the police. He had wanted to give him another call, but it just wasn't worth the risk, he'd explain it all when he saw him. There was only a few more days to go.

The weekend at the Adelphi passed without any significant incidents, and George Brooks was casting his eye over Monday's arrivals. There was a large check in for the Federated Sands dinner that evening, but there were sufficient vacant rooms from the previous evening to allow a reasonable movement in the room inventory of accommodation. He'd been through the breakfast room and greeted a few of the better known guests, Lord and Lady Palmer was there with Mr and Mrs Blenkinthorpe. They had chatted about their horse that was running the next day at Newbury. As he had left the room he noticed that Marker was sitting in the far corner gorging himself as usual. He didn't know that the detective was on his last few weeks, and thought that when he was General Manager he'd put a stop to all these meals that he was forever eating.

Putting the day's arrival sheets to one side he thought about Sandrine again. He was pretty sure that he had seen her in that bar with Wildblood's son. He was a familiar face as he had met him when the Restaurant Manager had asked if the hotel could take him on as a waiter. And it was his birth certificate he had seen in Sandrine's in-tray. It was then that he slowly made the connection. Cynthia Hampton, he'd heard the name from Andrew. Cynthia Hampton was surely Andrew's mother, and therefore Eion Wildblood was Andrew's half- brother. He bet Andrew didn't know that. And what was Wildblood doing with the Chairman's wife? Well, he rationalised, it was pretty obvious what Wildblood had been doing. The next question was what Miss Parte was doing with Eion Wildblood. Knowing Sandrine, he thought, that was pretty obvious too.

When Marker had seen Brooks in the restaurant he hadn't liked the look he'd received back from across the room and had slipped a fish bone into his mouth from his Islay kipper. It had taken a moment or two to get it dislodged and gingerly put on the side of his plate. However something fortuitous came from the experience. He'd remembered that DCI Bowen had asked him to get some more information on Brooks and his relationship with Andrew Bulling. He decided to pay Brooks another visit that day and took the opportunity to knock on his office door after the morning meeting. There was no reply. Never one to put off by a lack of response, he tried the door handle and it opened. He left the door ajar and stood near the desk.

Brooks' diary was open, and the detective flicked the pages to look at the notes section at the back of the book. There were a number of telephone numbers that had been written in. He spotted Andrew's name and number.

Moving the pages back he took the opportunity to look a few days further back from the day's date. There, on the Tuesday of the preceding week, he spotted the name of the same travel agent he had used to buy his ticket to Jersey. Brooks had made an appointment. He turned back the pages to where they were originally-. He then took another look at the certificate from Lausanne Hotel School that hung on the wall. He made a mental note of the date it had been awarded and then felt as if he should look in the desk drawers, but then his attention was drawn to a small pack of photographs that were still in the film developer's wallet. It was partially hidden under a buff file that was on top of the filing cabinet. He slipped the wallet into his pocket. Safer, he thought, to examine them when he was back in his office. He could return them before it was noticed that they were gone.

At that moment Brooks arrived.

'Can I help you Marker?'

'Yes, I found the door open so hope you wouldn't mind if I waited for you.'

Brooks wasn't sure if he had closed the door or not. But he did mind him in his office uninvited. Marker continued:

'Difficult times we live in. The police are asking me if there is anything I can help them with in their pursuit of Andrew Bulling's kidnappers. You told me you knew him at hotel school. How do you think he will shape up under a threat like this?'

'Oh I think it will be tough but he's reasonably strong.'

'What do you think his father will say when he's released, I assume they will pay the ransom.'

'Oh he doesn't get along with his father, so that will be interesting. I imagine that security will be a worry in the future.' Brooks replied.

'I suppose it will be good for you to see him as you are such good friends.' Marker looked at him and Brooks didn't like the inference.

'I haven't seen him in years.'

When the detective had got back to his office he pulled out the photo wallet he'd taken. There were some reasonably good pictures of Sandrine, and most interesting were the ones of her lying topless on what Marker assumed to be Brooks' sofa. Then the last in the pack made him sit up.

It was a recent picture, and it was of Brooks and Andrew Bulling sitting in a pub, and beside them was the man who had murdered that prostitute together with another character whom Marker didn't recognise. He had assumed that Brooks only knew the murderer casually, but now Andrew Bulling seemed to know him too.

He put the photos back in the folder and would take the first opportunity he could to get them back to Brooks' office. It was a shame as he would have liked to keep the two or three of Sandrine laid out so provocatively. They would just have to live in his memory.

He made his way back to the lobby. When he was next to the Hall Porter's desk he pulled out his Arrivals list and searched for a name that required a senior manager to meet on arrival. He found a suitable candidate.

He signalled to Fellowes the Porter to come over.

'Can you ring Mr Brooks and tell him that Mr Poigestre, the organiser for the Federation Sands dinner is on the forecourt and wanting to check in.'

'Oh! Mr Poigestre, I hadn't seen him.'

Fellowes was unlikely to see anyone unless they held out a pound note or two.

'Well he's sorting his car out with the doorman.' Marker lied.

The Concierge picked up the phone and dialled Brooks. Marker made his way across the lobby and towards Brooks' office. He passed him as he got to the top of the steps and they ignored each other. The detective had less than a minute for Brooks to find out that he had been called in error, but it was enough time for him to get back to Brooks' office and return the photos.

It had gone rather quiet for DCI Bowen who was not making much headway with her investigation into the kidnap, but she had made some progress on how Sir John Bulling might have killed his first wife. Sitting on her desk was a blood stained helmet.

'You see Sloane, I've done some research.'

She was holding the shattered hemet in her

hands as her number two, who was seated opposite her, adopted a pose to suggest earnest interest.

'If you drop a crash helmet off a coffee table it probably doesn't do much damage. But drop it out of a first floor window and it's a different story. You can't tell if it's damaged or not by looking at it superficially. You have to look inside. Now no one was especially keen to look inside this helmet at the time because it was full of blood but I've had it gone over by our forensics people who've taken the two parts of it, separated the inside padding and found this.'

DCI Bowen tossed one part over to DI Sloane and pointed at a straight line along where the helmet had split.

'I've had an identical helmet tested to breaking point and the outer shell doesn't break like this – not in a straight line. The skin polymers don't work like that. Hit it hard enough and it shatters in a star formation. The only way this could have split along a line was if the skin was scored from the inside before the helmet was hit. Our friend Bulling must have done this to the interior of the helmet sometime before Cynthia Bulling put it on for that fateful trip.'

Sloane looked mildly interested.

'Sabotage? Seems a bit unlikely. Do we know it was exclusively her helmet? Even if you're theory is right it's a risky business assuming it will break on impact. He's much more likely to have been pissed and seeing her unconscious hoped she'd die whilst he meandered off. How could you possibly prove that it was Bulling who weakened the helmet?' Sloane asked.

'I don't think I can. But I think I have enough to put some pressure on to our friend Sir John. Let's see what happens when he's confronted with it. He'll be surprised I have the helmet from all those years ago. I'm going to pay him a visit, it'll also be interesting to hear what he has to say about the kidnap. He hasn't been very communicative has he? I bet he's in it up to his puffed up ears.'

They took the station car back to Adelphi Hill. It was a dull summer's day, typical for anyone who lived in London who was thinking that one day the sun might shine through the smog. Their unmarked car pulled off the Embankment and parked up. They had deliberately arrived unannounced, ignored the doorman and went straight to the Chairman's office. He was out. Bowen asked Diana to call Richard Marker while they waited the Chairman's return. The three of them met in the hotel tea lounge. After the order had been taken Bowen asked the hotel detective what news he had about the relationship between Andrew Bulling and George Brooks.

'They are clearly friends.' Marker was guarded.

'Yes Richard, we know that.'

Sloane and Bowen looked patiently at Marker who replied:

'I don't think that he's involved directly in the kidnapping but I suspect that this is much to the advantage of Broadman Developments. I am pretty sure that Brooks is paid by Broadman to be an inside mole. So there is a tenuous correlation.'

DCI Bowen moved forward in her seat. The tea was served and nothing was said until the waitress stood away.

'You think a substantial company like Broadman would set up a kidnap?' Bowen asked.

'Not exactly.'

Replied the detective:

'But I think some of the parties involved are pretty ruthless. I suggest you take a look at the track record one of their directors – name of Archer.'

Bowen wrote it down.

'How's your love life getting on Richard? Still

seeing Sandrine Parte?' The hotel detective was taken aback.

'What do you know about that?' he asked.

'I wasn't born neuron-less. If you seriously believe I would buy your story of a security clearance for someone that isn't in direct contact with hotel revenues you are a monkey's uncle.'

Marker blushed. He was, after all, burdened with a rather complicated love life, yet was not expecting a critical commentary on his relationship with Sandrine.

'She's useful, but I don't trust her, and it's not just what you told me about her past life, I think she has her own agenda, but I'm not sure where it's heading. So I'm working with her and whilst I admire her talents, I'm only looking at them from afar.'

The Chairman's secretary then appeared from the staircase and told the trio that the Chairman was now back and would see them. They made their way back down the corridor and into his office.

Bulling stood up as they all entered and indicated that they should all take a seat.

'I'm sorry for the interruption Sir John, but I wanted to get an update from you as to whether you have any news for us. We haven't heard from you since our last visit. What have you decided to do?'

'It looks dire and I think that I will have to pay the ransom. There simply is no lead as to where Andrew is, and even then, if it was discovered where he's being held there is the risk he would be shot in some kind of rescue attempt.'

Bowen considered this for a moment then asked:

'I presume that you have someone handling this because Richard Marker doesn't seem to know anything about your plans.'

She looked at Richard. He looked bemused.

'Marker knows nothing, it's not in his job specification to sort out my personal issues. And he's leaving us soon.'

DCI Bowen looked surprised and cast a look at Richard.

'Is that true?'

'I'm being fired because Broadman's have their own security department that will be taking over, or so the Staff Manager told me. It's confidential, only a few know apparently and that includes the Chairman.'

'That's unfortunate, you've been extremely

helpful to us.'

The DCI turned her attention back to the Chairman.

'It's not illegal to pay a ransom Sir John, but kidnapping is a serious offence and I want to catch whoever is acting behind this. There was a threat about the motorcycle accident you were involved with when you were driving and you effectively killed your first wife. Are you sure that this isn't influencing your decision? Surely you don't want it all raked over again?'

'I have nothing to hide there,' Bulling lied, 'and I take exception to your inference.'

'But you do Sir John, you told us you didn't understand the reference to the Willows in the anonymous note.'

'I'd forgotten that was the road where the accident happened.'

Bowen paused and considered Bulling's reply. She then said:

'I'm looking at the file on that incident. It was certainly a convenient time for your wife to die. The hotel was in the midst of another hostile bid. Just after the dog days of the end of the war when business was pretty poor.'

Bulling shifted in his chair and looked uncomfortable.

'It was an accident and the coroner's report covers all the facts.'

DCI Bowen made a few more notes and then abruptly stood up to leave.

'Thank you Sir John. We will be back.' The three left the office with the hotel detective trailing behind, a little mystified.

'What is it that you know that I don't?' Marker asked Bowen.

'Well we are pretty sure he's hired someone to handle the negotiations and he's going to pay. I'm also sure that some of the money is to pay for silencing someone who knows more about the motorbike accident than we have been told.'

The hotel detective considered this against what he did know and decided that on balance he still knew more than DCI Bowen.

After the police had left his office, the Chairman had picked up the phone to Hofer.

'The police came this morning unannounced. I've told them nothing but they seem to know that I am holding back on information. They also made some dark allusion to the accident. It's essential that we are sure the kidnappers know nothing more than was in the coroner's report.'

Hofer took this in.

'I think I can get that verbally guaranteed but that isn't worth much. I believe they are just playing on your insecurities. If there was anything more the police would know first, unless you can think of any piece of information that they have missed and someone else might have gathered.'

'Impossible.' Said Bulling, but thinking that Hofer might be right.

Marker decided that his next step was to pay a visit to his travel agent. He would like to know what Brooks was up to, probably booking his holidays, but it might be worth checking. He wanted to know everything that little shit did. He took his coat off the stand and made for the Strand exit. Crossing the road he made his way past The Adelphi Theatre and took a right turn into Bedford Street. There was an excellent Indian restaurant there and he paused to look though the menu that was posted next to the door. It looked exceptionally good and he'd read a fine review in last week's *Evening*

Standard. Marker enjoyed the simple pleasures of life, especially food, as his general corpulence affirmed. He wondered if Sandrine liked the odd tandoori.

He walked on to the travel agency and pushed through the door. He saw that the consultant he had used last week was busy with someone at his desk. So he waited by the brochure rack until that particular piece of business was concluded.

'Hello, it's me again.' He cheerfully greeted the agent.

'I'm thinking of joining George Brooks on his holiday that he came in to discuss last Tuesday.'

He took a punt at what was the most obvious reason for the meeting.

'George Brooks. Yes, let me think. He did come in and saw me initially, but he was talking Italy, not my speciality I'm afraid.'

'Oh' said Marker, 'did he leave then?'

'No, not then, I passed him over to Tania, she knows everything there is to know about Italy. She's been all over from Pisa to Palermo. I'm not sure what happened after that or if he booked or not. Tania's off today but I can look up her files.'

'That be great' said Marker. 'George asked if it would be possible for me to join on the same deal.'

The agent went over to the vacant desk and came back with a file in a plastic sleeve.

'Yes, here it is, the Hotel Eden in Rome, four nights with someone called Andrew Bulling. It's quite pricey, I think he's booked a suite and an adjoining room.'

Marker didn't want to appear ignorant of the date of the reservation, but it was essential he discovered it.

'Yes that's it. I would need a single room, but I'm stuck on which flight to go on. Did George book Alitalia?'

'No he's taken the BEA flight to Rome's Fiumicino airport two weeks from today.'

Marker exchanged a few more pleasantries before leaving. He also didn't want to appear overly inquisitive and he told the manager he would think it all over. It was indeed an expensive holiday and one that Brooks' bank statement couldn't support alone. The Hotel Eden was the best in the city and the booking was for the premier suite. The money has to be coming from somewhere, and that somewhere had to be Andrew's. The question was where is all that cash at this moment in time?

DEREK PICOT

Chapter 13

Hofer's arrival at Nice airport with his assistant Michael was uneventful. The BEA Trident had been a comfortable flight taking just over two-hours for the journey. But when they went down the aircraft steps they felt the heat and humidity of the Riviera hitting them like warm melted butter. It was greasy and clammy, a significant change from London, and they were glad they were wearing linen safari suits.

They took a taxi to Menton. The old Mercedes drove reasonably quickly and they were grateful for the breeze the open windows created in the back seats. The climb up over the mountain gave some relief but as they dropped down into the valley above Menton the heat returned with a vengeance. The old car pulled up outside their hotel and the porter took their bags. The room they were sharing had the view over the quay that they wanted. They decided to take a coffee across the road to watch both the *Gendarmerie* and the Police Municipal. This was an irritation to have two police forces. Hofer assumed that the former caught criminals, the other errant motorists. Only the French would complicate something as simple as one force keeping law and order. Every half hour the white Citroens of the Police Municipal drove past and checked the traffic was moving. The *Gendarmerie* patrolled in blue Peugeots and although more heavily armed did the same thing but more regularly. They passed every quarter of an hour.

After their coffee they took a taxi back to Monaco and met up with the boat hire company Hofer had selected. They rented a large wooden decked Riva. It was the fastest of all the speedboats on the Mediterranean. The V8 3000cc engine had a top speed of over 60 kilometres an hour with seating for six. Hofer produced a license, (of which he had a few in differing names) and paid in cash. They decided to give it a trial and set off down the coast with a plume of spray from the engine that looked like the giant cockerel's tail. The boat rode the waves as smoothly as a silk stocking rolling off a shaved leg. Within twenty minutes they were mooring back up in the Marina at Monaco. The *Beaux*

Art façade of the Casino was reflecting the afternoon sunlight high on the hill and they strolled over to the Avenue de Monte Carlo, just below the l'Hermitage and into Rothchild's bank.

There they met Monsieur Blot who had already received the suitcases that would take the gold bars. They finalised all the arrangements for the next day and made their way back to Menton with the boat. They wanted to look over the top end of the quay where the transfer was to take place. Mooring up the Riva, Hofer asked Michael to check out the two phone boxes that stood near the statue. Hofer had decided that it was going to be the only way he could reasonably keep an eye on the transfer and speak to his London office at the same time.

'Not good boss. One's out of order, but I have the number of the other.'

'OK' replied Hofer. 'Let's call London to see if it makes an easy connection and speak to John.'

Hofer walked back to the glass booth that was barely sufficient to protect the telephone from the elements. He picked up the receiver and spoke in French to the operator. He then asked for a collect call to his London office.

'Hello, John? Good. There's only one phone working here and I think we can do this one of two ways, either I connect collect – which takes time, or we could try to see if you can dial in direct to this number. Let's give it a try.'

Hofer hung up and stood by the phone. At that moment a passer-by stopped and made a move to use the phone. Hofer explained that he was waiting for a call. After half a minute no call had come through and so he decided to let bystander use the booth. That call took three minutes and when he had finished, Hofer called his office again.

'Well John – what happened?'

'The line was engaged.'

'Well I had to let someone else use it. Let's try again.'

The second time it worked, but it took near half a minute for the call to come in. This wasn't good.

Hofer took control.

'OK let's do it this way. I get Michael here in Menton to call the office collect ten minutes before we get to the handover. John, you will be at Victoria as discussed. From your phone box you also make a direct connection to our office. Let's get Maureen to handle both calls from her desk. She has enough lines there to handle it, although I'd have preferred to speak to you direct. I can see it's too risky to assume that we can dialogue between two payphones.'

After the call they made their way to the *Capitainerie* on the other arm of the marina where they booked a space for the Riva virtually opposite the Statue of St Michel.

Archer had arrived back in London and checked into The Adelphi. This time, unusually, he was without his wife or his mistress. The hotel detective had noted his arrival that morning and decided that he was going to keep a close eye on what he was doing. In the afternoon Marker had visited Mary in the switchboard and confided in her that he needed to listen in to any calls that Archer made. Mary was excited about any opportunity to be part of a real life investigation and willingly agreed. After all, there might be another dinner in it for her.

He had passed by the reception brigade leader after the morning meeting and asked to be called when Mr Archer arrived. At two that afternoon reception called the detective in his office and told him that Mr Archer's taxi had arrived. As Archer was being met by Brooks at Reception and taken to his river suite, Marker took the stairs to the switchboard and set up his clandestine post. Within ten minutes of his arrival Archer wanted to place a call. Mary wrote the number down and passed it to the detective. It was the flat at Benneton Street.

Mary put two plugs into the outgoing sockets on the board and rang the phone that was by Marker who was seated away from the main board. He picked it up, and then listened as Mary put the outgoing call through to Archer's suite.

'Hello Mr Archer, your call is on the line.'

The call rang on for another three-to-five seconds before it was picked up.

'Hello?'

'Hello Andrew. It's me. I am coming over to see you to check that you have all the details correct and you have learnt every part of your role. You are going to be free tomorrow but you will be on your own after you leave the office to make the rendezvous.'

'I'm fine with that. What have you done about the money?'

'I'll tell you about that when I see you, but I have set the account up in Jersey as promised.'

The call took less than a minute and then Archer hung up. Marker sat back and looked pleased with himself.

He wondered if he should follow Archer out of the hotel, but then thought better of it. Hardly any point. Better to stake out the flat tomorrow and follow Andrew to wherever he was going.

'Thank you Mary. Thank you very much. Just what I needed to know.'

And with that Marker sauntered out to the hotel corridor.

The Francisci brothers were equally a little busy. They had arranged for their two Algerian associates to visit them in Nice that afternoon to finalise the handover arrangements. It was a hot day and the Algerians had been picked up from the station in a black Citroen much favoured by the *Unione Corse*, so they were more than appreciative of the *Juliper* beers they were offered when they entered the café the Franciscis owned. They made their way to the back of the restaurant and before they entered a private room they were frisked by two large security men at the door. They had to leave their Glock revolvers by the desk that was just outside the entrance.

When they entered they showed the brothers their arm tattoos. The black head with a white bandana. The sign of the *Unione Corse*. Satisfied that these were friends, the elder of the brothers explained what was to happen. They would pick up a Chris Craft Cobra speedboat that was in the marina on the opposite side of Menton and drive it over to the *Quai Imperatrice* where they would be joined by a man with a briefcase that contained a gold testing kit. They had to be in place by 11.45am. The jetty would be sealed off by men at the street entrance for a period of about twenty minutes. At midday they would be met by someone carrying suitcases of gold bars. This man would have to confirm to others that they had met, probably using the phone booth on the quay. Opposite, observing from a room above the Restaurant Olivier, a small bistro with commanding views of the marina would be a lookout who would be calling London to advise on the progress of the delivery. The gold was to be tested before it was loaded. If it was approved, it was to be put into their boat and then driven at speed to Genoa, to the *Ponte Ex Idroscalo*. It will take two and a half hours. If there was a problem with the gold then they were to shoot the courier, put his body in the boat and dump it out to sea.

It all seemed so straightforward.

The men finished their beers, picked up half of their payment in US dollars and agreed to meet Francisci's men in Menton the next day. After they had left the café they decided to spend a little time at the other Francisci establishment that they knew. A discrete bordello in the old town. It was a good a place to spend as any other and some of the Moroccan girls were as expert as those in Algiers.

The next morning Hofer rose early and after a coffee and croissant with Michael they made his way down to the Riva. They gunned the engine and slowly reversed the boat out of its berth and set a course for Monte Carlo. They got there by ten and moored the boat at the refilling station. Whilst Michael refuelled, Hofer went over to the taxi rank and took a car to the bank. He completed the paper work and loaded the gold laden suitcases into the back of the Mercedes.

At the marina Michael had moored the boat near the slip and when he saw Hofer he pulled the boat over. Together they manhandled the heavy load on board and Hofer paid off the taxi. By eleven they were on their way, but Hofer was concerned about the time. The boat was much slower on the way back. The weight of the gold bars was adding to their journey time. As they rounded Cap Martin and entered the *Baie du Soleil*, the long bay just before the marina, it was already 11.45am. They didn't reach the *Quai Imperatrice* until it was just before midday. Hofer didn't show any external sign of stress, but his heart rate had increased. Taking his binoculars he spotted three men by the statue, and more alarmingly, one person in the phone booth.

They rounded the pier heads and he had a chance to look more closely at his target. Algerians and a nervous looking younger man dressed in a suit with a briefcase. The scrutineer he thought. Michael reversed the boat onto its mooring and Hofer took the ladder to the top of the quay. Michael kept the boat engine running and tied up with a quick release slip knot. Hofer reached the top and looked around. He saw that the quay entrance had been blocked by a black Citroen with the hood up. Two men were peering under the bonnet in a poor attempt to fix an imaginary breakdown. Turning his head back to the statue, the bigger of the two Algerians approached him and Hofer could see the outline of a pistol in his pocket. Without saying a word he showed Hofer his tattoo.

Hofer looked at the design and said:

'Reasonable needle job, but a bit blurred. We aren't armed. They didn't tell me you would be.'

The statement was ignored.

'Where is the gold?'

'In my boat. How do you want to proceed?'

The tension was as palpable as the humidity in the air.

'We want to test one bar from each suitcase. I will pick the bars.'

'Not acceptable,' said Hofer waving his hand, 'I will allow Dr. Brains here to go on board whilst you two bodybuilders stay here with me.'

The Algerian nodded and the thin man with the briefcase clambered down the ladder to the boat. Across the way, above the Restaurant Olivier a man with binoculars put them down on the window sill and reached for the phone. The line rang in London.

Michael stayed at the controls whilst the scientist opened each of the suitcases in turn and took out a gold bar from each. He then opened his leather bag and took out a strong electro magnet and a small phial of Nitric acid. He carefully inspected the hallmarks on each bar in turn and then connected the magnet to a battery. He held a meter in one hand and picked up the magnet with the other. So far so good. He placed the magnet across the bars. There was no reaction and it all looked clear. Then suddenly the needle on the dial flickered on the last bar. The thin man looked up at the Algerians with a look of concern. Hofer could see one of them put his hand in his pocket and tighten his grip on his pistol.

He ran another pass with the magnet. After a second trawl, there was no movement and the first reading was put down to the movement of the boat.

He then held up a small blade and made a slight score line along each bar. He uncorked the test tube of acid and poured a little into each indentation. He was looking to see if the acid turned milky. It was a well-known test to see if the bars were merely silver coated in gold. Silver was also non-magnetic. Hofer and the heavies were looking down from the top of the quay. Everyone held their breath for a minute to see if there was any reaction. Hofer was nervous and realised he should have thought of doing this himself in the bank. But it was too late now.

∞∞∞

Andrew Bulling had heaved himself out of bed and was relieved that this part of the ordeal was almost over. He'd been over the file three times with Archer the previous evening and felt he knew everything. He tidied up where he could, and as the time was only ten o'clock he estimated he didn't have to leave for another half an hour. He pulled the nylon sheer to one side and looked out of the window left down the street. It was fortunate for Marker that he hadn't looked up the street as he would have seen the detective move quickly into a doorway out of sight from where he had been standing. He'd been there since early that morning, positioned at a café that had a good view of the whole street. However he'd got bored of sitting over several cups of coffee. He had enjoyed an excellent English breakfast which he had agreeably digested in the coming hours, but now it was time for a small constitutional. It was only by chance after he had left his seat to stretch his legs that he had seen the third floor curtain move.

This was it then, he thought. Bulling junior is about to move. He resumed his position at the café and waited. At 10.30 a taxi pulled up and Archer got out. Marker was surprised that he would appear but assumed that the fewer involved the better the security. Archer directed the cab to stay and Marker turned around briskly to see if he could hail a taxi. There was none in sight, very concerned he was going to miss them leaving he sprinted into Drury Lane where there was a rank. He grabbed the first taxi in the line and instructed the driver to turn and wait at the junction with Betterton Street. After a minute or so had passed Archer's taxi pulled out and the two cabs travelled in convoy to Victoria.

The first taxi stopped at the end of Victoria Street and Marker directed his driver to pull up twenty yards behind. Archer and a hooded man whom Marker assumed to be Andrew Bulling got out and made for an office block in Portman Place. Marker paid off his cab and wondered if his assumptions had been right. He decided to wait across the street. He looked at his watch. It was 10.50. He could hang around, but the office block was a big one with several entrances. The chances were high that he might miss them leave. Moving across the road he decided on a better vantage point and found one where he could see the lifts in the lobby through the glass frontage. He was rewarded as fifteen minutes later he saw the same hooded figure coming out of the nearest lift and make for exit. Marker stood his ground until he was certain that this was Andrew and didn't move until he saw which direction he was heading. Marker followed as he made his way up Victoria Street but not towards the mainline station, he went straight into the tube entrance a block north of the terminus concourse.

When he went down the steps Andrew suddenly realised that he wasn't sure which subway to take for the concourse. He had taken a wrong turning and chosen another exit to Victoria Street. He doubled back, taking Marker, who was following closely completely by surprise. He knocked into the detective without noticing him and ran back down the subway. Marker followed at a pace, but his weight was certainly not an advantage. Andrew raced through the passageways barging past people with large suitcases and women pushing prams desperate to find the right stairway to exit. He finally found the set of stairs that led to the main line station. But he was very late. The large clock that hung above the concourse showed it was almost fifteen minutes past eleven.

∞∞∞

Hofer was relieved when the test was done and completed. He agreed for the transfer to begin and called Michael up to get the phone line to London. At the same time the smaller of the Algerians went down the ladder to help the thin man with moving the suitcases across to their boat, leaving his partner on the top of the quayside. It was at this moment that one of the men that had been fishing of the harbour wall chose to walk over to the phone booths whilst Hofer and the Algerian were distracted looking down on the boats. He went straight over to use the only working phone. Hofer was annoyed he hadn't spotted this potential trouble earlier.

'No one move more gold until we have the line clear and agreed from London.'

Hofer held the Algerian by the arm.

The Algerian looked a little bemused. He said nothing, ignored Hofer and shook himself free. He walked over to the fisherman and pulled him away from the booth.

Across the marina, by chance, the Harbour Master had picked up his binoculars and was looking with interest with the proceedings that were going on under the Statue of St Michel. He had just seen someone physically pulled from the phone booth who was now in an argument with one of the trio that had been there sorting out what appeared to be the transfer of luggage between two speedboats.

It was now three minutes past midday and they were late. Hofer grabbed the phone whilst it was still free and dialled 'O' for the operator. At that moment the local fisherman took a swing at the large Algerian. Hofer could see the thin trace of blood coming from the gangster's nose. Without saying a word, the Algerian pulled out his gun and shot the man in the head. Blood and brain spurted everywhere, some of it hitting Hofer in the face. The man fell to the ground and mayhem broke out. The Algerian rushed for the ladder and scrambling down shouted to the men in the boats to leave the last suitcase, start the engine and go. Hofer dropped the receiver and came down the ladder a close second.

Across the way, the men who had been peering into the Citroen looked up startled as they heard the gunshot. They slammed the bonnet shut and got into the car just as a blue *Gendarmerie* car pulled up on the other side of the street. The curtains on the first floor of the Restaurant Olivier fluttered closed.

Hofer shouted for Michael to follow, but by the time that the two of them were in their boat the Algerians had already gone astern and were making a fast exit towards the pier heads. The Harbour Master was in shock at what he'd seen, but quickly recovered to radio his tender that was patrolling at the other end of the marina. Hofer gunned the engine and it spluttered. Damn he thought. Michael made it to the boat and Hofer tried again. The engine turned and half fired. He tried a third time just as the Harbour Master's inflatable came roaring around the far pontoon. The motor roared into life and he sped out after the Algerians.

The two *Gendarmes* got out from their car and approached the stationery Citroen. The driver wondered if he should move before they reached his door, but thought better of it.

'Everything alright? We saw you here twenty minutes ago and wondered if you've got it fixed. You've been blocking the quay entrance.'

The driver, who had a distinct North African appearance told them he'd finally sorted out the rotor arm for the spark plugs and it should now fire. A man crossed the street from the restaurant Olivier to join them and with that he turned the key and the engine purred quietly. The *Gendarme* saluted and stopped the traffic to allow the Citroen to get onto the main road.

Meanwhile, the Harbour Master had already called the Coast Guard and put out an 'all boats alert'. It wouldn't be long before the craft would be found, but he doubted the occupants would be in them.

Hofer's assistant, John, had arrived at Victoria station at quarter to ten dressed as a Post Office Engineer. He had promptly put the agreed telephone box out of order by attaching a sign and locking the door. He then waited in the coffee bar on the station forecourt and sat over a coffee until 10.30am. He had then walked back over to the box and dismantling his signage, unlocked the door and took up occupation on the pretext of testing the line. At 10.55am he dialled the operator for a collect call. He set up the call with the office and Maureen answered.

It all seemed to be going smoothly as they waited patiently for midday to arrive and the corresponding call to be received on the other line from France. The call didn't arrive and by

11.05 neither it, nor Andrew, had appeared. John was very worried. He had the phone in one hand and a picture of Andrew Bulling in the other. He frantically scanned the entrances but could see no one of the likeness in the photo. It was now 11.15am. He told Maureen that something must have gone wrong in France and that he'd wait another ten minutes before leaving. Just as he looked across to the tube exit for the umpteenth time he saw someone that he thought might be Andrew. He had reached the top of the stairs and pulled down the hood on his duffle coat. He excitedly told Maureen that he thought he had him in sight, and there was a tail following him. He would have to be careful as they might be armed.

Andrew looked around and appeared lost. Marker stood back from the stairs as John put the receiver down and opened the booth door. He slowly walked across the concourse towards Andrew. Like Stanley meeting Livingstone they shook hands.

'Andrew Bulling I presume?' John looked around anxiously for the man he assumed to be a tail as he spoke.

'The same' replied Andrew.

John was distracted for a moment as he had checked the photo he had in his hand. He still couldn't see the man that had followed Andrew. Marker had disappeared.

'You alone?'

'Yes, I think so. It's been intolerable, I've been held hostage handcuffed to a radiator for weeks. They held me right until I was pushed out of the tube, but I'm alone now.'

John was wary but had lost sight of what he assumed was the tail.

'Well I think you were followed but I can't see anyone now. Let's get you away from here. I have a car that's waiting in Victoria Street. We are going to The Adelphi.'

Richard Marker had seen where Andrew was heading and to avoid detection had taken the opportunity to move quickly to the shelter provided by a newspaper stand that had a large group of visiting German tourists gathered around it and which provided good cover. He'd watched as Andrew had met the man dressed as a GPO Engineer, and when they left arm in arm had followed them outside and saw them get into a large Jaguar. He made a note of the registration number and decided to go back to the hotel. It was a quick run on the District line to Embankment. When he got to the front entrance he wasn't surprised to see the same car parked up and a small crowd of well wishes gathering by the revolving door.

He realised that the ransom must have been paid. The question was how and to whom?

Whilst Michael raced the boat, Hofer closed the one remaining suitcase that the Algerians hadn't loaded and left behind. He did some thinking that was faster than the Riva. They couldn't be traced via the boat hire as he'd given a false name. He doubted that anyone had got close enough to get a view of his face except the boat hire agent, but the Harbour Master would have taken both the boat details as they roared out of the Menton harbour pier heads doing thirty knots in a five knot speed restricted area. The murder on the quay couldn't be connected to the gold as all anyone would have seen were suitcases being moved from boat to boat. Two thirds of the gold had now disappeared and he wasn't sure if Andrew had been released. His immediate plan was to ditch the boat, find a phone box and make a call.

He told Michael to pull into *Roquebrune Cap Martin* and they would leave the boat there. It was just before Monaco and was only a small harbour. They could get away easily.

Michael swung the helm to starboard as soon as he sighted the mole of the harbour and only slowed down to walking pace when he was in the safety of the long harbour wall. They drew up against the quay by some granite steps and tied the boat up there. Lifting the suitcase up the stairs they walked back along the quay to a set of phone booths that were at the other end. Hofer made a collect call to Maureen. It took five minutes of explanation, but Hofer finally established that Andrew had been released. He asked her to rebook their tickets out of Geneva for the following evening and to pay for thirty kilos of excess luggage. He didn't want to reappear at Nice airport or any other along the south coast. There would be a police watch all along the Riviera.

They grabbed a taxi and drove to Menton station. The train would take most the rest of that day and go via Marseilles to Lyon and then Geneva. It wouldn't be until midnight that they would be near the Swiss border.

It was late afternoon when the Press Conference

was held. Sir John Bulling had hastily arranged one of the private dining rooms to show his son off to those journalists anxious for a story to fill the next day's front page. Unsurprisingly, seated at the back alongside Richard Marker was DCI Bowen and DI Sloane. Sir John opened the meeting by saying that they wouldn't be taking any questions as Andrew was clearly exhausted and would need to fully recuperate from his ordeal. He had however prepared a statement that he would like to read out. He cleared his throat and began:

> 'I am delighted that Andrew has been released, and appears physically unharmed, but clearly traumatised from his ordeal. We are all very relieved to have him back into the bosom of our family. I cannot express how happy I am that he is here with us all now. I would like to record what a despicable act this was to kidnap someone who has lived a quiet life, and may I say, in a most abstemious way. His only fault being to have a family of some wealth that has been targeted by a ruthless gang of East End thugs. We expect the police to use their every resource to track down these dastardly perpetuators whoever and wherever they be.

Finally, Andrew will be taking some time to recover and I hope that you will have the respect to treat his privacy with journalistic professionalism.'

Sir John then put his arm around Andrew and together they both stood up for a series of pictures. The sea of flashbulbs that then exploded was if a tropical thunderstorm had struck.

After the pictures had all been taken, DCI Bowen approached the happy couple.

'Well done Sir John. I'm glad it has ended happily. In line with your sentiment, I want to use every resource available to me to get to the bottom of this complicated story. Let's start with a meeting in an hour.'

The two Bullings looked aghast at each other. Sir John then said it would be impossible.

'I must strike whilst the iron is still hot Sir John. If we can't meet here, then I can always arrest you on suspicion of perverting the course of justice and we can talk down at West End Central.'

'Put that way, I can see that we need to dialogue. Give me a few minutes with my son though please, we haven't had a chance to talk.'

Bowen agreed, but it was for that very reason

that she wanted an early meeting. She didn't want them to talk. She backed off and went over to Marker who was still sitting down.

'Well Richard. What do you make of that?'

Marker was still assimilating what he actually did make of it and was abstemious with his response.

'I think Andrew doesn't look to have had too bad a time of it. He wouldn't have come out of one of our wartime Egyptian lockups as well fed.'

The Detective Chief Inspector moved on and went to talk to DI Sloane.

Marker made his way over to Sandrine who was in deep conversation with some of the journalists. She was handing out printed copies of Sir John's statement.

'Yes it's wonderful news,' she enthused.'We had no idea he was going to be released. Completely unexpected.'

Not so. Thought Marker.

'Sandrine, when this is over, how about a chat in the Lounge Bar. I've got some news for you.'

The detective took her nod, mid-gush, to be affirmative and said that he would see her there at five.

∞∞∞

DCI Bowen waited in the Chairman's outer office. She chose to sit next to Diana who spent the time refining the polish on her nails with a manicure board.

The two Bullings had taken the opportunity to get their stories straight. Sir John wanted to make it clear that no ransom had been paid, and Andrew was anxious to impress upon his father that he had been having a savage time. Both hadn't really listened to each other's fabrication but were equally relieved to at least get part of their story in line between them before they met the Police.

When the red light turned to green the Detective Chief Inspector assumed that it was time for her to go in. She knocked on the door and entered whilst Diana continued the detail of her nail polish. Andrew was sitting across the desk from his father which left just one vacant chair. Bowen took it without being invited.

'Tell me Andrew. How did you get kidnapped in the first place?'

Andrew remembered all his notes.

'I was grabbed off the street in Fulham, blindfolded and then handcuffed. I don't know where I was taken, but I think it must be in London somewhere as the journey was not longer than an hour.'

'So it was unexpected?'

'Yes, of course!' Andrew became indignant.

'Oh I just wondered as you left your apartment as if you were going on holiday. Very neat for someone who had just popped out to Fulham. And then you left this item behind.' Bowen held up the book she had found between the cushions of his sofa.'

'I wouldn't take that on a trip down the road.'

He replied uncomfortably wondering what evidence he might have left in the book's pages.

'Yes, but why would you tear out the pages for the two days prior to that when you actually went missing? It wasn't because of some notes that you had made for your trip was it?'

'Of course not. I just split some coffee on the pages that day and I tore them out.'

'And you didn't leave them in your dustbin did you?'

'Oh I can't remember. I probably put them in my pocket to throw away later.'

Bowen was unimpressed. She had asked forensics to see what detail they could make from the impressions that had been left on the remaining page. They had made out what looked like train times and certainly no coffee stains. Turning to Sir John she asked:

'And you didn't pay a ransom?'

'No I didn't.'

'Well what a miracle we have here. Your son arrives back like a biblical parable, looking not too worse for wear and clearly not having to fight his way out.'

Turning back to Andrew she asked:

'And how exactly where you released?'

'They took me on the tube until we got to Victoria.'

Bowen could see that she wasn't going to get much of the truth out of either of them, and thought she would leave before she got angry.

'I'm going to leave now and you two can sort out your stories. I don't believe either of you.'

And with that she picked up her briefcase, put Andrew's book back in it and closed the door behind her.

She wasn't the only person left mystified as she headed for her car. Sir John had never considered the suggestion that DCI Bowen was making, and Andrew was deeply concerned that a ransom hadn't been paid.

Chapter 14

Richard Marker got to the Bar first and ordered a beer, Sandrine came about five minutes later and ordered a Daiquiri. Tony mixed the drink, shaking the mixture as if he was frantically waving a Chelsea scarf at Stamford Bridge. He then served it in a cone shaped cocktail glass and the measure came within a quarter of an inch to the top. It was a perfect blend. Sandrine took the drink from the table and tapped the detective's glass.

'Cheers!'

'Salute' replied Marker. 'So we know that all Andrew had to do was to get in a cab with Archer and drive to Victoria Station.'

'How do you know that?'

'I followed him.'

'So that is where you went this morning. How did you know he's be released today?'

Sandrine asked even though she knew as well.

'I saw Archer had checked in last night and put two and two together and came up with four.' Marker took a swig of his beer. Sandrine looked thoughtful and then asked:

'Well now we have to chase the money. Do you have any ideas?'

'You're the one with the contacts Sandrine. What do you think? Are we still a team? We haven't slept together since Saturday.'

She smiled and squeezed his hand.

'Missing me?'

'A little.'

He replied, when he actually meant a lot, and that warm uninvited feeling somewhere low down inside came along again. Sandrine changed the subject.

'Well the money is somewhere around the Mediterranean and I bet it won't be too long before it appears in Andrew's account. I've got his London details.'

'How did you get those?' Marker asked.

'Because I'm good at it.'

Sandrine didn't want to reveal the data that she had taken over the months she had spent with Brooks in his apartment. And she didn't want to tell Marker that Brooks virtually ran Andrew's affairs as he was so bad with managing money. Brooks had set an account up for Andrew Bulling at the same branch as he had for his salary from The Adelphi. For convenience it was Barclays, the same bank that he used for his untaxed money in Jersey.

'And how might we get our hands on any of that money when it does appear in the account? Get him to write us a cheque?'

Sandrine looked at him and wondered at his naivety.

'Richard, not done this kind of work before?' She asked. Marker looked abashed.

'No...have you?'

Sandrine looked smug.

'I've set up an instruction mandate using Andrew's signature. I have complete control over what happens to that account and he hasn't a clue. After that I have arranged a joint account in both our names and from there I have a further offshore account in my own name. Simply put, money moves for the single account to the joint and then out to a single again.'

Marker was impressed with her dishonesty. Sandrine was working the system better than a corrupt bank cashier. He wondered at her chilling ingenuity.

Sandrine changed the subject again.

'I wonder what Bulling senior is saying to Bulling junior and vice versa?'

At that very moment, in a different part of the hotel, the Bullings were indeed in conversation, and it was getting heated.

'You've cost the family a huge amount of money, and we've lost control of the hotel. Three generations of hard work thrown away on rescuing you from a bunch of hoods wanting you to pay your drug debts. And now we have the police suggesting that you knew you were going to be kidnapped. Andrew, if this is some elaborate scheme of yours to get me to pay your drug debts...'

Bulling had adopted his usual aggressive stance and loomed over his son who was sitting nervously. Andrew stuttered a reply.

'I...I...that is...that's simply not true. I have no idea who these people were. I owe money to no one. Looking at those kidnap threats it seems to me that you paid only because you wanted to silence anyone who was going to prove that you killed my mother!'

Bulling went puce.

'How dare you!'

He shouted so loudly that Diana, seated in the outer office, put down her nail file, walked over to the outer door and closed it.

'Look you little poof, I've paid a personal fortune to get you out of this and as usual you're just ungrateful.'

Andrew looked deeply offended. How he hated his father. Couldn't he show some sympathy?

'I don't have to take this,' he said, and getting up opened the door.

Diana looked up from her manicure, and he walked out.

At that moment Sir John's private line rang and he picked it up. It was Hofer.

'I see,' said Bulling. 'So we have Andrew released and I have some change! Well that is good news in part.'

There was a pause and then he continued:

'Yes, I understand, you will tell me the story when you are back in London. Long distance lines aren't safe.'

∞∞∞

Meanwhile the Algerians had tied up the boat on the quay in Genoa as arranged. There were two cars waiting to pick them up with the gold. A little distance away was one of the Francisci brothers who was with a small group that were smoking next to a phone booth. He was not pleased to see only two suitcases. A third of the money had disappeared. When the two Algerians had reached the top of the steps he walked over to the tallest and slapped him hard on the face.

'*Dov'è il resto dell'oro?* Where is the rest of the gold?'

The sorry story was re-told.

'*Merde cazzo.*'

He kicked the Algerians and went over to the phone booth to speak to his brother in Nice.

It wasn't long before the message was passed to Jeddah and the Sheikh was informed. Al Mukta picked up his line to speak to Archer in Leeds.

Archer answered his direct line immediately.

'Archer.'

He nodded and listened.

'I see Your Excellency, not good news, but it's not a complete catastrophe as we have two thirds. Get it converted and put into the Cayman account we discussed. That should take three days. I suggest you tell your team that as they only retrieved two thirds they will only get paid two thirds of the fee.'

Al Mukta agreed and passed the message back to Nice. There they made a call to Genoa. After Alberto Francisci heard about the reduced fee he went over to the Algerians and kicked them both hard again.

They then loaded the suitcases and the two cars went off to the back streets of the old town. There they stopped outside a small shop front. The top half of the display window was blacked out, on display in the bottom half was some cheap pieces of jewellery. A sign read '*Giovanni Bascioni, Mediatore di Pegni*'. They all paraded through the pawnbroker's front shop to the back office where a large elderly man sat with a green jeweller's visor pulled down over his forehead. He was balding and obese.

'*Hai I dollari?*'

Francisi had seated himself opposite Bascioni and asked for the dollars.

'*Sì, nella cassaforte. Vediamo l'oro*'.

The broker put down his half smoked cigar and told him it was in the safe. He moved over to check the gold in the two suitcases that now lay open on the floor.

'Non è quanto concordato'.

Not the quantity agreed. Francisci knew that it was less than they thought, but the deal was done.

They were asked to leave the room whilst he opened his safe, and when they returned, he had counted out $200,000 in used notes waiting for collection on his desk. Francisci took the money and re-counted it, he then put it into three bags. $90,000 in two and the last bag held $20,000 as their fee. They then left the same way that they had come in and the two cars separated. The Algerians were bundled into the back seat of the Fiat with one of the gangsters pushing a gun into the larger of the two's ribs. The car took a sharp turn left and disappeared towards Caruggi, the slum area of the old town. They had been told how to deal with them. Francisci got into the front car and drove off at speed in the opposite direction to deposit the funds. Within half an hour the two money bags had been deposited at the *Monte dei Paschi* bank – one of the oldest in the country.

∞∞∞

After he had left the Chairman's office Andrew went straight over to see George Brooks in his office on the mezzanine floor. He knocked on the door. Brooks called out:

'Enter.'

Andrew turned the handle.

'Good God! Andrew it's you!' exclaimed Brooks.

The door closed and George jumped up and came over to embrace Andrew. He gave him a long hard kiss. Andrew kissed his face and neck. They held each other close before Andrew eventually pulled back.

They both sat down and Andrew told Brooks the whole story starting from the call he's received from Archer and the trip he'd made to Leeds.

'I am going to be rich! I'm getting all the proceeds from the ransom that my stupid father paid. It's been an outrageous and audacious plan. In one stoke I have my inheritance that I was never going to get and my father has been booted out of the hotel. He's such a miserable bastard. He only paid because he believed that had something more on him. He's a murderer you know. Should be dead really. I'd so like someone to kill him.'

Brooks took this all in. He'd wondered about the kidnap and a possible connection to Archer, but hadn't worked it all out. So Archer had engineered all this to finally wrestle control from Sir John Bulling.

'I have some other news for you.' Brooks said. 'I think you have a half-brother who has no idea you exist. His name is Eion Wildblood.'

'Eion who?' Andrew asked.

'Eion Wildblood, he's the illegitimate son of Patrick, the restaurant manager and your mother.'

Andrew looked stunned.

'You mean my mother was having an affair with a waiter?'

'Looks like it. What's more your half-brother seems to have taken a shine to my dear friend Sandrine Parte.'

'What! The Press Officer you've been banging in your spare time?'

'The very same.'

This was all too much for Andrew to take in at

once, and he fell back in his chair and looked at the ceiling. After a brief pause he said:

'How do you know this?'

Brooks went on to explain the story of the birth certificate that he's seen by accident in Sandrine's office.

'What's she doing with him then?' asked Brooks

'Probably fucking him, knowing her propensity for youth.'

'I'd like to meet him. We might have a lot in common, and we certainly have a lot to talk about.'

The next day BCI Bowen was looking through the transcripts of the two phone taps that she had placed. She had taken the hotel detective's advice and looked more closely at Adrian Archer. She regretted she hadn't got his line bugged earlier. It had taken too long to get approval for a tap on his private line in Leeds and at the same time she was challenged to persuade her superiors that a tap on Sir John Bulling's private line might be useful too.

'So Archer is talking to some Arab Sheikh, he says two thirds are safe, presumably the other third has gone missing, whatever is left is going to a Cayman account. Is this ransom money? Could be, or it could just be another of his many business transaction. Can we trace where the incoming call was from? No?... Shame.'

Bowen looked across at Sloane who had now taken off his headphones and was shaking his head. Bowen continued:

'And what about Bulling's call? About the same time from a geezer called Hofer. Who is he? He tells Bulling that he has some change, what does that mean? Is that the other third of a ransom? Maybe, maybe not. Too much of a coincidence I'd say. Half an hour between the calls in London and Leeds. Okay, let's find out who Hofer is. Start looking at companies that offer kidnap assistance.'

Sloane got up from the chair and was just about to leave to his desk when Bowen added:

'Find out about this Arab too. Get Leeds to go over what they know about Archer.'

After he had left the office, the Detective Chief Inspector picked up the phone and asked for The Adelphi.

'Richard Marker please...Hello?...Richard? It's

your friend DCI Bowen. Andrew Bulling is staying at the hotel at the moment is that true? Yes? Well I want to see him down here at West End Central tomorrow morning. Can you get hold of him and fix it? Thank you very much.'

∞∞∞

The day after, the Press was full of the story. The tabloids had printed large pictures of Andrew, glass in hand, taken at the Press Conference. *The Daily Mirror's* red-top headline read:

Adonis of the Adelphi Toasts Freedom!'

Well, thought Marker, he was an attractive boy when he was made up. He tossed the paper to one side and rang Andrew's room.

'Would you like me to take you over this morning? Good, let's take a taxi at nine. I'm sending up the papers for you to read, you've made the front page in quite a few.'

After putting down the phone he called the Hall Porter to save the best of the day's press and deliver it to Andrew Bulling's room.

At nine they met in the lobby and took a black cab over to the police station. At the desk they asked for DCI Bowen and were shown into an interview room. After a few minutes Bowen arrived with Sloane in tow.

'Hello Andrew. Good to see you too Mr Marker. Please take a seat.' They all settled down and Bowen continued: 'You see Andrew, we are very keen to arrest those that were behind your kidnap, and to do that we need your help.'

There then began a trawl through all the events that Andrew had learnt by heart to repeat and which he now explained again to the best of his memory. The police were looking out for inconsistencies. Little slips that weren't the same when told the second or third time. The interview took considerably longer than Andrew had expected. The focus was on the detail. What was the description of the room he was held in? What had he been given to eat? How did he eat it if he was handcuffed? What was the description of the room again? And so it went on. Marker reminisced to himself of the similarities of this interview with the many he had witnessed in Cairo with the Military Police. If they went over and over the same facts they would eventually get to an inconsistency and with that one loose screw the whole assembled fabrication would fall apart. After two hours Bowen looked as if she was going to wrap up the session.

'What's your bank account?'

She shot the question from nowhere and took Andrew by surprise.

'Why do you want to know that?' he asked.

'Oh it's just procedural. Is there a problem letting us have it?'

'Why do you need it?'

'We want to see that nothing irregular is happening with it.' Bowen replied.

'No, I don't mind.'

Andrew's mind raced. What did they suspect? He'd have to get hold of Archer and make some fast moves.

When Marker and Andrew left the hotel detective could see that he had much on his mind.

'Must have been quite a trial?'

Marker asked aware that the only trial Andrew had had in the last two weeks was probably how to change channels on the television.

'It was difficult and dangerous.'

Andrew gave his stock answer and looked out of the cab window. The last thing he wanted was this amateur sleuth on his tail as well.

After they had gone, DCI Bowen sat together with DI Sloane and they went over the tape recordings they had made.

'He clearly is an amnesiac and he was never in a room handcuffed to a radiator. He keeps changing the colour of the wallpaper for a start. You'd have thought that if he had been lying on the floor for two weeks he might have got that right.'

Sloane finished his coffee and looked at Bowen. The DCI replied:

'You're right – more holes than a string vest. Well if he's lying, he's in on it – and he's going to have to be paid, so we need to watch the bank.'

Sloane passed over the account and sort code that he'd been given. It was fortunate for Marker that he was there because as Andrew had told them, he had made a note too.

As they got up to leave Sloane turned to the DCI and said:

'Hofer – he works for London Risk Management Associates. He's a specialist in handling kidnaps.'

Bowen looked at Sloane and said:

'Ring up security at Heathrow and see if he's been flying anywhere recently. Customs will have a record. Thank God we still have exchange controls on the border.'

∞∞∞

When Andrew and Marker had got back to the hotel they had gone their separate ways. Marker heading for the restaurant, it was lunchtime after all. Andrew went back to his room and picked up the phone. He dialled Adrian Archer's direct line.

'Hello Adrian? It's Andrew. Yes, yes I think I did a good job at the interview. Look the police want to see my bank account. No, no I don't know why, but I've nothing to hide. Well not yet anyway. Look can we move the money to a friend's account? George maybe? It might be safer. Okay. Let me get you the details. No need? You have them already? Okay, let me talk to him, but go ahead. After that can you help with setting up a new account for me somewhere? I can't have it sitting in Brooks account for ever. You will? Great. Where? Caymans. Good.'

There was a pause:

'What's that?...It's less?... Don't tell me. Why?'

When he put the phone down he was incandescent. Stupidity had reduced his pay out by a third. He was determined to get that back even if he had to get someone to kill for it. He dialled George's direct line in his office. Brooks answered.

'George I need my payoff to go to your account. The police want to look over mine. For some reason Archer tells me he has your details. I trust you with my life, and this amount of money is my life. Will that work for you?'

Brooks thought this through.

'How much will it be?'

'Only about two hundred grand. A third of it has somehow disappeared'

'Shit.' He paused. 'Okay, that's still a huge amount. I will make a call to Jersey to warn them. What do you want to do with it after it hits my account?'

'Move it again, but it will take some days, Archer has to set it up.'

By midday the next day Hofer and Michael had made it back to Heathrow and were waiting in the baggage hall. Their flight had been delayed and now the luggage seemed to be taking an interminable time to come through. Hofer was getting anxious. He had split what remained of the gold into two cases and each one now only weighed eighteen kilos. It was well below the weight maximum but an unpleasant thought played in the back of his mind like the discordant violin in a school orchestra.

Exchange controls. He wondered about exchange controls. Were customs on the lookout for smuggled gold. They undoubtedly were, but would they look in their suitcases?

They were standing in front of a large round carousel. Most of the bags had already been ejected from the central conveyor belt and there were only a couple of other passengers waiting with them who had been on their flight. It was looking challenging. Passengers from the Munich flight were joining them and some of the bags from that flight were beginning to arrive. The carousel moved on slowly round in an even circle. Finally as Hofer was looking around in apprehension that some authority might appear, the two suitcases came into view.

Michael retrieved them both and put them on a trolley. They joined the queue to Customs and entered the inspection channel. Just as they cleared the stainless steel counters an officer appeared from behind a screen and asked them to stop.

'Which flight have you come on?'

He addressed them both.

'Geneva.' Hofer replied.

'Anything to declare?'

'No, we haven't.'

He looked at them both, then looked at the cases. Hofer stood still and looked the officer in the eye. The Customs man looked as if he wanted to open the bottom case, but just as he was indicating to Michael to put it on the counter a colleague appeared at the door.

'Joe, have you a moment? I've got a Jimi Hendrix type in here and I need you to witness the body search.'

The officer looked at the two men and slowly got out his chalk to mark both cases as cleared.

They only sighed in relief when they were well out of the terminal building and standing in the taxi rank. Hofer gave the office address and they were in central London within the hour. When he got to his office desk he asked Maureen to call Sir John Bulling in his office.

'Sir John? Can I come over to your office so that we can talk?'

The meeting was agreed.

∞∞∞

Richard Marker was thinking how he was going to follow where the ransom money was as it flew through the banking system. Sandrine was obviously one ahead of him with her joint account set-up. If the money reached there who knew where it would bounce to next. He knew that Andrew Bulling and Brooks both had accounts at Barclays in Jersey and it was the place to start. Maybe a search of her locked desk drawer might reveal more. He decided to pay a visit. Later that evening was as good as any. He waited for the Press Office to be locked up. Sandrine had left earlier. On a date he presumed. The cleaners had arrived and were working through the offices, it seemed an interminable amount of time was taken in emptying the bins and vacuuming the carpets. Eventually he heard them move on further up the corridor to the Card Index.

Taking his master key, he opened the door and then securely locked it close. He didn't put the lights on, there was still sufficient light coming through the blinds from the sunset. Making sure that he didn't touch more than he needed, he circled the desk, pulled out the chair and sat down. He tried the drawer. It was locked. He took out a small bunch of skeleton Lowe and Fletcher desk keys and started to try them all in rotation. The fifth key worked and the drawer slid open. He searched for Sandrine's red diary that he had seen her refer to occasionally. It fell open at the most used page, a list of press numbers. He turned to the back cover and found what he wanted. Taking out his camera he photographed the cover and the three preceding pages. He recognised Brook's bank account number and a list of several others at the same sort code.

As he was putting the diary back he saw Sandrine's desk calendar and like any detective, couldn't resist the opportunity to see if there was anything of interest in it. He turned to the day's date. There was the letter 'E' alongside a 19.30 time entry. And the name of the restaurant, Bligh's in Covent Garden. It was worth a visit he thought and slid the calendar back, locked the drawer and left. He grabbed his coat from the office and went off to see who she was meeting. He walked quickly up the Strand and crossed over to Covent Garden, turning the street corner he recognised the green canopy of Bligh's. When he got to the entrance he ignored the bouncer on the door and strode into a noisy smoked filled bar that heaved as if it was a transatlantic liner in a force eight gale. His eyes toured the room and he spotted Sandrine on a barstool with a very young man. It didn't take him too long to work out who that was.

He re-traced his steps and went back to the hotel. Jealousy once again arose in his emotions. He wasn't her keeper, but there such things as loyalty, trust, monogamy, faithfulness, moral-fibre, and possession. Possession above all else he reasoned. He wanted to possess her. But then the reality of his situation sunk in. He only possessed her for the time that he was with her, and even then that time was no real claim to ownership. Realising with a heavy heart that finally his deep emotions for Sandrine were not meaningfully reciprocated he was left to ruminate on his own melancholy future.

He opened his office door and was greeted by the familiar stale smell of ashtrays and stale dog ends. He cleared a space on his desk and immediately set about how he was going to manipulate the Jersey banking system. It was going to be easier than manipulating Sandrine Parte.

The Adelphi settled down for the night. Most of the arrivals were in, and the reception office noted only a few VIPs were left outstanding. Mr Van der Fleit had duly arrived, this time with his wife, and as indicated in their confirming letter he had come in late, at nine o'clock. They had reservations in the Restaurant and they were particularly keen to see the new Cabaret that had been arranged for ten thirty. The Adelphi's sprung dance floor that was laid out in the centre of the room was surrounded with a variety of beautifully set tables at which sat numerous glamourous women with elderly men in dinner jackets. The tables gleamed with the reflection of individual candelabra. Fine silver cutlery sat on starched white Irish linen. The napkins were the size of small table cloths and enthusiastic gastronomes eagerly tucked them into their collars before indulging in plates of caviar and lobster.

The dance floor itself was the best in London and at the appointed hour, The Adelphi Orchestra would move their gold chairs back onto the stage that had opened up behind them and the floor would be cleared.

At ten o'clock, Mr Mrs Van De Fleit had changed and arrived downstairs at the restaurant podium. They were immediately shown to their discrete table that had been especially set aside for them and laid for two. Van der Fleit tipped the *Maître d'* before they had sat down. In his book it was always wise to show the type of generosity he was capable of before a meal. The service ran so much better with waiters who focused on the potential for the size of an additional tip that might come with coffee. This logic being based on the largesse shown when the menu was presented at the beginning. They cast their eyes over the *Carte de Jour* and just as their first course of chilled *Vichyssoise* arrived the lights were dimmed for the entrance of The Adelphi Dancers.

The band struck up and six gorgeous girls took centre stage dressed in much so plumage that they might be mistaken for a flock of flamingos. Mr Van der Fleit looked quite overcome as he was seated close to the girls as they performed high kicks in unison. He had to gaze heavenward to appreciate the extraordinary angle the lead dancer was able to achieve with one straightened leg that seemed to stretch as far as the chandelier.

The routine finished to much applause and the soup plates were cleared. The main act for the evening was Mireille Mathieu, the French *chantreuse*. The Van der Fleit's main course was served. A Dover sole for her and a large Entrecote steak for him, cooked just off medium. After another large round of applause, The Adelphi Dancers took to the stage again. It was at this moment that Van der Fleit decided to swallow a large piece of his steak whilst once again moving his head to a ninety degree angle. The consequence was instantaneous. As the girls legs swung upwards, he fell downwards. Right off his chair. Choking.

It took a little while for anyone to realise that he had slid to the floor and was turning a flaccid blue. Suddenly the waiter who had been carefully serving the large tipper realised that his benefactor was no longer at the table and that his legs were appearing from under the tablecloth. He rushed over and tried to pick him up. Van der Fleit was considerably heavier than the diminutive Italian could lift and as his wife put her napkin to her face and screamed the girls in the dance troupe broke step. Pandemonium broke out and the orchestra struggled on for a few bars, but the girls stopped dancing and the stage lights went dim.

Van der Fleit was dying. The *Maître d'* reached for his podium phone and asked the operator for the hotel 'First Aider' to come to the restaurant. Mary was in the switchboard and looked for the name at the top of the First Aid list. It was Richard Marker. She rang his office on the wild chance that he might be there despite the late hour. He answered, and grabbing the first aid kit he kept for such emergencies ran up the stairs to the ground floor.

Pushing his way through, he entered the small coterie of concerned people that had gathered around Van der Fleit. He noticed that the waiter was standing close, looking shocked but with the bill and a pen in his hand. This presumably on the hope that if Van der Fleit made it he was going to sign an even bigger gratuity. Holding his head whilst stuffing napkins under his head was another familiar face, the Night Manager, and in the background ushering some screens into place was Patrick Wildblood.

Marker took control. He pushed everyone away and manhandled Van der Fleit into a standing position. His head lolled to one side. He was gone. Marker placed his arms around Van der Fleit's torso and stood behind him. Holding his hands together and pushing his thumbs into the diaphragm of the sagging body he gave a stiff pull upwards. Nothing happened. The res taurant guests had gone quiet apart from Mrs Van der Fleit's sobs. He gave another huge tug upwards. Suddenly a large piece of meat flew out of the Boardman director's mouth. Van der Fleit took his first breath in several minutes and slowly regained his colour.

There was a mild round of applause. Mr Van der

Fliet was led away by the ambulance crew that how now arrived so late that Marker was surprised they weren't wearing pyjamas. The Adelphi Orchestra struck up again and the rest of the guests danced the night away. The briefest of interludes, however dire, were not going to disturb their night of fun. Marker went up to the Lounge Bar, had a stiff brandy and decided to park the Jersey banking system until tomorrow. He took the night bus home.

The next day Marker was called to the Chairman's office where he was surprised to see Van der Fleit and Sir John Bulling sitting together.

'Come in, come in.'

Bulling warmly welcomed Marker as if he was a long lost relative.

'Mr Van der Fleit has been telling me how you saved his life last night. Well Done. Charles, what do you say?'

'Thank you so much Richard. What on earth did you do?'

'The Heimlich manoeuvre sir. It's a well-known action when people are choking, which is what you certainly were.'

'Well you saved my life. Now tell me Richard, can I save yours? I understand from Sir John that our staff people have laid you off with the takeover personnel plan. Would you consider staying on? On an increased salary of course? We can't have people like you who make a difference, leaving.'

Marker was darkly amused by this turn of events.

'Let me think about it. But put it this way, I'd like to stay on until I have tidied up one or two loose ends I'm currently working on. It may take me a month or so at least.'

'Stay as long as you want to Richard. You have your job back and you can leave when you want.'

Marker got up to shake everyone's hand and left the office walking with his head a little higher than when he had arrived.

Chapter 15

Andrew Bulling was sitting in the station café at Waterloo and was engrossed in conversation with George Brooks. He had agreed to meet him there as George had come up from seeing friends on the south coast. They were surrounded by the guides to Rome that the travel agent had passed over to them.

'So it's the Eden Hotel? I'm sooo excited...'

Andrew could sound more camp than a scout outing. George continued showing Andrew the hotel brochure:

'I've upgraded to the best suite. The hotel is part of the same marketing consortia that we are in so we are going to be especially looked after. I've arranged a double and single adjoining. The Italians don't look kindly on queers like us.'

'I don't think anyone takes kindly to us except the little old lady that lives below me in Fulham.'

'It's because they are all Catholics and believe the Church has turned its back on sodomy.' Brooks suggested.

'Like you turn you turn around for me?' Andrew replied.

Brooks smiled at the analogy.

Andrew's expression changed to something darker.

'My father's told me he's cutting my allowance and that I have to get a regular job. He suspicious that I was somehow involved with the kidnap. That stupid policewoman took a certain line of questionning. Of course I denied it. I'm so angry. I'd like to put the frighteners on him. He'd be better off dead.'

There was an ominous silence whilst Brooks considered the point.

'You haven't met Eion Wildblood yet have you? When he finds out that your father killed your mother wouldn't he be angry too? He's had a pretty tough life. I wonder if he was left any money by your mother and if he was, who has it?'

'My bloody father, I bet, conniving bastard. I know that my mother left me money as I had it when I was eighteen, he was the executor. But what if he couldn't find or even know who

Eion was? Maybe he just kept the money.'

Brooks said that he would look up the Will at the District Probate registry. They finished their coffee and separated. Brooks took a stroll back over Waterloo Bridge and on to the hotel. Andrew, meanwhile, took the tube to the pub at the Boltons in Earl's Court.

When he got back to the Adelphi Brooks made a few calls and sent one of the page boys over to the probate office for the last Will and Testament of Cynthia Bulling *nee* Hampton. By the late afternoon he had the copy in his hand. It was dated 17 July 1947, and in it there were various bequests and towards the end there was a sum of £1000 to named as Patrick Eion Hampton. As anticipated the Executor was John Bulling who had noted that he could find no trace of this person and the probate officer had marked it as 'undistributed'. The money had then been given back in proportion to the other bequests. John Bulling had taken three quarters of it.

Brooks smiled and picked up the phone to Philip Wildblood.

'Wildblood? it's George Brooks. I remember that we turned your son down for a job. Nepotism or something like that. Look, with the change of ownership Broadman say that employing family members is now in order. Can I see him one more time?'

And so it was arranged. An appointment was made for Eion Wildblood to come over to see George Brooks on the pretext of a job with some interesting prospects.

'So Hofer came in from Geneva?' DCI Bowen cast a look at Sloane.

'I wonder where he's been.'

Sloane looked at his notes.

'Went out with nothing and came back with nothing, as far as we can tell. But here's something interesting. BEA say he flew out to Nice with a Michael Sheer, then changed his return flight back from Geneva. He also booked two suitcases as excess luggage.'

Bowen considered this.

'Nice is near to Monte Carlo, anything can happen there without the Monaco gendarmerie knowing about it. Also check out our mates in the *Surete* to see if there has been any recent excitement on the Riviera. Mind you the crooks down there are killing each other on a daily basis. You can't buy an ice-cream in Marseilles without someone stealing the cornet. Have a look with Interpol at Geneva too. With a bit of luck something happened there, I fancy a short break on the lake.'

Sloane left the DCI to her file on Sir John Bulling and went off to run up a large international phone bill.

∞∞∞

Hofer arrived at Sir John's office just before eleven and found Diana Spurling finishing the application of a new strawberry coloured nail varnish to her left hand. He put a large suitcase on the floor.

'He's on the phone,' she said, 'take a seat.'

And pointed to the row of three chairs that sat opposite her desk. After three minutes the red light on the top of the door frame turned green. Diana pushed the intercom switch.

'Mr Hofer is here to see you.'

She looked at Hofer and cast her eyes towards the Chairman's door. Hofer took this as a signal to enter. He picked up the case and knocked.

'Enter.'

'Good morning Sir John. How are you?'

'A lot poorer after your expedition.'

Uninvited, Hofer took a seat.

'Well I have some good news. Andrew is presumably safe and as well as can be expected? I read the papers.'

'He's an ungrateful shit if you must know.'

Replied Bulling. Hofer ignored the profanity. He was used to dealing with clients who had preferences for the venacular.

'Well the handover was not without its excitement.' Hofer continued after a brief pause: 'Someone got shot, the kidnappers panicked and left the last suitcase in our hands.'

'I hope it wasn't anyone you knew?'

Bulling feigned concern.

'No it was a passing fisherman I think. Entirely unnecessary. But the good news is that I have part of the gold ransom here. It's yours to deal with how you like.'

It was a windfall indeed, and one that Bulling was certainly not expecting. It might come in useful as a first deposit in his new off-shore investment company.

'So it all ended well then?' Bulling asked,'I assume that you will send me your account and expenses?'

'I've already left it on Diana's desk.'

Hofer then stood to leave and extended his hand. Bulling shook it firmly and clapped him on the back and as an afterthought added:

'Well done. Well done. Can't tell you how grateful I am.'

As Hofer left, Bulling passed Diana's desk.

Full of hubris his face puffed up and he gave a broad smile and exhaled:

'Diana, can you ask DCI Bowen to come over?'

When he inhaled he then smelt the strong odour of acetone but decided to ignore it. He was in too good a mood to shout at her this morning.

Now that Richard Marker was fully employed again, and on what appeared to be his terms, he was considerably more relaxed. So relaxed in fact that he had taken off his jacket, loosened his tie and was perusing the new Adelphi *Leons* menu that had been printed that day. His drab office also seemed to have taken on a new atmosphere, although that was only perceptible to Marker himself.

He put the menu down having decided on the avocado shrimp salad to start and then the *Tornedos Rossini* cooked *a point* for the main course. All to be followed with a *Peche Melba*. The Escoffier classic named after the Australian opera singer and now recreated by The Adelphi *patissier* in a more brilliant form as *Bombe Dame Nellie*.

He then looked at the timetable of Jersey flights which he had collected that morning from the travel agent. He picked up the phone and dialled.

'Hello, it's Richard Marker, we talked this morning. I'd like to book a day return to Jersey for Thursday this week please. Yes... Thank you. I will drop off the cheque this afternoon.'

He'd almost come to a conclusion as to how he was going to handle the financial opportunity that lay before him. But he had to determine one more thing. Was Sandrine counting him in or out of <u>her</u> plan? This was important because, despite himself he was still emotionally involved. So after the call he dialled the Press Office.

'Are you free Sandrine? Good. I will come straight on up.'

He reached the office within a few minutes and

walked straight in.

'Morning Sandrine. Mind if I close the door?'

'Be my guest. I hear you are quite the hero after last night.'

'Well, kind of you to say so. It's the Heimlich manoeuvre, I'd like to try it on you one day.' Marker smiled.

'As long as it doesn't hurt.' Sandrine smiled back. Marker continued:

'Sandrine. I was thinking about what you said last night in the bar. If, with your madcap scheme, you can get our hands on the money that is floating around. Are you cutting me in?'

Sandrine had thought about this before and she most certainly wasn't. Her plan was to get the money and run, she didn't want to sit and nursemaid Broadman Developments through slicing the hotel in half and making one part into a department store.

'Well of course, my sweet. How were you thinking we'd divide it considering that I'm the one with all the bank details and all you've done is follow the trail?'

Marker felt a pang of anger. He was hurt. This was not what he had wanted to hear.

'Remember that I know things about you Sandrine that could make your time here difficult.'

He instantly regretted the threat.

'Blackmail Richard? That's beneath you.'

But Sandrine wondered what it was that he might know. She hoped it wasn't anything to do with her dishonesty. She decided that if she was going to dip into whatever the proceeds were she would have to move quickly. Too quickly for the detective to catch up with her. She bit the end of her pen.

'OK it's a deal. You let me know when you think the money is moving and I will manage the bank. I will let you know when it's in my account. That way I will have control.'

If Sandrine actually got her hands on the cash, Richard could see she certainly would and wondered how that would complicate the issue.

'OK Agreed. Dinner tonight?'

She shot him a look that could pierce steel.

'After you leaned on me? 'Fraid not. I've got a date.'

Marker left the office wondering if it was with Eion Wildblood again. He bet it was.

DCI Bowen came over to see the Chairman later that afternoon, with DI Sloane in tow. After the pleasantries Sir John got down to the matter he wanted to discuss.

'Well Detective Chief Inspector, you've been very concerned that I've been paying a ransom for the release of Andrew. It is true to say that I have been in negotiation with the kidnappers and I have employed a specialist in the field to help me. I didn't want to involve you and your associates. Questions of security as you can imagine.' Bulling cast a glance at Sloane and continued: 'because it may have stymied the delicate plan that had been put in place.'

'And what plan might that be?' Asked Bowen.

'Well, we wanted the kidnappers to see we had the ransom which was agreed to be in gold bars, but we didn't want to hand it over. So we misled them. They saw the gold, released Andrew, and a diversion was created that frightened them off. They panicked and left us with the gold.'

With that Bulling walked over to the suitcase and opened it. The brilliance of £100,000 in gold bars lit the room with amber.

'So you see, no ransom was paid at all. The kidnappers had nothing. So I think that I have resolved the whole ghastly business rather well. I might even now buy back my shares!'

'And where did all this take place Sir John. I hope it wasn't abroad with all the strict exchange controls that are in place?'

'Well gold isn't a currency Inspector.'

'Detective Chief Inspector' Bowen reminded him. Bulling continued to gush.

'Well I'm not too sure, my specialist was handling that and I have a confidential agreement with him that I can't repeat any of the details that I haven't witnessed myself.'

Bulling was wondering if his priggishness was leading him into a hole.

'Well maybe I can tell you Sir John. Your specialist is a man names Hofer who works for London Risk Management. A kidnap specialist insurance company. We've been talking to Interpol today and we think it all took place in the old port at Menton. There was a bit of a kerfuffle we understand. An innocent bystander was shot dead. We don't know who was involved yet, but a bit unfortunate if that was your friend Hofer I'd say.'

Bulling blanched.

'I don't know anything about that at all.'

'Neither do we, yet. But I'm sure we are going

to find out. I'm glad you got your money back, but I hope it didn't cost any lives. It might make you and your scheme an accessory to murder.'

Bowen looked at Sloane and they made for the door.

'Good bye Sir John. As usual, we will be in touch.'

Bulling sat back in his chair and finally felt the fool that he was. Too smug to think things through. And what the hell had Hofer been up to in Menton? Bulling hoped it was just an awful coincidence, but he did have some of the gold back. Better not to ask too many questions.

The two police detectives made their way back to West End Central.

'Well what do you make of it all?' Asked Sloane.

Bowen turned in her seat:

'I think Bulling hasn't much of a clue about what happened. He wouldn't have invited us in if he knew what went on. He just wanted to stick our noses in it. Looks as if Hofer and his sidekick were involved somehow, but professional kidnap negotiators don't play with guns. Just not worth it. The French police have said that they think the guy got shot as he was interrupting a drugs deal. So nothing to do with a gold exchange. Apparently happens all the time. I'm going to give it a rest, although Hofer might have something for us on the kidnapper's identity. It's worth bringing him in on the pretext of smuggling gold.'

When they got back to the station they sent out a car to pick up Hofer at his office and bring him back for questioning. The car arrived there just as he was leaving for the evening and by the time he got to West End Central it was gone six thirty.

'We won't keep you long.'

The DCI had introduced herself and her colleague, Sloane. Hofer looked coolly urbane despite his exciting past forty eight hours. He was used to Mr Plod calling him in after the event.

'How can I help you Chief Inspector?'

'We know that you are on the Bulling kidnap and your client has taken the trouble to call us over to see a pile of gold he's sitting on. He tells us you have gave it to him having met the kidnappers and tricked them into leaving it with you. Why they did that only you know. So far. What I know is that you came in from Geneva last night and didn't make a Customs declaration.'

'You've not brought me in here to discuss my

taxes surely?'

Hofer gave Bowen a steely eye. The stupidity of Bulling made no impact on Hofer's equilibrium. Bowen could see that she was dealing with an experienced interviewee who if pushed would simply give no comment. She decided that she didn't want to go gardening by beating around the bush.

'OK Hofer. This is the dope. We want your help in getting to the kidnappers. For what you can give us we'll forget that we suspect you took a pleasure boat trip around Menton harbour and all the fuss you might have caused our French colleagues in the saucepan hats.'

Hofer considered his options. Now that Andrew Bulling was released and he had his fee, it was going to be better to cooperate with these two jokers rather than play the martyr at the stake.

'Alright. I can give you what I know, if you're going to forget my European holiday. But I don't know much.'

Hofer gave his opinion and circumnavigated any area that might have caused some embarrassment. DCI Bowen filled in a number of pages from her spiral notebook. It was fortunate that she was a fast writer.

'So to wrap this up' Bowen asked: 'You think

the kidnap threat was real enough, but we aren't looking for any East Enders, the accent was false. In France you were dealing with North Africans. You think Bulling only paid up because he was scared they had something on him, and you can't be certain that they didn't.'

She paused to think:

'So it's a French criminal gang involved for sure, and someone there who had United Kingdom connections. You think they headed for the Italian border. Shame. This is a professional job and we will have great difficulties dealing with the *Carabinieri* there.'

Then out of the blue she asked Hofer:

'Do you know an Adrian Archer? Director of Broadman and general all round dodgy bloke?'

'Never heard of him.' Hofer replied.

After they finished the interview and Hofer was on his way, Bowen turned to Sloane:

'Interesting?'

Sloane looked laconic.

'Well interesting for what he didn't say. He never talked about the circumstances of the Victoria Station handover for one.'

'Well,' considered Bowen 'He wasn't there, and I didn't ask him.'

'Perhaps you should have, his mate was.' Replied Sloane.

Bowen thought he was getting a bit too clever for her liking. Sloane continued:

'I think they cocked it up in France and I don't understand how or why the kidnappers let Andrew go.'

They both reflected on that and Bowen eventually said:

'Young Bulling said they took him on the tube and then released him. On the tube there is no way to check that the handover was going to plan. Did they just chuck him off the tube at Victoria? Maybe they took him up to the station and made a call from a phone box. That is assuming he was actually with someone. If he wasn't it would mean that he was in on all this and didn't need a chaperone.'

She walked around her desk and sat on its edge.

'Maybe he didn't take the tube at all, that's very risky considering his picture has been in the Press.'

Sloane looked up from his notes:

'Maybe they 'chauffeur drove' him.'

Bowen looked puzzled.

'Andrew Bulling's story so far is pretty inconsistent but before we put the squeezers on him let's go back to Archer. That taped call of his puts him under significant suspicion. Maybe he cooked up this little scheme with Andrew Bulling. And we need to see Hofer's man at Victoria. Let's hope he's not got an attack of amnesia.'

Sloane made up his notes and with that they decided to call it a day. DCI Bowen caught the bus to the Elephant and Castle in the hope of seeing her children before they got to bed. There was little chance of that as it was already well past nine. Sloane put on his overcoat and wandered off for a drink at his local pub.

Sandrine Parte was really enjoying herself in the darkest corner she could find at her local in Chiswick. Sitting opposite her looking elegantly cool was young Eion Wildblood. She had just got the drinks in.

'Cheers!' She tipped her Manhattan against his pint. 'What news?'

Eion looked across the smoke filled room and offered Sandrine a Rothmans.

'I've had a call from The Adelphi, Mr Brooks has asked me to come over for an interview.

Some change of policy with the takeover has opened up an opportunity.'

Sandrine's heart sank. It was going to be difficult to have a relationship with Eion if that happened.

'Are you going to go?'

'Nothing lost nothing gained.'

He flicked the ash from his cigarette and leant over to give Sandrine a kiss. She placed her hand on his cheek and flicked her tongue inside his mouth.

'I'd be a bit worried about that. It might make it difficult.'

'Don't worry,' he said: 'I won't take it unless it's buckets of money.'

'Let's go back to my place when we've finished these. It's almost closing time.'

Sandrine took his hand and placed it on her thigh very close to the top of her leg. Eion could feel the taughtness through her short skirt.

When they got to her apartment, Sandrine went to the bedroom whilst Eion made two small cups of espresso coffee. She came up behind him in the kitchen dressed only in a French negligee. He slid his hands behind and felt the round nakedness of her bottom. She kissed his neck and he turned around. He held her head in his hands and kissed her deeply.

'Coffee?' She asked when he let her go.

'I'm too hot for that.'

She led him to the bedroom, stripped him naked and then lay him on her bed. She then took her dressing gown cord and tied both his hands to the grill of her bedstead. It was an old trick of hers. She enjoyed this part the best. Slowly working her way down his taut muscled torso she licked his nipples and then took each one in turn and bit it. Eion murmured in delight. Then she moved further down feeling for his hardness. Gripping it firmly she slowly stoked it and put it into her red lipped mouth. Satisfied that she hadn't gone too far she then sat astride his chest and moved backwards until he was deep inside. It didn't take long for her orgasm, and she assumed that he wouldn't be far behind.

The next day Brooks had called Andrew Bulling and told him that he had arranged a meeting with Eion and could he make it that morning? Andrew was still bleary eyed and enjoying the luxury of an Adelphi bedroom rather than the dodgy double bed he had at his place, but he was enthusiastic to meet this new family member and see what he was like.

At ten-thirty Eion Wildblood was in the hotel lobby and the Enquiry Clerk called Brook's office.

'Send him up.' Brooks asked.

Eion arrived looking fresh and well presented as he had left Chiswick early to get back to his place to change.

'Eion, this is Andrew Bulling, you might have read about him in the Press.'

Eion looked a little surprised but smiled and shook Andrew's hand. He had certainly read all about the kidnapping and was astonished to meet the victim and knew that he was The Adelphi Chairman's son.

'Well, good to meet you sir' he said, 'you must have had a horrible ordeal.'

'It wasn't great.'

Andrew replied and indicated that Eion should take a seat and they all sat around Brooks' desk.

'Coffee?'

'A small one please.'

Brooks poured out the cups from a silver coffee pot that had been delivered with the best china.

Brooks felt the moment was right to address what he had found out from his evening foray into the Press Office.

'Tell me Eion, I think you may have just found out that you mother was Cynthia Hampton.'

Eion was surprised at this opening.

'Yes, that's true, I have, but what has that got to do with this job opportunity you told me about on the phone?'

Brooks looked across at Andrew and then said:

'I said opportunity, actually, nothing about a job.'

Eion looked puzzled. Brooks continued:

'Cynthia Hammond had an affair with your father and you were the result. We think that she met him whilst she was working as a model on an event here at The Adelphi. At the same time she must have met her future husband as well, because I am not sure if you know that your mother married Andrew's father, the Chairman of The Adelphi. Sir John Bulling. Or just plain Mr Bulling when they were together.'

Eion looked very shocked.

'No, I certainly didn't.' Eion replied.

Brooks continued:

'Clearly the relationship with your father continued for some time after the wedding, because before you were born, along came Andrew.'

Brooks paused and grandly swept his arm across to silently introduce Eion's new relative.

'This makes you and Andrew step-brothers. Now sadly, your mother died shortly after you were born and we aren't sure of her exact circumstances at that time.'

Andrew then took on the story:

'You see Eion I am a few years older than you and I do have a vague recollection that our mother was not happy in her relationship with my father. He's an egotistical bully and certainly didn't deserve someone as sweet as I remember her to have been.'

Eion was floored. This was an awful lot to understand.

'Do you know how our mother died?' Andrew asked.

Eion leant forward.

'I was told it was some kind of accident.'

'Yes, a motorbike accident with my father in charge of the bike. We aren't so sure it was an accident.'

Brooks and Andrew looked earnestly at Eion.

Andrew continued:

'I'm sure that my father must have known our mother was pregnant and knew it couldn't have been him. Perhaps she might have even told her. At the time the family was already in some turmoil as there was another hostile bid being made for the business.

If she was threatening to leave him, or indeed pursue a high profile divorce it would have been a very awkward situation. On top of that she had a number of Adelphi shares that if sold would have tipped the balance of ownership over to the hostile bidders.

That is why when the accident happened it was at a very convenient time and offered a solution to both the problems. Her infidelity and the prospect of her selling her shares.'

Eion looked non-plussed. Brooks then continued:

'Now, as a consequence of all this, we think Andrew's father began to wonder about the legitimacy of his other son, Andrew. Ever since he was a child Andrew has been rejected and even now has been denied his rightful inheritance.'

Andrew took in a breath and glanced at Brooks. Turning to Eion he said:

'Well, I believe that my father deliberately

killed our mother and staged the motorbike accident.'

Brooks then took a document from his desk drawer.

'This is the last Will and Testament of your mother Eion. In it there are several bequests amongst which there is £1000 for you. You've never received this because the executor notes that he had no means of discovering who you were. As a consequence your inheritance was given back to the main beneficiary. Do you know who that was?'

Eion sat with his mouth slightly open. Brooks continued:

'No? Well both the executor and the benficiary was Sir John Bulling, Andrew's father. He took the lot; lock, stock, and barrel. Eion, you are owned £1000 and twenty years interest. Do you want to have it?'

Eion regained his composure.

'This is all an amazing story. I had absolutely no idea.'

He stood up, took Andrew's hand shook it then embraced him. They stood together in silence. Stepping back he went on:

'I never knew I had any family except my grandmother in Ireland...' He was close to tears. Brooks offered his white hankerchief from his top pocket.

'Of course I want to have it!' He shouted.

'Well Eion.' Brooks carried on: 'We have a plan to get that money you are owed.'

Eion became suddenly animated and ignoring Brooks looked at Andrew.

'You mean the Chairman of The Adelphi murdered our mother? It's just incredible!'

'Not only murdered her, but failed to pass over your inheritance that she left for you.' Brooks reminded him, 'you are owed a considerable amount of money that as executor of the will John Bulling should have properly distributed. But he didn't and he simply sliced it up giving himself the majority.'

'That is outrageous.'

Eion's face had gone from pale to blush as he read the probate document for himself.

'I can see what you are thinking,' said Andrew. 'I've been treated in the same way, I've been locked out of the family business since he took another wife. I think our mother loved us both dearly and I believe it was her intention to leave my father maybe even move in with your father. I don't know if that was the case. If it was it would have been a huge embarrassment to him and that is why he killed her.'

'Why don't we tell the Police?' Eion asked.

Brooks replied:

'We don't have the evidence and the Coroner's court have already ruled that the motorbike accident was just that. An accident:'

'I'm going to confront him then!'

Eion who had momentarily sat down stood up again full of Irish anger. Brooks beckoned for him to sit down again. Andrew continued:

'Well, we have a plan. My father doesn't know you, but he knows both of us.' Andrew pointed at Brooks. 'Brooks and I are very close friends. We have had an idea that is considerably helped not only by your appearance out of the blue, but also because you have suffered similarly.'

Andrew then felt it necessary to embellish the injustice that he felt. He embarked on a fabrication about the circumstances of his kidnap.

'As you know I have been recently held at the hands of merciless kidnappers. My father reluctantly agreed to pay for my release, but he planned to put my life at considerable risk in an effort to keep back the ransom money. He devised a scheme where at the point of handover the kidnappers were tricked.

I was being held in London and was told on the day of my release that I was to be moved to a handover point at Victoria Station. As far as I can work out, halfway through the journey, there was a significant breakdown in communication. I had already been bundled into a car and held with my head on the floor under the back seat. We had been driving for a good half hour when they stopped the car to make a phone call and I heard them say they couldn't get confirmation. I assumed that things were going wrong. Then they said they would drive back to 'sort me out'. I assumed that meant they were going to kill me. Luckily chance was on my side and I saw an opportunity to escape.'

Andrew stopped to pick up his cup of coffee and took a sip. Placing the cup back on Brooks' desk he continued:

'I could just see through the rear passenger window that we were very close to Victoria. As the thug who had his foot on my neck had got out of the rear of the car when they made the phone call, I had a chance to make a run for it. He opened the rear door to get back in and I launched myself at his legs, pushed him over and ran the few steps to the entrance of the Victoria tube station entrance. They ran after me of course, but I was too quick and lost them in the underground subway. Knowing that there was some kind of handover on the concourse I decided to run to the most public of all places. Under the clock. It's an international meeting place and full of people. They couldn't touch me there. As they came out of the tube exit after me they stopped. They saw I had been luckily spotted by one of my father's negotiators.'

Eion was astounded.

'Well that is very brave, and none of this is in the Press!'

'No, because Sir John has friends in high places in the newspaper world and didn't want it known that he had put the handover at risk simply to get his money back. He's told me to say nothing and just say I was released without any trouble otherwise he will make my life worse than it already has been. So you see, he's quite ruthless. He couldn't care less about me. I was lucky to escape with my life.'

Eion, being a young man and somewhat unworldly, (despite an excellent track record in bed) swallowed the story like a hungry priest on the last day of Lent.

'So...' Brooks picked up the story. 'Andrew needs to start a new life after this terrible ordeal and his father won't help him. He needs money and his father now has lots of it. Some of that money is yours. Andrew wants to frighten him as much as he's been frightened. He wants to scare him rigid. So will you help him get some of the money that was never handed over? Would you like to help us do that? You can get your inheritance back and more.'

Eion liked that very much, and as a consequence played right into their hands.

'Good.' said Andrew. 'Let's meet this afternoon. Here's the address of a pub I know in Earl's Court...'

As he left the office he felt a rush of exhilaration. His London experience was turning out to be exciting and perhaps dangerous. He'd met a long lost member of his family, he was on his way to gaining an inheritance and he'd had some of the best fucks of his life.

Archer was finalising the arrangements for Andrew's payoff. It was deserved, but unfortunate that the old man had got his hands on some of it. Still Bulling junior hadn't had to do too much for it, and after the expenses there was still ten per cent in it for him too.

He picked up his direct line, and as he did so he heard an unfamiliar 'click'. He put it down again. He then lifted it one more time. The same thing happened. He then picked up the main switchboard line and this time heard nothing. His Army intelligence training hadn't been completely forgotten. A simple phone tap he thought, and then wondered how long it had been there and what he had said. None of the kidnap threats had been made from that line, but he had spoken to the Sheikh. He was going to have to be careful.

He went to his secretary's desk outside and lifted the receiver on her direct line. There was no click. He took the extension phone from his meeting table and plugged the cable direct into her socket and with the long lead took it back to his desk. He picked up the phone again. No click. He dialled.

'Your Excellency, it's Adrian. I'm calling on a new line, please take the number, same dialling code but the last four digits are 2467, not 2400 which was my previous direct line. How is the transfer of cash going? Good, as arranged, we are going to put it into George Brooks account at Barclays Jersey. When will that be?...The day after tomorrow? Excellent. No I'm not sure what happens to it then. That's Andrew Bulling's problem, are we secure that the transfer can't be traced from the Hungarian bank? Good, good. Speak soon.'

He then dialled Andrew Bulling at The Adelphi.

'Andrew, its Archer. Your transfer will hit Brooks account the day after tomorrow. Do with it what you will, it will be our last communication on this subject.'

Andrew said he understood and replaced the receiver. He would need some of the money for Rome and he would have to make himself scarce if their plan succeeded. He decided to go straight downstairs to see George Brooks.

'George!'

He had excitedly burst into his office unannounced and was surprised to see the hotel detective sitting opposite Brooks.

'Oh! I'm sorry, I wanted to speak to you about Rome, I'll come back later.'

Marker had been discussing first-aid training, but this intrusion by Andrew Bulling was revealing. The detective showed no reaction to Brooks and continued his monologue about how all the First Aid boxes were being perpetually robbed of Elastoplast. As he was getting near the end of his piece he pulled out his handkerchief.

'It's hot in here.'

Marker mopped his brow and moved behind Brooks who was still seated at his desk.

'Mind if I open the window?'

'Be my guest' replied Brooks.

After he left the office he knew he had to find out more. He had opened the office window as he had already decided he would get under Brooks' opened window from the flat roof so that he could listen to the urgent conversation that Andrew Bulling obviously wanted, and soon.

Happily and rather obliquely, part of his responsibilities was pest control, a job that encompassed vexatious humans and all other creatures that set up habitation in The Adelphi. It was one of those thankless tasks that didn't fit comfortably in anyone's remit, so it had been passed to him in the belief by senior management that as the Security department did little enough, there was space for Marker to hunt mice.

This gave him the opportunity to be in any part of the building on the pretext of vermin eradication. There had been a considerable number of pigeons nesting in the low alcoves of the walls above the restaurant roof and new preventative netting had been put in place. All the mezzanine offices had windows that looked out on to the same roof. Marker was about to scramble out of the access door and position himself just below Brook's window to wait for Andrew's arrival back in the office. But as he put his key in the access door Otto Klimp opened from the other side.

'Going out for a fag?'

He smiled at the hotel detective.

'Too much time on your hands Richard, you should get yourself a proper job. I'm looking for a boiler-hand at the moment, all that heat in the Engine room would help you sweat some of this off.'

And he took another poke at Marker's stomach.

'Look you fat arsed footplate stoker, just fuck off. I'm checking the pest control work. What were you doing?'

'Looking over the air handling unit. I'm just going back out but I have to get a part from the basement'

Marker calculated that he may have a spare five minutes and to get the Engineer out of his way he made a suggestion:

'Do you fancy a smoke?'

Marker calculated that he would need ten uninterrupted minutes to listen under Brooks' window. If he held the German up now before he left for the basement he would have enough time. He took the packet of Rothmans from his pocket and flipped the pack open.

Klimp looked encouraged by the filter tips.

'Ok – let's have a quick drag.'

The engineer pushed the access door open again and they were out on the roof some twenty yards from Brooks' window.

'So this kidnap lark has been a story.'

Klimp took a pull on his cigarette and continued:

'I've had to install a new safe in the Chairman's office. He's got a suitcase of gold bars in there. I reckon that he never paid a ransom. Conned them out of releasing his son without parting with the goodies. Clever bastard.'

Marker took this all in without showing any surprise, but he wondered how that had happened. Klimp bade him well for the rest of the day and the detective moved over towards Brooks' open window. As he went he checked the pigeon netting, pulling it here and there, tugging it taught in places. Finally he busied himself under the office window on the pretext of adjusting the net tension and as the window was some five feet from the ground he was certain he couldn't be seen. Andrew Bulling had already returned and was in animated conversation with Brooks.

'So the money will hit your account, and then it moves to the Caymans.'

Marker couldn't quite make out the muffled reply. Then Brooks spoke again.

'So we are all on for Rome?'

'Yes, that's fine. I may have to lie low if our plan to put the frighteners on the old man goes ahead, so that may push the date out.'

The voice was getting louder and Marker was sure that Andrew Bulling was heading towards the window.

'Lousy view you've got here George. Looks out over the air handling plant.'

Andrew leaned on the window sill and looked across the flat space. He lit a cigarette and dropped the match on the detective's head. Marker stayed pressed against the wall and waited. After a couple of minutes Andrew stood back and finishing his cigarette flicked his dog end at Marker's feet. It was fortunate that he didn't look down to see where it landed.

DCI Bowen was listening to the latest call that had come in from Archer's phone. An Arab had been on the line and Archer had cut him short. She wondered if he had guessed they were tapping his line. The caller had said that arrangements would have to change and that the transfer would be done physically.

'So what did he mean by that?'

She asked Sloane who was sitting with his feet up on his desk. She knocked them off and sat on the edge that his shoe leather had occupied.

'It means they are not going to use the banking system I imagine.'

'Well it puts us back to going nowhere then.'

'Looks like it boss, unless we get another tip from Brooks' phone. Something might pop up there.'

Bowen decided to ring Richard Marker and dialled his number.

She got straight through.

'Richard, Amelia.'

She felt the time had come for first names.

'Look we've been on Archer's case. I think he's involved as you intimated. I need your help. We think there is money sloshing around and some of it is coming his way, it may be from the ransom, it may not. If he checks back in to the hotel let me know. I want to find out what he's up to.'

The hotel detective asked her to hold the line whilst he ran through the next day's arrivals. He saw that he was due in.

'He's coming tomorrow with his usual arrangement. The whole caboodle, him, the wife and the mistress. Everyone except the cat and budgerigar.'

'Alright. Keep an eye on who he meets and what he does.'

Marker could see it might be to his advantage particularly as he knew that new arrangements were being made.

'Yes, that's fine. I'll do that.'

He put the phone down and wondered if he would say anything to Sandrine. They were, after all, supposed to be a team. But he decided that he wouldn't, instead he went up to see Mary in the switchboard. He found her straddling an impossibly small stool, her large backside flowed gently around it like an oversize raspberry jelly that was too large for the serving plate.

'Mary, can I ask you to help me in a little investigation? I know I can trust you. Yes? Good? Well I am wanting to know all about what Mr Archer is doing. He's due in tomorrow and I'd like to know who he is calling. Can you keep an ear open for me? Anything you pick up will be useful. Who knows? There might be another dinner in it for you.'

The thought of that was one of the very few dining occasions that Marker wouldn't especially be looking forward to but it would still be an opportunity for something gastronomic.

Chapter 16

The day had not started well for Alberto Francisci. There was, as he put it: 'A fuck up with the transfer of the gold bars' and now the word was out that the Genoa *Carabinieri* were making a nuisance of themselves at the banks asking about any recent large currency movements. More to the point, his bank. The *Monte dei Paschi*. The *Monte dei Paschi!* Imagine. Nothing, in his opinion, works properly in Italy. The Italians had assassinated the only two people who could run the country. Caeser and Mussolini. So he was now going to move the cash dollars he had intended to transfer though bank channels by courier. And he knew who that was going to have to be. He, Alberto Francisci himself. On top of that he would have to convert dollars to sterling at a ridiculous black market rate. Then there was the question of how to smuggle this all to London and through Customs there.

In front of him were two identical blue suitcases and a little old dark-haired Italian seamstress. She was busy unpicking the beige stitching on the silk linings. Later that day she would be even busier resewing it with the cash neatly distributed underneath.

'So Lorenzo, *tu grasso maiale.*'

He shouted at the hood who was standing nearest the door:

'Stop chatting *questa vecchia cameriera*, and get down to see Benito at the agency. Two tickets, first class, Alitalia. London tomorrow morning. Book The Adelphi Hotel, get a travel agency voucher for all the costs.'

Alberto was going on a trip. And how he hated flying.

The agency typed out the confirmation voucher, sent a telex to The Adelphi and he was booked. All that remained was a phone call to Nice. They would have to tell the Sheikh they were moving the money by hand in sterling and the London contact would have to advise them what happens next.

When Archer heard that the money was now coming by courier in hard cash he was not amused for two reasons. First the call from the Sheikh, despite his request to use another number had come through on his direct line which he was sure was bugged. Secondly he didn't want Andrew Bulling flashing quantities of money all over the gay bars of London. The Police would be on to him straight away. It was a good thing he had cut the Sheikh short. He hoped whoever was listening in wouldn't have got much. He eventually put a plan in place and decided to ring Andrew and went out to the pay phone on the street corner. He called The Adelphi. Fat Mary answered.

'Good Morning, Adelphi operator. Yes. May I know who's speaking? Yes, Mr Archer, I will put you through.'

Mary passed the call to Andrew Bulling's room.

'Andrew? It's Archer. There's a change of plan. Your money is arriving at the hotel tomorrow and I will be there to see that you receive it. It is yours, but it will be in sterling and I don't want you throwing it around London, and certainly not in lavish places of entertainment. Do I have your agreement?'

'Yes,' replied Andrew, 'that's fine. I'm around and I'm planning a couple of trips abroad...so I can change it when I'm out of the UK?'

Archer finished the call. And Mary pulled out the plug on her board. She immediately pulled another cord and plugged in the hotel detective's extension.

'Mr Marker, Mr Archer has been on the line from a call box. He spoke to Mr Andrew Bulling and this is what was said...'

Marker was stumped. All his running around Jersey banks was now for the birds. The money was completing a circle and arriving back where it just about started. As he was considering this the phone in his office rang again. It was DCI Bowen. They had been listening to Archer's incoming call from the Middle East.

'Richard? Good. Look we think that there is going to be some sort of delivery tomorrow that Archer is involved in. It'll be in two suitcases. We don't know what it is but the contact is someone called Francisci. Can we leave it to you? I'd like to know what they are moving. If it's gold we can bang them up for a long time. We will speak to the Border at Heathrow and check incoming names. Italians, so probably flying Alitalia but we don't know for sure. Anyway we will let whoever it is go through unmolested, I want to catch all the canaries in the cage but we need to get inside those cases when they get to you.'

Marker put his phone down and then dialled the travel agency to cancel his ticket to Jersey and whilst he was still considering how well all this might be playing into his hands, DCI Bowen was on another mission.

'Sloane' she shouted to her number two: 'I'm going to see Bulling senior tomorrow at his house in Aylesbury. I've just called his dippy secretary and she says he's taken a few days off. 'The strain' she says. Well it's the strain of having too much money if you ask me. I'm going to put it to him that he deliberately killed Cythia Bulling and I'm going to gauge his reaction. I'm going to tell him that he knew he had given her a damaged helmet and that he simply left her long enough on the verge to die. That'll get things moving.'

Sloane nodded and put down his notebook.

'What do you make of the call to Archer?' Bowen asked.

'Well that bastard is like a bag of liquorice all-sorts isn't he? Sort of sticky but with a lot of colour. And he's clever. Never says too much on the line nowadays does he? I think he's suspects we are listening. Marker will keep us in the loop. It'll be a mistake to go tramping all over him too soon with our hobnails. Let's see how things develop.'

Andrew had decided to introduce young Eion

to his friends at the Boltons. Not because he thought the Irish boy was also homosexual, although he was good looking enough to qualify, it was to borrow the 'frightener'. Well, not borrow it. Rent it. Andrew knew the 'Firm' quite well and they were the only people who could get him tooled up with a gun and a full magazine. He met Eion at Earl's Court station and they walked to the pub taking seats at the bar. At quarter past-four 'Epsom' Edwards arrived with a briefcase. He was an enforcer for the Krays and earned his nickname because of the racket he ran with bent jockeys at the racecourse. The transaction took three pints and one hundred cash. A very nice Colt that had not been used much either. Andrew reckoned it was a good deal, slapped Edwards on the back and left with Eion for his apartment at The Adelphi.

'So let's go over the plan again.' Andrew was sitting on the edge of the bed talking to Eion. 'Tomorrow you get the ten o'clock Marylebone train to Aylesbury and there you pick up the car that I am going to leave tonight in the station car park. I will put the key on the rear tyre. You drive to Cullerton Manor, our family home. He'll definitely be there tomorrow, went up yesterday for a few days' rest. That's a joke. Anyway, look at this plan I've drawn of the house. He spends most of his day in his study and you can get access to that here, from the garden.'

Andrew pointed the route out.

'The doors will probably be open, it can be hot up there in late summer, but if not knock on them until he opens up. Show him the gun to get him to back off. Fire a shot in the ceiling if he doesn't move quickly enough. The gun is only to frighten him. All you want is the gold that he is sitting on. It's probably in his office safe, he took it up there from the hotel when he left yesterday. The safe is hidden behind an oil painting, he has a key that he carries with him. Here, take this rucksack, gold is heavy – you will need your hands free. It'll be no problem.'

Andrew thought his new found half-brother was a malleable Irish kid, not much more about him, but he considered he could do the job and Eion was clearly very excited about the prospect. He hoped that the lad wasn't too much of a 'hot head'. If things went wrong it wouldn't be good if he was unpredictable. Still, reasoned Andrew, it should be reasonably easy, Eion would be masked up, undetectable. The gun made it very real. Then Andrew had another nagging doubt, perhaps he shouldn't have given him the Colt. Did he really need it? Guns can be a dangerous thing, with fatal results...

'When you are back in the car drive it to Iffley Road. Here are the keys to my apartment. Leave the gun and the rucksack there and then drive the car to Stamford Brook tube, dump it and take the train. I will meet you later at the Boltons to sort out your slice of the action.'

After Andrew had left, Eion rang Sandrine who was still in her office.

'Sandrine? I've met Andrew Bulling. George Brooks introduced me when I went over for that interview. Turns out there was no job but he wanted me to meet Andrew. What a surprise that was. You didn't tell me that my mother was married to the Chairman and that he was my half–brother.'

Sandrine was completely ambushed at this turn of events and wondered how Brooks had got the information and passed it on. Whilst she held the receiver in her hand she checked that she still had the birth certificate on her desk. It was there in her in-tray but in view. She then realised that she had been careless and he might have seen it when he passed by.

Eion continued:

'Really nice bloke. But he wants me to help him get one over on his old man. Can we meet tonight? I want to ask you about it.'

Sandrine was apprehensive as to what this might mean but readily agreed. They arranged to meet at seven at their favourite bar, 'Blairs' in Covent Garden. She was anxious for the rest of the day and she locked her office early to get to the bar in good time. Pushing through the early evening crowd she found a banquette on a far wall that was away from the noise of the crowd. Eion arrived just after seven. She gave him a slow kiss on the lips, puckered and gentle. He took a deep breath in. She was good. Very good.

'So', she said, taking a pose on the seat and offering him a Peter Styversant said:

'What's the news?'

Eion took a few minutes to tell her about the surprise extended family he had just met. Then he excitedly told her that the Chairman had tricked the kidnappers and how the gold was now all back with him at this country estate. By the time Eion had got on to the part about his lost inheritance he was becoming alarmingly emotional.

'I need that money Sandrine, my mother left it to me. And he killed her you know. He definitely did.'

Sandrine couldn't disagree. With all that she knew it looked a possibility. But she became alarmed when Eion went on to tell her that he was on a mission to threaten Sir John Bulling. The young Irishman was becoming very excited and she could see that in this mood he might be dangerous. And where on earth did this new version of events from Andrew Bulling come from? She doubted the kidnappers had been tricked but Eion was certain that all the gold was with the Chairman. It all sounded very implausible. Her attention was brought back to Eion. He was so agitated he was almost shouting. She looked anxiously around the bar to make sure no one was eavesdropping.

'I'm going to have him you know, I'm going to get my payoff. It's mine my rights.'

He looked earnestly at her. Sandrine thought quickly. If it was Eion's intention to frighten the Chairman into handing over the gold that had somehow ended up back with him it was going to be dangerous. She paused to consider all that she had heard and ponder this new twist of events. Was there a chance to take a share with whatever came back with her new young lover? She urgently needed money, she felt so guilty. An absent mother. She wondered if her daughter even remembered what she looked like.

'Be careful Eion. Are you serious? You are going to steal the gold he's got up there?'

She sounded incredulous.

'I don't want something happening to you.'

But Sandrine had seen a window of opportunity. If Eion was successful he'd need somewhere to hide both himself and his share. He wouldn't have a clue as to its real value and certainly wouldn't miss a part of it if some of it disappeared when she offered to launder it on his behalf. She liked that thought. A few days of vigorous sex whilst she shared her apartment with an attractive Romeo who had come into some serious cash. She pulled in a sharp drag from her cigarette.

'Look, if you see him tomorrow and it gets unpleasant you're going to have to lie low for a bit. Maybe stay at my place or something. God! You are going to have to be careful.'

After they finished their cocktails she kissed Eion again, gave him her flat key and wished him luck. She was going to go home and sleep alone tonight. Too much to think about.

Later that night, when she had pulled the bedclothes up tight, she mulled over what she had been told. She had heard what he'd said about Andrew's version of his remarkable escape and knew that not to be true. So why did Brooks and Andrew create this elaborate story to inveigle Eion? It must mean that Andrew didn't have the money from the ransom and was using his new found half-brother to do some dirty work.

Her plans to raid the bank and sequester Andrew's ill-gotten gains would be pointless if there was no cash going through the account. She would have to talk to Marker just to check out what he knew.

∞∞∞

The next morning DCI Bowen left Marylebone on her way to Aylesbury at nine-thirty. She wanted to pass by Aylesbury police station and see DS Mills again before making her way to Cullerton Manor.

Oblivious to the danger a visit by the police to Cullerton Manor might cause if they all arrived at the same time, Eion Wildblood had put the pistol in his satchel and made his way to the same station to catch the fast train. He arrived at Aylesbury just before eleven. Andrew Bulling had left a small Volkswagen for him in the station car park. He found the key on top of the rear tyre as agreed and got in the driver's seat. He pulled out a pencil drawn map from his satchel that he'd been given and checked the route.

It was a ten minute run and when he reached the house he slowly steered the car up the drive but took a turn that was very close to the house and which led to some derelict stables. He manoeuvred the car around and left the key in the ignition. Taking the overgrown footpath round the side of the stable block the rear of the house come into view. It was a sunny day and he could see that the French doors that Andrew described were open. He put on the balaclava that Andrew had provided, put the rucksack on his back and looking around, approached the end wall. The only sound were the birds in the distant trees. He walked up to the door and saw Sir John sitting at his desk with his back to the doors. He took the gun from his satchel and confronted him. He stood straight in the open doorway so that the bright sunlight blocked out his features. He held the gun forward with two hands.

'Get up you miserable bastard! I want the gold'. He shouted in his Irish brogue.

Bulling stood up and turned around in shock.

'Who are you? What the devil are you doing?'

He could only see the outline of the gunman who was hidden by the bright sunlight streaming into the study.

Eion instantly spotted the gold bars gleaming

in the sunlight. They were in an open suitcase against the near wall. Not even in the safe. He took a look again at Bulling's overweight blustering figure.

'Give me the gold!' he shouted again.

Bulling looked shocked but didn't move. Eion waved the gun around.

'I'll shoot you! Stand over there!'

Eion swayed back and pointed the gun at the far wall, Bulling moved back whilst Eion edged over to the suitcase, took off his rucksack and started moving the gold bars.

'Get back!' He shouted as Bulling held up his hands.

They seemed to flutter in the air. Eion turned around to transfer the last of the bars. He sensed Bulling moving again and turned quickly around to face him. Bulling had taken a step towards him.

He pointed the gun at his head, and shouted at him once more. Just then the door started to open and Lady Julia appeared. Eion panicked and yelled:

'Stay back!'

He swung the gun. Then inexplicably he pulled the trigger. Bulling fell back against his desk. It had happened in an instant. Blood splattered up the wall. The bullet had entered his heart and plasma was now pumping all over the large white ink blotter. Lady Julia screamed and ran over to her husband's body that was now slowly sliding to the floor. Bulling was moaning in deep guttural gasps.

Eion now pointed the gun at her.

'Don't move!'

He roared. She was hysterical. With shaking hands he slung the rucksack on his back and turning around ran out through the French doors. The rucksack was heavy, very heavy and he struggled to keep up a pace. The only thing he could hear when he ran was his own deep panting and in the distance that stupid woman and her screaming. He got to the car, flung the door open and threw the backpack onto the rear seat. Gunning the engine the car wheels spun on the soft ground, but didn't move. He slowed the engine and tried a higher gear. Finally the car juddered forward and he moved off back down the drive. Pulling off his hood he reached the gate and turned right towards Aylesbury and the A40 for London. As he gathered speed down the Willows a police car passed him on the other side. He slowed and saw in his rear mirror that they were turning into Bulling's house. They were very quick he thought. Impossibly fast. He panicked.

∞∞∞

DCI Bowen made it to the front door minutes after Sir John had been shot. She rang the bell several times but there was no reply. Together with her driver she walked around to the garden and could just make out the sound of distraught sobs coming through the open French windows. Bowen approached cautiously and looked in. There was a slight attractive woman whose whole body heaved in compulsive spasms as she lay hunched over the lifeless body of Sir John.

'Oh God, it's Lady Julia, and Bulling has been shot,' said Bowen.

∞∞∞

Alberto Francisci and his brother Carlo arrived at The Adelphi around lunchtime and the hotel detective had easily spotted them as they were dressed as if they were going to a dance-hall in Naples. Black shirts, light suits, patent shoes. Not the sort of clients that Timothy Patterson would have liked to see gracing his Axminsters. With them were the two blue suitcases that the Porters had commandeered as soon as the taxi had pulled up to the front. Carlo objected to the cases being taken, but Alberto told him it would be unseemly to be seen to be carrying their own luggage.

'*Che bastardo, sofisticato come un pescivendolo Napoletano.* You're as sophisticated as a Naples fishwife,' he whispered. 'This is a quality hotel. Here they will do everything for you, probably kiss your arse if you ask them. Leave the bags!'

Unfortunately their rooms weren't yet ready. Their travel agent hadn't advised the hotel of their time of arrival and the receptionist had pointed out that the hotel voucher was not properly filled in with these details. The receptionist asked the porter to hold the luggage in the luggage store. After they were deposited there the door was locked.

Marker had been called by the Hall Porter as instructed and made his way to the lobby as they came in through the revolving door. He had seen the luggage go to storage. Marker took the opportunity to go to the store and using his master key went in and locked the door behind him. He looked over the suitcases. He had a collection of skeleton keys that he had acquired over the years. They fitted most suitcase locks. He tried the first one. It didn't open. He looked at his watch, there was only a certain amount of time that he had to do this and he didn't want the prying eyes of the hotel staff coming in to the lodge. He then looked at the second case. Here one lock became undone, he glanced at his watch again and the sweat on his face was becoming prominent. It was as hot as the kitchen ranges in the store and he felt a long wet trickle down his back. He thought he really should lose weight.

He went back to the first case and tried a different key. This time both locks opened. Inside, the contents looked to be the usual collection of clothing and personal toiletries everyone would carry, albeit that there were more multitoned patent shoes and some pretty awful electric colours for the suits. He felt the suitcase lining and was pretty certain that there was something there. He took out a penknife and cut a small section of the stitching and pushed his finger inside. It felt like paper but it smelt like money. He closed the case and moved the trunk away from the door. He unlocked the lodge door and walked out into cooler air. So if this is the ransom, he needed to get hold of it. And quickly.

He went straight down onto the Strand. There, as the No9 bus to Piccadilly passed by, he ran to the stop and jumped on. He then got off at Trafalgar Square and ran up Lower Regent Street to the Lillywhite store. By the time he had made it to the luggage department on the second floor he was exhausted. He was, after all, carrying two stone too much. There, fortunately he found the identical cases and bought two. He made his way straight back to the hotel. It had taken him just over half an hour. He used his key again to access the lodge and put the new cases on to a vacant shelf. He looked around but the original cases had gone. Alarmed he retraced his steps to the Reception.

'How long before the Francesci room is ready?' he asked.

'Oh, it's ready and guests are in the room. Luggage went five minutes ago.'

Marker looked perplexed. Then he saw Archer in the lobby and a few minutes later the Italians joined them. Archer must have checked in when he was in Piccadilly. He watched them walk over to the Smoking Room and order some tea with Enzo.

Marker took his chance. He went back to the store, unlocked it and took back his two empty suitcases. He locked the store again and went via the staff lift to the floor the Italians were staying on. He checked the corridor was empty and then using his master key opened their bedroom door. He laid out the two cases and then using his duplicate keys again opened the original set that he had been delivered by the porter. He carefully replaced all the contents in the same way that they had been packed into the two new cases. He then re-locked all the luggage, placed the full ones back in their place and took the original, but now empty cases with him back to his office. On the way along the corridor he ran into Mrs Haul.

'Doing a little portering Mr Marker?'

She gave a withering look.

'If I can help out. Actually they are full of some old files from storage. I've taken a leaf from your book and I'm spring cleaning.' She looked doubtful.

'You might start with your office if you are doing any cleaning. That hasn't been touched since Miss Havisham was jilted at the altar.' Marker smiled and wondered who the dickens was Miss Havisham?

When he was safely in his office he took out his old army knife from his desk drawer and carefully cut open the lining of each case. It was the first time in his life that he had ever seen that much money.

∞∞∞

'Bugger' thought Bowen as she surveyed the scene. Most of the Aylesbury police station were now at the house and two policewomen were consoling Lady Bulling. She picked up the study telephone and dialled her London number. DI Sloane answered.

'Would you believe it?'

She complained down the line.

'I'm just about to arrest him for murder and then he gets killed minutes before I arrive. Look it's obvious this is about the missing gold, his wife in-between hysterics has told me that she had heard a commotion in her husband's office. When she went to investigate she opened the door and was confronted a young man in a mask waving a gun about who then promptly shot her husband and ran off with the gold.

Not much of a description. White, male, young, slight Irish accent maybe. So who are the suspects? Well Andrew Bulling may have a motive. Find out where he is. And then we have slippery Archer, but I doubt he'd put his hand to this. It's more likely those hoods who were tricked out of the gold in the first place. Maybe an IRA connection. I'm getting forensics straight on to this. I want you to get everything that we can find on who dislikes Sir John Bulling the most. There will be a long list.'

She slammed the phone down and went for a walk in the garden to cool down. After ten minutes she came over to the local DI who would be continuing the investigation.

'I have to get back to London. You know that Sir John's son was the victim of a recent kidnap. I think you'll find that the motive is the part of the ransom that was returned to him uncollected by the kidnappers. They are obviously the prime suspects, but we don't know who exactly they are. So I will keep on with that part of the investigation and up to date. In the meanwhile keep the Press out of here until we've completed the forensics.'

The local DI nodded and decided to post two more policemen on the gate.

The news reached The Adelphi an hour later and the hotel went into another yet another state of hysteria. It was becoming a regular thing. The staff were bereft. Fellowes, the elderly Hall Porter, rang Marker.

'It's like losing Nelson on the deck of the Victory.' He almost cried down the line.

Marker had little sympathy for Sir John but could see the analogy. Bulling, he thought, like Nelson, probably only had one eye on the ship. He half listened to the eulogy as he wondered who else would be calling to give him condolences.

Sandrine was scared. She had heard the news and guessed the worst. She was desperately worried that Eion was holed up with a gun in her flat with all the ransom. She decided that she had to put some distance between them. She wondered if she had really known him at all. Eion, a murderer. She couldn't go home alone, he might be there and just shoot her for what she already knew. She dialled the security office.

Marker picked up the phone:

'Richard? I'm scared. What do you make of it?' she asked.

'Couldn't have been Andrew,' he mused. 'He was here. I'd guess it has to be the kidnappers. They wanted the gold.'

But she knew it wasn't them.

'Listen Sandrine,' Marker continued: 'I am a little busy but I've got something to tell you about all this. Can we meet tonight?'

This played into her hands. Sandrine sounded

relieved.

'Yes, let's say six o'clock, I have to be home by eight. I left some dinner in the oven on the self-timer. Would you like to come home and have some with me?'

The detective was pleased with her reply. Maybe he was back in again. But the truth was Sandrine didn't want to face what she suspected might be waiting for her.

'Delighted.'

He put the receiver down and the phone immediately rang again. DCI Bowen was on the line.

'Just when I was going to arrest him for killing his wife the bugger goes and gets shot. Richard, what do you make of it?'

'I think it's someone who's gold digging,' he said. 'Those Mafiosi that you asked me to look into. I see they are with Archer. Maybe worth you coming over to see them both? Perhaps one of them shot the boss.'

Bowen thought Marker was as good at picking suspects as a blind man throwing darts.

'I'll be over. Did you trace any of the payola?'

'Nothing in the cases.' He lied.

∞∞∞

Eion was in deep shock as he drove into London. He wasn't sure of where he was going and in his panic decided that it would be too dangerous to go straight to Andrew's flat. But he had Sandrine's key. He parked the car a street up from her address.

He couldn't believe what had really happened. Had he really killed the Chairman of The Adelphi? He thought he had. His heart was still pumping adrenalin. He was so frightened that he didn't even feel the weight of the rucksack as he pulled it from the boot. He made it to her front door within five minutes. Pushing the bell he didn't expect a reply. Fishing the key from his pocket he had difficulty turning the lock as his hand was shaking so much. He pushed the front door ajar when it finally went in and ran into the passageway and up the stairs. He went into the sitting room and looked for a phone. He found it on the bookcase. Picking up the receiver he dialled Andrew's number.

'I've killed him. I've shot him.'

Andrew was instantly alarmed.

'You fucking idiot, that was stupid. Why did you do that?'

'I panicked. I shot him. I killed him'

There was a pause, then Andrew said:

'This is not good. Not good at all. No. No. Where are you?'

Eion ignored the question.

'I need to get rid of the gun.'

'I told you to leave it in my flat with the gold.'

'I can't it's too dangerous.'

Andrew knew he was right. Where was he? More to the point where was the payoff. He hoped that the boy wasn't going to do anything foolish.

'Alright, get you arse over here and let's meet now at the Boltons.'

Eion looked at the rucksack and realised that it was too incriminating to be seen moving around with it in his hand. He tusselled with the draw strings and pulled it opened. The gold bars shone as if lit from inside. He stood back. He had never seen as much wealth and wondered what his share might be. Maybe he could have it all and just run. Maybe that wouldn't be so clever. But he had a plan. He grabbed two bars and a shopping bag from Sandrine's kitchen and only took what he thought he could safely carry alongside the satchel with the gun.

Eion had flagged a taxi and arrived at the pub within twenty minutes. He hid the bag under the banquette and waited for Andrew. He placed the satchel on the table. Andrew arrived looking more than a little breathless.

'You have the gold?'

Eion had begun to have second thoughts about anything other than the share he had taken.

'It's safe for the time being. The gun is in the satchel'

'Ok – well Epsom Eddy will be here shortly and we give it back to him. Have you cleaned it?

'No, I don't know how to.'

'Fingerprints I mean.'

'Oh yes, I've wiped it a bit.'

'Why didn't you go to Iffley Road?

'I saw the Police arrive at the house in Aylesbury. I thought they would have it staked out.'

Andrew's heart raced. He couldn't afford to be implicated.

'Why in God's name did you shoot him?

The Irishman didn't answer.

'And where are the gold bars? Eion, don't mess with me. We agreed you would get your share. Don't think of running out.'

And that was just what Eion was going to do.

Andrew took the satchel and walked over the bar. Edwards appeared at the door and nodded to Andrew. They both went off to the toilet and came back a few minutes later. By that time Eion was long gone. It would be the last time they met.

Archer and the Francesci brothers had finished their tea. Archer returned to his apartment and the Italians went over to Fellowes the Hall Porter.

'We hav'a two suitcases we want delivered to Signor Andrew Bulling's room. He's 'ere isn't he?'

Alberto Francesci had a strong accent and his English was only phonetically understandable to those used to transacting with waiters employed in the Italian restaurants of Soho. It was fortunate Fellowes understood the language of Dean Street.

He confirmed Andrew Bulling was still in residence and would send up a porter in a few minutes. The brothers returned to their room. When they were outside their door they both stopped. The paperclip that they had put in at the top of the door jamb when they had left had fallen to the floor. Someone had been in their room. They slowly opened the door and looked around. Suddenly Mrs Haul appeared from around the corridor corner.

'Good afternoon gentlemen, I have just been in your room placing some flowers for you. It's Assumption Day and I know how Italians like to celebrate. I worked with several of your countrymen during the war. They were with your resistance.'

This brought an instant smile to Alberto. He had been with the Mafia in the war and had worked with the Nazis.

'Mind you, I always thought that communists were irreligious,' she continued. 'But not the lot I was training. So as long as you celebrate the holiday the flowers are yours to keep. They all died you know, my Italian operatives. We parachuted them in, but they were captured and shot by the Nazis.'

Alberto wondered if it was him who had shot them, but decided it couldn't have been unless they had been running a prostitution ring in Milan where he had had some trouble in 1942.

'Una donna con i cappelli tra i denti.'

A woman with hair on her teeth. Alberto muttered to his brother and hoped she didn't speak Italian.

So they thanked her and she went on down the hotel corridor. They closed the door and admired the flowers. Alberto put both cases on the bed and unpacked their clothes. He checked the suitcases were empty. A few minutes later there was a knock on the door. It was the porter who took then collected the empty cases and placed them on his trolley. From there he went up a floor and knocked on Andrew Bulling's door. There was no answer, so he opened the door and placed the two suitcases in the wardrobe.

When Archer had returned to his river suite, he picked up the phone to speak to Andrew, when there was no reply he called the operator to leave a message.

'Just put down my name, and then put the message as 'delivery made'.'

The switchboard operator wrote out the message and left it in the 'Messages out' box for the page boy to come around and post under the guest door in due course.

It was some hours later that Andrew returned to his room. After Eion's disappearance from the pub he decided to take a few drinks to mull over what he had said and worry about the suggestion the police might be closing in on his scheme. It was an hour after that when the page boy finally delivered the message. Andrew looked around his room and saw nothing, although he wasn't quite sure what he was looking for. He rang Archer.

'What does this delivery look like?' He asked.

'It's suitcases. Your reward is apparently in the lining.'

Andrew dropped the phone and looked around the apartment but saw no cases. He was too drunk to go through the whole suite.

'I will check this out in the morning. Maybe the Hall Porter has it. I've just got back. Sometimes they leave it in the luggage store waiting for a call. That way they get a tip. I'll ring you if I have a problem.'

He fell onto his bed fully clothed. He didn't want to have to tip anyone again today, the hotel was tip mad. He fell into a troubled sleep when he should have been dreaming of silver linings.

That evening the hotel detective took Sandrine to the Coal Hole. A pub just along the Strand that was, early evening, usually full of actors and actresses gaining a little courage with gin before their stage outing at The Aldephi Theatre or Drury Lane. Tonight was no exception.

'It's getting dangerous Sandrine.'

'I can see that,' she said.

'So you think it's Archer and his bunch of East End mates that put a hole in Bulling's head?'

Sandrine asked with an air of innocence that gave no betrayal of the fact she knew that her Irish friend was certainly involved. Marker put his drink down.

'I'm not sure, but it would put anyone in the frame who has a grievance against Sir John. There were a few.'

'Tell me,' asked Sandrine, 'Brooks saw Eion Wildblood yesterday on the pretext of offering a job. When they met he introduced him to Andrew Bulling as his half-brother and told him a version of events that, how do you say that in English? Was a 'cock and bull story' I think is what you say. Andrew's story considerably differs from what you saw of the handover. Now why would he do that?'

'So Eion Wildblood is his half-brother? You never told me you'd found that out.'

Marker was watching Sandrine's reactions carefully and she barely changed her expression. So he continued.

'What type of relationship are you having with young Wildblood Sandrine?

Sandrine felt herself redden.

'Well, I'm having a bit of a game with him, he's only a boy. But it has got a bit more challenging.'

Marker didn't think fucking young men was challenging. And if it was a game it couldn't be as challenging as chess. He wasn't going to let that remark pass by.

'Sandrine, I really thought that I knew you, and I now realise that I don't really know you at all. I had hoped that we had something that had some fidelity. Anyway I know I don't possess you, much as though I would like to. So your life is your own.'

'Oh Richard!'

Sandrine looked anxiously into his eyes. She didn't want to lose this relationship now. She only wanted to finish with him after she had the cash.

'You must trust me if you love me!'

The trouble was that Marker still did love her, but trust was another issue. He returned to her question.

'Andrew Bulling and Archer are in this together. Bulling to extort money from his father. Archer to get him to sell his shares. Andrew wants compensation and revenge for the way he has been treated. I think you will find that Andrew isn't yet finished with his anger and wants to use your toy-boy to further hurt his father.'

Sandrine thought that it was certainly true that Eion was being manipulated but couldn't conceive that he would have been capable of murder. And it certainly looked like that now.

The pub began to clear out. It was seven o'clock, the fateful half hour before a performance starts had arrived and all theatres demand the cast appear at the stage door. They finished their drinks and Sandrine began to feel apprehensive about returning home. She had a good idea of what awaited her. She hadn't heard anything from Eion and assumed the worst.

'You're coming home for my supper aren't you?' She asked nervously.

Marker wondered what had changed to make her so anxious.

'Of course, you invited me earlier.'

'Oh good. That's very good. Thank you.'
Sandrine was tense.

Eion had fled from the Boltons and taking the tube at Earl's Court had returned breathless to his bedsit. There he grabbed what belongings he had. Making sure his room was left empty he had made it to Euston with the gold bars he had taken and all that he possessed. By the time Sandrine and Richard were walking hand in hand up the Strand he was already through Birmingham on the train to Holyhead. He might just make the midnight crossing to Dublin.

The journey to Chiswick was uneventful and the tube full of late commuters. It was the end of the week and some had obviously been doing a little bit of late shopping. They got off at Turnham Green and walked the five minutes to her apartment. Marker had not been there before and wondered what her rooms were going to be like. Yellow, he thought. Predominately yellow. It was dark as they arrived at her front door and they went up the stairs. Marker could already smell the *fricassee* that he now knew was in the oven. Sandrine put the light on. Then as she opened the door she saw it. The rucksack with the glint of gold coming from the unfastened flap. Moments later as Marker came into the passageway, he saw it too, and instantly recognised the remaining part of the ransom. The apartment was yellow alright, but not the wallpaper, it was lit with the Chairman's gold.

Sandrine had feared that this might happen and was ready with her story. But she was more afraid that Eion might still be in her apartment hiding armed with a gun. She thought she knew him well enough, but if he could kill! She had moved behind Marker as he leant over to look at the rucksack more closely. He moved over to the bag and gave her a sharp look.

'This will need some explaining Sandrine.'

Marker loosened the draw string.

'Indeed it will,' she replied.

Over the meal she had prepared Sandrine told Marker about her relationship with Eion and how she had foolishly suggested that the Irishman could stay with her as he was having a problem with the landlord at his digs. She had no idea how the gold got there, but the only person with a key was Eion, and he must have either put it there or given her key to someone who else to do the same thing. She could only think that it had to be Brooks or Andrew who had got him involved.

'Someone will be back for the gold who has the key,' said Marker. 'It might be Eion, or someone else that is in on the raid at Bulling's house. And they will have a gun. It's too dangerous for you or the gold to remain here. I'm going to make arrangements for us to stay at the hotel tonight and we are taking the gold with us.'

This was not what Sandrine had considered in her plan, but if the opportunity came to split the gold bars she would go along with the idea. Sandrine was certain that with that amount of gold in her house someone would be collecting it and doing that shortly. She didn't want to be there when they did.

'Richard, if we take the gold and they come for it they will know it's me that has it.'

'No they won't Sandrine because I am going to smash the lock of the front door and make it look like a break in. When we get to the hotel I will call the police and tell them there has been a robbery and I have taken you to the hotel for safety. With luck Eion or his friends will turn up looking for the gold with the police crawling all over your place.'

'Are we going to share this little package?'

Sandrine looked longingly at all the gold in the rucksack.

Marker looked at her and thought about all her deceit.

'Of course we are Sandrine.'

Marker was surprised how easily he could perjure himself.

It was early the next day and DCI Bowen was reading her reports. She read one aloud to Sloane.

'The bullet that killed Sir John Bulling came from the same gun that killed Amanda Norton.'

'Who was she?' asked Sloane stirring his coffee.

'The prostitute at The Adelphi. It means that the phycostic poof we now have locked up must have rented it and it's been passed out for another job. I'd say it has to be 'the Firm' and it looks as if the Boltons might be a good place to ask a few questions...And I see there is a report of a break-in at Sandrine Parte's flat. That's unfortunate. I will talk to Marker about that. We must get on and find what was in the Italians luggage. Have we heard anything from Marker? He's a fair weather friend. Never calls if I want something in return.'

Bowen sent Sloane off to see what he could discover about the gun. He could start with Norman who was now safely locked up in the Scrubs. She needed to move fast and visit The Adelphi again, and this time not just to meet Marker, but to rendezvous with Archer and his Italian friends.

She arrived just before ten o'clock and rang Archer in his suite. He agreed to come straight down. They met in the Smoking Room. Enzo served them tea and then rang Marker to tell him about his unexpected guests. Marker was surprised that the police were moving that quickly. When Bowen had finished with Archer she asked Enzo to call Marker. They met in the lobby.

'Any luck from Archer?' The hotel detective asked.

Bowen looked unhappy.

'Well he's taking us nowhere and I haven't anything concrete beyond what I know from the phone taps I placed. I can't use that in evidence. Then of course those mafia boys have buggered off so no joy there. I know you checked the luggage. Still I'm making some progress with Sir John's murder. Same gun killed that girl. DI Sloane has just called me to say that our friendly barman at the Boltons tells us Andrew Bulling was there yesterday and met one of the fixers from 'The Firm'. I've an idea as to why he did that but it's going to be difficult to prove unless we trace the gun.'

'I see' said Marker. 'Very challenging'.

Bowen looked him quizzically:

'Are you sure there was no trace of the money that was to come in with those dodgy Italians?'

'None.' Marker replied.

Bowen gave him another look of suspicion but then she never trusted anyone to tell the truth.

'I hear there was a break-in at Miss Parte's flat last night and you reported it. What's missing?'

'Yes, I went over for dinner and found the door forced.'

Marker was surprised that she knew about the burglary report, but DCI Bowen was not to be underestimated. He thought quickly:

'She's lost a few personal items. A pearl necklace, jewellery of some small value. It'll be an insurance job unless you lot can turn something up.'

Bowen looked thoughtful again.

'She around?'

'Funny you should ask,' replied Marker. 'I rang her room this morning and there was no reply. I checked with the Night Porter who told me that she left early this morning. Probably gone back to check if anything else is missing from her flat.'

'Best left to the Chiswick station – they are virtually on the doorstep.'

They said their goodbyes and before the hotel detective went back to his office he passed by his mailbox. There was a handwritten envelope in Sandrine's handwriting. He tore it open. It was a note and a set of keys.

Richard, I have left because I am terrified. I am sure they will come for me. Please go and secure my flat. Let me have a share. You know how to reach me in France. Sandrine x

He made his way to the basement and opening his office settled into his chair and re-read her note whilst he toyed with the keys. He did indeed know her French address but had no intention of sharing anything with her and certainly not the gold. By the far wall the rucksack was still full. He'd doubted her story about Eion and suspected she was far more involved than she wanted him to believe. But it had been an excellent supper of *fricasse au volaille.* The tender legs of chicken had been beautifully marinated in a cream and mushroom sauce. That had been worth the trip alone.

She had, he thought, for her own reasons, been grateful that he'd been there. After they had arrived last night at The Adelphi Marker wondered if her regretful look of unhappiness when she said 'Goodnight' in the lobby was because of the loss of her young lover, or more likely that she saw her payoff disappearing. She had asked him what he was going to do with the rucksack. He had told her that he would keep it safe.

Sandrine had double crossed him more times than the pastry on a Bakewell Tart, but in a final act of kindness he would go back to her flat and make it secure. Then he would post her the keys, but there would be no share of the loot. He had plans for that.

He was startled out of his reverie when the phone rang. It was the Fellowes from the Porter's desk to say there was a problem regarding suitcases delivered to Andrew Bulling's apartment. There was a loss of some money and Andrew Bulling wanted to see him in the lobby. Marker smiled and looked in his drawer to see that it was still safely there.

'Tell him I am engaged and will meet him in half an hour.'

Marker put the phone down and despite the performance he knew Andrew would put on when he eventually got around to seeing him, he didn't think Andrew would be calling the police over his loss.

He turned to the question of what to do with all this cash and the gold bars. Better add it all up and see what it's all worth he thought. He locked the door and after counting all the notes and bars calculated that he must have most of the ransom in one place although there was a shortage. Probably commissions and expenses, but more likely pilfered he thought. He locked the money back in his drawer, hid the rucksack behind the filing cabinet, sat back and considered what he was going to do next.

Who should be the beneficiary? Andrew Bulling? The detective thought not. Then there was Archer from Broadman. Was it his money? Marker didn't think so. Sandrine was wanting a share but she wasn't going to get that and what about him? Surely, above all else he deserved it? But of course that wouldn't be honest. Then it came to him with startling clarity. That chance encounter with his post-war romance who offered him his first foot into one of London's most luxurious hotels.

He picked up the phone and dialled a number.

'Hello? It's Richard.' He had got straight through and heard the voice that rekindled his memories. 'I was so sorry to hear what happened.'

She had answered the phone very quietly and the detective remembered her softness from years back. He told her what loving her had meant to him when they had been together. And then he waited for her to pour her emotions over him and he listened with care and concern.

After a brief silence on the line he said:

'Julia, you helped me when I needed help the most. It was fate when we met just like that afternoon so many years before. I don't think Sir John ever considered for one minute that we knew each other. And certainly not as lovers. He gave me the job only because I'd saved you from being attacked in the street. Now listen carefully.'

He looked over his notebook and checked the address for the Bulling estate and then said:

'I'm coming to Aylesbury this afternoon, I have something to offer you.'

When he put the phone down he sat back and thought that with all the money Lady Julia's life was going to change for what had to be the better.

And his own life was overdue for uprooting. He still didn't have a relationship of any value. He was as likeable as he was ever going to get, his stomach like his love of gourmet cuisine was never going to fade and he had to accept he wasn't getting younger.

It was time for him to move on. He still enjoyed his life as a detective and was imaging time spent beyond the marbled lobby of The Adelphi.

He picked up the newspaper and re-read the 'Situations Vacant' column where he had circled that unusual opportunity in red ink:

> Luxury Restaurant Chain seeks Chief Security Officer with extensive knowledge in food and beverage operations
>
> Telephone: WHI 3434

Sounded an ideal position and who better would have qualifications like his to match? He looked at the size of his stomach in the mirror, picked up the phone and dialled the number.

DEREK PICOT

Acknowledgement

I'd like to thank Melanie Beharrell for her help and suggestions, and my editor, Rupert Prior for his patience and guidance. Appreciation also to Philip Lawless for his encouragment to get this novel into print.

The ideas for the story would not have been possible without the wide spectrum of personalites that I have enjoyed working with in my career. The meglamania of those in power, the heroism of those that work in the heat of the kitchen and most of all the long suffering service staff who endure the most challenging guests with humour and goodwill.

About The Author

Derek Picot

The author has managed luxury hotels on five continents. The 'Hotel Detective and his Lover' is his latest book and includes true life episodes that he has experienced around the world. He writes for international travel magazines and is a Master Innholder and Freeman of the City of London.

He lives in London and the South of France.

Books By This Author

Hotel Reservations

A light hearted reflection on the great hospitality mishaps and misfortune that over the years have befallen hotels and hoteliers from around the world. This collection of true life entertaining anecdotes will make you wonder if you can safely stay at an hotel ever again.

Printed in Great Britain
by Amazon